The Scientific Romances of
J.-H. Rosny Aîné

VAMIREH
And Other Prehistoric
Fantasies

The Scientific Romances of
J.-H. Rosny Aîné

VAMIREH
And Other Prehistoric
Fantasies

translated, annotated and introduced by
Brian Stableford

A Black Coat Press Book

Acknowledgements: I should like to thank John J. Pierce for providing valuable research materials and offering advice and support. Many of the copies of Rosny's works and critical articles related to his work were borrowed from the London Library. Also thanks to Paul Wessels for his generous and extensive help in the final preparation of this text.

Visit our website at www.blackcoatpress.com

Table of Contents

Introduction

This is the fourth volume of a six-volume collection of stories by J.-H. Rosny *Aîné* ("the Elder"), which includes all of his scientific romances, plus a number of other stories that have some relevance to his work in that genre.[1]

The contents of the six volumes are:

Volume 1. THE NAVIGATORS OF SPACE AND OTHER ALIEN ENCOUNTERS: The Xipehuz, The Skeptical Legend, Another World, The Death of the Earth, The Navigators of Space, The Astronauts.

Volume 2. THE WORLD OF THE VARIANTS AND OTHER STRANGE LANDS: Nymphaeum, The Depths of Kyamo, The Wonderful Cave Country, The Voyage, The Great Enigma, The Treasure in the Snow, The Boar Men, In the World of the Variants.

Volume 3. THE MYSTERIOUS FORCE AND OTHER ANOMALOUS PHENOMENA: The Cataclysm, The Mysterious Force, Hareton Ironcastle's Amazing Adventure.

Volume 4. VAMIREH AND OTHER PREHISTORIC FANTASIES: Vamireh, Eyrimah, Nomaï.

Volume 5. THE GIVREUSE ENIGMA AND OTHER STORIES: Mary's Garden, The Givreuse Enigma, Adventure in the Wild.

Volume 6. THE YOUNG VAMPIRE AND OTHER CAUTIONARY TALES: The Witch, The Young Vampire, The Supernatural Assassin, Companions of the Universe.

The first volume of the series includes a long general introduction to Rosny's life and works, which there is no need to

---

[1] *Le Félin géant* (*The Giant Cat* a.k.a. *Quest of the Dawn Man*) and *Helgvor du fleuve bleu* (*Helgvor of the Blue River*) will be reprinted in their original English translations in a seventh volume.

repeat here; the following introduction will therefore be limited to a brief account of the stories included in this volume, which will be supplemented by a more detailed commentary contained in an afterword.

Vamireh first saw print as a serial in the *Revue Hebdomadaire* in 1892, and was reprinted in book form by Kolb the same year. Rosny made no reference in his memoir *Torches and lumignons* to any prehistoric fiction in the list of projects he recalled working on in 1885, before making his first bid for publication with *Nell Horn*, but *Vamireh* represented such a stark departure from the pattern of his other publications that one is bound to suspect that it might have been written much earlier than its publication date. On the other hand, it is possible that he had been inspired to produce it by the sensational discovery in 1891 by the Dutch scholar Eugène Dubois of fossil human remains in Java—where Dubois, convinced that humans must have originally evolved in the tropics, had gone to specifically look for them, joining the Dutch army in order to obtain a posting there.

Dubois' discovery seemed to many observers to put the final nail in the metaphorical coffin of stubborn adherents to Biblical chronology, who maintained that all the evidence of "prehistoric man" found in Europe was either misleading or of sufficiently recent origin to be accommodated to Biblical chronology. Rosny, a determined evolutionist, must have been delighted by the discovery of what he initially assumed to be a specimen of the long-hypothesized "ape-man" *Anthropopithecus* (although Dubois preferred the appellation *Pithecanthropus erectus*, and subsequent taxonomists eventually reclassified his "Java man" as *Homo erectus*). Whether *Vamireh* was written as a response to Dubois' discovery or had been begun long before, it was almost certainly the publicity given to the discovery that encouraged its publication. Rosny followed it up rapidly with *Eyrimah*, which was serialized in the first five issues of *Le Bambou* in 1893 and then reprinted in the *Revue Hebdomadaire* in 1896, before being reissued in book editions

8

by Chailley and Plon—a success suggesting that the earlier work had been well-received, or at least considered very timely.

Further evidence of the success of *Vamireh* was provided when Rosny produced an abridged version of it for publication in an illustrated edition in 1896 as *Elem d'Asie*. Significantly, the abridgement disposed of much of the "background" material that Rosny had inserted in order to construct a broad image of the prehistoric setting, in order to concentrate on the story, which is a combination of a love story and an adventure story. The story in question partially inverts a formula that Rosny used in many of his adventure stories, in which the plot is moved by the abduction by savages of the hero's inamorata; in this instance, the hero is the initial abductor, and it is not until his pursuers recapture the prize that the tables are turned and he sets out to recover her. A similar inversion is featured in *Eyrimah*, where the narrative focus eventually settles on a male abductor and his pursuit, having started out as the story of the eponymous runaway slave.

The success of these two *romans préhistoriques* appears to have been brief, to begin with, not extending much beyond 1896. Indeed, the short story "Nomaï," which first appeared in the *Revue Parisienne* in 1895, represents a wry recantation of the assumptions made in the earlier stories, based on new thinking that Rosny had apparently developed in the course of writing a non-fictional essay on paleoanthropology, *Les Origines* (Borel, 1895). Both the essay and the short story flatly contradict one of the central assumptions of the earlier stories—a contradiction that was taken for granted in all Rosny's subsequent images of primitive humankind. For whatever reason, though, Rosny wrote no further *romans préhistoriques* for more than a decade, only returning to the genre after the pseudonym had been redivided, the two brothers who had been sharing it having decided to go their separate ways.

Once J.-H. Rosny *Aîné* had resumed his own literary identity, he made a concerted attempt to begin selling adventure stories to the new middlebrow magazines that had sprung up in imitation of the English *Strand Magazine*, and he eventually produced three more long *romans préhistoriques* in this context: *La Guerre du feu* (1909 in *Je Sais Tout*; reprinted in book form 1911; tr. as *The Quest for Fire*), *Le Félin géant* (1918 in *Lectures Pour Tous*; reprinted in book form 1920; tr. as *The Giant Cat* and *Quest of the Dawn Man*) and *Helgvor du fleuve bleu* (1930; tr. as *Helgvor of the Blue River*). The three stories included here do, in any case, form a distinct group.

Rosny was not the first French writer to produce *romans préhistoriques*; he had been preceded by Samuel Berthoud, author of *Aventure des os d'un géant, histoire familière du globe terrestre avant les hommes* [The Adventures of the Bones of a Giant: A Family History of the Pre-Human World] (1862) and *L'Homme depuis cinq mille ans* [Five Thousand Years of Man] (1865), and Elie Berthet, author of *Le Monde Inconnu* (1876; rev. as *Paris avant l'histoire*; tr. as *The Pre-Historic World*, 1879). When Rosny was first hailed as a French anticipator of H.G. Wells, however—which also occurred in 1896, when a volume entitled *Le Cataclysme* was issued, containing the story previously known as "Tornadres" (1888; tr. in vol. 3 as "The Cataclysm") and "Les Xipéhuz" (1887; tr. in vol. 1 as "The Xipehuz")—the fact that he and Wells had both written prehistoric fantasies was recruited as further evidence of their supposed kinship. Even so, it was not until the publication of *La Guerre du feu* that Rosny's contribution to the subgenre was deemed particularly significant; numerous other writers had contributed to it in the meantime, but none as effectively. Once *La Guerre du feu* had become established as a key work in the subgenre, however, Rosny's earlier prehistoric fantasies came to be considered an important, if subsidiary, component of his *oeuvre*.

A significant analysis of Rosny's contribution to the subgenre was published in the *Mercure de France* in 1923 as "J.-H. Rosny et préhistoire," by Jean Morel and Pierre Massé.[2]

---

[2] Morel, Jean, with Pierre Massé. "J.-H. Rosny et préhistoire." *Mercure de France* November 15, 1923. pp. 5-25.

The authors mention that other significant French contributions to the subgenre had been made by Remy de Gourmont, Edmond Haraucort, Pierre Louÿs and Pierre Mille (without naming the specific examples, which are decidedly peripheral in the cases of Gourmont and Louÿs), but rightly contend that Rosny's were more important as well as more prolific. More importantly, Morel and Massé attempt to analyze the sources on which Rosny drew, identifying three of particular significance: the French translation of Sir John Lubbock's *Prehistoric Times* (1865)—as *L'Homme préhistorique* (1876)—Nicolas Joly's *L'Homme avant les métaux* (1879) and Gabriel de Mortillet's *Le préhistorique* (1882).

Of the three authors cited, the one who seems to have had the greatest influence on Rosny was Mortillet—understandably, given that he was by far the most successful French popularizer of paleoanthropology and founded the first French journal dedicated to the science, *Le Musée préhistorique*, in 1881. Mortillet—a colorful character who had been exiled from France for many years in the aftermath of the 1848 revolution, which he had helped to prompt—had embroiled himself fervently in the controversies surrounding the antiquity of humankind following his return to Paris in 1864, inevitably weighing in on the side of those who opposed Biblical chronology, and contended that rapidly-accumulating paleontological evidence proved that human evolution extended back over tens of thousands of years into what geologists called the Tertiary period. He produced an influential categorization of the phases of human evolution through the Stone Age, based on variations of stone tools found at various (mostly French) sites, the five phases in question being identified as the Chellean, the Mousterian, the Solutrean, the Magdalenian and the Robenhaussian; this is the terminology that Rosny adopted in his prehistoric fantasies.

Morel and Passé observe that Rosny's image of prehistory remained anchored in the popularizations of the early 1880s, never progressing beyond the authors of the "period of enthusiasm" to take in the subsequent modifications made to

Mortillet's theories by subsequent paleoanthropologists such as Emile Cartailhac, Salomon Reinach and Alexis Bertrand. They do not infer from this that Rosny might have begun writing *Vamireh* in the early 1880s, while he was still living in England, but they do observe that the notion that there were several distinct species of humans extant in the Tertiary Era—which is so elaborately developed in *Vamireh* and played a significant role in many of Rosny's subsequent prehistoric romances and lost land stories—is an extrapolation of Mortillet's contention that there were three species of Tertiary "anthropopithecines," and the rather fanciful descriptions that he gave of them. (The controversial European specimens of fossil humans included several that were later to be gathered together as examples of "Neanderthal Man," but which still remained open to various imaginative interpretations in 1882.)

The other theories espoused by Rosny in his early prehistoric fantasies are credited by Morel and Massé to sources prior to Mortillet, as cited by him or by Joly. They credit the popularization of the thesis that an indigenous fair-haired European race had been defeated in war by better-armed dark-haired invaders from the East to the *Broca Conference sur les troglodytes de la Vézère* held in 1871, and the identification of the invading race with the "Aryans" hypothesized by linguistic theorists—in which they find the origin of the "Ariès" featured in Eyrimah—to Adolphe Pictet's *Les Origines indoeuropéennes ou les Aryas primitifs* (1859-63; reprinted in 1877). They suggest that the notion of secret metallurgists, similarly reproduced in *Eyrimah*, was probably drawn from Frédéric de Rougemont's *L'Age du bronze ou les Sémites en Occident* (1866).

Morel and Massé have less to say about the nature of Rosny's evolutionist ideas, although they do observe that he shows no considerable understanding of the ideas of Charles Darwin, despite his frequent use of the notion of "selection" and his incessant references to the inherent tragedies of the struggle for existence. Morel and Massé suggest that this might be because Rosny derived his evolutionist ideas from the writings of Carl Vogt, but that seems highly unlikely, and his true allegiance seems to be to the transformist theories of the Chevalier de Lamarck. When he wrote his early prehistoric romances, Rosny could not have had any inkling of the impending development by Henri Bergson of the quasi-Lamarckian idea of *élan vital*, which plays a crucial role in Bergson's concept of *L'Evolution créatrice* (1907; tr. as *Creative Evolution*), but he seems to have developed a notion very similar to it on his own account, which is vaguely sketched out in "La Légende sceptique" (1889; tr. in vol. 1 as "The Skeptical Legend") and tacitly underlies the great majority of his scientific and prehistoric romances.

I shall comment further on these points in the afterword, when I shall also offer my own commentary on the nature and imaginative sources of the three stories translated herein. One further matter that warrants comment in advance, however, is that neither Rosny nor any of his sources was able to rely on an accurate time-scale for the sequential events they described, their work being far in advance of the radioactive dating techniques that now permit a sophisticated calibration of the record revealed by paleontological and archaeological excavations. Rosny is therefore compelled to talk rather vaguely in terms of thousands or tens of thousands of years—figures which become much vaguer as they are occasionally extrapolated into even remoter regions of the past recorded by fossil remains. Although his imaginative reconstructions work on a more generous scale than Biblical chronology, therefore, they do not do justice to the actual antiquity of human and proto-human evolution—a failing for which he cannot be held accountable.

The version of *Vamireh* that I used for translation is a Plon reprint issued in 1926. The version of *Eyrimah* that I used is also a Plon reprint, issued in 1938. The version of "Nomaï" that I used is the one that appeared in the Plon collection *Un Autre Monde*, issued in 1898. I have no reason to think that any of these versions differs significantly from the original versions, or from any others.

Brian Stableford

VAMIREH

A Romance of Primitive Times

I. The Bellicose Night

Twenty thousand years ago, the North Pole was orientated toward a star in Cygnus. On the plains of Europe the mammoth was about to become extinct, while the emigration of the large wild beasts toward the Land of Light and the northward flight of the reindeer were coming to an end. The aurochs, the urus and the red deer were grazing forests and savannahs. The colossal cave-bear had perished in the depths of its caverns a long time ago.

In those days, the men of Europe, the tall dolichocephali,[3] extended from the Baltic to the Mediterranean, from the West to the East. More reclusive cave-dwellers than their ancestors of the Solutrean Age, but still nomadic, their technology was already advanced and their art sensitive. Sketches traced with frail chisels, timidly but faithfully, were the brain's struggle toward dreams, against the brutality of appetites. Later, when the Asiatic invasion came, art died out and that charming employment was only recovered after a long interval.

---

[3] 19th century scientists attempting to classify different human types often made use of the "cephalic index," a number derived by dividing the maximum breadth of the cranium by its maximum length and multiplying by 100. A cephalic index below 80 was generally reckoned to signify "dolichocephaly," and one above 80 "brachycephaly," although there were variant schemes with additional subcategories.

In south-eastern Europe, in the season of renewal, with the night two-thirds gone, the voices of carnivorous beasts were resounding in the ash-gray light of a large valley. In the intervals of silence, a river sang the life of fluids, the euphony of waves; the alders and poplars replied in whispers and intermittent harmonies. The star Venus was rising in the east. The procession of the immortal constellations was visible between the vagabond clouds. Altair, Vega and the Plough were rotating around the pole star in Cygnus.

While ferocious or fearful life palpitated in the darkness, hurrying to the celebrations and battles of love or nourishment, a thinking mind joined in. On the bank of the river, on the edge of a solitary rock, a silhouette emerged from the Humans' cave. He stood there, still and attentive, sometimes looking up at the Star of the East. Some vague dream or inkling of astral esthetics preoccupied the watcher, less rare among these ancestors of Art than many historical populations. His veins throbbed with robust health; the nocturnal breeze charmed his face; he enjoyed the rumors and clams of virgin nature fearlessly, in the full consciousness of his strength.

Meanwhile, a delicate light appeared beneath the star Venus. The boomerang of the Moon appeared, its radiance expanding over the river and the trees, dappled with long shadows. Then the form of the tall hunter, his shoulders covered with an urus-pelt cloak, stood out more clearly. His pale face, painted with lines of red lead, was broad beneath his deep and combative skull. His horn-pointed spear hung obliquely from his back, and in his right hand he was holding a massive oakwood club.

At the touch of the moonlight, the landscape seemed less grim. There were white wings fluttering among the poplars; paradisal corners could be glimpsed on the plain; there was a visible general palpitation, a timid protest against the ferocities of darkness. Even the voices diminished, the battle raging less ardently in the nearby forest, where the wild beasts' appetites for sex and blood were satiated.

16

Weary of immobility, the man walked along the river at the lithe pace of a hunter. After 500 meters he stopped, poised, his spear held ready at head height.

An agile silhouette appeared at the edge of a grove of maples: a red deer with ten-point antlers. The hunter hesitated, but the tribe obviously had abundant provisions of meat, for, disdaining the pursuit, he watched the animal move away on its slender legs, with its head thrown back, the entirety of its beautiful body, designed for running, launched into the reddish gleam.

"Llô! Llô!" he said, not without sympathy. His instinct anticipated the approach of a predator, some powerful cat on the prowl. Indeed, half a minute later, a leopard emerged from behind the troglodytes' rock, launching itself forward with lightning speed in immense bounds. The man got his spear and club ready then, attentively, sniffing the wind with his nerves in tumult. The leopard passed by like foam on the river, soon disappearing from sight. The hunter's delicate ears perceived its course over the soft earth for several minutes more. "Llô! Llô!" he repeated, slightly excited, striking an arrogantly challenging pose.

Minutes went by; the horns of the crescent moon were already clearer. Small creatures were brushing through the bushes on the river-bank; large frogs were croaking amid the water-plants. The man savored the simple sensuality of living beside the luxury of open waters, and the play of shadows and light; then he moved on again, his ears pricked, his eyes— accustomed to the semi-darkness—on the lookout for nocturnal ambushes. "Hoï?" he murmured, in an interrogative tone, as he took refuge in the shadow of a bush.

A noise of galloping hooves, vague at first, came closer and became more precise. The deer reappeared, moving just as rapidly, but less steadily, in its headlong flight. It was sweating, and its breath was too sonorous. Fifty paces behind was the leopard, untiring and full of grace, already victorious.

The astonished man, annoyed by the carnivore's rapid victory, felt an increasing desire to intervene, when something frightful occurred. In the distance, on the edge of the maples, in the full glare of the moonlight, a massive silhouette appeared—in which, from its 20 meter bound and its thick mane, the man recognized the almost-sovereign beast: a lion. The poor deer, mad with fright, made an abrupt and awkward detour, fell back, and suddenly found itself beneath the leopard's trenchant claws.

There was a brief, frantic struggle, and the dying deer made a choking sound. The leopard held itself rigid in alarm; the lion was approaching at a tranquil pace. Thirty paces away it came to a halt, with a growl, not yet crouching down. The quaternary leopard, large in stature, hesitated, furious about the effort made in vain considering the risk of battle—but the louder voice of the dominant beast reverberated through the valley, sounding the attack, and the leopard gave way, retreating without haste, with a mewl of rage and humiliation, its head stretched toward the tyrant. The other was already ripping up the deer, devouring huge chunks of the stolen prey, paying no heed to the vanquished animal—which continued its retreat, exploring the shadows with its emerald-gold eyes.

The man, rendered prudent by the proximity of the lion, hid himself scrupulously, but not fearfully, in his leafy retreat, ready for any adventure.

After a brief interval of furious consumption, the beast paused; anxiety and doubt appeared in its whole attitude: in the bristling of its mane, and its anguished wariness. Suddenly, as if convinced, it seized the deer firmly in its jaws, threw it over its shoulders and set off at a run. It had covered 400 meters when a monstrous beast emerged at almost the same spot where it had appeared itself shortly before. Intermediate in form and gait between a tiger and a lion, but more colossal, the sovereign of the forest and the savannah symbolized Force as it stood there in the vaporous gleam.

The man trembled, stirred to the utmost depths of his being.

After pausing under the ash-trees, the animal set off on the chase. It moved like a cyclone, covering the ground effortlessly, pursuing the fleeing lion westwards—while the leopard, having stopped, watched the scene. The two dwindling silhouettes vanished.

Again the man was thinking of quitting his retreat—for the leopard did not scare him—when things became complicated. The lion came back obliquely, having been forced to make a detour by some obstacle—a pool or a gully. The man laughed derisively, mocking the beast for not having calculated its flight better, and hid himself away again, for the colossal antagonists were heading almost straight for him. Slowed down by the detour and the deer's weight, however, the runaway was losing ground.

What should he do? The hunter inspected the surroundings; to reach one of the poplars he would have to run 200 meters; in any case, the *Felis spelaea*[4] could climb trees. As for the troglodytes' rock, that was ten times as far away. He decided to see what would happen.

He did not have long to wait. Within two minutes, the wild beasts reached the vicinity of his hiding-place. There, seeing that flight was in vain, the lion dropped the deer and waited. There was a pause similar to the earlier one, when the leopard had held the prey. All around there was the silence of the annunciatory hour: the interval when nocturnal creatures were going to sleep and diurnal ones waking up to the light. There was a faint glimmer of light, on treetops bathed in pale wool, on clumps of grass trembling in every blade in the hesitant westerly breeze, and around the entire perimeter, there

---

[4] *Felis spelaea* was a fossil cat first identified by Georg Goldfuss in 1810. It was often called the "saber-toothed tiger" or the "cave lion" before paleontologists settled on "saber-toothed cat." It seems reasonable to maintain Rosny's slightly awkward but entirely typical preference for the Latin term here, although I have occasionally substituted common names for other Linnean terms in the interests of reader-friendliness (i.e. "cowries" for *Cyprea lucida* and "periwinkles" for *Littorina*) when the references are merely casual.

was the vague confused natural ambush composed of arborescent frontiers, straits and silky bands of sky. Up above were the stellar night-lights, the psalm of eternal life.

On a mound, the tall and dominating profile of the *Felis spelaea* was outlined by the moonlight, its mane swept back over a pelt speckled like a panther's, its brow flat and its jaws pre-eminent. Once king of Chellean Europe, the species was now in decline, reduced to narrow bands of territory. Lower down was the lion, its breath hoarse, its flanks in tumult and its heavy paw posed on the deer, hesitant before the colossus as the leopard had previously been in its own presence, with a phosphorescence of mingled fear and anger in its eyes. Lurking in the semi-darkness, already harmonized with the drama, was the man.

Releasing a muffled roar, the *spelaea* shook its mane and began to descend. The recoiling lion, its teeth bared, released its prey for two seconds; then, in despair, its pride injured, it came back with a roar more resounding than its adversary's, and set its paw back on the deer. That was the acceptance of the battle. In spite of its prodigious strength, the *spelaea* did not respond immediately. Pausing, drawn back, it examined the lion, estimating its strength and agility. The other, with the pride of its race, stood upright, head raised. There was a second roar from the aggressor, a resounding reply from the lion, and they found themselves a single bound apart.

"Llô! Llô!" whispered the man.

The *spelaea* crossed the intervening distance, its monstrous paw raised. It met its adversary's claws. For two seconds the red paw and the spotted claw confronted one another, in the final pause. Then the attack was launched, a confusion of jaws and manes, accompanied by raucous cries, while blood began to flow.

At first, the lion drew back under the formidable assault. Soon disengaged, it launched a flank attack with a sideways leap, and the battle became indecisive, the *spelaea*'s speed nullified. Then there was the frenzy of living bodies, the quivering of giant muscles, the indecision of reckless—and thus ineffectual—forces, the bristling of manes in the moonlight, the unfolding of flesh like the palpitations of maritime waves, the foam of maws and the phosphorescence of wild eyes, the hoarse grunts like the sobbing of a storm in the oak-trees…

Finally, with a terrible blow, the lion was struck down, collapsing at full stretch; like lightning, the *spelaea* was upon it, slashing its belly open. It struggled, with frightful roars. It succeeded in disengaging itself again, its entrails hanging out and its mane red. Understanding the impossibility of retreat, and that the other would show it no mercy, it faced up to the adversary without hesitation, and re-engaged in combat so furiously that the *spelaea* could not get hold of it again for several minutes. The end was approaching, however; the vanquished creature's strength was decreasing rapidly. Seized again, and pinned against the ground, the lion's torture began as the stronger beast persisted. The lion's viscera were ripped out; its bones were broken between omnipotent fangs; its face was crushed and deformed…and its roars of agony echoed across the horizon, ever more raucous and weaker, soon dying away into sighs, coughs and a quiver of vertebrae. Finally, there was one last convulsion of the throat, a lamentable sigh—and the sovereign beast died.

At first, the *spelaea* persisted in rending the cadaver's still-vibrant flesh, in the voluptuousness of vengeance and the fear of a return to life. Finally, reassured, it cast the lion aside with a disdainful thrust, and roared its triumph and challenge at the shadows. Its shoulders and thorax were bleeding from large cuts.

The first light of dawn appeared, a filtration of quicksilver on the low horizon. The Moon's bow faded and became blurred. The *spelaea*, having licked its wounds, feeling hunger returning, launched itself upon the carcass of the deer. Weary, and too far away from its lair, it sought a retreat in which it could feast in the shade. The nearby bush in which the hunter was hiding attracted its gaze, and it started dragging its prey toward it.

21

Meanwhile, fascinated by the magnificence of the battle, the man was still contemplating the victor when he saw it coming toward him.

A breath of charnel terror and horripilation passed over him, without him losing his instinct for combat and calculation. He thought that, after such a battle, avid for rest and nourishment, the *spelaea* would doubtless pay no heed to his retreat. However, he could not be certain of that; he remembered tales told by old men late in the evening about the big cats' hatred of humans. Rare, and in continuing decline, they seemed to have an inkling of the role of primates in their extinction, and satisfied their confused resentment every time they encountered a solitary individual.

As these memories strayed through the watcher's mind, he wondered whether the shelter of the bushes or the bare savannah would be preferable if he were attacked. If the former nullified the speed of the beast, the latter made it easier to throw a spear and wield a club. There was no time for lengthy hesitation; the *spelaea* was already parting the foliage.

The man leapt sideways, his choice abruptly made. He emerged from the bushes by the easiest route, at right-angles to the gap through which the monster was entering. The rustle of the branches disturbed the *spelaea*, which moved around the edge. Seeing the human silhouette emerge, it roared. At this threat, with all thought of escape extinct, the hunter raised his spear, his muscles supple and docile, and took aim. The weapon quivered, and flew straight into the feline's throat.

"Ehô! Ehô!" cried the man, brandishing his long club in both hands. Then he stood still, solidly—a handsome human giant, a clear-sighted hero of the ages of strife.

The *spelaea* advanced, gathering itself, calculating its leap. With marvelous ease, the man moved aside, letting the monster pass by; then, just as it came back at an angle, his club descended like a mighty hammer and vertebrae cracked. A roar was cut short, and the fallen colossus abruptly became still—and the man repeated his victorious battle-cry: "Ehô! Ehô!" He maintained his defensive pose, however, fearful of a recovery, contemplating the beast with its open large yellow eyes, its half-meter-long claws, its giant muscles its gaping mouth full of the blood of the lion and the deer: that whole miraculous organism of war, with a pale belly beneath its yellow coat with black spots.

The *Felis spelaea* was quite dead, however; it would never make the darkness tremble again. The man felt a great sense of well-being in his breast: the swelling of an exceedingly pleasant pride; an enlargement of personality, of life, of self-confidence, which rendered him meditative and nervous before the luminous flowering of the dawn.

The first scarlet fanfares were rising over the horizon as the breeze increased. The small creatures of the daylight were opening their eyes one by one, the birds chirping their delight, turned towards the east with their little breasts swelling. In the fine mist, the river had a slightly dull tinplate appearance at first; then the splendor of the clouds plunged a shivering world of shapes and tints into the water. The tops of the tall poplars and the short grasses of the savannah trembled with the same ardor of life. Already the Sun had appeared above the distant forest; its rays poured over the valley, punctuated by the interminable shadows of slender trees.

The man extended his arms, in a confused religiosity with no precise object of worship, perceiving the force of the radiance, the eternity of the Sun, the ephemeral nature of his own being. Then he laughed, and repeated his triumphant cry: "Ehô! Ehô! Ehô!"

And the humans appeared at the mouth of the cavern.

II. The Horde

In the radiant morning, while the breath of the river and the savannah were regenerative and voluptuous, the embers of the first cooking-fire were dying at the mouth of the humans' cave. A hundred meters away, the Sepulcher-Tree[5] rose up, its branches full of pale skeletons of dead troglodytes. The gentle collisions occasioned by the breeze caused the aerial ossuary to send forth canticles of sighs and euphonious syllables, and one old man, squatting on his heels, his long-sighted eyes perceiving a few skulls in the shadowed branches, recalled the feats of a glorious hunter, a companion of his youth devoured by oblivion.

The scattered horde of Pzânns yielded to the charm of the moment. The children bounded through the grass to the edge of the water; among the mysterious willows, a half-naked young woman washed herself and her finery, braiding the vague unruliness of her hair. The males were busy with equipment for hunting or labor; almost all of them were heavy in build and muscle, with highly-developed skulls and combative energy. Warriors were crushing and mixing red lead with urus-marrow in flint bowls, and painting their faces and breasts with fine fiber-brushes, designing awkward parabolas, interlocking networks, vague representations of natural forms, rings and sets of radiant lines. Some of them were kneeling down, attaching barbaric jewelry to their necks, foreheads and feet: necklaces made of the canine teeth of lions, wolves, bears, aurochs and deer, punctured at the base; the backbones of fish; pierces of fluorspar with amethyst gleams; sculpted pebbles; and various fragile marine ornaments—cowries, periwinkles and limpets.

The horde represented a humankind already inclined toward the ideal, industrious and artistic, given to hunting but not warlike, which accepted the mystery of things without having yet submitted itself to worship, scarcely prey to vague symbolisms. Sons of the great dolichocephalic race dominant in Quaternary Europe, living in peace with other hordes, strangers to the oppressions of slavery, they were characterized by a coarse nobility, a grandeur and a generosity that

---

[5] Rosny inserts a footnote: "That is to say, a tree chosen by the nomads in which to suspend the skeletons of their dead."

would not be found again until the Neolithic.[6] Their territories were large, so abundant in nourishment that no instinct of direct appropriation or low trickery had been able to arise. The tribal leaders, equipped with no power of enforcement, freely elected and followed by virtue of their wisdom and experience, had not yet enthroned despotism. Only quarrels of love and emulation occasionally reddened the earth with human blood spilled by humans.

After the meal and the toilette, the women and those males who were not involved in today's hunt began their labor. Oh, what frontiers had been crossed in the cerebral realm since the flints of Thenay[7] and taciturn *anthropopithecus*, when the ancestral Chelleans appeared in the bosom of the fauna: the division of labor; the tradition of tool-making; sovereignty over nature; organization multiplying human strength; artistic drawings!

Several of them were sewing furs with fine eyed needles, using holes pierced in advance by means of pointed stones. Others were cleaning fresh hides with scrapers and scourers. A few, established in the open air, were hammering with pieces of stone or wood, sharpening axes, knives, saws and chisels. The sculpting, with little sharp blows, was carried out with marvelous skill and patience, causing points and blades slowly to appear; the artisans, familiar with their materials and endowed with the divination acquired by long practice, rarely failed to discover the favorable directions of percussion. Some

---

[6] Rosny inserts a footnote: "The second major period of the Stone Age, also called the Age of Polished Stone."

[7] Rosny inserts a footnote: "The first and crudest vestiges of human industry, attributed to a sort of ape-man or *anthropopithecus*, a precursor of our ancestors of the Chellean Epoch." The term *anthropopithecus* had been coined to refer to a hypothetical "missing link" between apes and men; it was sometimes applied to actual fossil finds, but only briefly, and was discarded when more elaborate classification systems emerged.

of them were engaged in even more delicate work, carving points, hooks and harpoons of bone and horn, thus equipping themselves with delicate and precise tools, which humankind would be unable to surpass until the Stone Age gave way to the Age of Metal.

Most of all, the needle expressed an ingenious industry: rounded splinters of bone, indented by notched flints, delicately polished and pointed, with eyes drilled by rotating points with calculated slowness, avoiding a thousand risks of breakage.

While the work began, a group of hunters met at the cavern entrance.

A young man with sharp eyes climbed up to the top of the crag to explore the view. To his left, beneath a vague, soft gleam of tarnished amethyst, the forest extended between the river and the horizon. Facing him were valleys, the gradual circles of steppes, a few low and gently-sloping hills, oases like water-lilies on a marsh, and the sinuous mirrors of fecund waters. Beyond, lost in the dusty light and the pallor of the clouds, was mountainous country. Everywhere, there were the diminutive profiles of animals grazing the plain; the hunter took note of a herd of horses and a herd of urus. In a resounding voice he denounced them to his companions, tracing the areas of the hunt with his finger. In response to his speech, they all went in quest of weapons: bows, harpoons, spears and clubs. Then, as they were about to leave, the old leader looked around and cried: "Vamireh!"

Then the young man who had vanquished the *Felis spelaea* appeared on the threshold of a cave. He hesitated between the desire to continue the preparation of a cloak made from the monster's skin, which he had begun the night before, and the desire to go hunting. Youth was triumphant, along with the appeal of the rejuvenated valley, the exclamations of his companions. He went back into the cavern, and promptly reappeared armed with a bow and a club—and the troop marched off in a northward direction.

Restless at first, their barbaric brains overexcited by the march and the fine morning, they gradually fell silent. Soon, from the top of a hill, the urus herd became visible to them. Several hundred of the large herbivores were in a triangular formation, with a circumference of about 2000 meters. The bulls with leonine flanks and stubborn heads were circulating among the heifers and young males with a heavy tread. The whole multitude realized the splendors of leisurely life, peaceful majesty and social strength.

At the call of the leader—the colossal bull standing at the most acute angle of the triangle—the other males grouped together for the battle. A wild intelligence—an intelligence atrophied in their Asian kin by a servitude that was already long—endowed them with tactical aptitude and spontaneity.

The hunters paused. Hidden behind a hillock, they discussed the plan of attack. The nature of the terrain and the disposition of the animals left room for two alternatives: to approach them simultaneously from the right and the left, taking advantage of a slanting series of hillocks; or to move around the plain and surge forth from a clump of fig-trees some two leagues away. After a few minutes, the majority favored the first method, for the other, although more productive in the case of success, was evidently less certain, because panic might scatter the urus before the ambush could be sprung.

The troop divided into two parties, one led by the old man armed with a carved staff of command, the other under the command of a middle-aged colossus.

On either side, the march was organized and regulated, wisely making use of the accidents of the terrain. The old man's group, slightly in advance, was drawing closer, to within bowshot, when the huge leader of the urus herd seemed to become anxious. Raising his red head, dotted with white patches, he sniffed the horizon and stood still, subjecting it to a profound scrutiny. Then he gave voice, as beautifully and as gravely as a lion. The scattered herbivores shivered and drew closer together. After a minute of suspicion and a shake of the spine, the conviction grew that the enemy was approaching—the implacable vertical enemy so well-known to the animals—and the signal for flight was given. The abrupt departure of the enormous caravan accelerated to a trot that made the whole valley tremble.

Abandoning cunning, the troglodytes climbed up the chain of hillocks that hid them. The most agile appeared at the summits; more than ten bowshots separated them from the laggards of the urus herd. The animals, no longer encumbered by new-borns, were moving away rapidly, but, as soon as the hunters bounded into action, there was no doubt how the expedition would conclude. The most ardent, true barbarians of a victorious race, unhesitatingly engaged in a contest of emulation, insensible to their leaders' orders. In a few minutes, three of them had arrived within bowshot and launched their arrows; one bull stumbled, with a mighty groan.

"Ehô! Ehô!"

More arrows flew; one of the bulls collapsed, and then a female. Five hunters were within firing range. Then, sacrificing themselves, two of the male ruminants came to a halt. The noble protectors of their race pawed the ground momentarily, their huge anxious eyes staring into the void, and then launched themselves forward. More arrows inflicted deep wounds, but the bellicose animals seemed insensible to them, drawing ever closer, and more reckless. Sure of their legs, the majority of the hunters were content to scatter, but two young men, moved by pride in their power and skill, exchanged a glance, stood still and waited, one with his throwing spear in his hand and the other with his club. Having become curious, and feeling a dramatic thrill, the others formed a semicircle.

The first bull, lowering its horns, charged straight toward the taller of the two young men at a frightful speed. The latter avoided it, with a smooth sideways movement, and plunged his spear into the animal's side. Bloodied, it almost fell, but it came back at an angle, less rapidly and more artfully. Even so, it missed its target, and again the weapon plumbed its entrails, more deeply and more cruelly. Tottering and falling to its knees, the urus seemed to be defeated, in a position to receive the final blow. As the lance was raised, however, it leapt up again, and its left horn lifted up the man. Carried on the convexity of the crescent, not on the point, the warrior got away in time, and his third, decisive thrust, full in the heart, assured him of his victory.

"Thérann has killed the great urus!" he howled.

Beside him, the contest was even keener. As Thérann killed his adversary, the other bull charged the hunter with the club. Recklessly standing his ground, the man brought his weapon down, and tried to fracture the beast's skull. Turned aside by a gesture of the horned head, though, and glancing off, the blow only made a partial impact and the bull lurched forward for ten meters, dragging the nomad with it. Trampled underfoot, with his belly ripped open, reduced to impotence, the wretch's entrails spilled out and his bones were heard to splinter. Then the blood gushed forth. Incurable wounds punctured his torso—and the hunters were so horrified that only a few arrows flew from the bows, fired by the best archers. Then, as the bull gored the body of the fallen man, several rushed forward, shouting loudly.

The monstrous beast did not wait for them. Perhaps sure of dying, but desirous of falling in battle, it ran proudly towards its assailants. Clouds of darts buried themselves in its handsome flanks without breaking its stride, and it suddenly reached a new antagonist—an old man slow to retreat—and knocked him over. A spear-thrust to the shoulder saved the man, and the supple profile of Thérann was interposed between the two.

"Thérann! Thérann!" cried the hunters.

Thérann avoided the urus's charge, but his second thrust, badly-aimed, hit a shoulder-blade. In his turn, he fell to the ground; in his turn, he saw the pointed horns lowered—and everyone thought that he was doomed. Then Vamireh surged forward, as agile as a salmon swimming upstream, his club upraised. He just had time to lift Thérann up and shove him away at random, while the troglodytes cried: "Vamireh is as strong as a mammoth!"

With a gesture, Vamireh refused all help; then, standing six meters from the bull, he spoke to it: "Go away, brave one, so worthy to live and create the great race of the urus, so worthy to graze the good grass of the plain for a long time yet!"

Immobile, the ruminant gazed at the hunter with its large blue-tinted eyes. Merciful pity whispered in Vamireh's inner being, regret for the grandiose beast sacrificed to the fatality of conflict. Meanwhile, painfully, without its earlier energy, its arteries depleted, the bull lowered its horns to defend itself, waiting for the human to attack.

Vamireh continued: "No, brave one. Vamireh will not strike the great vanquished urus. Vamireh does not want to deprive the plain of the brave one who would protect its race against the lion and the leopard."

Having fallen to its knees, the urus seemed to be listening to the hunter, in a vast and vague dream. Then its head shook; a feeble echo of a bellow quivered in its throat; it lay down, its eyes glazing over, and it exhaled its last breath upon the grass.

Thus the hunt concluded, in a grave melancholy; the five urus that lay scattered on the plain had cost the life of one son of the human race, for Wanhâb, son of Djeb had just returned to the world of things.

The Pzânn warriors had encountered the strength and courage of the urus once again, but nevertheless, in an indefinite sentiment of wisdom, they felt more sadness than anger. Agreeing with Vamireh's last words, they knew that the existence of herbivores was necessary to that of humans; it was by virtue of that profound sentiment that, 1000 years before the domestication of animals, they had learned to use all life moderately, save for that of carnivores and parasites, and to be magnanimous towards powerful males, in order that the herds of deer and oxen, and the caravans of hordes, would be fortified against the large predators.

III. Wanhâb's Sepulcher

In the evening light, when the Sun was transformed into a circle of embers, the elders emerged from the cavern, followed by the melancholy horde. Two young warriors were carrying Wanhâb's skeleton, and the red light shining on the pale skin and through the rib-cage was like a symbol of acute anguish, the sunset of the vernal day over the ruins of a young man, vanished forever into the abysm of metamorphoses. The horde moved slowly over the savannah, and the dull sobbing of the wife and the mother punctuated the taciturnity of the scene.

When they reached the Sepulcher-Tree and the bearers had climbed the hill, an old man came to stand next to Wanhâb and everyone waited for him to speak, because he was renowned for talking to other people. The old man stood still for some while, allowing ancient things to rise up in his memory: the confused syntheses acquired by his race, which was still entirely natural, not having conceived any mystery beyond material forms.

"Humans...Wanhâb, son of Djeb, born among us, was an intrepid hunter and skillful worker. The urus, the leopard and the hyena have known his strength. He has carved the bodies of beasts and has made clothes and weapons from them. He has forged tools from the benevolent stone. Humans...Wanhâb, son of Djeb has left life behind; he will hunt no more, no longer skin beasts or forge tools from the benevolent stone— and because he was a faithful and wise companion, we shall miss Wanhâb, son of Djeb."

"We shall miss Wanhâb, son of Djeb!" repeated the voices of the horde.

Then a weightier silence descended, and the heads of the troglodytes were raised to watch an agile hunter climb the Sepulcher-Tree. He slid from branch to branch, between the skeletons of ancestors. When he reached a free branch,

31

Wanhâb, son of Djeb was suspended by a braided thong, one end of which the hunter was holding, and the lattice-work body of the dead man climbed slowly up into the foliage.

Emanating from the warm horizon and the broad zenith was so gentle a languor, so charming a breath of life and so peaceful a majesty, that Wanhâb's companions, and his mother and widow, forgot the pain and horror of death. Finally, the skeleton, fixed in place, was swaying feebly among the other skeletons, and the horde dispersed into the dusk. On the headlands of the river and the crests of the low hills, contemplative natures tried to divide the light into a thousand ephemeral figurations.

Soon, only a nucleus of intimate friends and relatives still remained under the tree, and twilight overwhelmed the celestial glories. Another day disappeared into the depths of the past; another night revealed an infinite face. Shivering then, with embryonic imaginations mingling the ideas of death and night together, the humble prehistoric individuals faithful to Wanhâb added one more dream to the millions of dreams from which Worship was born, from the marriage of Fear, the Supernatural and Immortality.

Meanwhile, the young wife remained prostrate on the grass, her hair running between the stems, as the willow-flowers weep over the water-lilies in ponds—and Thérann the victor, Wanhâb's friend, took pity on her and felt his heart quiver, because the woman's tresses were beautiful and her neck was round and white in the final glimmers of daylight. He spoke gentle words then, and she looked up at him—and the promise of universal nature that everything recommences and that the wounded hearts of the young heal up in individuals who are still young, began to be fulfilled for her. She thought that Thérann was strong among the strong, and devoid of ferocity toward women and children—and when the darkness was victorious, they lay side by side, without moving or speaking, but sensing tomorrows rise within them, while the wolves roamed the savannah, the hyenas laughed on the river-bank and the great carnivores got to their feet in the fullness of their strength.

IV. The Islet

In spite of his youth, Vamireh, son of Zom, was the wonder of the Pzânns horde. A subtle and powerful hunter, handsome in build and as strong as an aurochs, he also possessed the mysterious gifts of art. The forms of animals and plants captivated his imagination. He was the one who roamed the hilltops alone and marched through the forest or wandered along the river in the dark, for the joy of discovering secret things.

The dolichocephali of Europe did not make fun of such men, and held Vamireh in profound esteem for knowing how to ply the gravers that carved bone and horn, and the chisels that carved wood and ivory in the round. Devoted to his art, he had become the most renowned artist of the tribes that came south-west in spring. For days or entire weeks on end, he removed himself from the midst of his companions, exploring the wilderness, laboring in some distant retreat, and the works he brought back from his wanderings were the delight of the horde. Neither his father Zom nor his mother Namir worried about these absences, having a diffuse faith in his good fortune.

One morning he embarked on the river and headed downstream in his slender vessel, which trembled at the slightest eddy, propelling it with thrust of his paddle. As the troglodytes' lair faded from view, the river broadened out, becoming shallower, and rocky outcrops dressed in mosses and lichens interrupted his progress. There, the deep bass of the current, the rumors of the pebbles and magical resonances sang the hymn of great waters; sometimes the blocks of stone were arranged in architectural symmetry, in halls open to the four winds, in which the voice of the abyss sang.

Along the virgin banks the forest extended, in edges of fragile willows, gray poplars, mournful ash-trees and birches on the mounds—and, behind them, the populations of giant trees, the cosmos of lianas and the war of little plants, the mystery of creative nature, liberated forces, renaissances in the humus, in partial shade like that of temples, and ambushes in which joy, terror and love quivered in perpetuity.

Vamireh abandoned his paddle, gripped by the solemnity of the spectacle, delighted by the vacillation of the shadows of trees on the surface and the savage scent of the place, while herbivorous muzzles slid between the tree-trunks and the foliage and groups of sturgeon swam upriver, shaving the erratic blocks of stone.

Meanwhile, an islet came into view. Vamireh started paddling again. He steered his canoe into an inlet on the southern shore of the little island, where he moored it among the willows. Frogs, water-fowl and a teal ran away. Vamireh parted the foliage and found himself in a clearing where the earth seemed to have been trampled, the wild grass intentionally dispossessed. A smile appeared on his face while he plunged his hand into the hollow of an alder. He brought out scrapers, blades, pointed flints, and fragments of bone, cord and oak-wood. For a few moments, he studied a statuette that was still vague; the top of the head, the forehead and the eyes were nearing completion. An esthetic, religious hesitation made him shiver.

"It will be finished before the full Moon."

Then he threw off his cloak, went to fetch the teeth and bones he had brought from his canoe, and hesitated for several minutes as to whether to continue the statuette or work on engraving. The fangs of the *spelaea* were particularly tempting. He picked them up and put them down several times over. With the sharp point of a flint he sketched imaginary contours, screwing up his eyes and biting his lip. Then, looking around and wandering about the islet, he seemed to be searching for a model: a tree, a bird or a fish.

34

He picked a flower from a cove—a huge water-crowfoot with a pale corolla—and examined it. An intelligent gentleness, a mental finesse in cerebral contact with nature and an artistic thoughtfulness furrowed his brow and his eyelids. He savored the large, discreetly-polished petals, subtle anthers and naked pink stem, besotted with their shape, with a voluptuous retina—especially the terminal lines, the contours that his graver could reproduce: the flower's frontiers. Posing it, wedging it with little branches, he tried to restore its natural pose and sharpened his instrument. Finally, taking one of the *spelaea*'s canines, in a profound absorption and with a grave passion, he began lightly to trace a profile, the outline of the crowfoot.

Sure and sensitive, his muscular and athletic hand lent itself to the work of Art; already, a graceful outline had appeared: the deployment of the petals, the tips of the anthers on their frail stalks. Excited, Vamireh paused, his lip held more nervously between his teeth, his eyes half-closed. The minutes having been well-spent, the flower seemed likeable on the fine ivory. The man laughed softly, squeezing his torso between his arms.

Soon discontented with a few lines, however, he erased them with the scraper and began again, while an irritation was born: a conflict, the moment when the labor became hard, imprinted with anger. With the gestures of a colossal child, reproaching his materials, letting his arms fall by his sides, he threw away the graver several times over. The stubbornness of his race soon brought him back to work so that he finished the sketch, succeeding in correcting the maladroit lines. Weary, he got up, no longer wanting to look at his work. Then melancholy invaded his brain, a humility in confrontation with nature. For a long time, he stayed by the river-bank.

It was a great era of fecundity; the water was filled with a tumult of inferior creatures, many having come from the sea, moving upstream. The equinoctial floods having ended more than a month ago, branches and uprooted tree-trunks had become scarce.

Noon came—the blazing Sun and shrunken shadows, the air tremulous with heat and ascending columns of air—but on the damp islet, beneath the willows and green alders, the hour was delightful. In the distance, on the river, a large horned animal appeared, which Vamireh recognized as an aurochs. Unhurriedly, he went to the river's edge, along a sort of stony jetty. His hunter's heart quivered at the sight of the enormous mammal; he admired its huge skull leaning down over the water, its long legs and its muscular chest.

"Ehô! Here's Vamireh! Vamireh!" he shouted to the animal, in a resounding voice.

The aurochs raised its head, astonished, and the nomad continued: "Vamireh will let you live!"

Having finished drinking, the aurochs went away. Vamireh had brought a slice of urus meat, cooked in advance for preservation. He ate it, let himself fall on to the ground and went to sleep.

After an indeterminate time, a light contact woke him up with a start. He saw half a dozen water-rats fleeing. He stood up with a single bound, his eyes dazzled, immediately thinking about the unfinished engraving on the canine tooth. When he picked it up again, he was pleasantly surprised; instead of the uncertain sketch he had imagined, it was a firm and precise design with elegant lines. He picked up the graver again, carefully deepened the lines, and then, hollowing out a suspension hole in the root of the tooth, he smiled with joy over his new trinket.

For today, however, his creative power was exhausted; he attempted in vain to resume work on the statuette; invincible yawns and a continual awkwardness accompanied all his efforts. Discouraged, he replaced his materials and tools in the hollow of the alder and raised his eyes to the sky to calculate the hour. Evening was still some way off, the Sun only halfway to setting, although a certain coolness was already descending as the shadows lengthened. Mosquitoes were hovering in columns; translucent clouds were forming above the forest. Then tedium began to weigh upon the dolicho's heart—

36

the tedium of excessively good health and accumulated strength. Formless promises wandered through his mind, desires for hunting, dangerous work and generation.

He was tempted by the distant region of the river's lower reaches, beyond the forests. Unknown to his race, he was overwhelmed by a keen, hazardous and childish curiosity in their regard. Why should he not go and see? In the boldness of his youth, inclined to sudden enterprises and accustomed to solitary wandering, the desire germinated, grew and became clearer in the burning imagination of the frustrated artist.

Then he carefully inspected his spears, his club, his harpoon and two rows of fish-hooks, assured himself that the waterway did not pose any danger to his canoe, picked up the paddle again and lightly re-embarked.

As he moved further downstream, the forest became denser, its banks less definite, made of muddy humus and mud excessively furnished with sylvan debris. The current, blackening, flowed more slowly, the blocks of stone having disappeared, and 1000-year-old trees loomed up intermittently. Large crocodiles slept on promontories and the clamor of parrots covered the august whispers of Life.

V. The Man of the Trees

When dusk engulfed the river, Vamireh realized that he had come a very long way within the confines of the forest. He roasted a few slices of a sturgeon that he had harpooned on the way and, his hunger satisfied, recalled the vague legends of the Pzânns.

Tâh, an old man of 120 winters, with a lucid memory, told of the crumbling of the mountains. Three generations before Tâh, the way south-east was barred by lakes and mountains that neither the Pzânns, nor any other race known to them, had ever crossed. Then the fires under the earth had trembled, and the flanks of the mountains had opened up. The abyss had drunk the great lakes. The terror of it had remained in humans. An entire generation had grown up, none of whom dared to cross over into the new lands. Then Harm, the great hunter, followed by Tâh's father and brave young men, had ventured into the defiles hollowed out by the cataclysm—and thus were the great savannahs of the south-west discovered...

Sitting under an aspen, his breast stirred by these memories, Vamireh wanted to be one of those like Harm, who found distant lands. He remembered a sequence of other legends: the story of the adventurous Pzânns who had attempted to cross the forest 100 years ago, some of whom had disappeared without trace, while others came back with tales of the river running on forever between great trees, and perils increasing with every day's journey.

None of that discouraged the nomad, however. His curiosity and his courage were excited by the nocturnal rumors, and all the traps that he perceived extended in the shadows. He remained beneath the aspen for a long time, sleeplessly. When tiredness finally weighed too heavily on his flesh, he went back to his canoe, pulled it up on the bank, and then, having found a dry spot, spread out his *spelaea* hide. Turning the canoe over, he covered himself up with it, shielding him from immediate surprises. With his club in one hand and his spear in the other, he dozed off.

On that night and the ones that followed, Vamireh was not attacked by carnivores. It was not that the monsters of the shadows did not prowl around his canoe, but none of them attempted to force a way in. Vamireh camped on islets as often as on the wooded shores. In the abundance of everything, there was no lack of the meat or fruits that sustain human strength.

More than once, confronted by the interminable forest, from which large streams came to join the river, he felt sad and regretted his adventure. He knew that the return journey would be more difficult than the outward one, and the stories of people who had not come back troubled his memory. His heart filled with tenderness at the thought of Zom and Namir, his parents, and his younger brothers and sisters. To be sure, Namir and Zom had sometimes waited for him for two or three quarters of the Moon, having become accustomed to his departures, but how long would the journey last this time? Many obstacles had accumulated—especially the rapids that Vamireh could no longer pass through, where he would have to carry his canoe along the bank. Between the mangroves and the undergrowth, over tangled bends, amid reptiles and wild beasts lying in ambush, these passages had been difficult—but the very obstacles, as he overcame them in greater number, pressed him to persevere, for fear of having endured perils without any reward.

One morning, he woke up while the birds were finishing their hymn to radiance, and the reeds were rippling in the undergrowth like light rain. A rustle of branches attracted his attention. He saw a shape the color of ash-wood approaching, with a swaying, jerky gait, crouching down on its hind legs. It was larger than a panther. At the sight of its four hands, its face, its circular eyes and its delicately-trimmed ears, a memory stirred in Vamireh—words spoken by Sboz, who had penetrated further into the forest than any other Pzânns. In the peculiar creature with the long arms and the powerful chest he recognized the Man of the Trees.

A stranger to the peoples of Europe, and almost to those of Asia, every period pushed the species further back into the tropical lands: the profound southern forests conserved a few scattered families, here and there, 100,000 years after the exodus of their race.

A surge of sympathy ran through Vamireh. Standing up, he uttered the greeting cry of the Pzânns. The Man of the Trees stopped anxiously, his round eyes searching the thick curtain of foliage.

Vamireh pushed the branches aside, abruptly exposing himself. "Hoi! Good luck to you!"

The Man of the Trees stood up. Covered in downy fur, the hair on his head sparse, less tall than the nomad but broader in the shoulders, he seemed to be endowed with a formidable strength. Vamireh was astonished by his fearsome features—the enormous jaws and the eyebrows fused above his yellow eyes—and by his dark and grainy skin, without suffering any diminution of sympathy or pleasure in seeing a fellow human after a week of solitude. Accompanying his words with a gesture he went on: "Vamireh, friend…friend!"

The Man of the Trees growled, parting his lips, evidently suspicious of the other's intentions. The nomad, realizing that speech was futile, attempted to communicate by means of gestures, with no result other than increasing the stranger's suspicion. Refusing to get excited, Vamireh took a few steps forward—but then, his eyes tremulous and clenching his enormous fists, the Man of the Trees struck his chest and threatened the troglodyte.

The latter became indignant. "Vamireh does not fear the lion or the mammoth…nor the ambushes of men…"

The Man of the Trees growled again, but without making any move toward the Pzânn, simply by way of self-defense. Seeing that, Vamireh fell silent, his curiosity increasing as his anger disappeared. They contemplated one another for some time.

The pause seemed to inspire some confidence in the Man of the Trees. His features relaxed and a herbivorous placidity appeared in his ponderous face. Though less analytical than Vamireh, he too perceived the presence of a fellow human—but vague instincts, perhaps ancestral memories or atavistic fears, did not render that presence agreeable. Did he sense that once having been, in the course of the Tertiary Era, the equal of the tall Dolichocephalus standing before him, poverty and poor habitats had condemned his race to die while the other was victorious? Were the dolors, revolts, nostalgias, perpetual migrations and battles lost written in his flesh? Had all of that been transmitted from generation to generation, from blood to blood, vaguely awakening dreams of ancestral life returning to hereditary fibers, worth as much as direct and precise memories?

He stood there sullenly, his amber eyes scrutinizing Vamireh, but less suspicious.

The Pzânn, having run out of gestures and concluding that communication was impossible, went back to his canoe in order to refloat it. As he reached the river he turned round and saw that the Man of the Trees had followed him, and was watching him curiously. When he finally re-embarked, a certain benevolence showed on the ashen snub-nosed face, and the hairy arms sketched a vague friendly gesture. Vamireh replied to it immediately, cheerfully, excusing the forest-dweller his suspicion.

For a long time, while the frail vessel drew away, an attentive face remained immobile among the mangroves—and what panic dream, what impression, as wild and confused as the riverside undergrowth, was wandering through the brain of the Fallen, within the sluggish skull of the Man of the Trees?

VI. The New Country

Yet more days elapsed—and still the forest! Vamireh was beginning to doubt that it would ever end. Why should it not be the frontier of the world? The rapids were becoming less frequent, however. Save for the attack of a panther that fell on him from the crown of a tree, the entrails of which he had ripped out, the torment of tiny creatures that harassed his flesh, and the threat of snakes, Vamireh had only had to cope with the ambushes of the inanimate, the perfidies of the marshy ground and the tangled plants of coves. Ever more adept at detecting danger, simply by virtue of the appearance of the water and the ground, he became accustomed to laughing at these obstacles, a greater pride surging in his heart and his flesh.

By the 60th day, however, the vegetation appeared to be thinning out. Two or three gaps appeared: regions of new growth where the trees were smaller and the centuries-old colossi rarer. By means of other indications—the presence of animals that liked open spaces, and the nature of the soil— Vamireh was able to anticipate the success of his enterprise.

Two days later, his last doubts vanished; the left bank displayed old steppes scarcely transformed into forest, where the trees were ever more widely spaced.

Toward the middle of the 68th day, he moored his canoe in a carefully-selected creek, armed himself with his spears and club, and undertook an expedition of discovery on foot, in a westward direction. The ground was firm; grasses and small plants were increasing dominance over the trees.

After a few hours, Vamireh arrived at the top of a hill overlooking the region. To the north was a dark green landscape tinged with purple and black: the oceanic forest through which the enchantments of Light flowed, to which life clung innumerably and subtly. To the south, the steppes opened up, punctuated by oases: country seemingly made for hunting and free circulation—the new country that Vamireh had wanted to find, and the appearance of which inflated his breast triumphantly. Laughing softly, he thought about the surprise of the Pzânns when he told them about his journey, the blissful delight of Zom and Namir.

He stayed on the hill for a long time, lost in ecstasy—but the firmament overhead was becoming more agitated. Two huge black clouds fused, rimmed by phosphorescence. Anguished, gyratory updrafts gripped the plants, and thunder rolled majestically over the forest. Vamireh loved that storm; his entire body breathed in its force and movement, emotions concordant with his state of mind. When the waters of the sky began to rain down, he received the cool inundation sensuously.

The fever calmed, however, as the ragged clouds were consumed by the atmospheric warmth and broken up by electric shocks. The grasses were scarcely able to hold on to the rainwater; the avid earth drank it all up. Vamireh marched delightedly through the post-pluvial landscape.

The last vestiges of woodland disappeared. Nothing remained but the immense steppes, dotted with clumps of bushes. The scattered clouds threw ephemeral curtains of light shade over the ground from time to time, refreshing the view.

Dusk was approaching now. Vamireh stopped on the edge of an oasis as darkness fell, and spent the night there. He set off again the following day, resolved to return if he was not overtaken by some adventure, having discovered what he desired: new hunting-grounds. The tracks of urus and aurochs, red deer and horses, assured him of the fecundity of the region, and he anticipated a great expedition of young Pzânns for the following year.

When two-thirds of the day had elapsed, however, he was overtaken by a rather considerable adventure. It was during a halt, while the nomad was just finishing off a brace of quail that he had killed on the way. Sheltered in a cluster of fig-trees, he saw a woman coming toward him.

Dressed in bark-fibers mingled with savannah grasses, she came closer. Vamireh hid himself more carefully; the wave that broke within him, from his heart to his brain, bore anxiety and charm. The certainty that she was young was verified not only by her increased visibility as she approached, but by her rhythmic stride, the supple sway of her hips.

At 30 paces, she was revealed as scarcely nubile, a slender virgin with large eyes. Vamireh was surprised by her dissimilarity to the familiar daughters of Europe, with their elongated skulls and strong build. Her face was slightly rounded, as pale as the clouds in spring; her hair had a sheen like that of pools on starless nights; her short stature had more in common with that of ash-trees than poplars; and her entire bearing, the shape of her lips, as well as that of her forehead and the form of her eyelids, was suggestive of a distant race— of a humankind that had developed for hundreds of thousands of years without any contact with the nomadic hordes of the West.

As a herbivore, estranged for centuries from regions where predators prowl, retains the atavistic instinct of recognizing a tiger, Vamireh perceived the distinction between his own organism and that of the adolescent girl. He divined that he would find entirely new things in this corner of the world to which his caprice had led him, and that premonition of the unknown made him anxious, hesitant to fall upon the prey of sexual attraction.

A prickling sensation passed through his flesh, like the effect that the approach of a storm has on the nerves of a bird. In his barbaric imagination, however, lashed by electrified blood and all the amorousness of May, the foreign woman seemed infinitely desirable. A child of art, inclined to the sensuality of contrasts, he was captivated by her long black silken eyelashes, her tremulous gait, the precision of her contours, the charming animality of her eyes—and his resolution was made.

While he hesitated, though, the passer-by had skirted the ambush and was already 100 paces away. Vamireh leapt out, with the rapidity of a stallion.

Turning in response to the sound, the young maiden saw Vamireh coming; fearfully, with a plaintive cry she tried to flee. She ran lightly though the long grass, but with no hope of escaping the mighty hunter. Twice or three times she changed direction, trying to slip away at a tangent into clumps of bushes. He gained on her continually, only held back by the pleasure of seeing the fugitive's hair floating in the wind and the curves of her charming young body flexing. Finally, she sensed that he was right behind her, the wind of his breath on the back of her neck.

She stopped and turned round. With panic in her eyes, and her breasts turgescent beneath the grasses of her garment, she raised her eyes imploringly, with a stream of confused speech. The nomad stood motionless in front of her, listening, soon convinced of the impossibility of understanding her language, more rapid and more sonorous than his own—but the language of nature, the terror inscribed on the woman's lips and eyelids, moved him to pity. The new impressions experienced by his physiology became less sharp and more profound, sketching a crude poem, and brutal sensuality retreated before tenderness.

Did she understand? Had she an instinctive sensation of her triumph over the tall fair-haired man? Less tremulous, she continued to murmur syllables in which an indecisive malice was mingled.

He attempted to reply, to make her understand that he did not want to be terrible. Attentively, she observed the gestures he sculpted; they were new to her. A daughter of races with no plastic arts, worshipful races, she was only familiar with ample and monotonous movements distant from nature.

Even more than by the signs, however, she seemed surprised when Vamireh, taking off one of his ivory ornaments, offered it to her. Not without mistrust, she studied the lines engraved on the little plaque—the flight of an urus pursued by a predator—holding the work upside down, uncomprehendingly. With a smile, the nomad set about giving her directions, and miming the design, troubling her even more.

Vamireh's eyes, however, and his interjections, gradually reassured her. She began to smile too. Then, with joy in his heart, he placed his hand on the woman's shoulder.

She recoiled, her mistrust returning.

"Vamireh is good!" he murmured.

Suddenly, she started, and clapped her hands while gazing at the horizon. Following the direction of her gaze, Vamireh saw, to his annoyance, a group of men approaching at a run.

With a slightly mischievous gesture, the woman suggested to the man that he should run away. Taking hold of his weapons, he counted the newcomers; there were 12, armed with large bows and lances. Given the impossibility of fighting, he was seized by an angry despair, his pride wounded by the frustration of his idyll.

"Vamireh is not afraid!" he said, boldly—and as the foreign woman moved away, he went after her and took her by the arm.

She struggled, and cried out in a loud voice. He dragged her toward him recklessly, lifting her entirely off the ground.

Terrified at feeling herself as light as a kid goat against the nomad's torso, she defended herself without violence, with timid jerks. Taking flight in spite of his burden, he tried to run, and contrived a surprising rapidity, excited by the shouts of the pursuers—and for the first, he was victorious. Those who were chasing him, belonging to a thickset race shorter than his own, did not seem to be pursuers of prey—men with the legs of predatory beasts, like the occidental dolichocephali. They were agile, though, and they would doubtless tire more slowly than Vamireh, unless he relinquished his burden.

He scarcely thought about that, moved by a keen desire to fight. He ran in an easterly direction, toward the bank where he had left his canoe. Even supposing that he kept up the same pace, it would take him at least half a day to reach it—a long time after nightfall, after which the Moon would rise to its zenith.

After the first few minutes, the young woman abandoned all resistance. She was a woman, after all, carried off by a male who was not ill-treating her; a curiosity had began to arise, such that she allowed herself to rest her head and upper body on Vamireh's shoulder. In the distance, on the savannah, she could see the men of her tribe, and was able to make out their gestures.

They were armed with large bows and light arrows, dressed in cloaks woven from vegetable fibers and animal wool. She compared them vaguely with Vamireh, clad in the fur of the *spelaea*, armed with his club and spear. Undoubtedly, she wanted them to win, but would, however, have liked to save the life of her abductor. A certain vanity, a feminine impressionability to which male violence was not an insult, Vamireh's strength and the attraction of the unknown floated through her semi-barbaric mind, scattering promises.

An hour of the hectic chase went by, during which Vamireh continued to increase his lead. Softer and more oblique, the sunlight lent an amber tint to the savannah, and the shadow of the hunter and his prey extended immensely toward the east. Suddenly, as he looked back, Vamireh could no longer see his pursuers. He climbed up on a mound, and perceived them more than 5000 meters away.

Triumphant laughter welled up to his lips and he cried: "Ehô! Ehô!" Then, to the young woman, he said: "Vamireh is the stronger!"

She turned her head away, offended by his laughter and his cry. He sat down. They remained silent for five minutes. Vamireh's breath, initially hoarse and panting, became regular, his pectoral muscles rising more rhythmically. Then he murmured a few words. She opened her eyes and their gazes met. The man's was calm and tender. She lowered her eyelids; a malicious and disdainful feminine temerity appeared in her face. Vamireh was disconcerted and charmed by it, finding it even more delightful. With less conviction, he repeated: "Vamireh is the stronger!"

Already the pursuers seemed much closer; it was necessary to resume his flight. He started to increase his lead again, and it seemed evident then that it was the others, not him, who would tire first. Besides, their company, which had stayed together thus far, was breaking up, three or four of them being too exhausted to continue the chase. The rest remained more or less closely grouped, none of them attempting to go on ahead of his companions, held back by the mystery of the adventure, and the tall stature and extraordinary agility of the dolichocephalus.

The daylight dwindled further; the yellow hour arrived. On the savannah there was a less vibrant silence, a cool and melancholy atmosphere—a restful phase. The sparse oases spread life around them. The mosquitoes flew above the moist surfaces in huge columns. A euphonious rustling began everywhere, the chirping of small birds. It was an interval of safety and well-being, when the diurnal animals no longer had to fear predators on the prowl, in which the large ruminants were lying down on the plain in welcome security, in which something of the youthfulness of the morning reappeared in declining daylight.

Vamireh's run became slow and lumbering—but behind him, it seemed that the pursuit had been abandoned. At the extremity of the horizon, the silhouettes of the bowmen had vanished, and the hunter tried in vain to catch sight of them by climbing a small hill. For the second time, he took a rest, and put the foreign woman down. She remained standing beside him, melancholy, understanding the futility of any attempt at flight. He felt too tired, at present, to express his triumph, and was also anxious, for he felt that he no longer had the strength to start running again. Even so, he consoled himself with the thought that they too must be exhausted.

They remained there, without saying a word. Dusk fell. With august slowness, the universe of colors died away with the sunset and Vamireh shivered as he saw his companion bow down, extend her arms toward the horizon and speak to the disk of the Sun. A son of the priestless Occident, vaguely superstitious but devoid of religion, he did not understand what the oriental woman was doing. He watched her curiously, perhaps anxiously. When she had finished, they remained there for a while longer, until the Moon rose.

"Come on," said Vamireh, then.

She understood the gesture, and walked beside him, unresistingly. In the solitude of the night, when the wolf and the jackal were beginning to howl on the steppes, he would be protection. She had a more profound admiration for the huge club thrown over his shoulder, attached by ligatures. She already felt an embryonic intimacy and trust; her resignation was not as grim. Taciturn and weighed down by fatigue, he did not have his former ardor; the blood of May, full of generous molecules, had wearied in his arteries.

Their silhouettes went on for a long time, while the prehistoric Moon rose. The steppe was already more thickly covered with oases, the trees were multiplying into groves, advertising the proximity of the forest. The moonlight was already more silvery upon the grass, and Vamireh thought that his companion must be hungry and drowsy. He was particularly thirsty.

"Rest!" he said. "Vamireh will watch out for the beasts!"

Submissively, she sat down, beneath three stout fig-trees full of the perfume of spring. The Dream was flowing between the branches: the eternal dream of the Moon and the Stars; the daughter of the orient plunged her confused soul into it. She was aware of the fragility of her being. Her family and her tribe, the evening fires, the priests and the herds of Asiatic cattle haunted her, tormenting her until tears came. Alone as she was, though, she was not moved to hate the man who had stolen her, being all too well aware of the fact that he was her only barrier against the formidable night.

In the open, Vamireh watched the surrounding area attentively. The profiles of cats appeared at intervals. A deer fled in the distance. Sniffing the air, a wolf approached the three fig-trees. Almost immediately, the form of a frightened hare bounded away. Launching himself at an angle, Vamireh reached the point at which it would be closest to him; then his spear was raised, and whistled through the air. The little animal rolled among the grasses. As the hunter bounded forward, the wolf took flight, and the man went to collect the hare.

He skinned it rapidly and suspended it from a branch. Then, piling up dry grass and desiccated branches, he took one of the flints with which the dolichocephali made fire from his bag. He laid out some exceedingly dry fibers, and struck sparks. After a few attempts, the flame caught, tiny at first. Then fistfuls of combustible materials were skillfully arranged, and the hare began to roast.

The Asiatic woman bowed down to the firelight as she had to the setting Sun, with a similar chant. Impassively, Vamireh roasted the hare. When it was done, he offered it to his companion, and they ate in silence.

The meal was brief; one of them was too tried and the other too emotional to eat much—but a keen thirst tormented them, and it was therefore necessary not to think of stopping for long before having found water. They set off again.

After less than 1000 paces, Vamireh began to hear the rustle of a stream, and a little watercourse soon revealed itself, from which they drank.

"Sleep!" said the man.

She understood the gesture, and scrutinized Vamireh fearfully. In the pale moonlight, his face was sad and weary, not at all ferocious. She sat down with her back to a birch-tree, and closed her eyes, but she was still mistrustful and struggled against her tiredness. Its force defeated her, unconsciousness overtook her and she succumbed to the quotidian semi-death.

Sitting on the bank of the stream, Vamireh contemplated the facets of the water, the tangles of vegetation and the mullions of the willows interposed before the Moon. A dream as vast and peaceful as the night drifted through his brain. Softened by fatigue, his entire adventure appeared to him in slow, profound and tender notes. The Moon's ascent, the howling of beasts, the fluid murmur and the arborescent phantoms looming up on the steppe seemed to him to be dispensing time and space. In order to have carried away the maiden, he had felt that she was his, to the same extent as the *spelaea* skin that was hanging from his shoulders. As the firmament quivered, though, and the trees were transmuted into moving physiognomies, Vamireh sensed in his turn the weight of the environment; his mind retreated as his flesh submitted to drowsiness. Vaguely, he dragged himself under the birch-tree, took hold of the young woman's garment and curled up on the grass.

Time passed, and the Moon began to descend along the course of its decline. It was less than 30 degrees from the horizon when Vamireh woke up. With a glance, he assured himself of the presence of his companion, and then stood up, exploring the steppe. Nothing suspicious was evident there, and he concluded that the pursuers had abandoned the young woman, or that their fatigue, more considerable than his own, had forced them to rest.

As he felt his mood lightening, and his strength coming back, he decided to improve his chances further and get under way again. A quarter of the hare remained, which he divided in two with the aid of his flint knife, one part of which he ate. Then, having dipped his head in the stream, he remained still for a few minutes, contemplating the sleeper.

She had curled up on the ground. Her delicate head was resting on her shoulder. Her entire body, folded up in zigzag fashion, had an exotic charm that disquieted Vamireh. An afflux of blood throbbed in his temples; his savagery awoke entirely and he leaned over. What instinct, what poetic gentleness, raised him up again, full of pity?

Incapable of analysis, he was no less sensitive to impressions; he shook his companion gently to wake her. She sat up slowly, alarmed, her eyes confused by sleep. Then her perception of the situation returned, and she became sad, gazing somberly at the moonlit steppe and the descent of the reddening Moon into the occidental abyss. A vague joy penetrated her, though—the sensation of approaching daylight, the energetic appeal of good fortune in young flesh—so she did not refuse the summary meal that Vamireh offered her. Her appetite having come back, she even took pleasure in biting into the roasted thigh of the hare.

Charmed, he gazed at her lupine teeth, the hair flowing along her neck and a mysterious suggestion of maternity mingled with the young prehistoric man's increasing love.

Looking at him furtively between her lowered eyelashes, she accustomed herself again to the hunter's presence, finding him even more handsome and powerful than the day before— but the sacred memory of her tribe interposed itself between them, and filled her with regrets.

VII. Pursuit

Shortly after dawn, Vamireh and his companion finally reached the river. The abandoned canoe was still in the bush where he had hidden it; he only had to lift it on to his shoulder and put it back in the water. When he tried to put the foreign woman into it, however, she manifested a violent revulsion. It was almost necessary to force her. Furthermore, as soon as she was embarked, the resignation of her Oriental fatalism returned.

Sticking close to the bank, where the current was manageable, Vamireh began to move slowly upstream. The hour was delightful, in the oblique sunlight, not yet hot; all of nature was rejuvenated on the steppes.

Increasingly numerous trees announced the proximity of the forest. Vamireh hoped to reach it before the Sun was halfway to its zenith. He had only been paddling for half an hour when there was an alarm. His keen eye perceived a distant company of humans and animals on the steppe.

After a few minutes, there was no more room for doubt. They were men similar to those of the previous day—the same, in all probability. Thanks to the curtain of trees, there was every chance that they had not seen the canoe immediately, while Vamireh, much closer to the curtain in question—for whom, in consequence, every gap was an observatory—was in a position to follow their movements over the sloping surface that led to the river.

They were, in any case, not moving swiftly; they often paused, and it was soon obvious to the nomad that they were following his trail, with all the halts that such a mode of pursuit involved. Vamireh concealed his impression from his companion, and started paddling more ardently, with the intention of reaching the forest and disembarking on the other shore.

After a few minutes, however, the young woman perceived the new arrivals in her turn, and her features became animated. An exclamation sprang from her throat, and then, turning to her abductor, she looked at him in a humble and pleading manner. Embarrassed, he lowered his eyelids—but he was overtaken by resentment, and a wild determination that made him say, as he had the day before: "Vamireh is the stronger!"

She stiffened herself, apparently indifferent, keeping an oblique watch on the others' approach. Vamireh calculated that if he could be out of sight when they came close enough to the bank to see the details of the river through the bordering vegetation, they would be forced to hesitate between three possibilities: that he had gone downstream, that he had gone upstream, or that he had crossed the river and continued his eastward course.

By maintaining the present velocity of his canoe, it would be possible to reach a long and narrow island covered with trees, which he perceived about 2000 meters upriver. If he veered to the right there, it would become impossible for the pursuers to see anything. Estimating the distances and respective speeds, Vamireh could only arrive at the approximate result that his salvation would depend on a matter of ten meters. He therefore gathered his strength for a supreme effort, and moved rapidly toward the islet. At the same time, though, the others were nearing the river.

At one moment, his anxiety became immense; one of the Asiatics had just stopped, and, putting his hand to his forehead as an eye-shade, seemed to be looking in Vamireh's direction. From the manner in which the hand fell back, Vamireh deduced that he had not seen anything, but he was convinced nonetheless that the curtain of trees must already seem less opaque to the others, in order for one of them to attempt to peer through them.

Fortunately, the islet was getting closer. A few more strokes of the paddle and Vamireh would reach the point. Then, suddenly, having understood the desperate maneuver, his companion stood up in the canoe and started shouting. Powerless, Vamireh supplied the last paddle-strokes, rounded the promontory, and then, finally invisible in the shadow, he moored in a little creek and stood up furiously.

"Shut up!"

His rough hand lifted the young woman up and shook her. Afraid and overwhelmed, she fell silent, her fatalism returning. For two minutes he remained angry, his temples hot;

then he calmed down, certain that the cry had not carried, and resumed studying the steppe.

He definitely had the advantage. The others, moving more slowly and hesitantly, had reached an area where urus tracks were mingled with the traces of Vamireh's passing, and were evidently unable to explore the river. Vamireh pointed them out to the Oriental woman with a triumphant finger.

"They'll never get you back—never!"

Forcing her to sit down in the canoe again, he took up the paddle and continued upstream, sticking close to the island.

For an indeterminate interval, the little vessel advanced in silence. The islet broadened, filled with a hectically tangled mass of vegetation, its trees devoured by lianas. Colossal toads and web-footed wading birds were revealed periodically. Through the vernal incense, the perfumed joy of corollas, the scent of humus, damp wood and reptilian organisms emanated from the shadows. There was a whole sequence of capes to double, and water-weeds to impede the canoe. The arching branches of alders and ash-trees brushed Vamireh and his companion, and the trembling reflection of things rebounded from the waves, simultaneously dressed with a more discreet grace and a vertiginous distress.

Vamireh had completed half his course in this fashion when the islet began to thin out and get narrower ahead. The water became bluer. Eventually, the point appeared, and the river became broad and limpid, the forest outlined at a distance of 3000 meters.

The nomad thought that, by staying to the left, the imposition of the insular outcrop would surely keep him invisible, so long as his adversaries had not reached the region of the river bank opposite the center, on the assumption that they had continued the pursuit. Even if they were to move to the other bank—in which case the peril would be greater—he would probably reach the forest region without having been seen, and there, the hindrance to their progress would give every advantage to the vessel moving freely over the waves...

VIII. A Night Beneath the Branches

Night again! Life vast and minuscule, the mystery of forces, forested places, the collision of molecules and living beings, the inexhaustible wriggling in the earth, immobile cold-veined organisms looming up, shivering in gusts of air, the prowling of the avid, the anguished and the amorous—and a pale amber star drifting in the solitudes of the firmament!

Vamireh had constructed a temporary shelter between mossy blocks of stone, covered and sealed with thick beams of wood interlaced with lianas. The fortress was solid, and if any wild beast attempted to violate it, Vamireh would have the time to stab it mortally, through the interstices, with the point of his spear, which was anointed with a subtle poison and sheathed in an ash-wood staff.

About midnight, a scraping sound awoke the nomad and he looked out. Wolves were prowling near the shelter and a panther passed through the constellations of light and shadow. Meanwhile, raucous sighs rose up. Vamireh perceived the silhouette of a tiger, which was devouring an antelope that was still alive.

"Elem!" he murmured.

The ferocity of the night entered very gently into his soul. The word that he had pronounced was his companion's name, which he had obtained during the midday halt, when he had pressed her with gesticulatory questions. This was the third night they had spent in the forest, without the nomad knowing whether or not he was being pursued. The flight had been harsh, the river full of treacheries and the forest of ambushes, but he had overcome all the obstacles. Now, its vicissitudes came back to mind, mingled with his companion's name.

"Elem! Vamireh is Elem's master!"

He contemplated her as she slept. A flow of pale moonlight through the cracks in the shelter interlaced with darkness

55

on the maiden's face. Vamireh quivered before the blurred profile, reconstructing the pale features. As they had fled, while he had struggled on her behalf and against her, and he had multiplied the things he had done to please her, she had become more precious to him. His growing tenderness had coincided with subtle pity, and the delicacy of sentiments hitherto unknown. Although he had decided stubbornly to press on to the end of his adventure, and wanted Elem regardless of what she wanted, in spite of any and all perils, he felt, by way of compensation, full of mercy and patience. Only the imminence of a danger, the fear of losing her or of dying, could move him to the brutality of a troglodyte.

Then again, he felt a slight religious fear of her. She frightened him with her silence and her large eyes, motionless for hours on end, her mysterious prostration before the evening and morning Sun, and the words that she spoke then, slow, monotonous and musical...

Branches crackle; heavy footfalls are audible in the clearing. The wolves disappear. Beneath the branches, supported by the round columns of its legs, with white tusks sparkling in rays of moonlight, it is the Quaternary colossus, the great mammoth in its decline. Some slight anxiety or spring fever is agitating it with a desire to refresh itself in the waves of the river. It advances in a sovereign manner, and even the tiger retreats, carrying off its prey. Shivering, Vamireh admires the enormous beast. He has a respect for it inculcated by the elders; he knows it to be valiant but placid, and he knows the melancholy story of its decadence.

"Llô! Llô!"

It advances further, its large head profiled more clearly in the semi-darkness. Vamireh makes out its mane and hide, its sober trunk swaying synchronously, and its enormous flanks. It scrapes the shelter, draws away and vanishes in the direction of the river—and Vamireh crouches down, thinking that he might get another hour's sleep. He closes his eyes. He dozes off, his thoughts becoming dreamlike and then drawing away, and his respiration similarly marks his slumber.

Then the black eyes of his companion open. She listens to the forest; she sighs. Thoughts of escape haunt her. What if she dared, while he is asleep, to unpick the branches of the shelter and flee westwards, toward the lands of her tribe? But Vamireh would doubtless hear her and wake up—and she trembles at the thought of his cry of anger. Meanwhile, a smile comes to her lips—feminine mockery—and she senses that she is no mere victim. She has seen him embarrassed and timid; she has seen him suppress barbarous desire.

She understands all that as well as the daughters of the human race that will live in the distant future; she has a knowledge of it that is both confused and subtle. For that reason, her fear is mixed with indulgence—without her being able to forget, however, those among whom she has spent her childhood, the individuals of her race and her family, and the young males who speak her language.

Oh, if only she dared! But even more than Vamireh's wrath she fears the ferocious ambushes that surround her in the great carnivorous forest; she calculates her helplessness without her abductor's club and spear.

IX. The Nascent Idyll

In the days of feverish flight, when the blond giant roused her from her slumber in the bright morning, and in the nocturnal alerts, quivering in anticipation of the hunt, the idyll was born in Elem. Through her dark eyes, a dream dressed the entirety of the sylvan surroundings, and Vamireh moved through it, while her native steppes and their pastoral tribes melted away, losing themselves at the confused horizon of memory.

Even stronger, however, grew the instinct of final resistance, the dread of his fecund loins, the desire to be safe, for a less disturbing fate—and even while their union was sketched out in habitude, in the contagion of bodies, they seemed further away from one another, grim and concentrated.

Sometimes however, the captivating hours, of midday for the flesh and dusk for the mind, broke the charm of indifference. Then the brunette girl, warmed by the sultry contact of the air or lulled by the vague rumor of the dream, felt a surge of sharp desire, abandoned her eyes to those of the man, and surrendered to a slight intimacy. Some roaring wild beast, some thunderclap or sudden nocturnal dread would throw her against him.

Sometimes, he persuaded her to sing the melodies with which her tribe accompanied their labor. He listened to them, following the measure, surrendering himself to the music of the unknown tongue, utterly charmed in his savage candor. Like a stammering child he took up the song, lending mysterious articulations to it—for he was the one who was learning the foreign language, already adept at naming objects and vocalizing movements.

For her part, she interested herself in his weapons: the spears, of which he used several species, some with bases split to accommodate a shaft, some with points wedged in a hole in the shaft; flat or rounded harpoons; daggers and scrapers. She was most excited, however, by the fine eyed needle, and its reindeer gut thread—things unknown to her tribe, which, although it possessed the art of weaving vegetable fibers, only employed awls.

She was no less open-mouthed at his sculpture and the engraving, frightened by the patience required, the sureness of the notches and the verity of the depictions. She listened curiously to Vamireh trying to explain the Pzânns' way of life; she followed his pantomimes indicating dimensions, miming ceremonies and describing dwellings. Once, she learned the fate of women; after much effort, she understood their distribution in families under the direction of the elders. She was astonished by it, for she was accustomed to monogamous tribes, periodic unions with friendly tribes, children raised by their mothers, fathers serving both as chaste guardians of wives and vigilant protectors of children. The abduction of young women was customary, so the anger of the Orientals had not been aroused by Elem's kidnapping but by the fact that Vamireh had committed that offence without any preliminary alliance—and, in addition, the masculine horror of a distant race.

They understood one another so poorly, however, that any detail was impossible. The long hours went by marching, hunting and cooking. They became close to one another, and acted in common, like two children released by the vast forest. She was submissive to all strategic necessities, almost humble in letting herself be guided, but remaining reserved at every halt, in an attitude compounded out of fear and coquetry.

He retained a mysterious dignified gentleness, sometimes sad, abrupt with inanimate objects, snapping tree-branches, running after wolves and panthers, but never violent with her. When a perilous passage presented itself, and he took her in his arms, the embrace submerged his heart in a flood of passion, but he maintained the humility of the lion before his mate, a nobility of barbarian aristocracy. In any case, in the faraway caves, trials preceded espousals, an already-exquisite comprehension of fecund apprehensions of loves, griefs and joys, vanquished fevers, intimate struggles destined to become the great battles of future humankind.

Vamireh accepted the trial that would increase in complication, the slow seduction, the felicities gradually extracted, without overly gross triumphs—by virtue of which, more than anything else, the generations of his descent would in time be glorious.

X. Combat

Since dawn, the canoe has been gliding through the abundant freshness on the broad river. Powerful daylight streams through the gap opened on high by the interruption of the foliage. In the distance there is a chain of islets, and the image of trees close to the river-bank—their black shadows and their quivering lives—possesses a vertiginous beauty. All around, the forest is like an alternative darkness with a thousand gaping openings, populated with all the sounds of life: a formidable covert of the eternal struggle; a protector of adversarial races, propitious to attacking traps and defensive ramparts; a common storehouse of foodstuffs for fructivores and carnivores, reptiles and birds.

Vamireh is holding his notched harpoon, desirous of catching a fish. A quietude has possessed him. After the long hauls of previous days, the necessity for rest often involves him in his petty tasks: the repair of weapons or clothing; the quest for animals with delightful flesh. This morning, he is enthused by fishing. Twice already he has missed his victim, for the water creatures are quicker to flee into the wake of his boat than a man's hand can throw.

The harpoon plunges for a third time, and Vamireh, holding on to the shaft, darts the sharp point at the side of a young sturgeon. The fish wriggles and jumps; the barbs prevent the weapon from being dislodged, but the electric bounds of the prey create a considerable risk of the lines breaking, and Vamireh has to maneuver skillfully to avoid thrusts that are too sharp or too perpendicular.

He paddles with his left hand, pushing his prize in front of him to the river's edge; there he digs the harpoon in more deeply, finally lifts it out, and throws the bloody sturgeon on to the bank.

He hastens to prepare the meal. Soon, eaten into by the flames, the dry branches and herbaceous stems have made a heap of gray ashes in which his prey is buried. They emerge with their flesh tender and tasty, and the young people devour them.

Slightly torpid after the hearty meal, their eyes explore the diversity of things. They are quite a way from the bank, in a circular clearing bordered by enormous beech-trees. The undergrowth is abundant, working to recover the hiatus pro-

60

duced there by some ancient catastrophe and to repair the integrity of the forest. Large Compositae open up, with a bitter scent, and colossal barbed and bristling thistles thrust upwards, superb and terrible.

Elem and Vamireh are dreaming quietly, in perfect peace, when an arrow suddenly passes within a meter of the Pzânn. His expert eye discovers human silhouettes behind the trunks of the beeches. These silhouettes soon emerge, and a volley of arrows flies. In this moment of peril, instinct throws Elem into Vamireh's bosom, while the battle is joined, as the enemies—seven in number—approach swiftly. Thickset, they are men of the Orient, with infernal eyes. They know about Vamireh's speed, and they fall upon him in such a way that he cannot escape their thrusts. Already their bows are flexed, their poisoned arrows ready to follow their deadly trajectories—but raised voices advertise the danger to Elem, and all hands abandon the bows in favor of the spear.

Proudly, Vamireh looks at them, and his battle-cry stirs the hearts of the bravest. He recognizes his enemies as members of Elem's race, large-skulled, brown-skinned and dark-eyed. Tattoos ornament their foreheads and arms; a robust old man is leading them.

Vamireh has picked up his spear. The brown men shelter behind the nearest trunks. Then Vamireh puts his arm round Elem and begins his retreat toward the river, where he hopes to be able to embark…

At an order from the chief, the arrows fly. The Pzânn wards them off cleverly, and accelerates his flight—a very good tactic, which annoys the Orientals, for three of them race forward. Vamireh's spear strikes the most agile however, and the Pzânn gives voice to the great triumphal laughter of his race, thinking that the two survivors do not have the strength to fight him…

His club whirls in the air, challenging them; his robust chest emits hoarse cries; his arm takes pleasure in the extermination.

The chief sees that his kinsmen are doomed, and orders them to wait; in response to the imperious words, they obey.

A pause. The Asiatics hide among the huge thistles, cutting off the retreat to the river. In a bellicose melancholy, Vamireh sees once again the obscure colonnade of the gray beeches, the eternal semi-darkness beneath the frail lattice-work of branches, while the Sun lights the large clearing and the incoherent mass of undergrowth from which the Orientals are watching their enemy. Through the fever of the battle, there is an impression in the Pzânn's long head of the burden of the conflict, the fear of losing Elem again, of finding himself in the petrifying mutism of things for the long days of his return.

He no longer has anything to throw but the harpoon. The Oriental captain wants to mount a co-ordinated attack in which, if one has to die, the others at least have a chance to avenge him. Dispersed, in order not to offer too easy a target, they rush the kidnapper all at once…

The harpoon fails to claim a victim, the horn having detached from the shaft too soon—but Vamireh finds a new resource in an ovoid flint that he carries on his person. He uses it as a projectile, which strikes the aged commander. The latter collapses, stoically, struggling silently against the pain. He conquers it, gets up and rejoins his men; his features express anguish as well as hatred.

Vamireh tries to flee again. He grabs Elem and bounds away. Arrows follow him—one wound and he is dead. In any case, burdened by Elem, having only a restricted field available, a few steps in advance, he will be caught at the river's edge before he can reach open water. He puts the young woman down, setting her free. Full of anxiety for the Pzânn, she does not run away. He understands, and, with one last thought of Zom and Namir, in the caves and on the plane, he engages in battle…

At close quarters, where the use of arrows is impossible, the fight begins badly for the Orientals. One lance is broken by Vamireh's club, another is seized by him, and he makes use of both his weapons at the same time, with terrible ambidexterity.

Retreating or advancing, according to opportunity, he succeeds in holding the five brachycephali at bay, and even wounds one of them slightly in the chest—but these maneuvers have taken him away from Elem. He sees her in enemy hands, and sets out to recover her. A lance opens a wound in his side, and blood flows. His formidable revenge breaks the skull of an Oriental and knocks a second one down, his shoulder fractured, while the chief receives a stab-wound in the thigh.

The Pzânn is weakening, though; the last vestiges of his strength are required for self-defense. Elem screams loudly while the men of her race prepare the ultimate assault, and while the heat of battle causes the old warrior to drag himself forward to attack the wounded enemy. It is the end. Vamireh gets ready to flee. His club makes one more sweep, claiming one more victim; then he hastily picks up a lance and a harpoon. He runs to the river, reaches the canoe, leaps into it—and three strokes of the paddle deliver him to the current.

His adversaries weigh up the hazards of an aquatic battle. The chief forbids them to take the risk. Then they all take up their bows—but it is futile to fire, for the canoe disappears behind an islet.

XI. Vamireh

Lying in the bottom of his little boat, Vamireh closed his wound with his hand. Congealed blood covered it. He waited an hour for a favorable opportunity to return to the bank, for the loss of blood threw him into a limbo of dreams, a sort of gentle semi-consciousness, in which clear perception of his body evaded him. Things whirled around, as if thin and fragile, while his breast became lost in the delight of a warm, asphyxiating crushing sensation.

Then the crisis passed. With the fever of illness, his strength was reborn. The Pzânn was able to take his canoe back to the bank, go ashore and gather the balsamic leaves and resin necessary for a dressing. First, he washed his wound in the river; then he put his lips to it, and applied leaves steeped in resin and a broad band of hide over the top. This bandage, solid enough to resist any strain, permitted sufficient evaporation and even allowed passage to suppuration. After eight hours, it would be necessary to renew it, but in the meantime, thanks to the aromatic leaves and the resin, there was little danger of complications.

Vamireh felt a great relief; the vague fear that he might have been fatally wounded disappeared, and he felt a considerable pride, a joy of victory. Voluptuously, he appeased his thirst and his hunger, and then went in search of the wood necessary for the fabrication of new weapons. He soon found shafts: a dozen small ones for spears, one large one for the lance. As he worked on them, he was gripped by the temptation of having a bow and arrows in the Oriental manner, in fire-hardened wood. The shaft of the bow was flat but broad, with a tiny round notch for directing the arrow. Vamireh uprooted a young ash-tree, whose extremities he burned, then spent long hours scraping the wood in order to thin it out, making alternate use of fire and flint.

The Sun set before he was able to finish, and he realized that it would take at least two days, not counting the work of sharpening the arrows. So, while seeking out the best nocturnal refuge, he promised himself that he would finish the lance, the spears and the harpoons first, in order to equip himself in advance against any attack. That was improbable; the Orientals, with their two dead and their wounded—of whom the chief was one—were hardly likely to open hostilities. They would go back to the steppes as quickly as possible, taking the young woman with them.

Vamireh smiled in thinking that they did not hold her conclusively, and he was late going to sleep, enfevered by stratagems that he formulated for getting her back.

When he woke up the next day, a great weakness retained him on his bed. The scarring was beginning. He could scarcely drag himself to the river-bank, where he went back to sleep as soon as he had taken a drink, at the risk of being devoured by predators. The Sun had reached its zenith when he recovered consciousness. He quenched his thirst again. His head was thumping, his veins throbbing, and his mind was dazed.

He understood that the day was lost, resigned himself to it, and fortified himself in his canoe close to the river's edge. With pauses in which he drank, as if in a dream, darkness lay upon his life until the following dawn. He was close to oblivion. All night, his robust chest was agonized in the darkness. The periodic crises followed one another like tidal waves. With the dawn, however, came calm; sleep restored him, and Vamireh woke up hungry at midmorning.

He checked his bandage. All pain had gone; the flesh, almost knitted as well as before, only had a slight sting; the redness had disappeared from his breast. His head was free.

Vamireh set off in search of food, armed with his only two remaining weapons, a harpoon and a lance. The undergrowth offered few resources at that moment and, in any case, he had to lie in ambush, for he could not muster any speed while wounded. Three hours elapsed in which nothing passed by but small carnivores with repulsive flesh, and hunger was already beginning to torment the hunter's gut terribly when a herd of hinds appeared, led by a fine male elk. They were dangerously large prey, but all the more seductive because the male's antlers would furnish everything he needed by way of points for lances, harpoons and spears.

At that moment, Vamireh regretted deeply not having a bow that would permit him to attack at a distance, for male elks often avenged the murder of their mates determinedly. This one was a colossal deer, as large as our present-day horses, and its antlers expanded above its head like the branches of a defoliated beech: two forks to begin with, and then a large rack garnished with curved points.

The troglodyte, under cover, drew nearer to the group with infinite precaution, but the distance was still too considerable to hope that he would be able to use his only harpoon successfully, so he waited. The animals were grazing and playing, and a hind eventually strayed within arm's reach of the man. The harpoon flew and struck home. With an agonized cry, the animal collapsed, while the herd whinnied and fled into the thickets, leaving the male immobile, scrutinizing the thick foliage.

After a minute, the huge deer approached the victim and pawed the ground nervously, torn between a desire for revenge and the fear of the unknown. Meanwhile, lust for the superb antlers haunted Vamireh; in a reflexive and entirely unhealthy movement, he emerged from cover, his lance at the ready and the *spelaea* fur in his hand.

The herbivore hesitated, its oblong pupil lost in the dream of the forest; but the man was already recoiling, and the beast's instinct detected a weakness in him. Immediately, with its head lowered almost to the ground, it charged the barbarian. He watched it come, and stepped aside, suspending his heavy cloak from the forked antlers; then, while the deer was getting rid of the encumbrance with a mighty shake of its head, he stuck the lance in between its ribs and shoved it all the way to the heart. The animal fell.

Vamireh fell down too, exhausted by the effort—but he soon got up again, lit a fire, and cooked a piece of the hind.

When his appetite was satisfied, a great sadness overwhelmed him. He had lost Elem. He saw her again, even more precious than before: her brown eyes and her expression, grim and tender at the same time. He recalled the vicissitudes of the battle, in which she had not abandoned him. His gaze searched the undergrowth for her, and he felt a constriction of the heart that soon became intolerable. He shouted the young woman's name, ardently imagining means of getting her back.

The woods fell silent in the warm hour. The sunlight mirrored on the river formed showers of little ellipses through the limited density of the trees. The crowns hung like great clouds, and the space enclosed by the high branches, full of scattered gleams of light, had confused gaps and deeper gulfs. Refined by pain and solitude, the sight of these things agitated the troglodyte's inner being to the point of suffering. He experienced alternating desires for sleep and art, and recalled a day's work in the caves, when he had sculpted a staff of command—and that brought back the urge to make new weapons.

Armed with a delicately saw-toothed flint, he set to work. By nightfall, he had detached the antlers from the head. A slight fever gripped him again then, for moving his arm back and forth had irritated his wound. Being idle, and not being able to sleep, he conceived a desire to mount an expedition to recover Elem's tracks. He slid into his canoe and went downriver.

The night hid him in the vast darkness. The river seemed the voice of silence, an exceedingly low whisper, broken only by the croaking of isolated frogs, hoarse and mournful. In the alternating surfaces of shadow and reflection, the sweeping and sure flight of blind bats appeared and disappeared incessantly. The strip of starry sky extended above the trees plunged an abysm into the waves.

A few strokes of the paddle brought him level with the bank where he had fought the Orientals; then he abandoned himself to the current, hiding his silhouette in such a way that the canoe might seem from a distance to be a rootless tree-trunk. To begin with there was a wilderness in which the fauna remained quiet, then vague indications appeared of a fearful presence. Finally, he perceived heaps of stones marking the location of graves and, an hour later, the flames of a fire denounced his adversaries' encampment.

For a long time, Vamireh watched. Elem must be lying down on the other side of the fire. One warrior, who raised one of his arms into the air from time to time in order not to fall asleep, was on watch. The firelight projected his gesture as a gigantic shadow across the river. The Pzânn clutched his harpoon, and calculated the possibilities of an attack, his fever and his weakness pushing him to recklessness.

The rumor of the woods grew as the breeze increased. The water was brightened by a pale phosphorescence, a background halo limited by distant branches and inlets crammed with reeds. The play of the clouds continually changed the surface of the waves, throwing a leaden veil over it, or turning it into a trembling night-light or a stream of constellations.

Vamireh's inner being was animated by a drama. Beyond the fire, her face in the firelight, Elem showed herself. Oh, to get her back, to carry her off as before! But the internal effort made him feel his ill-closed wound, and his powerless arm. In a few more days, he would regain all his strength; in the meantime, he could follow the trail and choose his moment. Gently, he set the harpoon down, took hold of the paddle and, before returning to his latest refuge, let the current take him to the other bank. There, he paddled prudently, at a speed that was almost negligible at first, but increased gradually.

An hour went by. The canoe was making slow progress, although Vamireh kept close to the bank. In addition to the current, he was obliged to battle the algae in which his prow became entangled and which stuck to his paddle. He was about to put in to shore when a sort of channel through the reeds attracted his attention, He steered his boat into it and, for a short interval, navigation became easier again—then the channel was blocked by water-weeds.

In the hope of finding open water again within short distance, the feverish Pzânn moved the obstacle aside and went further in. Unfortunately, there were only small pools covered with lentils, reeds, algae and bulrushes—to the extent that the man was overtaken by an extreme lassitude, and had to lie down momentarily in the bottom of his canoe.

The night wore on. A presentiment of dawn paled the sky and the cries of sylvan cockerels sounded in the thickets. The faint speech of pointed leaves brushing together and ruffling like feathers, the splash of an otter and the eternal rumor of the river, punctuated by clear notes, were the only sounds of the wilderness. Everything seemed to be plunged into a gray semi-transparent mist; the black fringe of the forest on the far side of the river was hardly perceptible between the waves and the pallid sky.

Vamireh sat up. An extraordinary torpor was numbing him, urging him back to sleep. He felt an urgent need to contrive a shelter, and measured the distance to the bank. It seemed considerable, all the more so because the vegetation was even thicker. For a moment, he thought of abandoning the effort and sleeping in his canoe, but it would only require a single movement to overturn the vessel, and his wound would not permit ample swimming strokes. Resigned, he headed back toward the bank, aided by his paddle, bloodying his hands on the sharp-edged leaves of the reeds, pulling and pushing the frail canoe, extremely tired, with frayed nerves, making long pauses.

Day broke, and everything seemed extenuated: the water, the sky, the forest. The broad river emerged from a horizon of mist, and lost itself in mist again.

He reached the bank. As he disembarked, separating the tall stems, he saw a panther battling with a very young mammoth. The pitiful little herbivore was trying in vain to repel its adversary with its trunk. A female was visible in the distance, running impetuously to the aid of her offspring, and the trumpeting of a male in the reeds announced that he was about to swim to the bank. With one bound, however, the panther set itself on the back of the elephant cub; its claws were already raking the thick hide, and its fangs reaching for the belly when the compassionate nomad intervened.

Scarcely had the harpoon drawn blood from the spotted coat than the panther retreated, growling. Meanwhile, the vast head of the male mammoth emerged, almost at the same time as the female appeared.

Then the panther darted into a thicket, and the enormous proboscideans, swinging their trunks, drew away. Vamireh watched them diminish into the distance, touched by their good fortune and their strength. Then he hauled his canoe up on to his shoulders, went into the trees, and expended the last of his strength in collecting thick branches for the consolidation of his refuge beneath the boat. Feeling heavy and unsteady, he began wedging the most suitable branches for that purpose in the ground at the foot of a tree—but he had to interrupt his work; a greater torpor overwhelmed him, and while he was trying to sit down he rolled unconscious into the Nirvana of sleep.

XII. The Mammoth

In a clearing between beech, oak and elm-trees, sedges and rye-grass grew, mingled with daisies, woolly groundsel and dioecious nettles. Beneath the seed-heads of the grass, amid the leaves, flowers, stems and roots, the society of insects proceeded, a material sketch of the intellectual society of human beings, practicing physics and chemistry, the industrial use of tools and acids, creating the auger, the borer, the saw, the spatula and the die, digging with spades, perforating with caustics and hollowing the tunnels of mines, forging social habitations, diving-bells, swords and armor, producing light, silk, fabrics, wax, sugar and honey.

Dawn found them all at work. The large Magdalenian flies took flight at acute angles in the first rays; wasps visited corollas; enormous butterflies swayed on their velvet-covered wings; clouds of mosquitoes came back from the river to take shelter under the leaves; legions of ants carried off aphids, stamens, seeds and all the debris of minuscule vital battles; tiger-beetles lay in wait for prey in their pits; finely-ridged dung-beetles sought carrion in which to deposit their eggs; boring-beetles hammered their foreheads into the bark of elms; crickets went to sleep, wearied by excessive vibration; earwigs raised their pincers in the depths of corollas; and agile ground beetles pounced like tigers on smaller scarabs.

The forest seemed wary of the unconscious man. The zone circumscribed around the Sovereign biped by the hearing, sight and sharp sense of smell of the ferreters of the roots

70

and branches began gradually to decrease; pointed noses, delicate ears, black pearls of bulging eyes and long antennal moustaches scrutinized the essences emanating from the human, realizing his weakness. Rats approached, enticed by the thongs imbued with bone-marrow; then came the curious heads of dormice and squirrels, on the lookout for the large Quaternary lynx in the forks of trees.

Time went by. Sunlight steeped the clearing. The stream of life increased with the radiance; the flies became more numerous in tracing the enigmas of their flight, the bumble-bees and honey-bees more rapid and more sonorous; the hunting of the birds more active in the branches.

Meanwhile, disappointed in its nocturnal hunt and famished, a hyena limped through the thicket. Its nostrils perceived the odor of the human amid that of hide and grease. It came closer; the rats fled, and the carrion-eater, without emerging from cover, realized that the man was not dead. Hope, however, caused it to stay in the shade, half-asleep.

The long silky threads of light were still falling vertically through the gaps in the branches; the shadows reached their minimum and then began to grow again. Vamireh was still asleep, watched by the hyena. The birds became dispirited; the great trees rested voiceless; ants shook the blades of grass; hornets bent their bodies as they hung on to the frail stalks of florets; flies hummed relentlessly; and herds of roe deer broke branches with the rapidity of their running.

About two hours after noon, jackals caught wind of the fetid stink of the hyena and gathered in the part of the woods where it was. In their turn, they set up an ambush in a thicket, and in their gluttonous anxiety, their sinister calls attracted crows to the prospect of a large quarry. They came in large numbers, croaking, their black flock darkening the clearing momentarily; then they selected a beech in which to perch. From an altitude of 4000 meters, three vultures noticed the excitement of the crows and descended vertiginously into a neighboring tree.

These covetous individuals encircled the prostrate Vami-reh, distrustful of one another, the nocturnal species looking forward to darkness, the diurnal ones dreading the daylight's decline. A hesitation made them coy and watchful to begin with; then the jackals retreated, fearful of the hyena, and panic dispersed the vultures in a trice. Nothing deterred the crows, massed in their hundreds, their chisel-like beaks ready for any aggression.

They opened the celebrations; grave and comical on the branches of their beech, they began a sort of preliminary dance, advancing toward the extremities of their perches until one of them fell; that one flew back and forth for a minute, croaking furiously, then returned to the file. The squawking and the game alarmed the nocturnal individuals and when the vociferators descended on the man in a cloud, with a racket like a hailstorm in the forest, the hyena made off and the alarm spread to the jackals. The latter, however, moved forward myopically, sagacious and grotesque, their terrible jaws like a huge nose at the tip of the head, a blue-black sheen over their entire bodies.

Two meters from Vamireh, doubt set in; the crows ceased croaking, and the oldest held a conference in low gur-gling tones, alternated with dances. A movement from the Pzânn started the rout, however; the birds returned to the branches.

There was a pause; the hyena was heard laughing and the jackals weeping; then, in the re-established silence, the vul-tures' wings clicked heavily, and the three raptors jumped down to the ground. Their bald necks emerged stiffly from fine collars of white fur; their long gray heads were somewhat reminiscent of the head of a benign mammal: a camel, kanga-roo or antelope. For a long time, they stood like motionless sentries, the elbows of their wing-bones like high pointed shoulders, their necks appearing to spring forth from their breasts, their wings forming mantles garnished with fine dis-tinct fringes of pinion feathers. From a mighty race, their wingspan extended to eight feet; their powerful claws, avid to rake dead flesh, grasped animate prey in times of famine.

Were they weighing up the man's death-throes: the residue of his sovereign muscles, the rise and fall of his breast, and his bovine neck? They did not budge, but the famished canines, weary of waiting, began to creep through the bushes. Then the birds flapped their wings noisily; the frightened jackals stopped, and the oldest vulture marched toward Vamireh's blond head.

The untidy hair that had strayed over his face half-covered his eyes; his large blond moustache quivered in response to a feverish groan; and a sort of provocative laugh curled his lip amid the resigned forbearance of the folds of his mouth. His half-bared shoulder seemed to be made of polished stone; the twisted cables of his triceps narrated a poem of bundled muscle-fibers, harnessed in thousands to the same task. The *spelaea* fur hid his torso, where his tumultuous heart was beating.

The forest continued its labor of a colossal city, more quietly. Sated life, in all its forms, went to sleep in its lairs and nests, including the insects' tunnels. The crows, interested by the vulture's action, maintained a discreet queue; the jackals yawned and closed their dazzled eyes; the hyena dug in the ground with its forepaws; faint noises became audible—little cries, muted songs, the fall of ripe fruits—like the diffuse ticking of the clock of existence.

Meanwhile, the large raptor studied the Pzânn's half-closed eyelid through a gap in his hair; the sclerotic was visible. The instinct of a bird of prey is to peck out eyes; the vulture decided to do that. A slow approach brought it within range. Its companions also came forward then, and one of them placed a talon on the bare shoulder.

Vamireh's hand went unconsciously to the threatened spot, colliding with the bird's wing. The animal responded with a peck on the wrist. The wound awoke the man's defensive faculties; as if in a nightmare, his athletic fists found the vulture's neck, while he hid his face in the grass.

For two minutes the hooked claws dug into the *spelaea* skin, and then asphyxia prevailed, and death, without Vamireh's fingers letting go. Already, the vast wings of the survivors were beating the air, their bodies rising up to the top of the trees, hesitating for a second, and then escaping toward the sky through a large gap.

Having acted, the tall nomad fell back into his lethargy, to all appearances a cadaver, and the crows delegated ten of their number to clarify the matter. The others undertook a conference in which gurgling sounds replied to croaking sounds, with similar replies. The ten soon found out that the bulky prey was still dangerous, but the corpse of the vulture attracted them, and they explored it. The man was still holding that corpse in his clenched fist. With minute circumspection, inspired by their avian bravery, they turned the animal over and attacked the bald neck; a breach appeared and the terrible chisels dug into it; soon, only the raptor's head remained in Vamireh's hand. Then, taking hold of it collectively, they dragged their prize a few meters way.

The jackals thought the moment favorable. Yapping and howling, they were heard approaching, like a downpour in the foliage. The ten crows rose up, cawing furiously—but those up above were already falling in their hundreds on the spines of the carnivores, which were quick to flee in response to the unexpected aggression. The black flock remained master of the battlefield, and began to devour the vulture.

The hyena had stopped digging. The increasingly keen torsion of its gut moved it to audacity. Although still superb, the species was in decline, increasingly losing the offensive. This one was far from the monster of its kind, the elephant-attacking Machairodus, a meter long with a double row of teeth. Perhaps the giant hyena still dragged quivering herbivores into its caves, but in spite of its canines and molars—the most solid of any contemporary animal, capable of biting through the femur of an aurochs—this one, a spotted hyena, preferred to stick to dead flesh, or to dig moles, field-mice and other little diggers out of their tunnels.

It advanced slowly, lowering its tail and extending its head like a crawling animal, sniffing the man, more anxious with every passing second. At pouncing distance, it paused for calculation, staring at the throat, envisaging the choking thrust of the dog or the wolf. It did not dare, and scratched the ground nervously.

While it hesitated, the battle between the crows and the jackals was rejoined. The canines made a sortie, and this time they were able to recapture the vulture's remains, while their adversaries took flight. It was a meager quarry! Delicate and supple, their eyes blinking in the daylight, they carefully crunched the bird's bones. Their appetite roused, they considered the larger prey. The hyena did not oppose them; it even seemed as if both parties were encouraging the other to audacity. The laughter and howling overlapped, accompanied by darts, sideways leaps and suggestive exhibitions of canine teeth.

Branches were thrust rudely aside, wood breaking with a tempestuous racket; the bulbous head of a 15-foot-tall mammoth appeared. The colossus liked the clearing; its huge body paused there, swaying; it ripped up a few plants with its trunk, in accordance with some puerile whim. Then it lay down, lapsing into the semi-sleep of large animals, dreams flowing through its head of the inexhaustible sequence of shapes and movements that its eyes had drunk in all day long.

The hyena and the jackals, lurking in the profound depths of the vegetation adjacent to the clearing, suddenly beat a considerable retreat. A soft, heavy and ungainly animal slowly disengaged itself from the thicket and emerged into the light: a bear. The mammoth watched its approach placidly.

The plantigrade stopped, studying the proboscidean. Having woken up in its waterside den, the noise of the jackals had attracted it; at present, it was counting on the recumbent human for its daily meal, and it was expecting the elephant to remain neutral, knowing that it was placid outside the mating season. At first the calculation seemed accurate; the elephant got up as if to go away. Ten meters away from the man, how-

75

ever, it fixed its attention upon him. Its trunk turned in the direction of the body; it moved closer, sniffed and gazed down. Then it trumpeted in a threatening manner, and presented its tusks to the predator. The latter had the concentrated, blind and obstinate anger of its race. It growled, reared up on its hind legs in the shade of a poplar, and waved its clawed feet, the rictus of its lips declaring its thirst for reprisals. The trunk was raised into a semicircle, the tusks raked the ground, and, with the entirety of its gigantic body braced, the elephant waited...

They were two powerful beasts. The bear had its hairy arms, equipped with colossal claws, its canine teeth and its muscular jaws. Standing upright, it could seize and stifle an adversary. Its thick, loose skin was no hindrance against wild beasts, even leopards and lions; it could make use of its weight, and its slow gesture had a terrible precision.

The strength of the mammoth was, however, beyond compare. Its little eyes, unlike those of the bear, saw perfectly; its marvelous trunk surpassed in cleverness and musculature the arm of an anthropoid ape; its tusks, turned along the arc of a circle, ten meters long, projected like the horns of an aurochs. Its entire body, on its four columnar legs, beneath its russet woolly fur and its great black median mane, seemed supple and easy to steer. Everywhere, in the forests, the savannahs and mountain passes, it was the victorious sovereign herbivore, a descendant of the trunked colossi of the Tertiary: *Dinotherium, Elephas merodionalis* and *Elephas anticus*. Those three, along with the hippopotamus and the rhinoceros, represented the glory of the Tapirean Era, of the monstrous flora nourished by the gluten of plants: the triumph of huge skeletons and massive muscles; the triumph of armed peace, armor, horns, tusks and trunks, opposed to the carnivorous rage of rapid movers with canines and claws of steel.

Confronting the myopic plantigrade, the proboscidean was the first to weary of expectation. In its skull, bathed by great waves of blood, the intoxication of fury sometimes moved it to folly. It trumpeted loudly and charged. A tree saved the bear. It had time to climb up it to a considerable height. The other shook the vast throne with its shoulder, and the plantigrade needed to sink its claws three inches deep into the bark in order not to be thrown down.

The elephant persisted, and the bear suddenly tumbled on to its back. Fangs sank into the nape of its neck, and claws dug into the flaps of its ears. The pachyderm shook itself like an animal emerging from water, however, while its trunk gave its enemy an almighty slap.

The bear fell off, and rolled away like a furry ball. Grabbed by the trunk and caught with the tusks, it was lifted off the ground and thrown into a tangle of lianas; then, as the huge beast came after it, it got up and lumbered away.

The merciful herbivore accepted this denouement, and was already moving away when the bear charged again; this time, running blindly into the mammoth's trunk, it scratched and bit it cruelly. Trumpeting in pain, the mammoth bent its knees, then shook its head. That caused the plantigrade to lose its balance, and fall between its tusks. The trunk held it there to begin with, and then the immense ivories dug into its entrails. Then, again, the great columns of the legs broke its rib cage, and the bear exhaled its life in a supreme growl.

The infuriated mammoth persisted for a few seconds more, then threw the cadaver out of the clearing—and the hyena and the jackals had their meal.

Its vengeance satisfied, the proboscidean went back to the man. Again it sniffed him, and, taking up a position five meters away, it trumpeted. The female appeared, with the cub. All three of them took up positions around Vamireh.

Nightfall was not far off now. The large blue prehistoric flies sought the shelter of the foliage in their turn; the mosquitoes departed in clouds toward the water; the crickets resumed their vibrant ariettas; the ants dragged the last wisps of straw into their subterranean granaries. The tiger-beetle larvae slept in the depths of their pits; the dung beetles doggedly persisted in the burial of the corpse of a field-mouse; the chirping of birds died away in the branches; and the crows flew away. The diffuse rays of the Sun, redder and dimmer, lingered on the frail tips of groundsels and grasses; then they darkened further, no longer illuminating anything but occasional bright wisps. The grass still emitted a phosphorescent gleam, though, and the mammoths gravely collected these last luminosities with tranquil eyes, while a sinister clamor emerged from the undergrowth, of jackal calls and the laughter of the hyena, gorged on the flesh of the gray bear.

The vast darkness eventually arrived, spreading the cloak of its mystery over the forest and the river. Fireflies glittered in the bushes; nocturnal moths with fleecy wings soared, followed by blind bats; owls screeched in the hollows of oaks, and the voices of predators were heard proclaiming their murderous triumphs. More than one leopard, and more than one pack of wolves, caught the scent of the recumbent human, but none dared disturb the invincible family of the huge hairy mammoth with the bulbous forehead.

Until four hours after dawn, they persisted in their watch. Then Vamireh emerged from his long torpor, refreshed and fortified as if by a bath in the river on a torrid day. He stood up, stretched his arms and inflated his chest, and suddenly perceived the departure of the proboscideans.

That departure linked up in his mind with the previous morning's adventure, and he shouted words of welcome to the mammoth without knowing how much he owed them. He found out a short time afterwards when he discovered the cadaver of the bear with the broken bones, and his heart was deeply touched.

XIII. The Head

After five days of tiring marching, continually interrupted by pauses for rest, a considerable amelioration was evident in the Orientals' wounds. The sixth day's stage was serious and they were able to hope that they might see the encampment of their tribe before the end of the lunar period that was just beginning. The first to rise, the chief, had never uttered a word of complaint. The old man bore the injury to his shoulder robustly and stoically, as if local injuries had no influence upon his whole body. Every evening and every morning, he treated and dressed his men's wounds and his own, applying herbs in order to reduce inflammation, and reciting words more beneficial than balm.

By day, Elem followed the troop, grimly and silently, but she often woke up in the night, remembered, and wept. Her primitive soul missed the tall nomad, his pale and gently energetic face, his broad shoulders and his imperious muscles— not to mention his anger, his delight, the intellectual superiority of his blue eyes, his preoccupation with art and work. All of that touched her flowering flesh, stirring the affinity of races for propitious hybridization. She sighed with love, while the hours turned in the firmament, dreaming of escape with the dread of being immolated by her kin.

They had already taken umbrage at the praise she accorded to the Pzânn when they questioned her. Only the chief, a thoughtful interrogator, undertook a tranquil enquiry. He was avid for details of the strength, agility and, most of all, the industry and artistry of the wild man, and the mores of his distant country. His hatred, mellowed by age, was drowned by the attraction of the enigma. He regretted that the tall blond man had not been captured. Perhaps he knew exactly how far the forest extended, where the river came from, and where the Earth touched the sky.

More ferocious in their mores, and less artistic than the tall dolichocephali of the western plains, the Orientals had been quick to accept sacred hierarchies. On the fertile plains of the East, they had dreamed of the immobile and monotonous pastor. Their social organization was more advanced, but these races did not have the future of the flexible, willful, hardworking and individualistic races of Europe.

Nomads and hunters, the Orientals already took advantage of the vegetable kingdom; they prepared nourishing pas-

79

turelands with various seeds and thus succeeded in maintaining their stability. Harvests of hay permitted them to nourish several herds of horses and Asiatic cattle, kept prisoner in enclosures, for the scarcely-tamed animals refused wholesale domestication and could only serve as food.

All that, and the fertility of the region, rendered the journeys of the Asian brachycephali less extensive than those of the European dolichocephali. A transitional fauna inhabited their forests, in which species that had emigrated from the Occident were already found: rare varieties of monkeys, jackals and fallow deer, mingled with the beasts of the cold steppes: mammoth, bears, hyenas, aurochs, urus and musk-oxen. With the first frosts, an exodus began of the monkeys, jackals and fallow deer toward the great woodlands of the South; in the summer they came back.

On the Savannahs of the East, the Asiatics had made alliance with dogs, whose villages were widely spaced—dogs that were less defeatist than anthropoid apes, strong in discipline and intelligence, which sided with humans in the war against the predatory beasts, and helped to hunt urus and horses, in return for a share of the booty.

Like humans, the dogs had understood the benefits of social existence; they had deliberative assemblies, male armies, leaders turned gray by the pressure of time. In legendary times they had been terrible enemies of the nascent race. The forefathers of the Neanderthals had already crushed the face of the lion and tamed the Dinotherium with the inverted tusks; the world already trembled on hearing the slow footfalls of a dreamer of the civilizing genesis sketched in the insect world, while the dogs still defended their realm—and who could have predicted the outcome, since anthropopithecus stuck to family groups, to the primitive horde, while the other was confederating its tribes, enlarging its fatherland, raising armies, fortifying its settlements and teaching its children?

The gray-haired old men, the wisdom of nomad tribes, overcame savage instinct, competing with one another in passing on their knowledge of things, penetrated by the mystery of things, attempting primitive explanations of the phases of the Moon and the rotation of the stars. The alliance with dogs was due to them, and they encouraged attempts to domesticate insects, birds, the urus, the horse, the bear and the wolf. That held a significant place in their annals. They knew the caprices of animals and that, while some yielded to force, others preferred death to restraint. They traveled considerable distances to see the Rain tribe, in which the sorcerer Nadda raised bees, and the Moon tribe, in which a young warrior climbed on to the back of stallions, and the Thunder tribe, in which three bears lived among humans.

The Oriental chief, remembering all this, was increasingly chagrined at not having become acquainted with Vamireh. How much better it would have been to make peace with these bold and industrious blond giants! The two distant peoples communicating over long distances would have enlarged the fatherland of human beings. Unknown countries would have been explored: the opening of the great abyss, the lands of the horned elephants, the water-beast, the giant serpent—all that legend had told for centuries.

He protected the young woman. Not only did he forbid any violence in her regard, but he accorded her complete freedom of movement. By day and night he let her wander, whether she went on ahead or fell behind, and he repressed the protests of his men in so firm a manner that they no longer dared to say a word.

Elem was grateful to the old sorcerer. As the days went by her grief matured like a fruit in the summer Sun. When she was alone she raised her arms toward the Invisible, pleading and praying. Her attentive eyes explored the river—the friendly river on which the Pzânn's boat had carried her for weeks on end. The sight of aquatic plants and stray mists on the horizon intoxicated her and stifled her. A desire to die and a profound instinct of survival, of blood too red and vivid, ready to spring from her veins, a spirit of revolt and madness, all remain fundamental to our amours, rendering them disturbing, mortally loving and desperate.

On the 17th day, however, things calmed down.

In the mists of dawn, she thought she saw Vamireh's canoe among the reeds. It was distant and blurred, but with all her primitive energy she convinced herself of the Pzânn's presence. Several times, during the march, she almost gave herself away, beating the undergrowth and lingering on the bank. Distraught and thoughtful when the time to stop for the night arrived, she could not go to sleep, and beneath her half-closed eyelids her gaze searched the darkness.

XIV. Recapture

That night, while the troop slept, the sorcerer read the hectic stream of the life of branches in the flames of the fire. Flames: numerous and subtle colored entities, leaping and crackling, tinted with fine blue, bright yellow and red; creeping and vibrant when running over embers, tall and undulating over twigs, lost in frontiers of smoke, which, in places, flare up and tear apart. Flames, from which a thousand chimeras surge: caves, forests, great sparkling lakes; a transient world that unknown breaths excite or extinguish; a world that becomes angry, and calms down, and becomes furious again; tamed and redoubtable; a devourer of forest submissive to a child's hand.

"Greetings, fire," said the Oriental. "More beautiful than your enemy, water, gentle to the Earth that you fecundate, and gentle to humans, whom you caress with warmth…"

He seemed profoundly meditative. Perhaps he had glimpsed the great marvel of the future, the era of metallurgy. Already, in parts of the world where stones had been melted by heat, little solid ingots were found in the ashes. Everyone guarded these metal strips carefully. They came in various colors: yellows, grays, whites. By striking them with stones one could shape them, or hammer them into blades—but such blades were fragile, pliable or brittle, and no one could yet see them as a rival of stone, bone or horn.

"Fire runs in our veins," the old man murmured, reverting to mysticism, "and that is why our mouths fume, like a brazier on which water is thrown." He breathed in voluptuously, proud of that thought, and his heart swelled as he contemplated the darkness. The firelight blotted out the stars of the zenîth, but on the horizon of the river, they sparkled numerously and delicately. "The fire of the Moon, and that of the stars, is a fire as cold as the human gaze…"

He fell silent. The nocturnal clamor of the forest seemed less noisy. A lion roared in the remote distance, and its beautiful warrior voice rang out from the depths of the abyss to echo in the mountains, powerful and infinitely grave. There was not a breath of wind. The bright surface of the river was toned down everywhere by heavy masses of leaves; anguish radiated from the shadows.

These things caused the old man to shudder. He stood up. The light of the fire illuminated the whole of his thickset silhouette. His anxiety increased when he saw that Elem's eyes were open, and he listened. A faint noise like that of a crawling animal reached him from the profound darkness, soon joined by an abrupt rustle of leaves, and then a slight dry click, as of one pebble against another.

"Get up!" he cried, his bow pointed toward the suspect location.

An arrow emerged from the covert, grazing the chief's head—and the Orientals were not yet on their feet when Vamireh, with a single bound, arrived next to the fire. The old man fired an arrow in his turn, but it went astray to the Pzânn's left. The latter, his club aloft, was about to crush his sole adversary when Elem intervened, imploringly. Immediately, the tall nomad moved toward the men on the ground, and his gesture made it clear that he would kill the first aggressor. Sensing defeat, the Orientals awaited Vamireh's command. The old man looked at the intruder fearlessly, signaling to his men to remain calm.

"Speak, and prefer justice to violence."

Vamireh understood that he could dictate his terms; his mime indicated that he wanted Elem.

"Go!" said the old man to the young woman. "But why take the daughter of our tribe by force? Let your blood be mingled with ours, and let peace unite the Sons of Light with the man from the unknown country."

Elem took Vamireh's hand, speaking softly, and drew him toward the sorcerer. He let her do so, captivated by the Oriental's earnest and dignified voice—but behind them, the other three abruptly got to their feet, with enthusiastic cries. Vamireh thought there had been treachery, seized Elem and started to run away. Some distance away, in the darkness, he stopped.

"Old liar," he shouted, "your voice sings peace but your mind wants war; Vamireh does not trust you." He armed his bow and took aim.

Elem interposed herself again. The deflected arrow vanished in the darkness.

Then the others armed themselves—but Vamireh disappeared while the chief sadly put a stop to the pursuit. "Don't run to death. He could not understand my words, and your cries frightened him."

The fire received new combustible materials, and while the flames burned brightly, the Orientals went back to sleep, distressed by the incident in which their naivety in thinking that they had been understood had rendered the chief's prudence futile.

XV. Reinforcements

Dawn was expanding over the forest and the old man was still undecided. It was now impossible to fight the wild man with any certainty of victory; his far superior strength put open combat out of the question, and any ambush would fail by virtue of his prudence. Reinforcements could only be obtained from tribes more than two weeks' march away. Should he reconnoiter the enemy territory and come back with an army? Might some insurmountable obstacle present itself, though? Did the forest have an end?

Long were his prayers and the rites that gave voice to his thoughts. In the pale flames of the fire and the arabesques of the branches his gaze sought the answer to the enigma, but he said nothing; tribal wisdom holds that a prudent chief act without causing the inexperienced caprice of the young to hesitate. He picked up his weapons, studied the direction of the shadows, observed the flight of certain birds, and then took his companions away.

They soon understood that they were marching southwards. Great plains extended in that direction all the way to high hills—infertile plains into which rare explorers ventured; it was dog territory. A little further to the east, after a journey of six days, they would have been able to meet friendly tribes. The young ones were astonished, but said nothing.

The journey proceeded, punctuated by brief halts. They maintained their direction until dusk. The night was bad; torrential rain poured down on the forest four hours before dawn. The fire was extinguished, and their soaked bodies shivered in every gust of wind. It was necessary to construct a shelter, and the daylight was already bright when they got under way again.

The four sullen men were no longer talking to one another. Everything radiated ferocity; the rain pierced all shade; the earth impeded their feet with heavy mud; the prowling of predators in the thickets was a perpetual threat. A pack of wolves began to follow them at a distance, in anticipation of a death. Snakes multiplied, ominously suspended from branches. The dread of winter whipped up their appetites; it was necessary to fight wolves for a slain hind. Nostalgia for huts and caves filtered into the Orientals' hearts, requited by dreams of the joys of the hearth. The old man alone remained impenetrable, bowing his head beneath the downpours and accepting the contrary fate.

The second night was particularly cold; fortunately, they discovered another clearing, on the edge of which they succeeded in maintaining a fire of twigs. They got under way again early; the moss on the trees and flocks of birds flying toward the plains were again sufficient for orientation. They were less certain, though, forced to make numerous halts. The young men looked at one another furtively and somberly, obstinately turning their faces eastwards. Around the eighth hour, they began to exchange words in low voices, and appeared to be animated by a leaven of revolt.

Meanwhile, the old man marched on, robust and proud. He began to think aloud, gravely, and even to laugh with a sort of enthusiasm. Sagacious, by the standards of those primitive times, he seemed to be gifted with a far and double sight, and a revelatory inner voice.

In the middle of the day the Sun pierced the clouds. A warm and sweet-scented mist rose from the ground. The old man extended his arms and shouted prayers at the star, then turned to his companions.

"Who has the right to exempt himself from obedience? If the Council wants your hut, you must surrender your hut; if it wants your arm, you must surrender your arm; if it wants your life, you must surrender your life. Am I not, in spite of my age, the strongest of us and the cleverest? Your hair is not white and the Spirits do not speak to you as yet. Curb your pride, or it will bring great misfortune upon you!"

Repentance and terror filled the souls of the young men then; they prostrated themselves and yielded once again to the authority of experience. The chief announced that they would reach the edge of the forest at twilight, as confirmed by the presence of large migratory quadrupeds, lovers of the plain.

They felt safe again, and hopeful, in spite of the rain, the dark forest and the increased numbers of wandering predators. Six wolves perished under their poisoned arrows; the rest scattered. The humans seemed to have regained the scepter—but the cataracts fell even harder, and an impetuous wind rushed through the treetops; the predators emerged from the shadows, anxiously, and the maltreated humans became lamentable again.

The wolves regrouped; the laughter of large hyenas in the undergrowth became sharper. The approach of dusk redoubled the hostile voices, the clamor of hateful lives. The Orientals started trotting. The breath of wolves panted behind them; the wind blinded them with volleys of dead leaves. The eyelid of the night closed rapidly upon the torment. Then the chief stopped.

The wolves with phosphorous pupils closed their circle more tightly. They howled, their lips pulled back over sharp fangs. They had few arrows left; it was impossible to make a fire. It was necessary to resign themselves to march by night, with infinite precautions. In any case, the edge of the forest would be their salvation. Slowly, keeping the wolves at bay with spears, the three Asiatics continued on their way…

After the third hour of darkness—the ninth since noon—they perceived a clearing opening on to the plain. The chief formed the rearguard, his desiccated fibers full of resistance, still petrifying the confused wolf-pack with his gaze, but ready to succumb.

To the victorious shouts of the humans, a distant barking responded. The wolves howled in profound anguish; then a rustling became audible in the thickets, the friction of hundreds of invisible bodies, abrupt volleys of yapping and the defeat of the wolves, followed by their flight, in the midst of growls of rage and cries of helplessness and agony.

Then the tranquil Orientals reached the limit of the forest. There, in a troop under the leadership of a captain, their allies the dogs were waiting for their friends.

XVI. The Rain

The diluvian period of summer, which covered the Quaternary sky every year, was approaching. The wind freshened
then; cold often killed flowers and fruits on the branch, and
immense consecutive famines exterminated the fructivores.
The rivers and streams overflowed. Humans cloistered themselves in highland caves, well-provisioned, and hibernated,
passing the time fabricating tools and weapons.

In anticipation of these evil days, Vamireh paddled all
day long. Elem, conquered and submissive, helped. The
cooked flesh of red deer served as nourishment, with the addition of wild fruits, fresh roots and eggs stolen from belated
nests. Vamireh watched over Elem tenderly, and their nights
on the fluvial shores had the immense poetry of childishness.
They were well-protected against the torrential rain; the canoe,
supported by four pillars, served as a roof; large branches were
distributed on every side, and the *spelaea* pelt sealed the
windward side. It was during this time that the tall western
nomad became the spouse of the daughter of countries unknown.

The crackling rain—the loud noise of the forest peppered
by the invasion of the drops—was already presaging winter
and the joy of the Refuge. The first cold spell confirmed the
prognosis. Vamireh, deprived of clothing in favor of Elem,
shivered in the precocious north wind. The next day, he was
obliged to spend the morning hunting for some furry beast. A
bear was ambushed, its heart traversed by a spear-thrust. Its
brain, combined with the brain and bone marrow of a reindeer,
served to imbue the hide, which had been well scraped in advance, stripped of its fat and tendons.

From then on, they were both warm while they slept.
Elem, delighting in the comfort, laughed softly, infinitely confident, but Vamireh remained anxious about the imminent
deluges of rain, which would render the forest uninhabitable.
The predators, more aggressive, and the dangerously hungry

wolf packs, would amplify the eternal battle in the thickets; weapons would be broken in the perpetual conflict. It might be necessary to stop over for weeks in some cave to make more harpoons and spears, not to mention the nocturnal harshness of temporary encampments and the ferocious downpours beneath the open sky.

However ungentle the beginning of the diluvian period might be, they could reach the caves by the end of July, but only by making haste and making use of every day. Vamireh was not remiss in that; from dawn to dusk his vigorous hands plied the paddle. Unfortunately, the canoe suffered some damage, and it was necessary to spend three days carefully repairing it.

Finally, they took to the water again. The swollen river, stained with mud, was already overflowing its lower banks. The current offered more opposition; it was necessary to keep to the side; large floating tree-trunks were an ever present threat, along with terrible tangled masses of algae.

Elem spent the greater part of the day wrapped up in her fur, in a daze as the water went by. Meals were her principal occupation. In order to take them, they moored the canoe in an inlet. Thanks to a provision of twigs kept under cover, the fire flamed well enough to finish cooking a portion of deer, a wading bird or a fish harpooned en route.

The cold dry climate of the Magdalenian Era on the steppes of Europe, although ameliorated in the south-east, nevertheless involved the sudden return of cold before the autumnal equinox. That return gave rise to partial migrations among monkeys, fallow deer, jackals, rodents, and wading birds. Anthropoids then retreated toward the tropics, while the mammoth herds arrived in greater numbers and the forefathers of the Indian elephant, the descendants of the great Chellean *anticus*, came down from the mountains.

Vamireh sometimes stopped paddling when a herd of fallow deer or jackals appeared on the bank as he was passing, but he was veritably impassioned by an exodus of monkeys along some defile, or when they swung through the treetops from one islet to the next to reach the other shore. Flowing in their hundreds, with stormy shrieks, they were seen swinging out and leaping 20 meters, catching hold of branches and leaping again. Their faces grimaced, as if moved by thoughts; they made very human gestures, scratching their foreheads, picking off their lice, sitting on their backsides, peeling fruit with their fingers and teeth. Vamireh found their ornately-bordered ears, their forward-directed eyes, the dexterity and intelligence of their movements extremely charming.

One day, a furious mother threw her child on to the ground. The young monkey, injured, moaned in vain; the others seemed reluctant to burden their column with an invalid. Moved, the tall nomad ran to pick up the infant. He found it whimpering, clutching its breast. Placed in the warm, with fruit nearby, the animal became docile. It liked to sleep in Elem's lap, to install itself on Vamireh's shoulder, to catch water in its hand and to quarrel with its reflection in the river; the mere sight of it, mobile, full of caprices, devoted to little games, made Vamireh's heart swell.

Was there a race of human dwarfs? On this matter, he interrogated Elem, and learned that their language was unknown, that they lived like animals. She mentioned the men of the woods, however, constructors of huts, and Vamireh remembered the creature with the amber eyes, spare hair and furry body that he had encountered previously.

One day, at the hour when a vague redness trembling in the daylight announced the setting of the sovereign star, Elem uttered a scream and the Pzânn's paddle ceased stirring the waves. Humans had appeared on the right bank. They were small in stature, with curved spines, and a sad and humble ugliness was fixed upon their faces. Armed only with ancient clubs, black hair gathered in little tufts hung down to their chins.

"They're worm-eaters," Elem murmured, in disgust. "In summer, they go into the forests and nourish themselves on soft creatures hidden in shells. In the rainy season they go down to the sea shore, and no sacred tribe tolerates their prox-imity."

Vamireh observed the "worm-eaters" feverishly. Their jaws were pre-eminent; their foreheads sloped gently down to their enormous brow-ridges. The backs of their heads, en-larged, seemed too heavy; their hips were not arched and they leaned on their clubs to assist them in walking. For a while they searched among the aquatic plants for roots and stoned fruits, all depositing their finds in a heap in front of the leader of the troop. Along their route they had been collecting un-ivalve mollusks, tubers and edible leaves, so the pile was al-ready considerable. When dusk was very near, they grouped around the chief, and the latter distributed the food equally.

"They're fair!" murmured Vamireh, satisfied. Then, see-ing them light a fire, he yielded to sentiment and steered the canoe toward them, making fraternal gestures. They were ex-cited at first, but the small number of the newcomers calmed them down. They contemplated the tall nomad and his compa-nion silently and gravely. The man's stature, unknown in the Orient, amazed them. They were, however, prompt to sym-pathize with him, although they maintained a visible mistrust of Elem, who reproduced the type of their most ferocious per-secutors.

There were no women among them. The latter followed them at a considerable distance, in confused hordes. Spring brought the sexes together in traditional locations, then the male bands abandoned the female bands for the summer, au-tumn and winter. They were defeated. Sprung at an early stage from the anthropomorphic matrix of the Tertiary, entered into the *external* ways of humankind by the adoption of weapons and social methods, having progressed too far from the animal to re-enter it abruptly without weakening, they were doomed in confrontation with the vigorous younger branches of organ-ic potential[8]—that singular force which abandons the higher

---

[8] Rosny's "*espérance organique*" (which I have translated as "organic potential"—although "organic hope" would be more

type of red man in confrontation with the Aryan. Relegated, moreover, to the arid steps or the depths of forests, physically weak and ill-equipped for hunting the rapid sylvan fauna, they were falling gradually into vegetarianism, skilful in discovering buried tubers, recognizing edible stems and roots, provisioning themselves with stoned fruits and watermelons, grains and sunflower seeds and fond of all mollusks, spending winters on the shores of the Caspian Lake or the Black Sea, living by rudimentary fishing.

An adorable instinct of generosity rendered the life of the individual precious to the mass; the strictest equality regulated divisions and everyone devoted himself to saving his brethren from the claws of predators. By virtue of that, they were still the masters of the lion, the bear, the leopard and even anthropoid apes. Their fear of the brachycephali, the hunters of the fecund steppes, was immense, however; they had seen their kinfolk perish in thousands beneath arrows and spears. They never approached within six days march of enemy encampments, and even avoided solitary groups.

Vamireh captivated them with his puerile laughter, and his generosity in offering them food supplies from his canoe: slices of venison and sturgeon, and ducks' eggs. These provisions too were carefully shared out, to the Pzânn's delight. The latter, having made a present to the chief of a fox-fur, was dumbfounded when he saw the fur carefully cut up and a piece of it offered to everyone. His hearty laughter, and his attempts to make the absurdity of such a practice understood, induced some distrust in the "worm-eaters," but their terror of Elem was even more manifest, as was the disgust experienced by the young woman, so Vamireh decided, regretfully, to leave.

They re-embarked—but when he was some distance away, hidden by the reeds, he watched for some time, making

---

crudely literal) is not exactly equivalent to what Henri Bergson would subsequently term *élan vital* [vital spirit], but has some similarities to it. The implications of the concept are discussed further in the afterword.

whispered exclamations. The worm-eaters stoked up their fires and huddled around them, and after constructing a small hut out of branches, into which the chief slid, they squatted on their heels in the open, burying their faces in their knees, with the palms of their hands on their heads, and went to sleep.

The Pzânn then conceived a great pity for the fate of his inferior brothers. When he put into shore the murmur of his lips was full of bitterness. He remained in a somber mood during the evening meal, and was late going to sleep. Having risen before dawn, he watched the departure of the worm-eaters. He saw them swim across the river and move on eastwards. When they had disappeared, he uttered a melancholy sigh; then he woke his companion and set the canoe afloat.

Four days of laborious travel went by. On the fourth night a storm unleashed its fury, trees came crashing down, the waters of the river rose up in enormous waves, and the entire forest trembled. Sheltered beneath a rocky ledge, Vamireh slept, peaceful and resigned. Elem spent the night praying, imploring the Unknown for mercy. The insinuating force whistled through the thickets, bent the tall trees, and confused voices launched cries of help.

The storm died down before dawn. The day was mild; the Sun appeared between the clouds; the forest resumed a warm and humid life. The broad, mud-tinted river, abundant and tranquil, was charged with the debris of the previous day's battle. Fish that had swum upriver began to descend toward the sea. They swam in shoals, close to the surface, exhausted and physically depleted by the labor of reproduction. The weary Elem slept; the light-hearted Vamireh paddled toward his distant fatherland.

In the course of the monotonous hours, the idea of the distance to be covered and the speed of their progress soothed the Pzânn's brain. He was scarcely more any longer than an extended will, an organism plunged into a fluid dream of water and air; the splashing of the one and the endless caress of the other sent his flesh to sleep. Immobilizing his memory upon a few words, and upon the images of his father, his

mother, his valiant brother Khouni or his young sister, capering like a kid goat, without his being able to contrive the effort
to link the two elements together and imagine them speaking.

Some six hours after noon, however a troubling phenomenon became manifest, and the tall nomad's entire attention
was drawn to it.

XVII. The Relatives

Swiftly running animals—red deer, fallow deer and
elk—were arriving fearfully on the edge of the river and crossing over. They formed considerable herds, prey to a herbivorous panic. Their number increased as dusk fell, horses and a
few urus mixed in with them.

Startled by this strange flight, Vamireh searched in vain
for a simple cause: fire or migration. He stopped paddling.
Elem murmured incantations. The animals' gallop increased.
Wolves, jackals and foxes joined in with the deer, the cattle
and the horses. The shaking of the undergrowth revealed the
passage of smaller animals: hares, polecats, marten and pot-
ters. Finally, the carnivores appeared: lithe panthers and lumbering bears. In the distance, monkeys—scrupulous sentinels—sounded cries of alarm, and that clamor ran through the
treetops like a storm-wind, crossing the river and expanding
into unknown regions.

A beautiful night was promised—there was no threat of
storms, no symptom of bad weather—but the flight of the animals, like some elemental prodigy, stirred up ominous expec-
tations in the minds of the man and the woman. All their voices, in the serenity of the sunset, were vibrant with enormous
dread. Sowing the contagion of fear, Vamireh did not perceive
it as the fear of animals before nature, but as the fear of creatures before other creatures: an exodus of vanquished races,
the discouragement of a species confronted by the dominant
species.

He was, however, obliged to take measures against the extraordinary threat, to guard against the possibility of their being crushed by the blindly stampeding herbivores as they continued to run through the darkness. Vamireh spotted a little island where ash-trees were growing in the middle of the river; he directed the canoe to it and lit small fires there, thus putting them out of immediate range and in an excellent position to see everything.

Neither he nor his companion thought of going to sleep after their meal. Upstream and downstream, the flow of animals had ameliorated. Some risked crossing the river, others were following the banks—and the second maneuver had the curious particularity of operating inversely in the two directions; the animals downstream were heading downstream, while those upstream were heading upstream, as if they were fleeing the area of the forest that terminated almost exactly opposite the island.

XVIII. The Worm-Eaters

The worm-eaters were marching in the direction of the Great Lake. Although generally dreary, their foraging took on a certain gaiety at the beginning of each stage. They scattered then and, the morning pickings remaining individual, exclaimed over good finds, childishly showing off their booty of truffles, snails, sugary umbellifer-roots or bittersweet fruits.

Beneath the long black tufts of their hair, with their jutting muzzles and the disposition of a few clumps of hair on their cheeks, they bore a closer resemblance to some kind of dog than an anthropoid ape. Their short arms, their rounded torsos and the vague barking of their laughter completed the analogy. There was, moreover, a legend circulating among the brachycephalic tribes that a race of dog-men must have existed in the Far East, gradually destroyed by true men, the descendants of the water-beast, the sole legitimate possessors of the Steppe and the Forest, the River and the Great Lakes.

Playing thus amid the vast tree-trunks, chasing one another through the bushes with their bellies overfull, their backs bent, sometimes trotting on all fours, they retained the instinct of orientation that guides migratory animals. Their language was reduced to a few sounds signifying fear, joy, hunger and thirst; the rest was animal miming, and also occult communication, the empathetic flow of terror or anger.

The elders were guiding them, without ferocity, two of them commanding an advance guard of scouts while another—the oldest—brought up the rear. When crossing the territories of large predators, the leaders brought the cohort together with sharp cries. Then, with clubs at the ready, a surprising courage and solidarity allowed them to confront a bear or a leopard without trembling.

In the afternoon they collected the common provisions, which they ate in the evening before going to sleep. Each of them carried his portion of the booty without biting into it. The division was made next to a stream or a spring; they ate and drank soberly, and then they all went to sleep, worn out by their journey, their dreams as vague as those of a lion or a wolf growling in its sleep.

They went on. The damp forest poured its shade over them. Grave and puerile, their attention continually strayed, their poor laughter switched on and off like will-o'-the-wisps floating over marshes. Their life proceeded in short bursts of emotion, sketches of thoughts, the artifices of abortions at the breast, in lineaments of memories and anticipations. Whether the rain bathed their hard skulls, the wind whipped the napes of their necks with cold lashes, the thorns made their feet bleed, or parasites by the thousand burrowed into their epidermis, they accepted it. An entire heredity of resignation had accumulated in their skulls.

Through the ages, ever since the advent of the men with long arms, they had ceased to progress; they stayed as they were. There was no longer any future for them; the vast Earth disdained them, and yet, Life exhausted its means, hardening their epidermis, raising fleeces on their breasts, sliding layers of fat around their bellies. The circle of rival races became ever tighter, though, and these poor human antiques would certainly not outlast the carnivorous beasts, for they had been disarmed by the long crisis of transition in which muscular strength had been solidified and altered in accordance with the adaptations to the external world made by the brain.

In the semi-darkness of the undergrowth, they had companions in exodus to which they were not accustomed to do any harm: numerous groups of fallow-deer and jackals heading southwards, or swarms of rodents heading eastwards. They replied to the trumpeting of the placid eastern elephants and little wide-mouthed horses whose military herds crossed their path with long cries.

On the night of the second day of their journey, the chief was sleeping in his hut of branches, the nocturnal fire was about to go out and the squatting tardigrades[9] were huddling together against the cold, when a sentry's cry brought the entire company to its feet. The word designating a lion ran around, and a great terror caused teeth to chatter. As the chief gathered the strongest, however, they huddled together, cudgels raised.

The redoubtable silhouette of the lion came into the fire-light and paused momentarily before the war-cries of the humans. Whether it had failed in its hunting, however, or preferred the flesh of primates to that of other kinds of animal, it crouched down, executed a prodigious leap, and fell upon the company. They had retreated, opening their troop according to an ancient strategy, and more than 50 clubs rained down on the beast's skull, muzzle, eyes and spine.

The lion moved sideways, reared up on its hind legs, and felled four enemies with three thrusts of its claws. The others,

---

[9] Rosny is using "tardigrade" to mean sluggish in a general sense, rather than in its stricter biological meaning, which refers to creatures of the sloth family.

animated by the battle, became more audacious, their clubs falling more rapidly upon the bloody nostrils, and the Hercules of the group broke the beast's paw with a single blow before ten other blows paralyzed the hind legs.

Vanquished, the lion tried to flee; rendered ferocious, however, the worm-eaters would not permit it to do so. They rushed it all together, and while some held the feline down, the others attempted to kill it. They did not succeed in that immediately, and were subjected to terrible thrusts, but in the end, the chief having thrust his club into the depths of the gaping mouth, the lion began to choke. Savagely and vindictively, they finished it off.

It transpired that two companions had lost their life during the adventure, and that five others were grievously wounded. The dead, extensively mourned, were deposited in the bushes, and the wounded cared for attentively. At dawn, when they resumed their march, the worst-affected were carried. In spite of their losses, the tardigrades were not without pride at having defeated the redoubtable antagonist once again, and they carried their clubs joyfully, exchanging gestures of triumph and confidence.

The forest seemed better to them. Their bare feet bounced off the ground more rapidly, their unbowed stature became almost vertical and their poor eyes shone. Underprivileged as they were, there was no doubt that, had victory only been possible, an expansion of vitality would have enlarged their skulls—but their victories remained confined to the animal world. Like a material pressure, like a ligature about the arteries or a degeneration of the lungs, the fear of the brachycephali shriveled them up, immobilized and annihilated them, even from afar—and the circuit of their ideas was limited to that of their habit, either because they dared not think about what they could not accomplish, or because they were unable to think about what they had not accomplished.

About halfway through the day, the advance-guard of 15 men abruptly fell back. They were in an interminable oakwood. Everyone was hunting for truffles; wild boar were abundant, fleeing before the travelers, and legions of avid flies were buzzing around the truffle-hunters' heads. Going back and forth, pausing to dig, the advance-guard had spotted a family of anthropoid apes.

It was rare for apes to attack the worm-eaters, especially when there were no females in the column; on the contrary, a sort of fraternity animated the great apes, and the tardigrades had found them precious auxiliaries against bears and cats.

A council was held. It was decided to send a small delegation to the men of the trees in order to assure them of their peaceful intentions. That delegation, carefully monitored, attracted the attention of the anthropoid apes with cries of joy and benevolent gestures. Bewildered at first, they soon seemed to recognize allies; they signified that by means of grave gesticulations, and advanced slowly. A few minutes later, the two companies were united. The worm-eaters offered a meal of truffles, stoned fruit and edible leaves. The men of the trees accepted these things with pleasure, for their dietary regime was identical to that of the tardigrades.

Afterwards, the two disinherited races remained silent for some time, observing one another. Their nature appeared to share a common foundation of melancholy, but the melancholy of the great apes seemed heavier than that of the tardigrades, as if it were proportional to muscular strength and the amplitude of the torso. The humans, therefore, were the first to start laughing and the first to start playing, while the apes remained serious and meditative. One of them, however, was stirred by a distant memory inspired by the analogy of circumstances. It launched into a laborious explanation. Leaning forward, the tardigrades listened without being able to understand, but the memory appeared to plant a seed in other anthropoids, and they joined in with the first.

The confusion only increased until one of them took it into his head to pile up twigs and to indicate the dancing of flames. Then the worm-eaters understood that they meant fire, and, full of pride, the chief drew the necessary spark from two pieces of dry wood. When the light came, the darting of yellow tongues among the blue spirals, the men of the trees remained fearful and alarmed for a time, while the tardigrades laughed out loud.

There was a gentle communion of pariahs on the frontiers of animality, a reciprocal pleasure in finding out more about one another's consciousness, and a curiosity as to the progress each had accomplished in the disposition of matter. They parted as friends, the tardigrades heading eastwards and the anthropoids southwards, after a mutual exchange of gifts; the humans had given clubs to the apes, the apes had given eggs stolen from the highest nests to the humans.

The separation only took place after three hours, when the worm-eaters saw the first symptoms of the flight of the animals that had made Vamireh so anxious. At first, they were the ordinary occupants of the habitat—red deer and wild boar—so the tardigrades did not worry unduly, but a few hours later, they saw their companions in exodus, the fallow deer, moving in considerable herds. Then, seized with panic in their turn, they turned back.

XIX. On the Island

Elem and Vamireh were chatting in expectation of an extraordinary event. The Pzânn was able by now to understand and express the fundamental ideas of the language of the brachycephali, but, although he had questioned the daughter of the Orient intensively, she had found nothing in her memories that might clarify the situation. Her superstitious skull entertained ancient legends of the "water-beast" chasing all animate creatures out of the forests in order to fill them with humans. The animals had been saved by the "horned elephant" that reigned over the mountains. The "serpent"—the rival of the water-beast and the enemy of humankind—had opposed it with the disgusting creatures that ate worms, which the sacred tribes were annihilating...[10]

These things had little appeal to the nomad's mind, and even caused him some revulsion. Did not humans live on flesh, and would the savannah and the forest not be miserable places without animals? Then again, he could not imagine an invisible beast! His doubts shook Elem's beliefs, although she continued to murmur the appropriate words, in order to obtain the protection of religious practice for herself and her lover— and that was how it would be until the day she died, and longer still if destiny granted her children, for mystical things, though slow to be born, are like the pigmentation of skin or the form of skulls, which only Time can transform or annihilate.

Leaning over the river, they waited for darkness. It was slow in coming. The dusk retained a glow that was weak and dazzling at the same time, doubled by reflection. In that glow, the banks seemed very distant, and, with respect to the forest, like a frontier of dawn set against eternal darkness. Fleeing animals were moving there, their black bodies outlined in vivid streaks, rounded or inflexible spins, hairy or smooth, their heads long and slender or large and broad, the pointed antlers of the red deer, the palmate spread of the elk, the undulating

---

[10] Serpents and "water-beasts" of various kinds are featured in various creation myths, but this invented myth is only slightly reminiscent of the Vedic myth found in the Mahabharata, presumably recorded by people who shared a common ancestry with the "Orientals" featured here. The association of serpents with evil is, however, much later in origin than the creation-myths that involve them (the association of the serpent in Eden with Satan is, of course, a Christian fancy). Rosny would also have been aware that the Merovingian kings who were the first rulers of the Frankish kingdom that became France traced their ancestry (according to the seventh century *Chronicle of Fredegar*) back to a Bestia Neptunis [Marine Beast] called the Quinotaur [Five-Horned Bull].

mane of the horse, the supple and serpentine trunk of the elephant, the heavy humped back of the bear...

When darkness finally fell, the trees and the river slowly engulfed by the shadows, there was an observable pause. Becoming rarer by the minute, there were soon no more than slow animals, vermiform insectivores or carnivores fleeing the nearby habitat. The attention of Vamireh and Elem increased then, and they perceived a rumor similar to the howling of wolves or the plain of jackals.

Almost at the same moment, a considerable company of worm-eaters appeared on the shore. They seemed harassed, bent double, and covered in mud and blood. They were carrying numerous wounded individuals in their arms. Confronted with the impossibility of crossing the river with the latter, their distress increased. Rearguard scouts continued to emerge from the woods with every passing minute, with gestures of alarm, but no one budged. No one could think of crossing the river without the wounded, and many of them were preparing their clubs stoically for a last stand when Vamireh leapt into his canoe and headed toward them.

The troop he had encountered four days earlier recognized the blond giant and manifested their joy. The others, worn out by fatigue, watched the man approach dazedly. He touched land and made signs to indicate that he could transport two wounded men in his canoe. Those who remembered him obeyed him; the others passively trusted in chance.

Vamireh made 15 trips; by then, all the wounded were on the island, and the others swam to join them. Vamireh shared his provisions with them. He killed three fleeing fallow deer with arrows, and a little wide-mouthed horse. The reassured worm-eaters went to fetch the prey, and skinned them rapidly, according to the tall nomad's indications.

Vamireh, saddened by Elem's disgust, felt sorry for them. He hastened to dress the wounds of the injured, and showed all of them where they might shelter for the night—for the worm-eaters curled up to sleep immediately after the meal.

Then Vamireh rejoined his companion in observation at the other tip of the island.

They talked in whispers. Elem proposed that they should continue upriver that very night, but Vamireh objected that tree-trunks carried by the current after the previous night's storm would break the canoe. He also objected on behalf of the worm-eaters, who were under his protection. She resigned herself, and took up her well-protected place in the canoe, covered by a bearskin. For his part, he remained awake, feeding the fires. He finished skinning the animals he had killed and cutting them into quarters, which he then cooked in order to preserve them.

The darkness had invaded everything. He could scarcely make out the two banks of the river. From time to time, he listened more attentively. The rumor, previously capricious, sometimes coming from the right and sometimes from the left, became more distinct. Sometimes, too, it faded away but always became audible again, at a closer distance. A slight wind rustled the leaves; the firelight was reflected from the facets of the waves; at intervals, there was the splash of a diving body and the breath of a swimmer, then silence and solitude beneath a clear and starry sky, with no Moon.

Eventually, a human silhouette appeared at the edge of the forest and moved confusedly through the shadows. Almost immediately, there was a low undulation, as if made by hundreds of bodies, and a tempestuous racket of loud barking, reinforced by echoes: a flood of life and noise breaking the silence of the Darkness.

Having distinguished the voice of the dogs of the great sterile plains, Elem, alarmed, ran to Vamireh's side and murmured a word that the Pzânn did not know. The worm-eaters also woke up, and all of them, in the firelight, came in search of the nomad. Tall and serious, he attempted to pierce the shadows, to take account of the threat that was making Elem and the tardigrades tremble.

During their slow retreat, the worm-eaters had been attacked by the dogs. Ordinarily, the animals respected the an-

cient humans, whose migrating bands passed through the canine villages. On several occasions, however, the Asiatics had
made use of their quadruped allies to track the wandering tribes, and, fearing a battle of that nature, the worm-eaters had
retreated rapidly. On the way, they had encountered other
groups of their own kind, with the result that their number had
increased to several hundred. They had defended themselves
strenuously and had almost always succeeded in driving back
their terrible enemy, when, half a day from the river, after a
long rest, they had been attacked again. The number of their
assailants having further increased, they had suffered considerable losses in that last battle. Then, convinced that their
adversaries were moving slowly, guided by the Asiatics, they
had hastened their retreat. Having arrived at the river's edge
that evening, frightfully wary and burdened with the wounded,
they had fully expected to die, when Vamireh had saved them.

Surprised in their sleep by the dogs' cries, they rallied
around the tall nomad as their sole protector. The latter assembled their chiefs. He allotted each one of them a battle station
on the shore of the island, instructing them to gather their men.
For each individual, he raised one of their ancient clubs above
his head and brought it down on an imaginary enemy. That
was very well understood, and they all drew courage from the
Pzânn's excited face, from his beautiful eyes shining with
pride, and from his vast chest, inflated with the expectation of
the battle. He had the fires built up, then ran back to resume
his observation.

The opposite bank did not remain dark for long; the
flames of a vast fire soon illuminated it. Then, some distance
from those flames, almost at the frontiers of the red light, Vamireh saw the dogs. Elem pointed them out insistently, told
him how numerous and ferocious they were when led by humans, their organization into villages, their alliance with the
brachycephali. The Pzânn listened avidly. Becoming less fuli-
ginous, the firelight bathed the quadrupeds in light, and, seeing that they were more like hyenas than wolves, with their

104

large jaws, their tall stature and their athleticism, Vamireh understood how dangerous an adversary they must be.

His attention was deflected, however, because a human silhouette interposed itself in front of the fire and a voice rose up in the midst of the great silence, carrying over the water. Vamireh and Elem recognized the voice of the Oriental chief.

"Man from an unknown country," it said, "listen to the words of the man whose hair is white and to whom the spirit of wisdom speaks in his solitude. My words want peace. Allied with the dogs, however, we can envisage war without fear. What can you do, man from upriver, against the innumerable legions of the Beast, aided by our arrows and our arms. Accept peace. Let us exchange the blood of our veins."

With Elem's help, Vamireh understood this speech. Entering into the light of a fire himself, he shouted an acceptance. "The Pzânn salutes you, old man. He has listened to the daughter of your tribe and is ready to exchange his blood with yours. Take the Beast away, then, and spare the lives of the worm-eaters."

On the other bank, the three young men drew near, and the group of brachycephali became animated. They could not fraternize with the sons of the Serpent. The old man was inclined to clemency, but an excited fanatic among the young men preached the implacable will of the "Water-Beast" and the law of the sacred tribes—and all of them, full of hatred and disgust, were convinced.

The chief came forward again. "Why is a brother human taking the side of the vile Being? Let him leave that prey to the dogs, which are more worthy."

Vamireh was revolted. "The Pzânn would not dare to show his face to other Pzânns if he abandoned his allies. The Pzânn wants peace, but he wants it for all those who are with him."

A further conference took place between the Orientals; all the young men, more desirous of a victory than a peaceful outcome, favored war. The chief did not dare oppose them directly, but he reminded them of Vamireh's strength, and also spoke of the glory of an expedition to the North after the winter, and the necessity of making peace with distant peoples.

Two of the young men seemed convinced, while the fanatic obstinately lowered his eyes. He even went to the bank and aimed a poisoned arrow at one of the worm-eaters, saying: "The Council has said: *let your arrow never hesitate to strike down the foul*"—and the arrow described its mortal trajectory, hitting the tardigrade in the shoulder.

The man's cry of pain was accompanied by the blond man's cry of anger, and a rumor of disapproval among the Orientals.

"Man," shouted the old man, "forgive the ardor of excessively young blood."

Vamireh, however, shaking with indignation, replied: "My blood is young too, and cannot forgive such perfidy!" He had already taken up his bow, and his unexpected arrow struck the aggressor in the chest. Then he ran to the wounded tardigrade. His companions were sucking blood from the wound, thus removing the poison. Vamireh procured a quasi-antidote—alkaline leaves whose sap he squeezed over the gaping cut, and which he then applied to the wound, still moist.

In the Orientals' camp, the old man attended to the wounded man. The latter persisted in shouting insults at the worm-eaters. They were all deeply offended, in fact, because the nomad had struck a man to avenge an ignoble creature.

XX. Assault on the Island

The truce lasted for some time. The Orientals withdrew their fire to the shelter of the undergrowth. The dogs were invisible, but their howls sounded thunderously in the undergrowth. The crouching worm-eaters had gone back to sleep, save for a few resistant old men.

Vamireh fortified Elem's retreat with the aid of thick branches and prepared his weapons. The smoke of fires floated over the water, amid the ruddy firelight. No more talk of peace had been heard. It appeared that both sides were preparing for the imminent battle.

While he worked, Vamireh kept watch. Once, he thought he perceived the silhouette of an Oriental, who stood up some distance from the water and disappeared into a thicket. On another occasion, a pack of dogs came to drink. Nothing suggested an attack, though. He hoped that the Oriental chief would wait until morning and resume negotiations.

He had just set down his 12th poison-dipped arrow beside him when there was a rapid movement, and he saw a black mass of numerous bodies swarming on the river-bank.

"Ehô! Ehô!" he cried, while the tardigrade sentries woke up their companions.

In the distance, the impetuous dogs were leaping into the water, and they were seen to be coming in their thousands, their phosphorescent eyes gleaming in their damp heads, their immersion raising the water level along the coasts of the island. Silent and terrible, they swam intrepidly through a hail of stones, bones and pieces of wood that greeted them.

Vamireh, assured that there were no men among them, put down his bow and took up his club. Elem, armed with a lance, could defend her shelter. The tardigrades, encouraged by the Pzânn, displayed a very firm attitude, arranged in little groups, backs to the center, with plenty of room to wield their cudgels.

Before they could come ashore, the dogs were struck on the head so vigorously that they retreated out of range. Soon, however, they were seen to separate into two solid columns, one of which swam toward the poorly fortified tip of the islet, which Vamireh alone defended, while the other resumed the direct offensive. The haste of the tardigrades to protect their savior almost rendered the tactic effective, but Vamireh refused help energetically, obliging everyone to return to his post.

The column directed against him had scarcely reached the shore when the Pzânn's murderous assault sowed terror among them. His tall stature, his gigantic club and his formidable manner of smashing skulls, the rapidity of his movements and his authoritarian voice, plangent with the highest humanity, appeared to have a quasi-superstitious effect on the beasts. Gripped by panic, howling, in total disorder, they allowed themselves to be driven back.

Meanwhile, the invasion of the second column had succeeded—without, however, succeeding in disconcerting the strategy of the worm-eaters, who were still united in groups and defending themselves without weakening. The losses on the dogs' side were considerable, although 20 of the tardigrades were rendered *hors de combat*. In sum, the beasts sensed that they were beaten, when poisoned arrows launched from the other bank claimed two victims. That sowed some terror, and caused the groups on that side to draw closer to the center. The dogs redoubled their ardor, and within a minute, the number of wounded humans increased terribly.

After his victory, however, Vamireh had perceived the presence of the Asiatics firing their arrows, almost in the open beyond the bushes. His bow flexed in its turn and he dispatched several arrows. The Orientals were obliged to retire behind large tree-trunks, where their fire became sporadic. They contented themselves with shouting encouragement to their quadruped allies. The latter, replying with loud barking, assailed their enemies more furiously.

The situation was turning bad, inasmuch as the column repelled by Vamireh had obtained a foothold on the far tip of the island, and were bringing reinforcements. The poor tardigrade humans thought that they were doomed; their war-cries became lamentable, like agonized plaints—but the tall western nomad was already bringing the aid of his arm, and his club ploughed a large furrow through the muzzles and broken spines. On every side, the beasts took fright, anxiously recognizing in that voice and that strength the voice and strength of victorious races, so effectively that the tardigrades regained the advantage, and the dogs, driven back into the water, returned to the Asiatics' camp.

The intoxication of the victory inflamed the eyes of the worm-eaters. Turning to the blond man, they sang a hymn of triumph. Vamireh responded with mighty shouts. On the other shore, on the edge of the centuries-old forest, the furious baying of the dogs and the curses of the Orientals replied. The night was filled by the tumult, its echoes spreading terror. The two enemy troops sang of their invincible courage and promised further conflicts.

The tardigrades hastily bandaged up the wounded and placed them, for safety's sake, near the spot where Vamireh was camped with Elem. They cleared the islet of injured dogs, some of which succeeded in drifting to the other shore, while the others completed the process of dying.

Vamireh had rejoined his companion. Still filled with disgust by the worm-eaters, she had remained in her shelter without having had to defend herself. Now Vamireh told her about the victory, the number of victims, the ferocity of the assailants, and the probability of further battles. She listened, meditative and weary of the adventure, desirous of imminent peace. She said that she hoped that there might be negotiations at dawn, and the nomad approved—but he refused any concession with regard to the tardigrades.

Weary, Elem finally went to sleep. Three-quarters of the worm-eaters also slept. Vamireh stayed awake.

XXI. The Defeat

Time passed; the wheel of stars rotated in the calm depths of the river; wounded dogs howled; the Orientals' fires burned behind the foliage, illuminating the black tangle of branches and the frail density of the sylvan heights.

Vamireh went down to the river, and remained there for a few moments, as if to take the opportunity to make a conciliatory speech—but an arrow flew through the air and he was obliged to move back. Other arrows arrived; they traced slow parabolas and fell almost harmlessly in the center of the island. The Pzânn collected them, glad to see the enemy munitions depleted. The Orientals rapidly realized the disadvantage of their fire and ceased. In response to their cries and exhortations, the dogs reappeared. Their pack swarmed on the bank, barking furiously. The vague silhouette of a man loomed up momentarily among them, then crouched down. Another silhouette appeared on the bank, on watch. Finally, a human voice rose up from the river, denouncing a swimmer. The Pzânn concluded that this time, the Asiatics were accompanying their expedition.

That rendered the assault more serious. He had all his men woken up immediately, armed six of the cleverest old men with harpoons with fixed points and solid spears, supplemented in his own case with a lance and his club, and took up a good position for keeping watch. The dogs had just jumped into the water. Immediately, the human presence was revealed in a new strategy: three columns formed up, one heading slowly toward the front and another toward the point where Elem was, while the third, allowing itself to drift, rounded the island in order to attack from the rear. Then Vamireh, desirous of concentrating the defense, had the point opposite to the one where he was camped evacuated and had the other side of the island manned. He arranged his forces in such a manner that everyone could retreat toward his position if necessary. Then, lance at the ready, he waited.

The Orientals could not be seen. Their goal must be to direct the attack, only engaging in it personally at the decisive moment, and only then to maintain the rear-guard. They had probably blackened their faces in order to hide themselves more effectively among the dogs' heads. The frontal column paused ten meters from the shore, maintaining itself against the current, awaiting a signal from the company on the far side of the island.

When the signal came, the entire army attacked at once.

The courage of the dogs seemed to have increased. The bluish glint of their eyes irradiated the darkness and their fangs gleamed. As before, they suffered considerable losses before being able to come ashore, but as soon as they had suc-ceeded in doing so, a number of the tardigrades in the first rank perished, seized by the throat. The others' heroic defense put hundreds of dogs *hors de combat*, preventing a catastro-phe, and the battle resumed its normal course, the advantage alternating.

At the outset, observing the absence of the Pzânn, two of the Orientals had moved forward and supported the attack, first with arrows and then with light lances. The alarm of the contact had terrorized the worm-eaters and they would un-doubtedly have been routed if the six elders armed with har-poons and spears had not waited courageously for the Asiatics. Swiftly surrounded by a menacing circle, the latter had un-derstood the imprudence of confronting poison-tipped wea-pons and had beaten a retreat; since then they had only inter-vened with spoken instructions and by firing arrows at oppor-tune moments.

In Vamireh's vicinity the dogs, urged on by distant voic-es, had succeeded in their invasion. Vamireh did not wait for them; he attacked them with so much vigor, his club and his lance obtaining such a large number of victims, that the ani-mals could scarcely sustain the initial impact and fled, expos-ing an Oriental armed only with a spear. Vamireh broke the frail shaft of his adversary's weapon with a single blow; then, seizing the man by the scruff of the neck, he threw him to the ground, stunned, tied him up, put him in Elem's custody, and ran to help his allies.

They were holding on victoriously, but the dog-pack, continually renewed and encouraged by the voices of the Asia-tics, was persistent, and the moment was foreseeable when fatigue would prove fatal for the humans. Initially, they all retreated before Vamireh's war-cry, but then the assault was reorganized, because the Orientals directed the battle more actively from the shadows and greeted Vamireh's arrival with a volley of arrows.

The six elders armed with harpoons and slender lances regrouped, and faced the attack boldly, ready to support any maneuver by the tall nomad. He joined the advance-guard, trying to reach the Asiatics. He could not do it, for the beasts opposed him sternly in spite of the sweeps of his club.

Then, an incident occurred that threatened disastrous consequences: the worm-eaters who were defending the shore in the rear flowed forwards. That started a panic, and rendered Vamireh's presence indispensable.

The battle continued in deepening darkness. The Orientals dispersed the fires whenever they could, in order to increase the courage of the dogs. The tardigrades abandoned the darkest places, falling back toward the burning fires, which they maintained carefully.

Numerous wounded men lay moaning there, closing frightful gashes with their hands. They had mostly been bitten in the thighs or calves, while the dead had had their throats ripped out or their bellies torn—and the red blood caught the light of the fires garishly as bellicose shouts mingled on all sides with screams of pain, the cries of lives lost, the howling of the beasts and the raucous panting of human breath.

The canine mass emerged incessantly from the undergrowth into the light. The sharp cries of the Orientals, rising above the tumult, enraged them; they were struck down in hundreds, but they penetrated the defenders' ranks, biting and sowing terror.

The worm-eaters, already nervous of contact with the men from the great steppes, whose courage was maintained solely by Vamireh's presence, were also aware of approaching exhaustion, their arms becoming less prompt to raise their clubs, and were inclined to concentrate in numerous groups. Vamireh noticed that. With a terrible effort, he forged directly ahead, forcing the dogs to retreat; then he signaled to the elders armed with harpoons and spears to follow him. They came, and the strongest of the remainder joined them. From then on, that small, solid group bore almost the entire burden of the assault, while the rest, massacring the excessively bold dogs, succeeded in dispersing flank attacks.

Eventually, during a momentary calm, the Pzânn made it understood that the fires were to be built up, and a rampart of fires soon protected the bulk of the army. The flames spread, reaching dry grass and brushwood, setting clumps of bushes alight, to such an extent that, once they had retreated behind that barrier, Vamireh and his troops were able to get their breath back.

The dogs were frightened. The Orientals, knowing the beasts' mores, decided to go around the barrier. To do that, it was necessary to go around the tip of the island, for the enemy's flanks were protected by exceedingly thick vegetation, in which their scattered forces would be disadvantaged.

Anticipating this maneuver, Vamireh posted more than 300 tardigrades in the principal defiles; on his orders, they tried to light fires there, by transporting brands that they covered with smaller twigs, but they were unable to obtain that result before the dogs arrived.

The quadrupeds' attack, relatively half-hearted at first, was exasperated by the approach of the Asiatics. Many of the worm-eaters, tired out, abandoned their clubs and fell back on animal instinct, defending themselves on all fours with teeth and fingernails. Curiously enough, the dogs were initially disturbed by this new mode of fighting—but they were gradually able to take advantage of it, especially by courtesy of their numbers, which permitted three or four of them to oppose each man.

At that moment, Elem came to join Vamireh, and her words seemed more efficacious than her blows. Recognizing her as a member of the friendly race, the dogs were visibly disconcerted, and it required the intervention of the Orientals to drive them forward again.

In the renewed battle, two arrows grazed Vamireh's skull and shoulder, and then a thrown spear cleaved the breast of a nearby tardigrade. Understanding that he was visible from the shadows, and that he could not reckon with the dogs if he

113

could not get rid of the Orientals, Vamireh, having regrouped the worm-eaters and commanding Elem to take cover and restrict her interventions to words, disappeared into the undergrowth.

He orientated himself by means of the Asiatics' voices, and after a few minutes found himself close to them. Dogs surrounded them, readying to launch themselves forward. They were relatively fresh troops, held in reserve for emergencies. The animals scented Vamireh and denounced his presence—but he was already bounding forward. He threw them into disorder with mighty blows and hurled himself on the Orientals. The latter—the old man and one young man—fled, after having each thrown a spear, abandoning their arrows.

The Pzânn caught up with them and raised his club, but it fell on empty space, for they had sidestepped as rapidly as panthers. The impact with the ground caused Vamireh to lose his weapon. With a blow of his fist he knocked the younger of his enemies down, but then the old man opposed him with a spear, and their eyes met.

"Go," said Vamireh. "I know that you are good; I would not like to take your life."

The chief made no response. He continued to retreat, his spear at the ready, until he saw his companion get up; then he fled. The Pzânn accelerated his run, and overtook the Orientals, obliging them to veer sideways. He threw the young one in the water, grabbed the old man's spear, and obliged him to swim in a similar fashion.

At this retreat by the humans, the dogs howled in distress. The disarray extended to the distant packs. Vamireh assisted it by uttering cries of victory. Encouraged, the tardigrades took the offensive; the packs retreated in disorder, soon in panic. The Pzânn and his allies remained masters of the isle.

A thousand dogs had perished, and there were now only two Asiatics.

XXII. The Fire

The island was on fire, but the wind drove the flames in such a way that they could camp without danger on the point where Elem's shelter was located. All the tardigrades gathered there and installed their wounded there. The young woman, moved by the courage of those poor folk and the services they had rendered to Vamireh, had overcome her disgust, and helped bandage the wounded.

Expressions of joy spread like ripples on a pool over the sad faces, weighed down by weariness, whenever Vamireh or his companion passed by. The majority were asleep in their favorite position, and within their heavy slumber the night-mare of the battle remained vivid; they uttered cries and dull barking sounds, raising frantic faces between their arms and advancing their heavy jaws.

Vamireh had recovered the captured Oriental. After per-sistent but futile efforts to break his bonds, the man had rolled all the way to the edge of the river, with the intention of throwing himself into it and reaching the other bank. He had hesitated then before the violence of the current, and had tried to gnaw through the thongs binding his legs, but had not com-pleted the task before the arrival of the Pzânn.

Flames were rising up, splitting the darkness. Flocks of birds nesting in the high branches fluttered through the glow; the stars disappeared behind spirals of smoke—which, lit from below, seemed white, shadowed like clouds, full of gaps as profound as abysms. Under the pressure of the wind, the fire became a thread, elongated in undulating skeins, palpitating like living organisms, which, in phases of extinction, gave birth to the abrupt alarm of a rockfall or a thick rain of embers: a solid condensation of the darkness.

The darting red tongues quickly took hold again, avid for conquest; their twists and turns carried along the crackling of dry fibers and explosions of superheated sap, and sparks fell back abundantly from the treetops, languishing somewhat, like

115

a dribble of droplets—a shower of murderous anger—and died out. In the mirror of the waves, everything came together, the symmetries of the undulant flames, the smoke and the ascent of fictitious embers fused with the fall of the real ones.

When the light fury of burning gas rose up from a clump of bushes, bearing away fine sheets of vapor, the arborescent forms were outlined in pale obscurity, sizzling in every gust of wind, as if traversed by alternating waves of light and darkness. In the denser undergrowth the fire brooded, low, slow and ponderous beneath bitter clouds of humid smoke, then screamed, exploded and burst forth, biting into the slender branches and curling foliage, flaming over the dry grasses, stroking the thick-boled trees for a long time, and abruptly dispersed in detonating sprays, in which its forces seemed extinct.

From their encampment behind the bushes the Asiatics watched the island burn. Their own situation was scarcely brilliant. They had tried in vain to lead the dogs in a third attack. Their weapons were lost, save for those of the wounded man, which they had been obliged to reserve for an ultimate defense. Anxious, besides, for the fate of their missing brother, and with the prospect of being abandoned by the dogs, the young ones sensed impending annihilation, and regretted not having trusted the wisdom of the chief.

The latter, fatalistic and full of resignation, said nothing, hunched over the fire, his grave features distorted by grief. The others spoke to him humbly, talking about their confusion, and the necessity of coming to terms with the enemy. He listened to them silently for some time, then replied.

"Young men, the wisdom of the council, transmitted from father to son, advises that peace is proposed at the beginning of a war, when the army is strong, destinies are unknown and no humiliation can result from it—but it informs us that it is necessary to die in the hour of defeat, and not to expose ourselves to the sarcasms of the conqueror. At the time of peace you wanted war, and at the hour of war you want peace. It might be that our enemy, who has shown wisdom as well as

116

courage, will prefer the certainty of a treaty to the final hazards of combat. Perhaps the fire will oblige him to quit the island—and, if he is going to talk, he will talk then. If not, we must prepare for victory, death or flight."

The dawn tinted the east with a pale lilac. The fire, as if afraid of the daylight in which its splendors would be drowned, leapt up more ardently into the treetops in higher flames, roaring like a buffalo herd assailed by predators, or crackled, dry and cruel, in small explosions, like noisy clouds of locusts destroying cereals, or acid legions of ants marching upon villages. Its bright serpentine helices embraced the large trunks, reaching the shriveled leaves first—which, rapidly devoured, fluttered incandescently in the morning breeze, like butterflies of light and swarms of maddened wasps.

It was exceedingly hot; anxious in their sleep, the tardigrades retreated further toward the extreme tip of the islet. Vamireh studied the fire meditatively. He had made sure of his canoe and his weapons. Elem was asleep in the shelter. The little monkey was clinging to a branch, awake like its master, fearful of the glare and the noise.

As the thick leafy branches fell victim to the fire, however, the fiery flakes became increasingly massive. They described narrow curves, excited by the wind of their fall, twinkling like the stars. While they were still falling they seemed flexible and vaporous, but they struck the ground hard, fizzing and sending forth angry jets of sparks.

The Pzânn had untied the Oriental's feet, and he woke Elem up in order that she could serve as an interpreter.

"Ask your brother," he said to the young woman, "whether he thinks the time for peace has come."

"Death cannot frighten me," said the Asiatic.

"I know that you are brave," said Vamireh, "but a man is not a coward who saves himself while saving his brothers."

"Mine are not vanquished!"

"No," said the Pzânn, "but there are only two of them, and the beasts have learned to fear us."

There was a long pause, during which the Oriental reflected.

The dawn increased slightly, the delicate tint of lapis lazuli changing to turquoise. An aqueous half-light reigned in which the horizon of the river was unveiled. Everywhere, the trees, the sky and the river banks seemed extremely fresh by comparison with the vibrant dryness of the fire. The Pzânn wanted to resume his voyage over the green face of the water, to go up the giant river, with its forests and its rocks, the broad mouths of its tributary streams, the roar of huge cascades and the thin voice of little waterfalls, the lashing streams of rapids, the shade of narrow passes and chains of islets, the clarity of vast channels...

Meanwhile, the flames continued their ferocious roasting, paling in the nascent daylight, convulsing in vast tongues or expanding in delicate tissues suspended from lacy networks of branches.

Far away, in the sylvan depths, the baying of hunting dogs was audible, and that drew the Oriental from his meditation. He saw that Vamireh had also taken account of the absence of the beasts and the facility of a strike against the enemy camp. "What do you want me to do?" he asked the Pzânn.

"Talk to your brothers," the latter replied.

The Oriental stood up and walked to the edge of the isle, followed by Vamireh and Elem. He shouted the tribes' summons: "Ré-ha! Ré-ha!"

The brachycephalic chief immediately emerged from cover, followed by the hale young man. "Is our brother a captive of the man from the unknown country?"

"He is a captive."

"Is he asking us for help or vengeance?"

"No, the man from upriver is asking for peace."

"Let him untie your hands, for the counsel requires that you speak of such things as a free man."

The Oriental conveyed the old man's desire to Vamireh. The Pzânn hesitated momentarily, fearful of perfidy; then, without saying a word, he released the bonds. The captive did not move, merely raising his arms gravely above his head.

XXIII. Return

Past the chains of islets, beneath the shadow of trees and through the broad open channels, the little canoe remounted the stream, swollen by downpours. Elem and the little monkey played or slept, while Vamireh paddled all day long.

Peace had been concluded with the Orientals. The dogs had gone back to the arid savannah on the edge of the forest. The poor tardigrade humans had been able to finish their lamentable exodus to the Great Lake. The Asiatics had opened veins in their arms and their blood had been mingled with Vamireh's blood. In the name of the sacred tribes the old man had repudiated all war, and Vamireh had made a treaty in the name of the tall western nomads. In the spring of the following year, at the third full moon after the equinox, the Pzânns would send forth 30 hunters chosen from among the most intrepid, with Vamireh for a leader, and these men would come to meet an equal number of their allies, led by the old man.

Whether the wind whipped up the water into scaly waves, or the rain peppered it with drops and covered it with little leaping bubbles, the canoe still made progress northwards from dawn to dusk. The belling of stags, the trumpeting of mammoths and the growling voices of lions saluted the passage of the frail little vessel and the human enemy. They went on and on past chains of islets, beneath the shade of trees, through the broad open channels.

And Vamireh thought about the worm-eaters, about their profound sadness when the moment of separation had come, their heavy muzzles, the vague barking of their laughter and tears, the infinite gratitude in their eyes, and how long they had remained with him before being able to tear themselves away. From the top of a small hill he had saluted their departure with a cry of amity, and they had responded with their humble marching-song. Obstinate in the fraternal unity that was all that stood between them and the large predators and the anthropoid apes, they carried their wounded with them.

Past the chains of islets, through the broad open channels, the weeks went by; sometimes the Sun poured down its ardent gentleness; sometimes the north wind, the keen last of winter, rose; sometimes there were hectic squalls. It was necessary to shelter in coves, in propitious caves, losing entire days until they cleared.

Vamireh's breast was swollen by a great pride, however, for he had vanquished the ambushes of nature, the aggression of ferocious beasts and the ingenious attacks of men. Beside the evening fire, he heard once again the old man of a hundred winters, Tâh, telling tales of the crumbling of mountains, the ripping of the ground, the abyss drinking the great lakes. He saw himself greater than Harm. On warm evenings, the story of his journey, murmured by centenarians would thrill the hearts of the young: the traps of the river, the perversity of snakes, the ferocity of predators, the Man of the Trees, the new country, the thickset folk, Elem, and the worm-eaters. And the old men would say that it requires an invincible will to vanquish homesickness and the terror of long solitude!

More sunny days and abrupt downpours, the river green or muddy, the current stiffer or less rapid, and waterfalls…and always the canoe, avid to return, with Elem playful or asleep and Vamireh sweeping the paddle back and forth…

The rains became imminent: the endless rains. The tribe, taking refuge in the highland caves, would not leave the savannahs of the south-west before the middle of autumn, and Vamireh would find Zom and Namir, his parents, his valiant brothers and his young sister, capering like a goat-kid. Humble before the old folk, he would introduce them to his bride from far away.

Past the chains of islets, beneath the shadow of trees and through the broad open channels, in the decline of the Magdalenian Era, while the north pole gravitated toward Deneb, the diamond of Cygnus…

EYRIMAH

Part One

I. The Lacustrian Villages

About 6000 years ago, on Lake Re-Alg in present-day Switzerland, villages on pilings were strewn like islets at the mouth of a river, abundantly populated by dark-haired people of short stature with round eyes and large heads. They were Asiatic invaders, people who had filtered into Europe during the Hiatus,[11] from the great forests and rivers of the Rural Plain, through the valleys of the Caucasus.

The fair-haired people with long skulls who had roamed the savannahs of the Occident in the Stone Age had retreated northwards after centuries, following the reindeer and the mammoth, to preserve in the frosts the vigor and audacity that would ensure them a sovereign place in the history of the world. By virtue of numbers and their more advanced social organization, the Asiatics had vanquished their adversaries, and, being ferocious conquerors, had often exterminated rivals of whom all trace had disappeared in various regions for thousands of years.

---

[11] Mortillet and other paleoanthropologists of the early 1880s thought that there had been a "hiatus" between the "age of carved stone" and "the age of polished stone," although the notion had been largely rejected by the early 1890s; Morel and Massé cited Rosny's references to the hiatus as evidence of the fact that he had not read more recent work in the field, although it is a minor issue of no real significance.

Those tall nomads with the long heads who had not fled northwards had been driven back into arid peninsulas on the edge of the Ocean and to the summits of mountains. The tribes maintained themselves on the plains by productive circulation, or were respected by invaders, to the extent that, by virtue of the conquest of some and alliance with others, a new race was born, of medium height with rounded heads, which often combined blue almond-shaped eyes with dark hair, or fair hair with round brown eyes.

That hybrid race, in which extreme types were still found, according to the rule, soon became dominant. For a long time, however, in lands hospitable to the coexistence of two families, the Asiatic type and the European type conserved pure forms. Thus it transpired that in parts of Switzerland, the low plateau nourished the victorious manufacturers, agriculturalists and herdsmen, while the summits and profound gorges concealed descendants of the autochthons of the cold Magdalenian Era, hunters of bears, chamois and ibex.

One evening at the end of May, the lake extended beneath the light of the setting Sun. The profiles of mountains loomed up in the north over the marvelous waters bathing in a spectacular crepuscular light, which filled the west. Life seemed slow, fixed in the dream of light that was terminating the Earthly day, and any man of that time, standing on the promontory of a village, would have sensed the innocence of things—the forces dormant in his brain as well as in nature.

Over hundreds of leagues of forests and the nudity of the immense plains, free animals still laughed at humankind: urus and aurochs, wild boar and large deer, wolves and foxes. Otters undulated in the rivers; bears guarded their insurmountable passes; countless birds populated the frail density of trees; snakes wound the resplendent helices around thin trunks; and the insects were as ardent as if their world were still in balance with that of humans.

It had been a warm day; the lacustrians were resting outdoors in the cool air, only a few of them occupied in repairing weapons, constructing furniture or grinding the flour of the future with the millstones of the day—a small one atop a larger one. No one was allowed to be idle during the day, work being established in law. In the evening, activity expanded to conversation, games of chance and fetishistic practices.

A crier in the streets called out the names of the elders appointed to replace those guarding the bridges. Innumerable elm- or pine-wood pilings supported a vast trelliswork of slender branches. The houses were of various sizes, according to rank or wealth. The doors were closed by transverse bars and the windows were often fitted with thin fabric woven from linden-fibers. Each contained many small items of wooden furniture, imported marine trinkets, polished agates, decorated bones and, in particular, fine weapons, cooking implements, ornamental vases, mills for crushing cereals and frames for weaving flax or linden-fiber. The hearth consisted of a trough of four stones, with a fifth for a base. Already, in sum, a small familial world of complex objects testified to intimate joys, a household living by means of a thousand chores: an ant-like attachment to the hut in which the produce of effort accumulated, to the village that offered protection from common enemies, and to the fetishes that dispensed good luck, providing security against disease and death.

The Sun was setting, its dying light fusing with its image in the water, a colossal bird opening its wings over the fiery horizon; everywhere, flames as short as a sheep's fleece in autumn ate into the illusory mountains; a few downy bands outlined promontories on the pale waters; three grottoes flared up and melted by turns into the clouds.

The blonde slave-girl Eyrimah and Rob-In-Kelg, the son of Rob-Sen, contemplated these prodigious things without attempting any analysis.

Rob-In-Kelg was just 17 years old; as bellicose as his father, the most powerful colossus of Re-Alg, he was proud of his body. Already, the redoubtable muscular strength of Rob-Sen had appeared in his young frame, but his face was gentle in its pride. While still a child, he had been captivated by Ey-

125

rimah's blonde hair and the strangeness of her character. Lacking the dexterity and assiduity of her companions, she seemed to live outside of things. He, whose ancestors had been manufacturers and agriculturalists, steeped in the religion of luck and laws of property, saw utility and conquest everywhere.

The young captive from the mountains gave a grace to things, being endowed with a more liberated power: a creative spirit, a genius that was less perfect but vast, in which the future was about more than material things. If In-Kelg had a passion for Eyrimah's dreams, she, in return, admired his promptitude and certainty.

Sitting on the edge of the platform, their legs dangling over the water, their dreams are as different as their children would have been if he had married a lake-dwelling brunette and she a young man from the blond mountain tribes.

War and terror, nocturnal landscapes and ambushes, blows struck, wounds, booty, miraculous weapons, luck and victory, herds on the mountain pasturelands, slaves to harvest the wheat or the barley—such are the dreams of In-Kelg. For the lithe and changeable Eyrimah, everything—the lake, like the jumble of villages, the trees on the shore, the long curves and denticulations of the mountains, In-Kelg's bristling hair, brown eyes and mouth—is graceful. Penetrated by things and penetrating them, she surrenders herself to a quest for slight and merciful adventures, without making any significant effort to combine the various threads of her ideas.

In-Kelg is reminiscent of broad daylight, avid brightness, cock-crow, harvest-time, ewes with woolly fleeces; Eyrimah offers, instead, moist June dawns in the forest, drifting mists, soft light, trees branching to infinity, free and capricious animals.

They were sitting thus on the edge of the water, in the sweet fragility of spring, when In-Kelg said: "I shot a crow on the highest branch of an oak with my arrow, when the great Wid-Horg had missed it!"

Eyrimah looked at her friend, her sincere admiration clouded with sadness. "You'll become stronger than your father," she said, "more dexterous than Slang-Egh, and a faster runner than the lean Berg-Got. Then you'll be scornful of your friend, and you'll choose a wife elsewhere."

In-Kelg looked at her as a young master; she was resentful of it in spite of her enslavement. A pride that had grown over the years was vibrant in her flesh. As slender as a birch-tree, she was known to be more untamable than a virile wolf, and the chief, who had captured her as a little child, had once wanted to kill her because she had refused to obey him. Just as she was not as quick-thinking as her companions, her face remained more child-like, her white skin, her features as delicate as flowering grass and her exceedingly soft blue eyes full of innocence. Her love for In-Kelg was changing at the approach of puberty, anxiously preparing for the crises of passion that were like April storms in the forest, when frenetic hands of branches shake the open splendor of corollas. She dreamed of sacrifice, offering the overabundant blood in her veins to her lover. More than anything else, he loved to talk about his youthful exploits before her feminine tenderness.

While they were sitting in silence, the evening mist swallowed up the distant villages. There were dark shadows beneath trees with haloes over their branches. A man emerged behind them, heavy-jawed, his eyes lying in ambush beneath his bushy and brutal brows. He stood there watching them, watched in his turn by a thickset colossus with a broad serene face. The man with the massive jaw was Ver-Skag, Eyrimah's master; the other was Rob-Sen, In-Kelg's father.

The night grew darker, and then a large red Moon emerged from behind the jagged summits, as if vomited forth by some monster.

Her passion growing, Eyrimah placed her hand on the young man's arm. "Can the slave Eyrimah never become your wife?"

"If my father buys you from Ver-Skag," In-Kelg said, "or you run away and I recapture you!"

She thought about that, annoyed to be a slave that he could not take without lowering himself—but In-Kelg continued: "When I am entirely a man, I shall want no other than you."

She shivered, and raised her eyes toward him—and then Ver-Skag grabbed her, roughly. In-Kelg moved as if in opposition, but Rob-Sen stopped him. Then Ver-Skag took Eyrimah away with him.

Side by side, Rob-Sen and In-Kelg gazed at the lake; the young man was in a somber mood, because Ver-Skag had almost beaten his friend. Having thought about In-Kelg's love for the blonde captive, Rob-Sen reproached his son for that love. In-Kelg defended Eyrimah—her courage, her art of penetrating dreams, which rendered her precious to Vi-King, the high priest—and Rob-Sen listened, torn between the annoyance of an ignoble marriage and the desire to obtain an alliance with the mountain-girl for his son. He had been pressing for it for years, almost alone in wanting it, so rigorous was the hatred between the two races.

Thirty years before, Rob-Sen had followed the aged Teb-Sta, his maternal uncle, in founding a new settlement, according to custom. Now that Teb-Sta was dead, Rob-Sen was the foremost among the founders, yielding to no one except the priests. The colossus loved the village, the lake, the mother isle and his entire race in his own powerful fashion; he was the flower of his family, one of those men created at a time when a nation is approaching a dangerous apogee, when the future trembles before it and the past glorifies it.

In-Kelg admired the lake silently, respectful of its victorious beauty, and the moonlit night penetrated both of them with a grave ardor, while life, close to its conclusion, excited the village.

II. The Flight

The bridges had been raised. The village, gradually over-taken by sleep, fell silent. The children were in bed, a few women were finishing baking flat cakes of bread on beds of superheated stones, and a few men were praying before fetishes when a watchman's cry resounded over the water in sonorous circles, as far as the neighboring villages.

Everyone surged out of the huts in a disorderly fashion, even the women and children; only the swift and stout men, however, armed with lances, axes or bows, advanced as far as the series of bridges, with raucous shouts full of wrath or alarm.

Far away on the shore, almost out of bowshot, there was a company of about 15 men, moving furtively. At first, they made no reply to the shouts of the lake-dwellers, but when an arrow had been fired from the village they advanced to the water's edge, and the cry that emerged from their throats echoed like the mountain lairs.

The lacustrian chiefs, hard and headstrong, forbade the firing of arrows. For several minutes the crowd was swayed by various sentiments, primarily led to vanquish fear with fury: hundreds of squat bodies with cunning and cruel eyes, imbued with bellicose electricity, the rage of worker-bees against an enemy of the hive.

Meanwhile, the men on the shore now appeared in the moonlight. They were quite tall, with long torsos and slightly short legs; they were striking their immense breasts with their free hands, and roaring, as if in challenge and reproach. Their shoulders bore furs of chamois, ibex and bears; long blond hair fell over their cheeks; an inexpressible nobility surged forth from their appearance like the grandeur of the mountains where they lived.

At the sight of them, the lacustrian multitude was possessed by a rage even more profound than before: the rage of the conqueror against the beauty of the vanquished. Prompt and ferocious, drowning remorse in fetishistic practices, the desire for its absolute destruction made them howl in shrill voices. Knowing that they were more numerous and better-armed than the adversary, the majority would have engaged in battle, without any thought of the consequences.

The chiefs did not think like that, however. They knew about the wars of old, the courage of the mountain men—and besides, a few of them were fearful for their wealth. They imposed silence on their men. When a few protested, they struck them roughly. Then the darkness reigned again, for the mountain men also fell silent. Following custom, a priest advanced along one of the bridges and raised his hand in the moonlight.

A few common words, introduced to the lacustrians by the vanquished autochthons, served for the exchange of ideas. Gravely, almost sadly, the mountain men declared their peaceful intentions, but affirmed their intrepidity. They scorned insults; they would not permit anyone to attack them.

The priest replied that the lake-dwellers were the stronger, and that they could raise an army and assail the vagabond tribes of the mountains. Then, one of the tallest fur-bearers set himself ahead of his kinsmen on the shore and said, angrily, that the lake-dwellers would not risk themselves on the summits, and that the life of every mountain man would cost the lives of a thousand adversaries.

The chief Ver-Skag, a somber brute full of dreams of massacre, shoved his companions aside and brandished his axe, which glittered like a wave in the moonlight, murmuring insulting and warlike words. The priest stopped him, and said that there were 50 villages on the waters, that more than 200 had been built on the low plateau. Every time the mountain men had come down they had met defeat. Why should the vanquished speak like conquerors?

The heavy sentiment of their weakness must have weighed upon the mountain men, for they fell silent and huddled together, approaching the shore in mute mistrust.

The priest went on, reminding the mountain men that they did not have the right to trespass on the territory of the lacustrians when the wheat had been sown, or when the herds were beginning to be put out to pasture. The howls of the hate-filled crowd supported the priest's words, polished axes being displayed over their heads, the points or arrows and lances bristling in the night.

The clamor increased further when the tall mountain man marched to the very edge of the lake, his breast laid bare. All the priests raised their hands disapprovingly, however, and the ferocious multitude calmed down, listening. In the calm, the deep voice of the blond chief confirmed the peaceful intentions of his troop. They had been surprised by an avalanche, and obliged to cross the low plateau.

The lacustrian chiefs opposed this speech with insulting quibbles. The prudence of their wealth, the rising of spring sap, and the bellicose and avid blood of their race were all working within them simultaneously. They recalled the days of glory and booty with grunts of enthusiasm and covetousness. But the men of the mountains spoke the names of their allies, and when the lake-dwellers found that they were the powerful villages of the great western lakes, they shivered in hatred and terror.

The great western lakes, their shores and the neighboring plateau, were the possessions of a triumphant people introduced through the mountain gorges, a young nation. The old round-headed tribes, long preserved from all contact with the mountains, who kept the autochthons imprisoned on the heights, had retreated before the legions of the new men, which had brought with them a more advanced technology, a stronger warrior discipline and voluminous muscles.

The cunning and prudence of the race was, however, incarnate in the priest, inspired by Rob-Sen; he invited the mountain men to come into the village. They hesitated at first, then, with the cordiality of their vast hearts, they crossed the bridges that the watchmen lowered for them. The mute crowd was as sullen as a woman on a bad day, when the blood that oppresses her bloodies her dreams, but when a conference was held between the priests and the chiefs, it expanded in rapid

131

speech, like a blocked-in river whose channel has suddenly opened, and which makes the pebbles tremble.

The awakened children were playing noisily, the dogs barking furiously. In-Kelg had sought out Eyrimah again and was holding her hand, telling her how sad he was. Delighted by the young man's anxiety and the jealous supplication of his voice, she was slightly mutinous, looking at him with her admirable eyes, which were laughing in the moonlight.

Ver-Skag, annoyed by the peaceful outcome of the adventure with the mountain men, left the group of chiefs, saw the idyll, and was gripped by a rage of frustrated masculinity. The blonde girl fled, and Ver-Skag, seeing her disappear into the house, stopped in front of In-Kelg with an affected scorn.

"This very night," he sniggered, "Eyrimah…"

"Be careful," said the young man. "If you dare to touch Eyrimah…"

"I'm not afraid of you, or your father." He drew away, however, either because he was afraid of In-Kelg's attitude, or because he preferred to savor his vengeance for a longer interval, or because he thought the moment inopportune.

The conference between the chiefs and the mountain men came to an end. The disorderly crowd went back home, with grim glances at the mountain men, who were drawing away along the shore.

Ver-Skag growled like a threatened dog. His little round black eyes revealed his anger with no more nuance than the pupil drowned in the smoke of the dark iris: anger as heavy as his spade-like hand, the flattened curve of his shins or his jutting jaw. He lingered in his doorway, saluted by the more ferocious members of the tribe, who observed his mood. He saw the last silhouettes disappear into the shadows; he heard the last quarrels, the foot-stamping of human beasts preparing for bed, and then he went in, feverishly.

A small window, opened on the side opposite to the prevailing wind because of the heat, let in the moonlight. Eyrimah's legs were in the light, and a kind of halo encircled her pretty face. She was feigning sleep, a ladybird's trick, in order to avoid blows or scolding words. He stood beside her, the mire of his being aggravated like an estuary by the tide. It was a dark desire, mingling the horror and poetry of turbulent tides when the acid of fevers floats amid burned vegetation, phosphorescence wanders over the viscous debris of inferior life-forms, the surface is obscured by a plethora of lentils and newts, and tadpoles swarm over the greasy mud.

Eyrimah sensed a body between her and the light, then a warmth, and harsh breath upon her face. She opened her eyes.

Ver-Skag was kneeling down, with a broad sardonic smile. Eyrimah read within it the confused danger that either attracts or terrifies a woman. She slipped away, silently running to the doorway. There she was overtaken, dragged backwards and thrown to the ground.

She struggled and howled, biting and clawing, until a thickset silhouette emerged into the room: Ver-Skag's wife! Instantly, the latter began to utter cries of fury, the rage of a mole encountering an intruder on its territory. She hurled herself upon the chief, opening the nape of his neck with her canine teeth, ranking his forehead with her nail, and—most of all—stunning him with insults.

He stood up, with fearful hatred, raising his fist, but dared not strike her, sensing that she was more cruel and determined than him.

Eyrimah took refuge in a corner, while the man and the woman confronted one another. Then, her jealousy less immediate, the woman relaxed. She let herself be beaten, knowing that she would draw new strength therefrom, compounded from Ver-Skag's reaction and his grievances against her. The calculation was sound; the chief went into the other part of the house—but he warned Eyrimah that she would be his, not In-Kelg's, for that was his right as her master, and he would exercise it. When he had said that, he fell into the legendary sleep of brutes, from which the history of fables has drawn so many resources.

The young woman remained thoughtful in the frosty moonlight. A creature of finesse, cerebral energy and contained, world-conquering power—which are to crude muscle-power what heat and light are to hammer-blows, infinitely surer but restrained by finer and more scrupulous laws—Eyrimah felt that she was capable of vanquishing Ver-Skag, barring the kind of accident that crushes a judicious insect beneath the stone that it is hollowing out. If Ver-Skag used a modicum of violence, she was lost—and by virtue of that fact, the centuries-old effort of balancing force with cunning rose up within her.

She resolved to run away—but Ver-Skag had closed the door and the window; the noise she would make in opening one of them would awaken the man, and danger with him.

The frail corollas of modesty had blossomed within Eyrimah since she had seen In-Kelg's anxiety, and she was trembling with a fever of love and dread. Crawling toward the door, she paused in front of the room where the chief was asleep. He must have heard her; he turned over in his sleep and muttered a few threatening words. She went back to her bed, full of anguish. A few agonizing minutes went by, and then a glimmer of light appeared in the mists of her memory; she remembered that there was a hole in the wall of the hut, in the most distant corner. She resolved to get out that way.

Slowly, she located the fissure, enlarged it somewhat, slid her slender body through it, and was outside. Clever as she was, though, she risked being seen if she went through the village—nor could she get across the bridges. She decided to aim for the bulk of the island opposite the bank, and in order to do that with the least danger of being recaptured, she crawled to the nearest edge of the latticework and let herself down into the water.

She was underneath the platform of the huts, in the cavernous space where the pilings hung down like stalactites in a grotto. The damp, the reek of mildew, the darkness and the retreating wave of swimming rats, could not prevail against the youthful excitement of her courage.

In places, the moonlight extended broad beams or passed through in slender rays. The lake was warm. Far away, reduced in size by the distance, in strips as bright as the bark of birch-trees, whiteness unfurled, marking the end of the latticework.

It was impossible to swim. Swinging from one piling to the next, the blonde girl moved forward laboriously. She touched soft and repulsive algae extended along the wood; bats escaped through a loophole; alarmed fish made the water seethe and stirred up wakes of pale fire where they passed through the light.

At the densest part of the colonnade, Eyrimah hesitated; she could no longer see any but rectangular windows of light, the tunnels of subterranean animals everywhere, ominous and confused, pilings like twigs of undergrowth, and a few mollusks overhead, like flower-heads. Her bare arm, abruptly striped with light, looked like some marvelous serpent, and the heavy curtains of the splashing waves, breaking on her upper body, wrapped a cold embrace around her slim legs, the figure beloved by In-Kelg.

She ended up reaching the underside of a street, where a broader tunnel extended, illuminated in the distance by a tiny blue rectangle. There she could swim, her slender hands supported on the surface, her feet pushing her along silently. The beams of moonlight, more numerous, enveloped her in a mobile pattern, picking out her pale eyes within the pallor of her hair. The water seemed to be sloping upwards toward the lunar rectangle, which grew larger with every stroke. A dull plaint, like the sound of snoring, emerged from the confused pilings with the splash of a wave thrown from one space to the next.

Eyrimah was frightened, though, for footfalls were audible on the latticework overhead. She feared that it might be Ver-Skag. She caught hold of the nearest piling and waited.

The Moon must be close to its zenith now, for its brightness was visible on the lake, but scarcely extended into the tunnel through the rectangle, while it projected rigid sheets through a number of slits, which the water broke up with its ebb and flow. A breeze got up between the pilings. The waves broke into a thousand facets, in which the rays danced, as agile

135

as aquatic insects on the tide. The lacustrian cave, the grotto of the stalactites, was reminiscent of a hearth on a winter's day, when wasp-like sparks fly from the desiccated twigs.

The child's heart was beating in her breast like Oceanic waves. As savage as a she-wolf, undiminishable by anything, as swollen as a storm that will not burst, the instinct of modesty circumscribed her life. She had no fear other than that of recapture and rape; rather than surrender she would have let go of her pillar and drowned herself.

The running footfalls stopped. A shadow was projected over the edge of the tunnel; a body hung down. Hidden among the pilings, Eyrimah heard oars, and then saw a boat. She thought that it might be some merchant on his way to another village, and she resumed her progress silently, reaching the opening.

Already some distance away, the vessel was moving through the moonlight. The lake was splashing abundantly, the blades racing through the water, and then emerging slowly; the pure light, quivering, caused the long trail of moonlight established in its wake to vibrate in zigzags.

She got her bearings. She was opposite the bridges, where no watchman was stationed during the night. Considerable numbers of solidly-moored boats were oscillating in the waves. At first, she thought about taking one and reaching the shore by that means, but Ver-Skag might be on the lookout; he would surely see the boat and catch up with it. She therefore resolved to swim away, and let go of the pilings, sad to be leaving the wooden islet where she had spent her childhood, and especially sad to be going far away from In-Kelg.

Fatigue paralyzed her arms in the colder open water. The waves hampered her; her head scarcely emerged, rolling in the folds of the waves; her wet hair was plastered over her face, shoulders and arms. The reflected image of the Moon fled into the distance. She kept her eyes on it, and followed it. Small and delicate wrinkles were crumpling the image like a supple fabric. Outside the furrow ploughed by the star, the lake was dark, like molten tin seen from an angle, while the shores seemed as blonde as Eyrimah's hair.

Weary and imperiled as she was, she loved the grace of the trees, where clear droplets seemed to be cascading; she thought about the gray trunks of linden-trees, rough and warm, where she might place her crumpled hands. She swam more rapidly, her frail body gliding through the water, while her head protruded a little further—but a hint of fever reddened her cheeks; the shore seemed terribly distant.

She felt a desire to rest her head on the waves and go to sleep, for her arms were numb and she was having difficulty breathing—but for five more minutes her muscles sustained her. Then her little fingers opened, and her mouth skimmed the level of the lake, going under. She struggled for another minute, desperate to reach the shore, and then she sank and disappeared, only her hair remaining afloat, like long algal fronds.

Under the water, however, instinct reanimated her. She stiffened, and swam on her back, almost without difficulty—and as her ears were exposed, she heard a voice drifting through the rumor of the wind.

"Eyrimah!"

She recognized Ver-Skag's voice, as raucous as a voice of stone—and then another voice, young and clear, like the voice of a spring, also called her name. She was glad that it was In-Kelg, but she was afraid for him. She regained her strength. Her arms ploughed through the distance that separated her from the shore, hid her wet body in a crease of the bank, and gazed at the village where the two men had their backs to her.

Soon, the night was disturbed by a dispute. Clenching her teeth, the girl from the North saw fists raised, a mime of combat—and then a third person, thickset and enormous, intervened. She knew that it was In-Kelg's father, and heard the giant threatening Ver-Skag. No longer afraid, she rejoiced as she followed the scene with feminine malice. After two minutes of quarrelling, the colossus hurled himself upon his adversary; the body of Ver-Skag was thrown into the lake, and then the victor drew his son imperiously back to the village.

Eyrimah remained where she was, scrutinizing the darkness, anxious to find out what had become of Ver-Skag. Soon, a black head appeared on the surface, drifting toward the pilings. Eyrimah was not entirely displeased by that. She recalled her common life with the chief, tenderly. She was glad that he was alive. She had the great resignation of virgins, the desire for sacrifice.

Fearful of the watchmen, she crawled through the thick grass and reached the trees. Beneath their cover, she was no longer so cold. Although she had eaten as usual, her adventure had made her hungry; on the other hand, she had no desire to sleep. She therefore resolved to march until she discovered some thicket or rock in which her experience signaled the presence of eggs. First, she wrung out her meager linden-fiber tunic; then, drier and somewhat rested, she set out.

The Moon was going down, growing as it sank and less pale; the Earth had a melancholy thrill, as if the lazy night were stretching itself, sure of its morning.

There was nothing but long climbs and short descents in the ever-lengthening shadows and the bluish pallor of the moonlight; then she stopped in front of an opening near the top of a rock, where thistles grew and from which tumbled the tangled tresses of wild vines. It was almost inaccessible, the rock-face being steep and arid, but Eyrimah, sure of discovering eggs there and perhaps capturing some bird, felt herself attracted to the hole as to a gulf. She therefore climbed up to the summit, and then looked down. Her entrails were crying out. Ardent life claimed recompense and effort, new blood. She sought in vain for another place where there might be nourishment. There was fleecy grass everywhere, the lacustrians' carefully-protected meadows, already invaded by their flocks.

Before her hunger-enlarged eyes the night was hallucinatory: the resplendent bowl, the pearly disk where mist trembled; the vast Earth invaded by sheets of darkness; the lacustrian dwellings on the great lake; the wavelets reminiscent of the undersides of linden-leaves; and the voice of life a prodigious flux within her.

She leaned over; the tresses of the vine fell gently, intimately. It seemed impossible to her that things might be insidious, and only the vertigo that retains young animals still gave her pause. Finally decisive, she suspended herself from the rock—but then she became frightened of falling, sensing the void beneath her feet. She remained still for some time; then, wearying, she gave in. Her fingers opened, and she fell the length of the declivity. Fortunately, the upper part of the opening overhung; her body overshot; only her head and upper body intruded into it to some extent. When she touched the vine she gripped it hard, with grim instinct, thus slowing down and eventually stopping her fall. By hoisting herself up a little, she moved into the hole and wriggled inside it.

A confused joy overwhelmed her, of safety attained and audacity rewarded. At the back of the hole her fingers encountered warm feathers. A bird struggled violently, and escaped through the opening, followed by a second. Eyrimah regretted the lost prey, but was consoled by finding a small heap of eggs, which she recognized as fresh. She ate them immediately; then, satisfied, she curled up in her little niche and went to sleep.

She awoke at dawn. She remained motionless at first, numbed by cold, looking out over the landscape. The Moon was like a little round cloud, about to disappear. The daylight was rising in the far distance, down below, behind the trees, in a faint dust the color of forget-me-nots—which made the lake into a white-bordered hole, while darkness and mist were still consuming everything else.

Putting her head out of the hole, she studied the rock. She found that she was a long way up. The smooth stone below offered no escape. She could not think of going back up. Initially despairing at the idea of dying of hunger in the hole or breaking her bones in a fall, she ended up discovering a narrow ledge contiguous with the threshold of the opening. A hundred meters away, that ledge reached the lateral slope of the rock, which was not sheer. Hanging on as best she could to projections, and plunging her convulsive fingers into cracks, she made her way along the ledge, tormented by the sensation of falling backwards. She made her escape, though, proud and full of the joys of the rising dawn, which was trembling over the mountains and the lake.

Within the broadened horizon, 50 villages were visible over an extent of about two hours' march; the remainder were lost in the mist, along with the water. She observed an unaccustomed movement of boats between the villages and the villages on the shore. Directly beneath her, at the place where a stream departed from the lake and where the principal township stood, the boats were massing as in times of war.

Fearful for In-Kelg, whom she knew to be reckless, she retained the hope that it might be a fishing dispute, an argument between two neighboring villages, or that, even if it was a war, the adolescents would not take up arms. As she continued walking, however, she arrived in the vicinity of a meadow and saw that the livestock had been reassembled during the night, and were already descending toward the lake—with the result that she found herself in a deserted region, save for a few old horses, a few sick cows and a few capricious goats that had fled from the herdsmen. Then she became sad, thinking about the distant island and the boats. There was a slow procession of boats through the light mist, like a flotilla of ducks. She watched for some time. Finally, the bluish mist lifted, melting into the sky. Eyrimah saw the signal of the lacustrians' Grand Council, and understood that it was war, and wept. That did not, however, diminish her fear of Ver-Skag, nor persuade her to return to her old life.

When she finished weeping, she felt hungry. With a few agile bounds she caught a she-goat with dangling teats and drank for a long time. Satiated and restored, she laughed at the Sun and the mountains. Her intoxicated young blood swelled in her veins, making her light-headed. She was like a goat-kid in love with peril; she marched through the gullies and the rubble of landslides caused by bad weather. Savagely, she savored the gulfs, the clefts and vertiginous declivities. The soul of the mountain was within her, its rough and complex life, the shadow of its damp gorges, the dry wind of the plateau, and the pride of the stone that time carves and hollows out, dying slowly in its beauty, more profound every day.

Soon she reached the neutral zone that separated the mountains from the lake-dwellers' territory. The memories of her early childhood were vibrant within her, confused but moving. She was dazed by a joy of savage freedom. Bounding ibex or chamois disappeared amid the rocks, and sometimes a slender animal would pause, gazing at the frail girl for a long time.

The mountain quivered beneath the midday Sun. Eyrimah, sheltered by a rock whose foliage extended a delicate fleecy shade, went to sleep for a couple of hours.

When she woke up again, she had an impression of the grace of things as tangled as the brambles along her route, but profound and prodigious. She had a sensation of grandeur among the shapes, of inhabiting a god larger than the one of the lacustrians; she leaned her little trembling soul over the edge of the nature in which she had the splendor to be.

She crossed the region of the plateau. All around, wheat, barley and rye were sown on suitable ground. Dogwood, cherry-trees and wild plums were disseminated through the fields. Pear-trees and apple-trees, already improved, were grouped in primitive orchards. All the nourishment of the villages of Re-Alg was there: the oak plantations productive of sweet acorns; the hazelnut-trees, the pines whose oily and resinous nuts were eaten, the yew-trees, the raspberries, the mulberries whose fermented juice dispensed drunkenness.

Asiatic cattle, mingled with indigenous urus, sheep and goats were grazing the meadow-grass. At that time, the urus and the aurochs, retreating to the forests, were beginning to decrease in confrontation with humans; the wild boar had surrendered, transformed by captivity into pigs; the lion, the leopard and *Felis spelaea*, fleeing from the active race that tracked them, had reached India or Siberia, while the mammoth, the reindeer and the wapiti lived among the beeches of the North.

She marched until dusk, losing herself in blind pathways. Through the maze of the mountains, by deceptive trails and dry stream-beds suddenly terminated by an immense waterfall, her weary young flesh discovered the terrible charm of the eternal effort of the eternal journey, and the patience of the ant, along with the courageous anxiety of the migratory nightingale and the obstinacy of salmon going upstream.

In the afternoon, the sky became covered with low clouds, which soon deprived the valley of sunlight. She was at a considerable altitude, alone with the bears and the chamois. The warm and humid wind whipped her gently, her hair streaming behind her or returning to slap her cheeks, and its breath bathed her face in a powerful dream, sending all chagrin to sleep.

When the Sun set behind the clouds, the eternal chimera was ignited by the false mountains and the immense strands, its gleams transformed into devouring fires; then, as flowers of light blossomed, with naked petals of green and orange, Eyrimah stopped climbing. She installed herself on a high ledge, the only convenient place to sleep, and before the daylight was entirely gone, she was lost in sleep.

A rumor woke her, while the humid Moon, very high, was wandering amid the clouds, pouring light from one blue lake to another, amid the slow movement of the sky. She listened.

A deep sound, a trumpeting sound that she recognized as a voice from her distant childhood, was drifting through the high valleys. The quivering rock amplified the sound in the hollows of its abysses, duplicating it from the walls of its gorges. Soon, the night was full of the somber music. The alarm spread through the empty spaces from summit to summit. It was joined there by the glimmers of highly-placed fires.

Then Eyrimah thought of war, the emotion of women, the conceit of young men, the tranquil firmness of old men, the departure into the darkness, the quickening of hearts, the broad hymn of combat, the gripping and heroic precariousness of life.

A torrent ran nearby as soon as the Sun melted the snow, and a fine torrent it was, which had crumbled the stones beneath its violence, carrying enormous blocks away. Dry now, it testified to its passage in crenellations, peaks and rounded pebbles, the tooth-filled mouths of nocturnal monsters. Periodically, the Moon illuminated its bed, but vast sheets of shadow cut through the brightness rhythmically.

The blonde girl shivered slightly, for the darkness drank up the warmth. She stretched herself, and moved about in order to counter the numbness—and suddenly, in immense terror, collapsed on her stone.

Three men clad in animal furs and armed with lances had just appeared, and one of them, climbing an eminence, sounded a trumpet. They did not notice Eyrimah, and drew away, chatting—but two of them went off together, while the third continued on his way alone, pausing from time to time to blow the trumpet.

That encounter excited fear in her at first, and then a sweeter sentiment: a childhood memory, vague but not erased—and she had understood the meaning of the few words that the blond men had spoken.

As a slave among the dark-haired folk down below, she had been ashamed of her blonde hair and blue eyes, of which her companions made fun. Every time she had been able to perceive the high mountains from the low plateau, her heartbeat had quickened. She was filled with pride by their noble appearance, their robust and wild aspect, glad to have the blood of a heroic race in her veins. Had it not been for In-Kelg she would have run away a long time ago, even though the mountain men, in order to avoid war, did not welcome fugitives.

Here, however, her instinct had prevented her from crying out to the three men. She wanted to present herself to women first—and in her vibrant little head, the words of the forgotten language emerged. She repeated them, imploringly, with tenderness and terror. She had woken up completely.

A few large clouds were running across the face of the Moon; in the conflicting winds, the clouds melted like snow in spring and the star moved through hidden reefs and eroded inlets; its light sprang from craters filled far in advance by its radiance, or overflowed from behind fleecy masses in gleams finer than the bark of birch-trees, the silvery undersides of aspen leaves, pheasants' throats or tresses of pale hair.

Eyrimah wanted to get down from her stone and continue on her way, in search of a village. But another shape was outlined on the bed of the torrent—a slow and ponderous form. A bear was walking in the moonlight. Standing up on its hind feet, it walked thus for some time, a beast at play, and then fell back with a broad sweep of it head. The stones and the Moon appeared to amuse it; it rolled pebbles and rolled over itself, presenting its belly to the Moon.

The young woman, paralyzed by fear, did not move, following the animal's casual game with her eyes. Then the bear became suspicious of its solitude, exploring the surroundings with its nostrils. It caught the odor of flesh; two minutes later, it had discovered Eyrimah's retreat and began to climb the rock. It lost its footing at first and fell back, but at the second attempt its claws gripped the ledge.

The girl's screams, and the small stones she hurled at its muzzle caused the dim-witted and playful beast to pause, but not for long; it began to hoist up its formidable bulk, and at halfway had already eclipsed In-Kelg's frail lover when a stone struck it in the chops and a voice from down below called out, in the language of the mountains: "Come on!"

The bear made haste to descend, growling, then weighed up its adversary. It was familiar with humans and mistrusted them, not only by virtue of the mistrust transmitted by an animal to its descendants but by virtue of having been wounded

144

itself in a fight. It therefore went away, unhurriedly, sometimes turning its head toward the aggressor. The latter, a tall, grim mountain man, shook his lance, annoyed by that retreat, and threw stones at the beast, arrogantly shouting: "Come on! Come on!"

The insulted bear stopped, and the man persisted in provoking it by throwing stones at it. "Come on! Come on!"

The bear came. Obscurely enraged by the challenge, perhaps it felt the need to demonstrate that it was courageous and dangerous. Some distance away, the bear reared up on to its hind feet; approaching in that manner it looked like a gigantic human. Then there was a vague annoyance in the man, and in beast and man alike an apprehension of the taciturn adversary—and in the beast, a fear mingled with the confused instinct that its species was to be annihilated by the prodigious strength of humankind. Stones cracked by frost, rain and the violence of the torrent, full of sharp-edged holes and clefts, surrounded the scene. In three places valleys were visible in which oak-trees fleeced the gentle slopes. Eyrimah, grateful, praying, loved the tall blond kinsman who was challenging the monster. She found in him the instincts of heroism that were stirring within her, a nobility that the thickset lacustrians never attained.

"Come on, then! Come on, then!"

The slightly tremulous words vibrated on his lips like a learned bravado, a pride alimented by the tales told in the evenings, hatred of the last two livestock-thieves, the bear and the wolf, and a rivalry not yet extinct in the echoes of his savage soul.

The bear spread out its forepaws, distended its claws, and opened its maw. It showed its redoubtable fangs, in a hateful laugh. The man thrust with his lance, twice, but missed the bear both times.

Eyrimah's convulsive muscles were too taut for her to move. In the horror of the moment, everything seemed to her to have come to a standstill; she could scarcely distinguish the bear from the surrounding rocks, whose breaches and sharp projections also seemed to be the maws of monsters full of avid fangs. The great lance thrust for a third time, though, sinking into the beast's throat, and the duel turned in the man's favor. Eyrimah, surrendered to anguish, collected herself, while the bear, in frightful agony, broke the ash-wood shaft. It seemed to tear itself free, however, vomiting up the sharp point, and fell upon the man, embracing him savagely. A blow from a bulbous bludgeon, which the mountain man was holding in his hand, caused it to recoil.

There was a pause.

The mountain man's chances had decreased, the lance having been the best, the only means of fighting the bear. He would not admit defeat, however, and, sacrificing his life, he lifted his axe, carved from Alpine rock but unpolished, and shouted: "Come on! Come on!"

The beast did not move forward. Blood was running from its lips over its fur, but the wound could not be deep or dangerous. A dull fury, mingled with dread, shone in its poor eyes, and as the mountain man amplified his bravado, the bear turned tail and fled.

Eyrimah had come down from her rock and placed herself at the man's side. When the beast had gone they both sat down and, breathing heavily, rested without saying a word.

Through an open breach, a vale extended beneath the moist light, and it was as if a light snow were settling on the brushwood, on the pine woods and on the corners of rock. The two young people gazed at it, gradually recovering from their emotion, but not yet daring to speak.

Eyrimah found her companion young and admirable; he thought her agreeable, surprised that she was of his race even though she wore a linden-fiber tunic. A tender desire overtook him, further excited by the recent struggle and the solitude. He smiled at the blonde girl, and leaned over her gently. She smiled too, full of gratitude and trust. Then he leaned more insistently, and kissed her fresh lips. She struggled, wounded, but he squeezed her harder, holding her in his strong hands like a little bird, murmuring tender words, with a smile that was sensuous and determined.

There was a madness, a fear clouded by sadness and weakness, a vague struggle against the instinct that floats like submarine vegetation beneath the multiplicity of being. Amorous appeal mingled with resistance, concern for In-Kelg with panic abandon: a whirlpool of the soul swallowing, pell-mell, the polished corollas of modesty and the red fruits of desire, as her whole being rose up like a river in flood.

Deep down, by virtue of the troubled impulses of her will, In-Kelg prevailed. An abrupt energy having detached her, she took three rapid strides; then, seeing that the man was not following her, she waited for him to speak. As he remained silent, she begged him, telling him in badly ordered words about her captivity, her desire to be put in the hands of women.

Unmoving, he listened to her in profound astonishment, and his response was benevolent, for the pale maiden had captivated more than his flesh. She understood that by the humble tone of the man's voice, and they walked side by side, without fear.

The sound of the trumpets was still spreading through the mountains. He explained that the war was against the lake-dwellers. She told him about her escape, her hope of being adopted by the mountain tribes.

After an hour, they reached a cluster of huts on a plateau protected by rocks. A large fire was burning on one of the rocks, maintained by women and children. The young mountain man called out in a loud voice: "Dithèv! Hogioé!"

Two young women came forward, surprised to see the unknown woman in the linden-fiber tunic. The man told Eyrimah that Dithèv and Hogioé were his sisters and that his name was Tholrog.

Hogioé took Eyrimah by the hand and led her to one of the huts. The fugitive was astonished by the poverty of the dwelling, doubly lit by the Moon and a pine-wood branch that Dithèv planted in the earth in front of the door. It was not the little familial world of lake-dwellers, with furniture and pottery, separated into rooms, with wardrobes and floors, but merely a round space with large unpolished stones for seats and earth underfoot. The walls were, however, ornamented with furs, ibex horns and weapons.

In sum, in spite of the impression of savagery, liberty and a return to her childhood, Eyrimah was disappointed. Hogioé and Dithèv, tall girls, noble in their attitude, did not have the apparent subtlety, the prompt dexterity and the confident gestures of the lacustrian brunettes. Dull and slow, their generosity could not expand to the lacework of ceremony; the dishes that they offered Eyrimah, coarse and abundant, were piled up in front of her, and were almost all of meat, accompanied by a few pine nuts.

While she ate, and drank the pure water of Alpine springs, her fortified heart swelled. She threw herself into the arms of Hogioé and Dithèv, and suddenly, in the returned caress, sensed her powerful race like a grave history contained in song.

She wept, sobbing the story of her captivity, her flight, the loss of In-Kelg, the dream enlarged by her journey, by the mountains, the sheer slopes, the peace of the sky, the slumber of the wind and the anguish of danger. The two tall girls held her close and, in answer to a profound instinct, let her weep, feeling sad themselves, their lips tremulous.

Tholrog came in. The maiden's affliction made him anxious. One does not let guests weep; the roof is cursed under which a stranger's tears flow—but Eyrimah's face appeared through her hair, and her smile strayed over the clarity of her features.

Hogioé told Tholrog that the young woman had a heavy heart, but that she was content with her welcome. He was still vague, desiring the maiden ardently, like a tree that is preparing with all the sovereign skills of love, in the secret swarming of its roots, the harmonious network of its branches and the manufacture of its leaves, the precious vases of its flowers.

Anxious and breathless, he took her to a fire where men and women were listening to a robust old man. Hogioé and Dithèv kept her between them. Tholrog sat down facing her, eager for the sight.

The man who was speaking looked at her for a long time. He was Tholrog's father, renowned for reading faces. In the capricious light, shadowed by smoke, the pale and sensitive girl suddenly astonished him, and he admired her in silence, with the presentiment of patriarchs before beings who surpass their time. His large long head, with its mane of hair, turned toward his son. "This one's heart has spoken!"

Tholrog went pale; he dreamed of winning Eyrimah by the death of his rival, and by his exploits. She had a soft smile for his father, and the old man's majesty sympathized with the young workman's proud spirit, at an interval of half a century. Excited by her youthful presence, he resumed talking to the men and women gathered around the fire, and Eyrimah, attentive and delighted, far from the active and unemphatic lacustrians, heard a story to make the mountain tremble.

III. The Massacre

Wet through, full of bitter resentment after his fight with Rob-Sen, Ver-Skag remained sitting on the platform where he had climbed back up. The night, the moonlight on the lake, the charm of things steeped in a radiance more delicate than sunlight, which made the Earth seem a watery kingdom at the bottom of a limpid ocean, the soft breeze and the distant profile of the blue-tinted mountains with vast shadows set up a unique vibration in his head, amplifying his lust for vengeance, his need to make the bones of a human creature cry out, to experience the ponderous and profound sensuality of a massacre. It did not take long to bring forth the idea that he had nurtured as soon as he saw the mountain men. To cut their throats would avenge the theft of two cows, of which he ac-

149

cused them. It would put Rob-Sen in the wrong to unleash war, for Rob-Sen represented the party of peace. Finally, amid the disorder, a poisoned arrow might strike the colossus.

He got to his feet, and consulted his grim instinct. Vanquished at first by custom, dread of sorcerers and the fear of failure, a ruse soon came into his thick head like a glow-worm in a bush—a very small, quite simple glimmer of light in the opacity of his brain—and a smile of prideful and idiotic joy spread across his ferocious features.

Slowly, he walked through the village, knocking on the doors of houses. He soon assembled 20 men, and explained to them that the mountain men had come to spy on them, and that if they were permitted to come down from the mountains like this, in small groups, there was nothing to prevent them from taking possession of the village one night and cutting the throats of the defenseless warriors. Besides, had they not fired an arrow at the village? The enemy's audacity would only increase in response to such mildness!

They all thought as he did, because they belonged to the ferocious party, retaining the dream of their ancestors, a politics of strict reprisals. Each of them ran in search of supporters. When they were 50 strong, they ran through the village uttering cries of alarm. A crowd emerged from the houses. With loud cries, feigned anger and an eloquence skillful in sowing suspicion and fear, Ver-Skag and his allies exasperated the perfidious instinct of the multitude, his madness partly simulated and partly real. The women immediately set up a dastardly clamor, demanding the blood of the mountain men, reproaching the menfolk for having favored the enemies of their race.

Rob-Sen and a few chiefs of his party, trying in vain to mount an opposition, were elbowed aside and threatened, and Ver-Skag, at the head of the most ferocious, raised his polished axe over the head of In-Kelg. He stopped in response to the cries of lacustrians opposed to the murder of one of their own—for they were behaving like ants in the same formicary—but he led everyone toward the bridges.

The murderous frenzy carried away the human flood, and those that were calm at other times, were caught up in the whirlwind, furiously brandishing their favorite weapons—axes, stone clubs, oaken bows and flint-tipped arrows.

Rob-Sen and his allies, however, had gone to the bridges and were holding them, unarmed servants to the fore, then the free men of the party, and then the chiefs, of which Rob-Sen was the most powerful in stature. The mob demanded passage, without daring as yet to touch the chiefs—but Ver-Skag struck one of the servants with his fist, and they all howled like dogs at the Moon, the threats becoming more distinct and the circle of hatred closing further.

Armed with his lance and club, Rob-Sen, abruptly presented himself. Everyone recoiled. The chief declared his intention to prevent a war that was cruel and unnecessary, since the high plateau and gorges where the blond men lived were of no use to the lake-dwellers. A colossus, whose muscles calmed resentments, he added wise words regarding the need to be at peace with the mountain folk, in order to conserve their strength for use against invaders of the great western lakes. He and his allies had been preaching that politics for a long time: union among the lacustrians of the center; alliance with the mountain tribes. He spoke on the bridge, softly but forcefully. Charmed by his vigor, astonished by his prudence, conscious of the superiority of his foresight and his courage, the crowd fell silent, as a herd of hinds falls silent when the stag bells.

A murmur of admiration and regret replaced the shrill squealing and the furious demands when young In-Kelg, a symbol of the beauties of the race, set himself beside his father, his eyes sparkling—but Ver-Skag, and those who had fingers avid for fresh blood, saw that they would be lost if people listened to the colossus, and one of them, known for his eloquence, accused the foreigners at some length of having intended to set fire to the village. His anger, his feigned indignation, his clever allusions to the objects of old quarrels and the play of his physiognomy reanimated the crowd's rancor and thirst for blood. Ver-Skag and ten of his cronies were already marching forward, axes raised against Rob-Sen, when Vi-King, the priest, interposed himself.

He stood there, in the fading moonlight, an effigy of the old fantastical race. A troubled dream, the pride of a being who reckons with occult powers, the cruelty of nerves refined by excessively gentle climates and an intolerance of prompt syntheses quivered in his smile, in his dark, flat eyes, devoid of melancholy or gaiety, upon his brow, rigid and tempestuous, and in his hands, which were making sacerdotal gestures. He spoke as the law, as the species, as a voice of the collective will, a genius animating the crowd. His sole reservation was that it was necessary to exterminate the mountain folk to the very last man, in order that none of them could spread the news of the murder.

Rob-Sen was still opposed, but two more priests joined Vi-King, and the encouraged crowd, becoming impatient with the obstacle, growled and protested. Finally, the other chiefs stood aside. Only In-Kelg remained rebellious. Although the adolescents, on the whole, were in favor of the great adventure, he did not cease hurling invective at the crowd. His father silenced him, though. Both were frowning deeply, the chief in anticipation of the war against the western lake-dwellers, the young man furiously opposed to futile murder, and also anxious about Eyrimah, whom Ver-Skag might perhaps overtake as she fled.

Meanwhile, as the mass of warriors, women and children were surging forth pell-mell on to the shore, Ver-Skag sent out his most able scouts and swiftest runners; then, as the crowd was noisy and disorderly, he demanded silence, in order to take the enemy by surprise. They ran then with panting breath, all with the same fixed smile on their features, dark silhouettes possessed by a ferocious dream, their brains accustomed to bloody sensuality, the children as caught up as the rest of them in the toils of the drama. Silently running beneath the Moon, bathed by its soft light, they advanced toward the terrible unknown.

They continued thus for an hour, and came close to a little wood of oaks and elms. There, grouped in a circle around Ver-Skag, they became drunk on his hatred, increasingly haggard and frenzied, brandishing weapons whose weight in their hands gave them courage. The scouts Slang-Egh and Berg-Got soon came back; they were seen from a distance making signs of victory, and when they drew close to the chiefs they said that the mountain men were camped a short distance away under the trees, that they had lit a fire there, and that they were all asleep save for one watchman.

A silent rage swelled their heads; women and children prepared flint daggers for horrible tortures, and they discussed recipes for murder and means of prolonging agony: black practices infused in the blood of the race by torrid sunlight and sacrifices to fetishes and brought to flower, like venomous plants, in the rich soil of human fury.

Slang-Egh and Berg-Got divided the troop into two companies, of which they would each guide one, while Khan-Ut, the infallible archer, would go on ahead to the mountain men's camp.

As they came ever closer, the latter's sentry became anxious. Moving a little further away from the fire and his recumbent companions, he scrutinized the darkness. Just as he raised his arm in a gesture of surprise, Khan-Ut's arrow penetrated his rib-cage at the location of the heart. He could only utter a dull croak.

The two troops had taken up positions that overlooked the mountain men, and all those who were carrying bows and arrows at the ready waited, while the women and children stayed behind and the bearers of lances and axes moved round in order to come at the enemy at right-angles. The watchman's croak woke his companions one by one, but the first to stand up were struck down by arrows, and the others found themselves under the lances before being able to arm themselves.

During the attack however, four lacustrians lost their lives, and three mountain men got away, pursued by enemy bands determined to kill them.

Ten bound captives were brought back to the villages in the midst of a vindictive and howling crowd. For hours, their cries of agony spread out over the lake, amid the howling of dogs, the frightful delight of the women and wild dances—and when dawn broke, groups of torturers were still lingering over the bloody bodies, full of bloodthirsty hysteria and vile curiosity.

The dawn quivered over the world in fragile rays, and weariness overwhelmed the cruelest. The massed crowd, as silent as a child whose rage has suddenly calmed down, were consternated on seeing the priests bowing down for prayer to the Orient from which the race had surged. They all bowed down fervently, and regret for needless murder added its weight to love of the city; war, soon to be engaged with fury, seemed heavy after the fatigues of the night. With white faces and dull eyes they looked at one another, frightening one another, finding everywhere the irritation and the alarm of the crime, less sure of their accomplices and less sure of themselves.

Vi-King sang to the augured star, the light that was already steeping the mountains. A horse was led to the sacrifice. It was a spirited animal, with wild, enlarged eyes. It displayed its warrior profile and sparkling mane to the multitude, with its slightly thick lips, turned back with a nervous grace, and the nostrils of an animal once marine, in the proud coquetry of its bucking and prancing. It whinnied toward the shore, toward the crop-fields whose perfumes drifted on the wind, and a great laugh, as sad as a sob, shook the exhausted people. When Vi-King's lance penetrated its breast and the noble beast collapsed, an anguished rumor ran around the village. After the ferocities of the night, the murder of an animal penetrated them with horror, and they returned to their homes very pale, with heavy frowns on their faces.

The first meal, a few cupfuls of spirituous liquid extracted from mulberries and raspberries, hardened their hearts. The chiefs assembled in Wid-Horg's hut, he being the oldest of them, but they did not want to discuss the situation while

Rob-Sen was not there. After some hesitation, he came. He sat down in reproachful silence.

Wid-Horg described the murder of the mountain men and explained that war was now imminent, since three of them had been able to escape. He said that the war would be ruinous, the wheat having just been sown and provisions of forage almost exhausted. There was no possibility of defending the plateau. The enemy would lay waste to the fields and it was necessary to bring the livestock in without delay if they did not want them to be stolen.

The losses thus foreseen darkened the faces of the chiefs, and they were unable to find anything useful to say, their hearts weary, when Ver-Skag stood up. At the sight of him, Rob-Sen became furious. Taking advantage of his right as the older of the two, he cut off the brute's speech, and proclaimed his indignation.

This was not the moment to show themselves treacherous with redoubtable enemies, when the western lakes had just been invaded by a new race, powerfully armed. Ver-Skag would be the shame of the lacustrian tribes. Thanks to him, Lake Re-Alg would be lost, they would be driven back wretchedly into the mountains; instead of possessing the riches that accumulated in peace-time, they would live like the former inhabitants of the western lakes, presently established on the high plateau, assailed by the mountain men, or they would be reduced to slavery, tending the cattle and horses, excavating the quarries or fabricating the weapons and pottery of the conquerors. With the aid of the mountain folk, on the other hand, they would have been able to defend the passes; the enemy would never have got as far as Re-Alg. He, Rob-Sen, had said these things a thousand times. Were they so difficult to comprehend? Then why listen to a brute with a mind as disturbed as the water of torrents after heavy rain? Why abandon themselves to anger, like mad bees that kill themselves in wounding their adversaries?

Fists were waved at Ver-Skag. He was afraid, but, with his habitual obstinacy, he tried to defend himself. He said that

155

Rob-Sen was a coward, that he feared war like a woman. Had not the lake-dwellers defeated the mountain men a hundred times over? Why be afraid today? Were their axes less solid, their arms less vigorous?

"But what about the newcomers?" cried his companions.

He shrugged his shoulders. Newcomers had never before dared to venture as far as Re-Alg. Besides, why should these people come to the defense of miserable mountain folk? No, the war would be limited to Re-Alg and the summits. They would take possession of the high plateau, where the pasturage was excellent in summer.

There was approval from a number of the chiefs, but Rob-Sen reproached them for such great folly. Soon, when they went to the grand council in the city, let all of them be careful not to take lightly the prospect of war against the new people, and let them remember the day when the lake-dwellers of the West had told the story of their defeat. They had attributed it to their insouciance; instead for forming a confederation, of marching against the enemy *en masse*, each village had risen in is turn and its people had gone to break themselves against the aggressors armed with unbreakable lances and axes that did not shatter. Ver-Skag would answer one day for his words, and those who listened to the imbecile's voice would be like him, like thieves coveting a prize and not perceiving the owner's club over their heads.

Silence reigned for half an hour, and Rob-Sen, who knew his compatriots, knew that they were profoundly dubious. Beneath his muscles, his good red blood and his broad chest, he had a calm head, steady in thought and as sure as all his movements. There were people wiser than he, shrewder in their manner of speech, more skillful in the exercise of the bow and the lance—but he fired few arrows, and none missed their target; calm in the heart of battle, his arm never struck in vain. It was the same with his ideas: they were strong, judicious and clear. In that half-hour of silence he prepared his attitude to the grand council. His partisans would find him firm of gaze, with the intelligent strength that would attach them to his destiny, while the followers of Wid-Horg and Ver-Skag would reap nothing but anxiety and uncertainty.

Meanwhile, the people gathered outside the house were chattering like the tongues of leaves in the autumn breeze. The Sun was already pouring forth its hot rays, warming their heads, and legends were going through their ancient brains. How many similar moments had there been in the life of that active race, and was it not natural to relive emotions and recapitulate deeds formerly accomplished as people slide towards their ruin? Those round-heads, rapid in synthesis, were the solid nucleus of the world, but destined to fuse with other, more flexible beings. Perhaps they had the prescience of a greater victory in the land of their adversaries, a victory symbolized by the beauty of the vanquished—and perhaps that prescience discouraged thought of an inferior beyond, causing them to maintain themselves energetically, to reproduce themselves, in order that, if they were not to transmit the poem of the civilization, at least its elements would not perish, and that everywhere, throughout the centuries, their resistant and concentrated body and mind might be found in the elegant skeleton, the tender flesh and the fluid thought of Northern humankind.

A boat, coming from the island where the grand council was held, attracted attention. As soon as it was sighted, a man went into Wid-Horg's hut and spoke to Rob-Sen. The chief announced that his son In-Kelg was coming back from the island carrying a message. The furious Ver-Skag complained that the young man in question, his personal enemy, had been sent as a messenger, and would certainly have slandered him. Many of them then used this pretext to criticize Rob-Sen, for they had steeped their hands in the blood of the mountain men. They gathered around the chief, who waited for them, surrounded by his faithful followers. Wid-Horg demanded why Rob-Sen had made use of a child with a loose tongue. Rob-Sen replied that In-Kelg was wiser than many men, and that he would have said nothing beyond his commission. The two parties measured up to one another for a moment longer, but

157

no one thought himself capable of taking on Rob-Sen's sovereign muscles. Even Ver-Skag retreated with the others. Rob-Sen watched him angrily and scornfully, and both of them murmured muted threats when In-Kelg came in.

His father asked him to speak straightforwardly. In-Kelg raised his arm and said that in anticipation of the war, Rob-Fer and Rob-Set, his uncles, Wid-End and Kor-Ting, the chiefs of the principal city, and the priest Mana-Lith had decided to gather the chiefs of all the villages of Re-Alg. Vi-King was to transmit the signal. Then the chiefs went out, and the men, women and children of the village, along with the excited dogs, accompanied them to a spot where the platform had no houses, in the middle of which an exceedingly tall mast rose up. As the crowd shouted, demanding news, Rob-Sen suddenly extended his arm. A large square of gray canvas floated over the island.

"The Grand Council!" murmured the crowd.

That made a religious impression on every heart—but Vi-King attached a large piece of canvas like the one undulating above the island to a thong, and hoisted it to the top of the mast in his turn. Instantly, all heads turned toward the neighboring villages, and a vast clamor went up over the lake when they saw the Grand Council's order floating over three settlements.

Boats covered the lake. The chiefs were in them, bearing arms and offerings. The crowd, massed on the edge of the platform, threw weapons and items of pottery into the water as sacrifices to the aquatic divinities; some of them were finely modeled bowls, knives or beautiful axes, but more often, by virtue of cheating, they were old objects of no more use. Meanwhile, everyone was excited by the file of boats, cheering the chiefs whose names had resounded in previous wars. The people of distant settlements were weary from journeys of four or five hours, but they straightened up as they passed by, striking their breasts and shouting their names. The villages were singing the battle hymn; the growing fever even infecting the children and dogs.

Singers seated at various points recited improvised songs in vague couplets; some vibrated with the general joy, telling tales of triumphant war, glory and booty; others contrarily inspired and more original, wept for the death of warriors and the misery of women wandering around after the fire and pillage. In response to the monotonous music, the dogs howled plaintively, and the multitude, their souls suspended between hope and terror, became even more frenzied, attaining the elevated crises in which creatures forget themselves, becoming no more than a vast collective beast, ripe for monarchic orientation.

Soon, the flocking boats reached the island. The chiefs greeted one another, grouped between relatives from distant villages, and the assizes were held in broad daylight. It was a gathering of wild men. Force reigned within them and over them. They exchanged the glittering glances of provocative predators, reverted to animal ways, like herds of urus on the plains or bellicose groups of horses or chamois. They were simultaneously possessed by a pride higher than their valor and a personality more fluid, more resigned to death, as if they really had been absorbed into collective life—but they fell silent, for Mana-Lith raised up a sovereign fetish, displaying it to the four corners of the horizon.

He was an old, stocky priest. There was a fanatical tyranny and a covetousness in his round eyes, and he demanded sacrifices. Hair bristled then, and a fury like an excess of alcohol passed through the chiefs. They promised that each village would give one maiden, one goat, one ox and one horse for immolation. Mana-Lith withdrew. A quarrel broke out between two chiefs who had drunk too much fermented raspberry juice; they struck one another with their fists and gashed one another with axes. They were separated, and the growling crowd drowned out their voices—and Rob-Sen, one of the superior chiefs, spoke.

A hero of his race, he sensed its destiny more clearly than the rest. He repeated what he had already said at dawn about the mountain folk and the redoubtable invaders. He accused Ver-Skag of being the cause of the war. He asked whether it was admissible that a single man could oblige everyone to take up arms. He said that a man who did not have the strength to constrain himself for the sake of the general welfare should perish. Then he envisaged the war itself. He wanted it to be serious, important and decisive, to impose on the newcomers a terror of all aggression. Emissaries would be sent to the central lakes, as far as the great lake of Ten-III,[12] which lay to the north. Alliances would be demanded everywhere, and warriors obtained. From the next day onwards, it would be necessary to occupy the mountain passes, set up ambushes and take possession of elevated positions.

Ver-Skag got up, along with five of his followers. Interrupting Rob-Sen, he denied that there was anything else to be done than fight the mountain men of Re-Alg. Why send emissaries to the central lakes? The lake-dwellers of Re-Alg would suffice, and if Rob-Sen was afraid, then he, Ver-Skag would take responsibility for bringing the adventure to a glorious conclusion.

From the majority, fearful of Rob-Sen's vast project, there was the cowardly murmur typical of assemblies, the welcome for facile words, for impracticable hopes, annoyance at the idea of a long war, covetousness for rapid booty. Rob-Sen took account of these things, and was overwhelmed by sadness; the decline of his race sounded in Ver-Skag's false promises. Then came a giant's anger. He stood up, called to his followers, and proclaimed his wrath; he insulted the blind chiefs, more innocent than children and he marched toward Ver-Skag. There was a rumor in a hundred throats, like the growl of a storm over a forest. Ver-Skag, encouraged, awaited his adversary, and Rob-Sen, his gaze tranquil, was like a rock that divides the fore of a cascade. With one blow, his fist

---

[12] The significance of "III" is unclear; there seems to be no possible justification for employing a Roman number, but it cannot possibly be a phonetic improvisation.

knocked the brute unconscious; then he threatened Ver-Skag's followers with his axe, and they all drew back.

"I will assume control of the war!" said Rob-Sen.

His friends cheered him; the others, fascinated, fell silent. But when Ver-Skag was carried away, a group got up: the group of those who had massacred the mountain men, and who were afraid of putting themselves in Rob-Sen's power. They came forward, concealing their weapons—but Rob-Sen, bringing his axe down, split the skull of the foremost. In their amazement, they all sensed that a leader had come among them.

And Rob-Sen assumed control of the war.

Part Two

I. The War

Since the arrival of the warriors who had escaped the massacre, the trumpets had not ceased to resound over the mountain slopes, and great fires tinted the firmament red by night.

The mountains had accepted war ruggedly. Already, 500 young warriors were pillaging the frontier zones, stealing herds and ill-guarded fodder. They avoided any considerable battle, in favor of harassment and surprise attacks, massacring isolated troops and keeping watch on the enemy's large-scale maneuvers.

Kiwasar, Hsilbog, Tawr, Luighaw and Doukh dominated the assembly of the chiefs. Hsilbog was the most redoubtable of the chiefs for temerity and divination, as prompt to make decisions as to identify ambushes. Everything about him—his glacial gaze, which was undeceived in the crepuscular hours when shapes become confusing to humans, his rapid and violent expression, his warlike lips, on which the stubbornness of good leaders of men quivered, and his speech, as fine and strong as the pine-branch that draws its life from the cold atmosphere—was imperious, robust and dominating. His only fault was the desire to prolong victories—not that he stubbornly attempted the impossible, or that he lacked foresight, but that he wanted to push success beyond the mysterious limits that certain people sense but of which those who have more warrior spirit are unaware.

Kiwasar, whose leaden face shone less brightly in battle, was less prone to spot the enemy's ambushes or maneuvers, but he had a sense of the limits of what might be achieved. His gaze was reminiscent of springs that run in the shade, clear but devoid of brightness, his will as strong as the compactness of his forehead, but without violence and almost without any-

162

thing unforeseen. In the previous war, overwhelmed by superior numbers, he had not suffered any crushing defeat. He had been able to hold favorable positions, calculating his maneuvers in such a way that no decisive surprise was possible against him.

To Hsilbog unexpected victories were owed, and unlooked-for booty, but also less certain results and a few fatal defeats. The peace concluded by Kiwasar had been as unhumiliating as possible, and the mountain men admitted that the war in question would have been more lamentable with Hsilbog—or anyone else—as its supreme leader.

At the assembly of chiefs, Kiwasar was elected as supreme commander in spite of Hsilbog's cunning and eloquence. Hsilbog walked out of the assembly disdainfully, and avenged himself by a spectacular action. He left by night with 300 companions, took the lake-dwellers by surprise, and captured livestock and prisoners. The young chief Tholrog, who served under Hsilbog, had played his part, penetrating in an audacious move as far as the pilings of a village and abducting Rob-Sen's own daughter. At daybreak, Hsilbog returned to the mountain, having lost scarcely a dozen men, and made mock of Kiwasar's slowness.

Kiwasar had, however, thanks to the spies of Tawr, the most cunning of the chiefs, discovered Rob-Sen's plan of campaign against the allies of the West and the mountain men. He knew that the lake-dwellers' leader was proposing to take the plateau of Iordjolk by surprise or to force the passes of Oydahm. The occupation of either of these positions would paralyze the mountain men's freedom of movement, cutting off any maneuver useful to their enemies. The lake-dwellers had never succeeded in doing that before, but Kiwasar knew that they were going to mass all their forces and condense them into a formidable alliance. Moreover, their numbers had increased considerably since the last great war, while those of the mountain folk had remained static.

The divulging of this news fortified Kiwasar's authority. His orders were obeyed in the interests of supreme conservation, for everyone understood that if Iordjolk or Oydahm were lost, the very survival of the race would be compromised.

The mountain had 2000 warriors. Eight hundred, under Hsilbog, were designated for the defense of the Iordjolk plateau and the gullies leading to it. Twelve hundred remained under Kiwasar to defend the passes of Oydahm, on which the majority of the places of habitation depended. Kiwasar put the children, the old men and even the mothers into protective shelter. Hsilbog only took a few young women and girls with him, to encourage the warriors in the decisive hours of combat.

Communications between the two armies were assured by the narrow gorges of Borg.

Meanwhile, Rob-Sen's troops were growing in number every day. From distant districts, even plains that were beyond the lakes and mountains, he received promises of help. In spite of the pain that the loss of Eï-Mor caused him, he retained all his determination. He resolved to commence the great war. After a few uncertainties, it was the plateau of Dap-Iwr—the mountain folk's Iordjolk—that he decided to capture by means of an extremely rapid attack. With that objective, it was first necessary to insure himself against a surprise attack by the men—under Kiwasar—who were defending the other key to the mountains, the passes of Moy-Dhangh, called Oydahm by the enemy.

Rob-Sen sent 2000 men to advance on Kiwasar. That troop took the first defenses established by the mountain men's advance guard. Kiwasar, once alerted, moved the bulk of his men forward, while giving appropriate cover to the lateral positions—which were, in any case, almost impregnable—and Rob-Sen's 2000 men were obliged to stop at the entrance to Moy-Dhangh. Eight hundred mountain men, solidly entrenched, confronted them on the heights of three extremely steep and narrow corridors. A ravine was hollowed out between the mountain men and the lake-dwellers, planted with sparse chestnut-trees, punctuated with small patches of grass, where the assailants would be exposed to terrible losses.

It was dusk. The great trumpets were blaring out a savage music, a challenge as deep and dark as the approaching night. Rob-Sen, not at all inclined to attack these terrible forts, contented himself by placing his men in evident positions, and letting them file slowly over the plateau, multiplying the camp-fires as darkness fell. When he thought that he had convinced his adversaries of the great number of assailants and the necessity of leaving the entrance to Moy-Dhangh heavily guarded against them, he withdrew and had himself transported, lying on an urus-hide, to the part of the mountain that led to the plateau of Dap-Iwr.

He rested during the journey, even going to sleep, and when he arrived close to Hsilbog's advance positions in the middle of the night, he felt as vigorous in mind as in body. Three thousand men were waiting for him there, who had already captured a few positions the previous day. In accordance with orders received in advance, the army had been resting since dusk. Rob-Sen immediately gave the order to move off.

The Moon illuminated the landscape marvelously. Hsilbog's advance sentinels saw Rob-Sen's army approaching. They waited until the army was within bowshot and javelin-range, and started a deadly fire while well-covered. Rob-Sen accelerated the march of his advance guard, and the mountain men drew back.

An hour later, Hsilbog was told about the approach of a large enemy army. The mountain chief had 800 men. He hesitated between an immediate counter-attack—which the moonlight would facilitate—and taking all the measures necessary to make Iordjolk impregnable. In spite of the temptation of a rapid battle and a campaign commenced with a spectacular victory, great for one of his offensive nature, the memory of miscalculations made in the last war made him first take all the precautions of the besieged against a besieger. He divided his army in two, keeping 500 men for himself, and sent three secondary chiefs, each with 100 men, to guard the most redoubtable passes of the three routes across Iordjolk. That done, knowing that he was almost inexpugnable, he consi-

165

dered the possibility of undertaking a counter-offensive, which his intimate knowledge of the area rendered infinitely seductive.

To begin with, he wanted to make an approximate count of his adversaries, and sent out his best spies. From their estimates and those of the various advance posts that had retreated successively before Rob-Sen he knew at about the third hour of the morning that he must be facing between 2000 and 3000 combatants.

By that time, the men in question had surmounted the first, scarcely perilous, obstacles. They had just paused. Their leader was preparing a decisive plan; he had to risk carrying Dap-Iwr by sheer force, with the collaboration of fortune. In order to do that, it seemed necessary to Rob-Sen to engage the enemy everywhere and, after the outcome of the first attacks, to launch the bulk of his army at what appeared to be the most favorable route.

Rob-Sen's army was positioned on the slope of a valley into which the passages to the plateau emerged like three radii into the arc of a circle. The chief hesitated for some time over the division of his attacking columns. After interrogating prisoners, lake-dwellers involved in previous wars and spies adept at moving over the mountains—which the tribes always maintained—he finally decided to send 500 men along the dry stream-bed, 500 through the gully of Yor-Am and 400 by the third route. He kept half his army—1500 men—in his own hands.

When the decision was made, Rob-Sen wanted to increase the confidence of his men by making a great sacrifice to the war-god of Re-Alg. He summoned the priests. They advanced along a rocky ledge 20 meters wide, from which they overlooked the multitude. The color of their tunics was black. Their shaven skulls were trepanned. In their right hands they held extremely sharp agate daggers, in their left, oak-wood clubs. There were five of them, accompanied by assistants.

The moonlight, striking the ledge directly, illuminated their somber procession. Scattered around the sinister rocks were stands of tall pines, where the delightful mystery of near-darkness mingled with the snow of moonbeams, a few solitary oaks and clumps of beeches. In the distance, colossal profiles, was the symphony of mountains looming up like mysterious clouds. The Moon was motionless in the ether, along with the faint half-extinct torches of the stars. The lacustrian army, assembled in a vast descending avenue, was contemplative, in the murmur of a multitude thrilled by mystery. A shiver went through 3000 heads, their eyes shining in the pallor of the air, a wave passed through the human thicket—and the infinite purity of the atmosphere in which the sky, the mountains, the forests and eternal nature were bathing was a charm.

The high priest leaned over the crenellations of the ledge and cried: "Te-Laad made the Earth, and Ho-Than made the waters, and they set Ham-Dô to defend the Earth and the waters. Ham-Dô had children who populated the Earth and the waters, and the tribes of Re-Alg are among those children, and must exterminate the enemies of Ham-Dô who live on the mountain and those who live on the western lakes. Ham-Dô demands a great sacrifice and he will come to the aid of his children…"

Then, according to the custom of the lake-dwellers in time of war, Rob-Sen replied to the priests in the name of his army: "The children of Ham-Dô will offer five white stallions and five black bulls."

"Ham-Dô wants men."

"Which men does Ham-Dô want?"

"Ham-Dô wants five mountain-dweller prisoners. He wants to see their hearts quivering in their open chests!"

Deep down, Rob-Sen loathed the priests, having experienced their caprices and their tyranny; he was not, however, completely incredulous with respect to their power. Most of all, human sacrifices were repugnant to him. He hesitated for a few moments, prey to contradictory sentiments, in which faith, doubt and political calculation collided. One glance at the multitude decided him. There was an energetic approval in that moonlit mass, a violent and voluptuous cruelty, all the

167

hatred of the lake-dwellers for the mountain folk, combined with an implacable instinct of immolation. Belief, the words of the old omnipotent priest and the promise of victory linked to the satisfaction of an appetite would multiply the force of numbers, electrifying desire. Acclamations rang out.

Rob-Sen gave in, raising his arms toward the old priest. "Ham-Dô shall have the hearts of mountain-dweller prisoners."

On the chief's order, the prisoners were brought forth and hoisted up on to the ledge. The multitude jeered and insulted them. The victims replied, proclaiming the cowardice of the lake-dwellers and their imminent defeat. They were stripped of their animal-skins. Their white bodies were visible, maintained upright against the rock by their bonds.

With a practiced slowness, the priests opened their breasts. The army enjoyed their lugubrious plaints. Soon, great red floods were welling from the silvery edges of the rock.

Panting furiously, the lake-dwellers rejoiced in the sacrifice, raising their intoxicating faces; the sensuality of the murder excited them all by contagion. The enlarged wounds allowed the mystery of the internal organs to be seen. The sacrifices coughed more feebly.

With a rhythmic and rapid movement, the priests tore out the hearts, lifted them toward the Moon, still alive and beating, while the multitude howled in an extraordinary frenzy of carnivorous joy.

"Ham-Dô is content with his sons," the high priest finally shouted. "He will give them the lives of their enemies!"

Dawn was approaching. A delicate splendor was struggling in the Orient, between the gaps in the mountains. Fearful life was stirring among the beeches and pines. Then the red round furnace of the Sun posed on a solitary peak.

Rob-Sen, who had watched the sacrifice impassively, disposed the attacking columns. He kept In-Kelg close to him. In spite of his hatred, the latter was disgusted by having seen men of Eyrimah's race die in that way.

Trumpets were heard roaring on the heights.

Two hours later, the battle had commenced everywhere. The lacustrian columns, having chased away a few feeble advance guards, plunged into the most dangerous passes.

II. The Gorge

For 1000 feet, the banks of the dead stream-bed extended inaccessibly, 100 meters high, as smooth as ivory. The passage was covered in shadow; bats and other crepuscular animals lived there in abundance. A dismal breeze blew there intermittently; sometimes the voice of the wind sounded as high and profound as the sighs of a god of caverns. Overhanging rocks lined it in places, like meditative mammoths over an abyss. Only the evening sunlight, at the magnificent hour, plunged into it confusedly, brightening the flutter of the bats floating in the ether, as if on a rare wave, with a hint of red.

The dead stream-bed opened up to the west after a series of zigzags. To the east, the bed labored up a 45 degree slope, ending on a little plateau, uneven and initially difficult. By means of steep pathways, that plateau communicated with Hsilbog's camp to the right, and to the left with glaciers and the immense mountains. Rocky walls limited the view.

Tholrog was in command of the 100 men who had to defend that pass. He had also brought 15 women, in order to sustain the combatants in moments of weakness. That was the mountain-dweller custom; the proportion of women was generally inverse to the perils and difficulties. In an advance expedition like Tholrog's, only the young ones were involved, chosen from among the hardiest.

Next to Tholrog's sisters, Dithèv and Hogioé, stood the slender Eyrimah and the lacustrian captive Eï-Mor, Rob-Sen's daughter. By right of war, they were the young chief's slaves. Their graces mingled and contrasted, harmoniously.

Tholrog looked at the blonde girl avidly; confusingly, though, a little of his emotion was deflected to the other, the

169

marvelous foreigner whose beauty was somewhat enigmatic. He shook his head, savoring the harsh current of air that fell from above and the disquieting breath of the abyss. He was dominated by a need to act. He gave orders to accumulate stones on the high sides of the extinct torrent and on one of the edges of the little plateau. The mountain men set to work. The fortress was ready to crush the enemy; but anxiety strayed through Tholrog's mind.

Will they come?

As he believes that he will be able to repel any attack, the greatest possible good fortune seems to him to be victorious in front of Eyrimah. He thinks about that, impatiently, his eyes scrutinizing the darkness of the stream-bed, his ear cocked toward the west.

"Asberl! Tahmen!"

Two warriors approach, fine mountain scouts. They leave. An hour goes by; then the echo of rapid footsteps rises from the darkness. Asberl and Tahmen reappeared.

"The men from the lakes are advancing, in great numbers—the first are 500 meters from the dry torrent."

Then there is silence. Anxiety stirs in every breast, the awareness that no victory is certain, no position inaccessible.

A race often vanquished by weight of numbers, the mountain-dwellers are aware of the treasons of destiny by virtue of the elders' dark legends. They know that the mountains crumble, that the voice of a child can unleash an avalanche, that torrents cease to flow and that glaciers travel. Now, here comes death! Many will fade away, as the shade of a dead man fades away. Many of those who are tall and brave will be as cold as the pale summits, as still as the glacier-snows. And death will pass and pass again; they yearn to howl and sing.

Tholrog orders them to hide themselves behind the stones, without saying a word. He disposes them; he gives orders; the women are moved back 300 meters, into a cleft in the rock.

The landscape seems to be alone with him: the respiration of plants, the melancholy of the wind, the imperceptible life of the rock, in which forces flow so slowly that the rock seems eternal, the running of thin beasts, the soaring of falcons, the distant flow of streams and springs, insects gnawing their petty pastures or massacring one another in a crack in a pebble...

The sound of marching feet echoes. In the depths of the abyssal passage-way men are advancing: the lake-dwellers. At first there are 10, then 20, then 100, approaching with prudence. The first few pause, in terror of the silence, of the possibility of ambush. Night-birds and bats take flight. A dozen men advance as scouts.

The advance guard begins climbing the slope, but slowly, exploring every nook and cranny, every rocky outcrop. An imperious voice is heard; the men climb more rapidly; 30 others run to join them. Their woolly heads are visible, their prying eyes in red-painted faces, their pikes, clubs and bows. They stop to wait for their companions. Their mouths are anxious. One of them, drawing back, seems to have seen something. His hand rises to his eyelids.

"Blocks to the right and left," whispers Tholrog. His order is passed on in low voices.

The reconnaissance having been anticipated, the mountain men are not positioned at the most practicable entrance to the plateau. The first lake-dwellers are able to advance that far. They look around suspiciously, without seeing anyone. One of them speaks; Tholrog is able to understand his words. "There's no one here!"

Another makes a movement of alarm, though; his lips open over shiny teeth and his eyes grow wide.

"To the death!" cried Tholrog. And everything in the taciturn landscape awoke.

The falling of stone blocks was heard, and cries of horror. The mountain men surged forth, hurling javelins; then their bellicose trumpets roared. On the slope, 20 blond men hurled themselves upon the fleeing dark-haired men. There

171

was a brief battle, individuals whirling around, soft flesh opening, skulls smashing. Two lake-dwellers, instead of going down the slope, had recklessly run on to the plateau, in a mad rush, brandishing their axes. One of them, bounding at hazard, stopped dead, his face twisted into a rictus of mad and terrible laughter. Tholrog hurled himself upon him and knocked him down, but without killing him. The other took refuge in a cleft, his eyes filled with terror; his broad face imploring mercy.

It was death that came—a horrible blow of an axe-hammer; gray matter splashed all around, in pools of blood.

Down below, the boulders had crushed the lake-dwellers, and one could see soft pulp, red liquid, fragments of bone; panic drove all those still alive out of the sinister gorge. Only five or six round-heads remained on the slope: the number, the fury and the rapidity of the mountain men only permitted them a brief defense.

In the litter of limbs and heads, dark eyes, pale teeth and greasy hair only glimmered for a few minutes; then, their flesh rent, their skulls split and their necks broken, the lacustrians perished, finished off without mercy, torn apart and dismembered by adversaries in whom the overly brief combat left an excess of bellicose anger to dispense random carnage.

That rapid and overwhelming victory swelled chests. Voices resounded in the echoes of the stream-bed. Tholrog had the joy of a prize won from fate, of the certainty of a deed accomplished; full of pride, he watched the women come running.

From the shelter of the rock they listened to the combat; two or three came out, ready to join the men, to fight or to urge them on—but the bellicose rumor, the vociferations of attack informed them of the mountain-dweller's strength. They all came forward after the cry of triumph, and were met by Tholrog.

"They're running away," he said, with glorious calmness.

He told them the story of the battle. While he was speaking, Eyrimah trembled with other thoughts. Was In-Kelg

172

among the assailants? Rob-Sen's daughter, unfamiliar with the mountain language, watched the gesticulating young chief fearfully.

He sought Eyrimah's gaze. The sentiment of her beauty was suddenly mingled with the take of the victory. His voice became softer, his gaze sought the admiration of the large and tender pupils of her beautiful feminine eyes. Eyrimah kept her eyelids lowered, her eyes in the shadow of her long lashes; her delicate cheeks were as emotional as her heaving breast. The young chief was saddened to see her so distant; he was saddened by the white harmony of her neck, the abundant tresses of her hair, and the curve of her chin, as delicate as a distant snowy peak.

In compensation, he met the somber clarity of the eyes of the lacustrian girl, the adorable tremor in the trellis of lashes, finer than slender branches before the Moon—or, rather, before black pools in which the Moon is reflected. And although he loved Eyrimah, he nevertheless experienced a singular languor and warm pleasure before the bushy hair of Eï-Mor, like very distant fir-groves, her skin, delicate without being resplendent, and her attitude, full of sensuality within terror.

When Tholrog had finished speaking, he felt less sense of triumph; Eyrimah remained preoccupied rather than admiring. When Hogioé asked to see the torrent-bed, her brother consented. They all went, for barbaric life had not yet allowed the horror of blood to arise in them.

Silence had already fallen again. The mountain-dwellers, overexcited by the success of their avalanche, were adding all the stones of the plateau to the accumulated piles. Eyrimah saw the massacre, but could not recognize anyone; those who still had human faces seemed to her to be from a tribe distant from Rob-Sen's. The others were hideously disfigured. It was impossible that In-Kelg was among them, and the young woman's heart beat less heavily. Rob-Sen's daughter, perceiving the prisoner taken by Tholrog, furtively pointed him out to Eyrimah.

"He's not one of ours!"

"No," Eyrimah replied. "Don't speak to him!"

The daughter of the lakes had no need of this advice; her own people, more ferocious than the mountain-dwellers, had familiarized her with the peril run by captives.

Meanwhile, Tholrog, standing on a rock, spoke to his warriors exhorting them for the battles to come. His voice carried powerfully, his gestures were curt, his shoulders full of strength. Rob-Sen's daughter looked at him in astonishment; that hospitality toward the foreigner rose up in her heart which is the instinct to mingle races. The scorn preached by the people of Re-Alg for the mountain people was erased by the victory and the beauty of the blond men.

When Tholrog had finished, shouting burst forth, trumpets sounded lugubriously and war fever resonated in their minds. Tholrog could not help saying to Eyrimah: "Those down below shall never pass through the gorge."

She lowered her head and looked away. She loved the man who had rescued her in her flight fraternally, but the mysterious gift of her destiny was pledged to another human being. Tholrog felt anger overwhelming him. "They will all perish there," he said spitefully, but he calmed down before the dark softness of the eyes of Rob-Sen's daughter. He felt condescending and protective toward her, like the shade of a maple-tree over a traveler.

While he stood there indecisively, the sound of distant trumpets was heard.

"Our brothers are also fighting!"

His eyes plunged into the darkness of the stream-bed. A slight wind was whistling. An eagle was soaring beneath thin, pale clouds. The frightful cadavers of the lake-dwellers, some in sleep-like poses, the majority mutilated, covered in horrible redness—fragments of flesh, solitary hands, eyes torn out of their sockets, and split skulls from which gray matter protruded like some gigantic fruit—spoke of Death and Terror, the inevitable end of all those who palpitate upon the Earth. At the very bottom of the ravine, crows had settled, along with lean quadrupeds and insects; the faint noise of the feast was audible.

The scouts Tahmen and Asberl had gone back down, adept at gliding silently, as nimble as ibex and as sinuous as weasels.

Tholrog went to the lacustrian prisoner and spoke to him in his own language.

"Would you like to live?"

The terror-stricken prisoner, who had insectile eyes, the skull of a buffalo, a thick-lipped mouth, a forehead creased by a deep wrinkle between the two temples and nostrils like an ant-lion's pit, made no reply at first.

"Would you like to live?" Tholrog repeated.

"Yes," he said, with a vague relaxation of his features.

"Tell us what your people are doing, how many of them there are below the gorge, and how many there are at the other passages."

The prisoner hesitated; race-hatred heightened his fear, and the conviction that, when he had talked, he would be killed anyway. However, he said: "The entire mountain is full of our warriors…"

A mountain man armed with a club took up a position beside him, and Tholrog said: "If you don't talk, or if lies gleam in your eyes, that club will smash your skull. Tholrog knows how to read eyes!"

The lake-dweller looked into Tholrog's blue eyes, fearful of their glare, but reassured by their frankness. He talked abruptly, without pausing, risking everything for a slender chance of life. "I can't count the numbers. There are several tribes. Rob-Sen is leading those who must come through the gorges. Others are going through other passes. Those who are to attack you are 500. That's all that a warrior who is not a chief can know…" He fell silent, expecting life or death.

"Should I kill him?" asked the warrior.

"Yes! Yes" cried several voices. Axes and knives were raised; sanguinary faces jeered.

"The men of the mountain," said Tholrog, "do not bite in the cowardly fashion of the vipers of the lake. Tholrog has promised the prisoner his life."

There was doubt, and hesitation; then the chief's voice prevailed.

"Tholrog, son of Talaun, has given you your life!"

The prisoner fell to the ground. "Tholrog is strong! I am his slave!"

Rob-Sen's daughter was astonished by the chief's clemency. Eyrimah looked on tenderly, in the confused sentiment that the people of her race were nobler of heart than the lake-dwellers.

At that moment, the crows were seen to take flight between the overhanging rocks; the scouts were coming back.

"The enemy! More numerous than before!"

"They'll die in greater numbers!"

A handsome giant with ruddy skin and silver hair, Irkwar, who had grown up in a grim and bitter struggle against the pale peaks and glaciers, launched into a song of defiance with the mighty rumor of the trumpet. They all joined in, with the thunderous voices and bullhorns, which carried as far as the dazzling mountain summits.

"Dithèv, Hogioé," Tholrog ordered, "take the prisoner away."

Footfalls were heard. Thickset silhouettes were outlined in the pale mouth of the stream-bed. Their mass soon increased; sliding along the edge of the rocks, taking advantage of the projection—a strategy that made crushing them more difficult. Orders sent other silhouettes running. The bed of the extinct torrent filled with a swarm of silhouettes, like bears; they accelerated, counting on taking by numbers and speed a position impregnable to cunning.

"To the death!" cried Tholrog.

The boulders rolled. In spite of the lake-dwellers' strategy, there was a terrible crushing impact. As soon as the first besiegers reached the slope, the lapidation was redoubled, the blocks of stone carrying away entire files.

Heavy and dismal echoes, and the echoes of low voices, repeated the impacts of the stones, the screams of the dying, the clamors of the attack and the dull breakage of bodies and earth—but nothing stopped the attackers' first charge. They clambered over their fallen comrades; they arrived in lines, protected by huge shields of leather and wood. Scattered until they reached the slope, they renounced all tactics before the ripple storm of stones, climbing heedless of obstacles.

Tholrog watched them anxiously; the irresistible terror of the besieged before the besieger filtered into his soul. In the rear, he could see further columns running forward, driving back the rare runaways, encouraging the advance guard with ferocious shouts.

Halfway up the slope, for about a quarter of its length, the rocks overhung to such an extent that the lateral lapidation became less dangerous. The efficacy of the frontal assault was diminished because of an outcrop close to the walls and a few blocks of stone resting on heaps of bodies. The assailants, therefore, hastened to reach that sheltered spot; soon, more than 100 men were gathered there, frantic with the fever of the assault, while newcomers arrived incessantly.

The munitions of stones were beginning to run low.

Tholrog disposed a party of men to launch arrows and javelins. The lacustrians, furious at the difficulty of advancing, were unable to reply to that. Without pause, however, others were running forward; more than 200 men filled the sheltered space. They still had to climb the final quarter of the slope— 50 meters of bare and slippery ground, where the boulders rolled forcefully. There was a moment of doubt, of terror among the besiegers—and the well-positioned mountain men were still hurling their javelins and firing their arrows, occasionally releasing a well-aimed block of stone.

In response to the orders of their chiefs, and the pressure of the rearguard, the lacustrians finally quit their shelter, with ferocious clamors and the savagery of desperate animals. The

177

growls of the mountain men replied, souls filled with a sentiment of blind and mortal force.

III. The Victory

Tholrog gathered 60 men.

The combatants on both sides knew that it was the decisive moment. Tholrog and his 60 men hurled themselves into
the entrance to the valley, while the others continued rolling
down the torrent of stones. Long furrows of flesh and blood
cut through the company of the assailants; sudden gaps opened
up in their mass. Abruptly, they came into contact with the
besieged.

Irkwar, the mountain giant, struck the first blows; his
immense silhouette and the whirling sweeps of his club enthused the mountain men and fascinated the lacustrians. An
enormous shock caused them to recoil; the surge of hundreds
of men projected cadavers and living men pell-mell on to the
plateau. They arrived in a furious pack with crazed faces,
bloodshot eyes and frantic raucous voices.

Before that irresistible mass, the mountain men's advance guard retreated. Then, men dressed in vegetable fibers
and men dressed in animal skins, tall blond silhouettes and
dense dark silhouettes, clubs and lances, hammers and pikes,
smashed into one another in heated battle.

The warriors of the lakes had the advantage. The moral
force of the attack, the surge of those shoving from the rear,
and a certain disarray among the mountain men, weary from
maneuvering blocks of stone, accelerated the assault. Ten defenders succumbed to straight and very rapid thrusts of short
spears, while the powerful clubs and pikes only struck down a
handful of lake-dwellers.

At the same time, the launch of boulders became increasingly rare at the top of the banks, and without any great effect. Further bands of aggressors reached the slope and the

covered pass. Soon, more than 300 men were pressed into the attack, against less than 100 defenders. Only the narrowness of the entrance attenuated the savage thrust of that mass.

In a resounding voice, Tholrog cried: "All into combat!"

The stone-rollers came running.

Setting himself at the head of 20 warriors, Tholrog hurled himself at the lacustrians' flank, with a vast whirl of clubs.

His troop cut through, dividing the invading force in two, sealing off 30 round-heads in the ravine. Carried away by their momentum, they rushed forward, while Irkwar leapt forward to support his chief.

In response to the impact of the giant, the atrocious carnage of his club, and the ardent and mortal determination of Tholrog, there was a moment of stunned amazement among the lake-dwellers. That time was sufficient for those who had come too far forward on the plateau to be surrounded and massacred.

The plateau was free then; the efforts of all the mountain men were concentrated at the entrance. Their disarray had vanished, the moral force of the assailants was diminishing. To the rapid spear-thrusts, pikes, stone clubs and wooden clubs now responded frenziedly. Irkwar's massive hammer protected the center; everything went down before his thrusts, breaking heads and lances. A surge by Tholrog, leading a new contingent laterally, cleared the pass.

There was a tacit pause on both sides, a hesitation on the part of one to resume the attack, and on the other to emerge from their retrenchments to take the offensive.

Tholrog took advantage of the pause to rearrange his men. Of the 80 remaining mountain men he sent ten with Irkwar, and while they withdrew to the left he cried: "Javelins!"

A cloud of javelins rained down outside the fort; because of the configuration of the entrance, the lake-dwellers were unable to make much response. Their chief, moreover, understood the imperious necessity of taking the offensive; he forbade delay in firing darts and brought his men back to the as-

179

sault. Pell-mell, pushing one another and pushing cadavers, by an effort of the mass—condemning those in the front rank to death—they took the pass again and spilled out on to the plateau for a second time.

The mountain men did not lose their footing, however. Taking advantage of oblique attacks, striking down the new arrivals from the side, they accumulated a rampart of cadavers and wounded, which slowed down the mass—and so the battle went on, feverish and slow, impetuous and resistant.

Tholrog, confident in the bravery and stubbornness of his men, now that the moment of surprise had passed, had thrown himself toward Irkwar and his companions on the rocky banks of the stream-bed. They arrived behind a basalt column that overlooked the surrounding area; then, between the interstices and crenellations of the rocks, the chief showed Irkwar the enemy.

"Those directly below are unwary—a rock-slide might crush 50 of them and sow terror among the others. We have to detach the rock."

Irkwar shrugged his shoulders in discouragement. "That's impossible."

"It's possible. I've tested it—it can be overturned. When the lake-dwellers were staying under cover, it would have been futile—now, it's victory. We have to bring down the rock on their heads!"

Irkwar and Tholrog positioned themselves against the rock at a slight angle, in the direction of the ravine. Stiffening their muscles, they imparted a feeble oscillation to it.

"You're right, son of Talaun! With our companions, we can tip it over!"

"Do it!" said Tholrog. "I have to go back to join our warriors!"

On the plateau, the lacustrian flood was again overspilling the barrier of cadavers, driving back the mountain men, like a rising tide driving a river back into its mouth. It was the decisive mêlée. An unexpected effort, a surge more terrible than the rest might carry the position conclusively. The circle of mountain men was already reduced to 50; 40 were lying dead or helpless. Of the 500 round-heads, more than 200 remained, nearly 200 having been crushed in the stream-bed and nearly 100 struck down in the assault—but 220 men, 150 of whom were on a level with the defenders, was a force far more considerable than 500 fearful of lapidation in the gorge.

On seeing the new arrivals spill forth, in good order and full of ardor, Tholrog understood that defeat was only a matter of time. No maneuvering was possible in that hand-to-hand conflict, in which only the narrowness of the entrance was slowing down the mountain men's forced retreat. The forces were directly engaged and would remain so. The lacustrians had an accurate notion of the relationship of the two troops; the whole battle was taking shape as a powerful pressure, with breaking heads, punctured breasts and a vertiginous whirlwind of clubs and spear-thrusts at the point of contact.

Tholrog hurled himself forward. Rushing like a bull into the thick of the fight, where the lacustrians were least weary, then advancing more slowly, lashing out with both his shield and his club, he succeeded in pushing back the enemy's left flank, and enlivening the bravery of his own men.

"Courage!" he howled. "Irkwar will crush them!"

These mysterious words, and the partial retreat of the lacustrian left, put heart into the blond men. Before the renewal of their surge, the combat came to a standstill, the speed of the weaker party neutralizing the advance of the other. The further tightening of the combat caused all the blows to strike home, redoubling the carnage.

Tholrog and those surrounding him advanced at an angle into the enemy mass—but that impetuous maneuver quickly reduced the number of the mountain men on the plateau to less than 40 combatants, and although it inflicted heavy damage on the lake-dwellers, it further diminished the proportion of the number of the besieged to that of the besiegers. The advantage was, therefore, brief. Soon, the round-heads resumed the offensive, and their progress accelerated.

The mountain men's arms were weakening, and their courage too. Once again the dark-haired men were about to make the fair-skinned mountain race retreat. The bitter sentiment of fatality overwhelmed them. Even in the fury of combat, Tholrog and his companions had a lugubrious awareness of being the vanquished race, the race in decline in confrontation with another, better organized, more fortunate and more numerous.

As his own men were driven further back, in every direction, the young chief gave himself a few more seconds before summoning the women and Irkwar—before renouncing his last hope.

When we've been driven back another five meters, I'll call the women...

He had scarcely finished this thought than the retreat accelerated. He saw the beginning of the defeat. Angrily, his voice growling, he summoned the women.

They came, with their long blonde hair, their pale faces, their gentian-blue eyes, gleaming like snow; the superb Dithèv was in the lead, fully inspired with the bravery of her race, crying: "Sons of great warriors, children of the heights, will you not die rather than reappear vanquished before the old men or serve the cowards as slaves?" All of them, with loud cries, the youngest at the head, joined in with the men. The power of the race came with them, the ancient creation, Love, Hearth and Heritage. They brought 15 pairs of vigorous arms, and a fresh ardor; they put heart back into the vanquished.

Once again, the mountain men stopped the lake-dwellers in their tracks. Dithèv and Hogioé were seen bearing their slender grace between the blows, thrusting with a lance or raising a club.

Eyrimah, who had come with them, remained hesitant. Bewildered, she searched among the lake-dwellers for familiar faces, but found none. Terror and a confused ardor alternated within her. When she felt sure that In-Kelg's tribe was not present, the terror diminished, and mysterious voices murmured within her, impelling her to die with her own people.

Tholrog saw her, and was inflamed, his blows taking on a terrible velocity.

The interval of that fair female gleam against the red of the massacre was brief. Several of them fell, skewered by lances or javelins; the invincible drive resumed, a troop of lake-dwellers dividing the mountain-dwellers forces into two remnants.

It was the end, the disaster. Tholrog called to Irkwar. A moment went by; he called again.

Suddenly, Eyrimah experienced the vertigo of death. Her race spoke, overwhelming her with emotion, and drew her into the mêlée too, a poor tiny creature desperately caught up in the cataclysm.

Tholrog called Irkwar for the third time.

There was the rumble of a landslide, interrupted by the roar of trumpets, and then by screams of horror and agony— and the giant advanced, throwing himself upon the lacustrians like an aurochs on a herd of zebus.

At the clamor of trumpets, the fall of the basalt rock, the cries of agony and Irkwar's impetuous charge, the men of the lakes became anxious.

Already the giant was upon them, a reaper of death with inexhaustible muscles. All recoiled before his resplendent audacity. He symbolized the mountain, the terrors of storms, the hardness of porphyry, the depths of abysses. At his vast gesture, the cries of despair that went up from the stream-bed, the weakening of the dark-haired men, the male and female mountain-dwellers felt their power enlarged and increased.

Tholrog succeeded in gathering a dozen men and launching them forward like an avalanche—and the victory was there to be won, in the terror of one side and the confidence of the other. The balance of morale shifted: superstition and foolish terror ran from the mountains to the lakes, with the sentiment that after the women, the rock-fall and the arrival of Irkwar, other unforeseen circumstances would follow—and the aggressive force that had previously surged up so terribly, retreated and descended, adding the effort of its flight to the effort of the besieged.

Pell-mell, the lake-dwellers shoved their way down the slope, tumbling in the rout, massacred without difficulty, knocking down the weak themselves and trampling the wounded. Howling creatures, furious with terror, ran away through the blood or died beneath the shattering blows of clubs.

Frantic, pursued without pause by Irkwar's challenges and the long blasts of trumpets, 100 lake-dwellers escaped, scattering at hazard into the pathways, losing themselves in the unknown...

From the height of the plateau, Tholrog contemplated his victory. His heart swelled with pride. In the gorge, there was a grim sacrifice of heads, torsos and limbs, a continuous flow of warm blood, a stale and nauseating reek of living flesh.

They, at least, were hated individuals, of the abominable race that had vanquished, hunted and persecuted his own for 20 generations. On the plateau, however, randomly mingled with the round-heads, the dark hair, the thickset figures in fibrous tunics, were fair-haired warriors of the highlands, lying amid the blackening redness of blood and mantles of animal fur. Even more profoundly heart-rending, there were the cadavers of women, still young, the charms of their faces preserved in death.

Tholrog leaned toward faces that he loved, toward mouths that would never speak again, wide-open eyes that could no longer see the firmament at which they were directed, and an unsoundable regret rose up within his barbaric spirit—but he thought, too, that it had been a glorious victory, that 400 lake-dwellers had paid for the death of 66 mountain-dwellers, and that, at such a price, the people of the lakes would not be able to resist the fair-haired tribes. That past had been defended with glory; the enemy would no longer dare to exert its force, taking far away the terror of the massacre.

Tholrog also thought that, with so few men, it was necessary not to allow the pursuit to continue. His horn sounded the return.

Gradually, they all came back. The chief counted 25 warriors. The tribe would not refuse reinforcements, when Tholrog informed them of the carnage of the men of the waters!

IV. The Mountain

Tholrog waited for reinforcements.

Standing aside from the battlefield, where the blond warriors were finishing off the lacustrians and the last wounded mountain men were dying of poison or their wounds, he meditated, watching the warriors and the women come and go.

As Eyrimah passed by, his heart swelled to the maximum—and she aroused the terrible grace of lust, which causes insects to die and large predators to tear one another apart. Among the corpses and the blood, the young woman's grace overshadowed everything: her windswept blonde tresses, adorable throughout the ages; the delightful curve of her neck; the fine flame of her gaze; all of her captivating movements, like the undulations of birch-trees on a hillside.

The young chief contemplated her in an immeasurable bliss. She seemed stronger than the mountains and the lakes, more penetrating than the sacred word of the elders, more graceful than the flowers of the solitary vales.

He tried to talk to her. "You are brave, Eyrimah...the blood of the mountains is awake in you..."

But she lowered her delicate lashes, hiding her eyes. "I haven't learned to fight," she said, evasively.

"Eyrimah—do you prefer the mountain to the lakes?"

The bright gaze was raised toward him, then lowered again—and the young barbarian trembled, but no word that was within him could have expressed the immense sensation of harmony, beauty and all-consuming sensuality that gripped him.

Coldly, Eyrimah replied: "I ran away from the lakes!"

"Your heart is with the people of the mountain?"

"I ran away from the people of the lakes."

Her enigmatic reply and her attitude shocked Tholrog; when he said nothing more, she drew away. He was so emotional that he was quivering; a vague anger mingled with his love for the fugitive. He shook himself and marched off.

He soon found himself close to Eyrimah again. She was not alone; Hogioé and Rob-Sen's daughter were standing with her. Tholrog looked at the group somberly, and suddenly noticed that Eï-Mor was looking at him. He was the object of a gaze full of mystery, nostalgia and shadowy splendor.

The anger in Tholrog's soul disappeared. His gaze followed the foreign woman, the enigma of her gait, the infinite languor of her grace. Something unknown thrilled within him, in which he found an analogy with the large electrical clouds whose borders are so pale in the summer sky.

The Sun was climbing rapidly. It was nearly midday when Tholrog saw his couriers coming back, accompanied by a man-of-hidden-things—a quasi-priest of the mountain-dwellers' vague religion. He was clad in a bearskin longer than those of other men and his forehead was covered by a wolf's-head.

The man said: "Iordjolk is taken. Hsilbog is returning to Kiwasar. You will certainly be pursued. This is what Hsilbog says: since the best two routes are impossible for you, take the route over the glaciers and rejoin Kiwasar, or go on to the land of Ariès."

The man-of-hidden-things then explained that Rob-Sen, having been beaten, had returned unexpectedly to the plateau of Iordjolk and had taken it. Thus, one of the strongest positions in the mountains was in the hands of the lake-dwellers.

Exasperated, Tholrog gathered his men and began the retreat, abandoning the lacustrian prisoner. After a few hundred meters, the route they had to follow was barred by a wide pre-cipice. An enormous pine-tree had been laid across it. To pre-vent the enemy from crossing over, it was necessary to cast the tree down as soon as the fugitives had crossed the abyss.

They had not yet detached the tree when they saw the lake-dwellers appear, not by means of the dry stream-bed but along a path that connected with the plateau of Iordjolk. The mountain men combined their forces in a supreme effort. The lacustrians were only a few paces away when the tree col-lapsed into the abyss, with a terrible noise.

"Let the men of the waters pursue us!" cried Irkwar, ironically.

Eï-Mor and Eyrimah recognized In-Kelg among the pur-suers. Rob-Sen's daughter reached out her arms, shouting to her brother. Eyrimah, pale and paralyzed by emotion, sought the gaze of the young lake-dweller on the far side of the abyss. Tholrog saw that, and a grim anguish weighed upon his heart.

At that moment, In-Kelg shouted: "Our guides will be able to pick up your trail!"

"We'll die at the moment when you pick up our trail!" shouted Tholrog. His terrible gaze went toward Eyrimah; the young woman lowered hers, without humility—with the in-sulting pride of love.

Meanwhile, the scout Tahmen jeered. "Do your guides have the feet of ibex?"

With a clamor of defiance, the mountain men drew away.

They marched in the astonishing silence in which one can hear one's own life: the flux of blood and the breath of the lungs. The route was harsh. It rose upwards, interrupted by excavations and obstacles, between two gully-walls, sur-mounted by chains of rocks; it was like a tear inflicted in the primal era, a persistent cut in the hard granite flesh. The li-chens and mosses were sparse. They were in a dead and im-placable environment, crystallized, infertile and severe, sealed with the trace of immemorial things, contemporary with the world's origins.

On the jagged edges of the rocks high above, however, the Sun traced a jewelry of light; patient, industrious and cunning life profited from narrow refuges, clinging on with a humble and ingenious energy: a white fir-tree standing above the void; a gentian sheltered in a clump of short grass; myrtles lost in a cleft; indefatigable brambles; the reddish tufts and varnished leaves of Rhododendrons; a poor stunted forget-me-not; adorable saxifrage.

A timid ibex appeared, miraculously perched, and crossed an empty space with its huge bound, in which muscular strength competed with the prodigious surety of equilibrium. The exquisite animal lowered its large horns, savoring the liberated joy of overlooking the precipices, the vague animal poetry.

The great vulture of the Alps, the golden lammergeyer with the pale collar, opened its ten-meter wingspan, soaring in quest of its charming victim, the chamois. Buzzards, crows and eagles ploughed long furrows while a few poor snowy finches fled.

After an hour or so of marching, the way was blocked by a 60-meter-high wall. Seemingly insurmountable, it gradually revealed a vertical sequence of anfractuosities to which the mountain-dwellers' industry had added rungs. The ascent proved to be relatively easy, except for the difficulty of hoisting up a wounded man, Gateln, who was inert and feverish, wrapped in an aurochs-skin.

The gully came to an end thereafter; a circular space opened up in an amphitheater of needle-like peaks. There was a valley to begin with, then, limited by a frontal moraine, came the fan-like opening of a glacier. Threads of water silvered the valley in clefts. To the right of the moraine, a hole opened up in the rim of a gulf.

The valley was rugged, sown with erratic blocks of stone. Amid the grim indolence of the stones, fir-trees breathed in the light, their pagodas of branches terminating in sword-points. Offspring of hard ground, they were in harmony with the harsh surroundings. The breeze spoke a stony language there, almost the same as on the crags. The rigid trunks and leaves distributed a keen and consoling scent, the strong balm of resin.

Supernatural gleams filtered between the peaks; a pool seemed to be asleep in the depths; networks of snow illuminated shadowed corners. The rocks rose up like ancient beings, devoured by frost, heat and the invincible water. The wind murmured deep soft notes in long corridors; higher up, a clearing revealed pale mountains, linen robes extended over the heights, the taciturn splendor of glaciers and gorges.

The man-of-hidden-things came to his companions and said: "The ice-giants have transported these stones; it is necessary to ask their permission to pass through them, for they know how to punish those who forget." He took a javelin, whose point he sharpened, then threw it into the valley, howling. Grim-faced, with their arms folded, his companions looked at him fearfully, waiting for the giants to appear.

Nothing appeared, however, but an elegant herd of chamois, mingled with slender fawns. The humans watched them moving up to inaccessible escarpments, losing themselves among the abysses—flying, so to speak, from pedestal to pedestal, and galloping along narrow ridges. Each light little fawn, a child of tempests conceived in the winter storms, accompanied its slender mother. Already far away, they saw one matron pause, with two twin fawns, on a ledge decorated with a single gentian. She turned her pretty horned head toward the company of humans.

The man-of-hidden-things made a cross with two pikes. He brought out a little bag, from which he took some dead leaves. He threw ten leaves in all directions, and then howled ten times. Drawing a lump of rock crystal from his bosom, he caused a ray of sunlight to pass through it, projecting the marvelous colors of the rainbow in front of him. Then he intoned a mysterious plaint, and listened to the wind.

"We may pass," he said.

The mountain-folk crossed the valley.

Apart from trees and aromatic herbs, one might have thought it a desert. Invisible creatures were, however, keeping watch on the passage of the humans.

A marmot sentinel, sitting on its backside like a minuscule bear, interrupted itself while gnawing a root that it was holding in its forepaws. With a whistle, it alerted its companions, scattered around their common domain. They all ran back to their lair, staying silently in the little dwelling, all their senses alert to any danger. A pale hare had fled. With its piercing eyes, an anxious lynx followed the troop from afar. An old solitary bear with poor eyesight but keen nostrils, shielded by a circle of erratic blocks of stone, breathed in the numerous enemy odors that were passing over its seigneurial territory.

And other small animals, a discreet swarm of eyes, paws and ears, were disturbed by those who were passing by, but who did not perceive the numerous and secret life of the laborious valley.

The glacier was soon close by, eaten into by a resplendent Sun. A rumor escaped from it, confused voices mingled with elements, a conflict of forces—and also, toward the left, a faint and graceful ringing sound, like crystalline music.

"The giants are at work!" said the man-of-hidden-things.

It is true that the glacier was at work. It was collaborating in the great work of the weather. Destroyer of the mountain, a breaker of stones, a former of springs and torrents, it transported, excavated, engraved and polished, participating in making fecund soil for the valleys. Its ice cleaved or splintered, its drops of water dragged debris away. It was its forerunner that had once carried the erratic blocks of stone to the valley where it now maintained its separate domain.

The surface was melting, save for two or three pits of shadow; moraines were advancing, the largest stones reminiscent of verdant and flourishing islands, or oases sown with rustic grass and plants, others like heavy and somber reefs. Holes and wells were hollowed out by the Sun. The denser water continually descended into the depths, replaced at the surface by colder and lighter water. Some of the wells were pierced all the way through to the bottom, flowing through sub-glacial conduits—and it was the tumult of these flows that rustled, whimpered and sang.

To the right, where the water flowed torrentially, a large glacial cavern opened up, beneath bridges of ice and pillars resplendent with blue-tinted light, the water bore diaphanous debris, stroked by iridescent blades. Here and there, a ray of sunlight illuminated a blaze of gems, hardened a needle, or projected a sash in the half-light like a sheaf of incandescent lances.

It was a temple of solidified light, a temple of sapphires, colonnettes of lapis lazuli, capitals of crystal, into which refraction, here and there, cast rubies, amethysts, aquamarines, emeralds, topazes and carbuncles. Minuscule springs emerged everywhere, like singing worms, a thousand tortuous fountains that woke up in the sunlight and were paralyzed by night, gentle devourers of rocks and fecundators of tiny valleys.

Mounted on a crest of the frontal moraine, Tahmen and Irkwar explained that the glacier was merely a branch of a sea of ice. For the moment, it would suffice to cross a few hundred meters along a lateral moraine; they would then be able to walk along a ledge 2000 meters long, go back down on to the ice, climb over the rock and go across a section of the great glacier to rest in the cave of Môh.

The fugitives ventured on to the ice. The Sun did not reach the moraine along which they were passing; the ice there was solid. Sometimes it was necessary for them to traverse labyrinths or needles of layered ice, marvelously beautiful and bleak. Crevasses were rare, easy to go around.

Irkwar marched in the lead, on the lookout for ambushes, the treason of hidden abysses, holding the end of a long and solid braided rope, also held by those who followed him.

A gulf opened up, of vertiginous depth; it extended for a long distance, connecting with other, equally perilous crevasses. There being no possibility of a detour, Irkwar located a bridge of compacted snow and ventured forth upon it. There was a great and solemn silence—but the colossus slowly made his way across the dangerous passage, and then, with the aid of the rope stretched from one side to the other like a rail, the women also passed over. Only Rob-Sen's daughter manifested any fear, but she was able to overcome it. The most difficult thing was to slide Gateln across, lying on his aurochs-skin. They succeeded, however; the frail bridge over the abyss suffered no damage from the weight of all those people.

They arrived without further incident on the rock indicated by Irkwar. A ledge alternated thereon with narrow corridors. They could only march in single file; the abyss called to them with an insistent voice, vertigo attracting the mind like a whirlpool around a boat. From the depths of the shadows, the void seemed to be demanding its victim.

Rob-Sen's daughter looked away, trembling, fixing her eyes on the granite wall. They all walked silently. There was no sound, save for the echoing fall of pebbles, and Gateln's occasional plaints.

It was nearly three hours after noon when Gateln asked to rest. His voice was weak, his gaze wretched, his lips ashen. They were on a platform; the wall of basalt that cut off their view was cleft there by an enormous crevasse; they now had an abyss to the right and to the left, but the right-hand abyss was only a narrow gulf, exceedingly bleak and dark. The left-hand abyss opened on a miraculous dream of light and vastness. Gateln asked to be taken closer to it.

His mountain fatherland entered his pale eyes, all the way to his pain-racked soul: the entire country, plunging down and rising up again, pitted and pierced, jagged, sterile and fecund, pale and green, dull and silvery. The entire mountain, a taciturn world in which eternity seemed to be afloat, which devoured the minute, a gnawed skeleton whose tooth-marks and cracks were witnesses to destruction—and Gateln was moved by melancholy.

The breath of death stirred up his memories. He reviewed his life, fearfully. His life, alas, was there! It was in those great plateaus and massifs, the gorges, the peaks, the precipices, the pasturelands reminiscent of glaucous gems. His life was in those caves and crenellations; it soared between the needles of granite, the flanks of basalt, the cupolas, the pillars of gneiss or porphyry, the ravines, gentle or full of sterile rockslides, the jaws descending on the hillocks, the craters in which remained the lava of ancient fires, the pyramids and the cones standing like sentinels of eternity. And his life had climbed the argentine glaciers, the escarpments planted with black forests, the adorable gorges where fresh waters chattered.

With the immense fear of a simple soul, Gateln sensed that he was about to leave these things behind, that he would never see the plants that had so often opened the round of the seasons for him again. The huge chestnut, devoured by its offspring; the fir-tree, conqueror of the oak; side by side with the beech, hemmed with all the delicacies of its foliage; the larch of the highest forests of all; and the arolla pine, the magnificent battler of tempests, with its somber pride, which makes its slow and invincible sap in the cold where the fir is no more than a stunted bush...

And while his moribund eyes gazed at the layered forests, Gateln remembered the mosses in which one buries oneself as if in fresh snow; the meadowsweet in the woods; the golden showers of the Laburnum and the mountain-rose, adorably ephemeral; the tremulous Campanula; the proud and strong Rhododendron, and the rambling Anemone, which knows how to climb slopes and overturn obstacles. And the poor barbarian trembled with the desire that his life might not be over, and an infinite poetry—the poetry of children and animals—sang the sweetness of these things within him—and still his eyes were searching, alternately bleak and shining.

While his eyes shone, and his blood recovered a little of its violence, he reviewed rapid days and battles, and the pursuit of the maid who had become his wife over the fresh grass and around the thickets; he savored his mother's love and his father's strength. While his eyes became dull, and weakness descended upon his heart, he reviewed dawns and days and violet nights, distantly.

"Gateln has no more strength!" he murmured.

No, he had no more strength—and yet he could still see the vague lakes, the white threads of torrents, the resplendent fall of cascades. Above him, a few scattered clouds drifted, clouds soaring like swans, suspended like sheets of fabric, like the fleeces of goats, or so light and so diaphanous that it seemed that the breath of a child might carry them away.

Gateln was thirsty. He asked for water—the icy water that condenses on the rocks. There was none at this height, but they were able to melt a few pieces of ice for him. He drank avidly, then said, bitterly: "I can't see the villages any more."

Eyrimah looked at him with pity; many of them were moved by their companion's plight.

Suddenly, the man-of-hidden-things pushed everyone aside. "Death is mighty," he cried, "but one may sometimes chase her away!"

Armed with an axe and a javelin, he began leaping around the dying man making horrible noises. His axe whirled, and his lance stabbed at the void. He proffered objurgations, and then resounding threats, in mysterious, rhythmic syllables, terminated by sharp cries. Gateln suffered the racket patiently; a hope appeared in his gaze, as indecisive as the first thin line of the crescent moon emerging from the darkness.

The man-of-hidden-things continued thus for several minutes, amid the eager expectation of the mountain-folk. Finally stopping, he brandished the axe around Gateln's hairy head, and stared into the wounded man's eyes. "She is strong!" he said. "Let the warriors join in with me!"

A howling chorus had just begun, when Gateln sat up. "Look down there!" he murmured, in terror.

Everyone looked.

It was a fateful omen. A frail young chamois was standing on a narrow outcrop of rock. A great Alpine vulture was circling around it, moving back and forth, rapidly beating its vast wings, which bore it smoothly through the ether. The delicate quadruped, panting with anguish, raised its horns, facing up to the powerful bandit—and the carnivorous beast, not daring to swoop down upon its victim as yet, frightened it with its flapping wings and its bleak gaze.

This was after a long pursuit, in which the chamois, fleeing from peak to peak, had ended up on this frail haven on the edge of the void. Now the final battle had come, and the lamentable defense. In the moments of respite when the vulture regained its momentum, the chamois searched for a way out; it felt the rock, lifted its head. There was nothing accessible above it, even given its flying leap. If it attempted a descent via the imperceptible footholds by means of which it had climbed up, a single thrust of the lammergeyer's wing would have knocked it down.

The bird came back swiftly, screeching, wearying and paralyzing its charming prey.

"Gateln is the chamois!" murmured the wounded man. "Death is coming like the great vulture."

Suddenly, the vulture made up its mind. Taking to the field with a war-cry, it fell upon the chamois, struck it with its wing and beak, and tipped it into the void. The mountain-dwellers watched the antelope tumble into the depths, while the bird, wings half-furled, followed it with a murderous screech.

Gateln lowered his eyelids then, resigned. Like the poor chamois, he sank into the gulf. His heart would not race again, nor his eyes light up. Everything within him diminished and descended gently. He still had the strength to say: "Gateln has fought well!"

"The mountain will know it!" Tholrog replied.

Gateln went to join all those who, for hundreds of thousands of years, had lived and disappeared. His companions contemplated him, going to sleep as they would one day, with a beauty as cold as the winter sky—and Gateln, lying in a hollow in the rock, waited for the carrion-eating beasts to come and take him, to remake his life within themselves.

V. The Storm

They continued their march. It became increasingly difficult: all precipices, crags and vertiginous slopes. They passed through gorges over which vaults of ice were suspended, in which a shout might provoke an avalanche. They moved above the void on ledges so narrow that they could scarcely put both feet on them; then, extended leather ropes served as a hand-rail for the women and those enfevered by some injury.

The vegetation was even more stunted and plaintive, save for distant glimpses of a few meager fir-trees, crushed by the endless struggle, stocky larches twisted by effort or glorious arolla pines, proud and durable, and sometimes a small twinflower or a little sparse grass. A few raucous birds or furtive ibex passed by.

Then the desert resumed, pale and crystalline: the wintry cold and the beautiful silence; the ever present peril, with a strange tremulous sensuality. In the distance, mists formed— clouds on the summits. All the symptoms of wind and sky promised snow for the evening; it must already be falling lower down.

Tholrog kept close to his sisters, watching over Eyrimah and Eï-Mor. He protected them at terrible moments. He encouraged them with a protective severity. Eyrimah remained silent and reserved, with an inward gaze that irritated the young man. Eï-Mor was afraid, meekly obedient, replying softly. At brief halts, her face was raised anxiously toward her master, and the splendid melancholy of her eyes spoke of astonishment and supplication.

There were strange conflicts within her. In this perilous ascent with the enemies of her race, she experienced, in truth, apprehension, regret and fatigue, but she also found therein a dreamlike joy and a sentiment of the marvelous. Then, Tholrog hardly frightened her at all. She could not help looking at him at times when the route was easier, admiring his pale skin and the blue clarity of his eyes—and the sentiment of the unknown and unexpected refreshed every fiber of her being, so young, enchanting the adventure.

Sometimes, Tholrog spoke to the young women. "We can't rest before nightfall," he said. "We need to be sufficiently far away that your people can't overtake us during the night."

They understood the necessity of the flight. Vigorous beneath her apparent languor—and if not skillful, at least resistant—Rob-Sen's daughter was resigned to it. She was astonished that the chief thought it necessary to explain himself to his captive. When Tholrog spoke, Eyrimah drew closer to Dithèv and Hogioé; she always experienced a mixture of inclination, admiration and terror in his presence.

There was an accident two hours after the death of Gateln. The fugitives, rounding a bend in a passage, found themselves confronted with a frozen waterfall. On a steep slope, the ice formed a phantasmagoric chaos of truncated pyramids, twisted needles and blocks in the process of pulverization, down which masses of ice rolled at intervals, making an immense racket, in which the splendor and prodigious beauty of billions of facets and ridges was intermingled with the horror of the thunderous cataclysm of crevasses in formation and crumbling masses.

Leaning over this hectic solitude, the mountain-dwellers were intoxicated by the fury of the inanimate. One of them descended a little way, in spite of the warnings of his companions, and his foot suddenly slipped. He tumbled down to the bottom of the frightful slope. Scarcely had he got there, and his cry of fright had risen up from the depths, when a block of ice crushed him. His blood sprang forth in a red splash, his crushed flesh coloring the prismatic gleams with blue gems.

That death made the march even more somber. Eï-Mor, in particular, was in despair; she thought she was destined to die in the glacial desert of the mountains. Eyrimah felt scarcely more reassured, and the past that had been so hard was transformed by the deceptive grace of memory: oh, the warm lakes, the transparent mornings in which the lake sang the song of life, full of beautiful bright fish; the sounds of stone being carved, grain being milled; running through the grass or among the young foliage; the work of pottery, spinning, weaving, sitting outside the huts on the edge of the pilings...

The storm advanced in great clouds over the glaciers and the peaks. The birds of prey had descended to their eyries. The immense vultures had ceased to watch for chamois. A terrible penumbra limited the view.

Irkwar, Tholrog and Tahmren attempted to accelerate the fugitives' march. They were approaching a sea of ice.

First, there was a wild torrent between two smooth rows of needles and slopes, in which all the furies of the waters seemed to be rushing in silence. An impetuous surge advanced in a fantastic light, a sublime wrath of waves and foam—but it was only a representation of movement, all threat and swollen precipitation, advertising peril and power, but all was motionless between the high banks, walls of quicksilver, with great ruffs made for the collars of giants, blocks leaning over the abyss, ice-bridges astride the frightful walls of ice. And the silence was so prodigious that they all felt oppressed, solemnized, and they were all silent in the formidable peace of the landscape.

They were able to move alongside the river of ice for a while longer; then, as it broadened out, they either had to risk themselves on the surface, full of pitfalls and treacherous points or remain on an inhospitably narrow and stunted platform of rock.

At that moment, the storm descended in the vicinity.

Tholrog and Irkwar conferred with the warriors. Irkwar, highly-ranked among the hardiest explorers of the summits, knew the configuration of the heights and the glaciers better than anyone, and the perils of storms, avalanches and abysses.

"We can't stay here; the night would freeze us. We have to reach the caves of Môh before nightfall. Tahmen and I will guide you. We need to walk 2000 meters over the ice, then take a path through the rocks."

They were obliged to yield to his arguments and to set forth across the sea of ice covered with needles, peaks, ice-bridges, frozen waves and solid surf, traversing crevasses and labyrinths. To make things worse, the storm had reached them.

Rapid clouds descended; it seemed that the sky was absorbing the Earth. Howling winds spread out from all the mountains. The keen blades of the wind cut large fractions out of the clouds. There were silences, then terrible efforts, forces unleashed; the sky whirled above the peaks. The pale zenith displayed all the realms of gray and blue; it descended further. Subtle white flowers flowed within it, sometimes sown with furious gestures by squalls, sometimes arranged in bright bouquets. They stopped, and they reversed direction. Their finite delicacy, their network of minuscule petals, spanned the entire horizon.

Suddenly, the crisis arrived; the wind and the snow mounted a charge. In a sinister dusk, Tholrog and his companions were climbing the side of a glacier, with no shelter. All the rocks were smooth, eroded by the wind. The crevasse multiplied, increasingly perfidious, hidden by heaps of white snow, continually threatening to swallow the humans.

Irkwar and the lightly-built Tahmen, marvelous guides in a storm—the one by virtue of his lucid strength and cheerfulness in the cold, the other by virtue of the subtlety of his movements—warned them of traps, throwing out lifelines. Several times, for want of ice-bridges, they had to carve out steps in the walls of crevasses, descending into the abyss and climbing out again.

Tholrog, bringing up the rear, protected the women. They were marching courageously, but Rob-Sen's daughter was tiring somewhat, and often slipped, having difficulty keeping her balance on her tiny feet. Eyrimah had recovered the atavistic energies of a mountain-dweller; she moved forward, oblivious in the difficult but dreamlike struggle, excited by the freshness of the gusting wind.

The disorder increased. Tumultuous masses of air rushed upon them and collided with them; clusters of snowflakes glided like packs of white bears; the rocks were reminiscent of motionless livid aurochs; the great glacier sometimes resembled a desolate plain and sometimes a sea whose successive waves were breaking into dazzling foam—and over all of it, howling, roaring, trumpeting, mysterious whistling sounds and wild screams.

"Keep going!" cried Tholrog. "Another 2000 meters and we'll find refuge…"

Suddenly, in a blinding squall, he saw Rob-Sen's daughter slip and roll toward a gaping crevasse. He hurled himself forward, trying to grab her, but she rolled further; they both thought that she was doomed.

On the very edge of the gulf, however, the young man caught hold of the young woman. With one hand he grabbed hold of a block of ice; with the other, he held on to the brown-haired girl. Through the blizzard he could make out her dilated eyes, the terror in her pale face; a warm blast of energy shot through him; he hung on desperately—but his hand slipped on the ice. In his turn, he began a slow, inexorable descent. He thought that he was about to perish, but even so, he did not let go of the maid; their ardent gazes met, courage in the one, anguish in the other…

Then a hand fell upon Tholrog, and a rope was knotted around his feet. Several mountain men were holding on to it. Tholrog was safe, and he drew the young lake-dweller toward him with both hands.

Eventually, she was beside him, her youthful form disposed with an abandoned flexibility, her eyes terrified. The wind flung her hair around Tholrog's neck. He shivered, and saw depths more profound than any peril appear in the pale tempest. Still breathless, leaning against him, she had never been so frightened or so astonished; she could not understand why the enemy chief had risked his life for her.

Soon on his feet again, he set his companion down, sustaining her; all the howls of the storm could not abolish the sensation of the soft and delightful roundness of her figure.

The march became almost impracticable. At every step they saw men and women sink into the snow; a few stumbled, remaining buried for some time—but it was extremely dangerous to stay close to rocks; landslides and small avalanches threatened their lives there.

Irkwar, in his colossal splendor, enjoying the storm, was the chief here rather than Tholrog. His stature, his voice and the easy gestures with which he picked Tahmen up when the latter sank into snowdrifts, sustained everyone. He seemed to be the muscular sovereign of the mountains, his legs untiring and his blood red, his lungs made for frost and powerful respiration. Even Tahmen, so slender and agile, lost his sense of direction in that conflict and racket in the funereal dusk. Irkwar's strength and intelligence was redoubled, his instinct, orientation and divination miraculous. He avoided crevasses and recognized practicable routes, never losing the direction of the cave of Môh.

The slope began to climb more steeply. They went into an embranchment of glaciers, marching once again between two embankments. It was continually necessary to hollow out a route through snow accumulated on platforms. They were slowed down by a factor of ten. Suddenly, the wind blasted directly into the gorge, and frightful masses of snow came with it.

"All together!" cried the colossus.

They came together, huddling against one another; the avalanche arrived, a torrent of snow. Packed into a niche, the troop could not do anything but await the cataclysm. For an instant, the torrent flowed, and passed on. Not one of them escaped being buried. In the place where 30 vigorous individuals were standing, there was nothing any longer but a white surface stirred by the eddies of the storm: potent nature, the triumphant voice of the elements, the clouds opening over the peaks, the marvelous conflict of forces...

The shroud came apart, however. A pale silhouette emerged. He looked around with the tranquility of his great courage, and saw that the avalanche was not very deep. Already he was sweeping it away, causing heads coiffed in snow to appear; his trumpet excited the courage of those still buried. Thanks to their huddling together, the surface to be cleared was restricted; soon, almost all of them were in the open—and during that rescue of specters in the bosom of the interminable snow, Tholrog embraced Irkwar. "The villages shall hear of your courage!"

Irkwar returned the hug; he was emotional and troubled; there was a powerful fraternity in his blue gaze.

Meanwhile, Dithèv touched Tholrog's shoulder, saying: "Hogioé...and Eyrimah?"

Tholrog shivered. He looked toward the place where he thought he had last seen the two young women. The snow was deep and compact there. "There!" he said. With one bound, he was there, digging with his hands, aided by everyone else.

"Nothing!"

Fraternity, love and mortal anguish were amalgamated in his soul. He went on digging, and uttered a loud cry. He drew out a body—Hogioé!

Numb with cold, the young woman was reanimated. "Eyrimah is in there!"

Irkwar and Tholrog succeeded in reaching the stranger and extracting her from the sepulcher. She was weak, but not unconscious; the sight of her delicate face and beautiful eyes, powdered with silver, increased Tholrog's emotion—and the warrior's gaze said: *I'm the one who has saved you again!*

Eyrimah could not support that gaze; she lowered her eyelashes. Tholrog sensed how much further from him this daughter of his own race was than the lacustrian girl, how much more confidently and tenderly Eÿ-Mor's dark eyes had looked into his own.

It was necessary to resume the painful march, continuing to clear a path through thicker snows. Fortunately, the avalanche had cleared the heights of the mountain. They found the route over the rock just as steep, but less treacherous—and they finally saw the cave of Môh appear, where they would be able to rest from their long anguish and great efforts.

VI. Eyrimah and Eï-Mor

It is night, in the caverns of Môh.

Tholrog gets up, anxiously. The wind is making the snow and rock talk. Tholrog walks to the mouth of the cave, slides between the stones and moves aside the furs at the entrance. He is on an aerial promontory, as if posed in the glacial light that dresses the mountain crests and peaks, plunging into livid gulfs, heightening both the complexity and the mystery of the harsh landscape. The wind seems to be falling from the Moon.

The Moon is posed on the western summits, mediating above a cloud, hollowing out a river of light on the ice, a seeming highway of mingled wind and moonlight. Everything replies and calls out to the plangency of that wind; everything weeps, threatens or sings over the gulf and the stone. It is as if the entire landscape is populated by immobile wild beasts, crouching or standing, asleep or lying in ambush.

Tholrog is dreaming. His heart is young and full. It says things as enigmatic as the cold Moon, as tender as the water that flows underground and makes the rivers of the future one drop at a time.

Eyrimah is within him—and Rob-Sen's daughter too. They are like two delightful combatants; his soul is the field on which they are battling. Down there, where something trembled, where something has fallen, be it a lump of snow or a pebble, is that the pale girl or the dark girl? What does the Mountain think? What does the jagged edge of the Plateau say?

The wind increases, and Tholrog receives its cold thrusts with delight. His thoughts are animated by every crescendo of the storm, and mingle with all the responsive echoes. Nature enters into him with the two young women.

How supple she is in terror, the daughter of Rob-Sen! How warm, soft and fearful her eyes are, and how menacing her smile. When he held her, saving her from falling, when she trembled on the flesh of his bosom, when her hair fell around his neck, there was something that dominated the abyss and defied the peril of death.

But what of Eyrimah! Her gaze does not meet Tholrog's, even when she is afraid, even when he saves her. At the moment of peril, she draws further away from him. She does not hate him…but her white arms would not wrap around Tholrog's neck, fleeing him fearfully.

That makes Tholrog indignant. Is he not the one who saved her when she fled to the mountain? Should she not be his submissive and faithful slave? Anger beats within his breast. He wants the fugitive and he can have her. What does it matter whether she refuses, or is afraid?

Then, suddenly, he does not want her. He chases her away, feeling a hatred full of generous pride rise up within him. It seems that Eyrimah is recoiling before Eï-Mor's large indefinable eyes and her soft hair, resting upon Tholrog's neck. He opens his heart wide to Rob-Sen's daughter. She enters, victorious. A confused voice says that she will not flee, that in spite of terror and racial enmity, she will be able to come and give herself to him voluntarily.

Tholrog is mollified; his pride is appeased. And on a narrow strip of pale ice between somber silhouettes, he seems to glimpse the dark-haired girl, the mystery of her swaying hips, as beautiful and harmonious as the song of April handed down by the ancestors. Then, once again, there is Eyrimah, with the delicate chin, white cheeks and proud gait…and the son of Talaun is more indecisive than the rains of spring.

He continues his dream in the great counsel of winds and clouds, before the glaciers that extend into rivers, widening into deltas, pausing in lakes, great reservoirs of the waters of the Earth—and the visions of combat, flight and peril mingle, becoming confused with love, with the night and with the splendor of rocks eaten away by the drops of water, cleaved and carried away by the ice, with the crumbling, devoured grandeur of the immensity of holes and escarpments: the formidable ruin that is the mountain.

The storm eased during the night; the following day was clear and fine. The mountain-dwellers continued scaling the heights. When a third of the day had elapsed, they reached the rim of a gorge that would lead them to practicable paths toward the villages. While they paused, Tahmen the scout and Irkwar went down to explore the route. They came back in a hurry.

"The lake-dwellers are on our trail, and the route is blocked. We saw them 3000 meters further down, in a ravine—half a day away, given the twists and turns."

"We'll go on to the Ariès' lands, then," Tholrog replied.

A few hours later, the ascent having been concluded, it was necessary for them to descend again, perilously at first, crawling silently. Long columns of overhanging ice might have crumbled in response to excessive vibration. High walls of ice displaced a menacing splendor, their summits ablaze, their ridges decorated by the great luxury of the sunlight. Then they began to hear the delicate silvery and crystalline songs of subterranean water.

After more crevasses, gulfs, snowfields and corridors of blocks they ended up going through redoubtable gorges where the threat of landslides was ever present. The mountain became more helpful, the springs rustled, the verdure of fir-trees and grass decorated the little valleys; stubborn lichens colored the rocks; the ice and snow only remained in a few shaded places. There was life, the play of insects in the pure air, the vivacity of little birds and small animals.

All of them were saturated, indistinctly, with the same lukewarm joy. They turned to the harsh slopes, the magnificence of glaciers, the virginity of colossi; they felt the youth of their blood, the brightness of flowers, the swift flow of streams and torrents. Only Irkwar, perhaps, regretted the ice and the peril, the ferocity of the winds and avalanches lying in ambush.

After a long trek, they camped that evening on the threshold of the plain, a few hours from the lands of the Ariès.

The next morning, before the departure—while his companions were hunting—Tholrog went to bathe in a little stream. The weather was mild, especially after the cold days on the high slopes. When he came out of the water, he stood looking, with barbaric vagueness, at the patient and lively poem of existence: the whole of nature streaming, filtering, growing.

He was moved. The muted rustle of the stream replied to his thoughts. In the interstices of a young poplar, the alliance of forests of oaks and clear oases of birches was visible in the distance; beech forests climbed up to vanquish them with their mortal shade, as throughout the North, annihilating the oaks and birches as they moved to assault the old sylvan citadels.

Tholrog half-closed his eyes. In his warrior's body, still agitated by strife and peril, the advent of lust was terrible. It flowed like the young torrents of spring. The vast landscape was only one episode therein. Lying in the meadow, caressed by the grass, he reopened his eyes to watch a ray of light or an insect settle. The tiny leaves were trembling; the long trunks of poplars curved like the slender stems of rushes—and Tholrog thought about the young women.

They were there, a few meters away, behind the chestnut-trees. They were his captives. Their flesh was softer than moss, their eyes more profound than the scintillation of a star in the depths of a lake.

He got up and walked toward the women's shelter. Then a timidity prevented him from passing its limit. Standing on the strong rot of a chestnut, he could see his sisters and their companions moving around. He shuddered. His heart stopped like a stream before a dam.

Eyrimah came to the edge of the wood. Distracted, she attached a thorn to her hair. She arrived thus in front of Tholrog, and the lightness of her step, the contour of her cheek, the mystery of her face and all her youth entered into him as he watched. For a moment, he stood still; then an invincible impulse made him walk toward her.

"Eyrimah!"

She stopped, her gesture manifesting alarm. The man's gaze was authoritarian. She said nothing, full of a wild gentleness.

"Although you fled into the mountains, am I not the one who put his hands on you and saved you from hunger and the beast?"

"You are, Tholrog," she replied, with a tremor.

"I'm the one who saved you from the snow—am I not your master?"

"You are my master."

She said it with sincerity; in her savage soul, she would have liked to obey his command, to bow down before his words and his warrior's mouth—but she wanted to keep herself for another, for the dark-haired head and somber eyes of In-Kelg, the fearful and hidden joy of gazes meeting.

"You shall be your master's wife, Eyrimah!" said Tholrog.

She became paler than the water-lilies of the lakes. In a troubled debate, she was the docile slave and the virgin; she had a womanly inclination to yield to force and the willful desire to retain the power of choice. Tholrog appeared to her, alternately, as a chief whose orders must be followed and an enemy who rules by the sword. None of that had any expression, any language for the poor girl. She recoiled, a large tear cooling her anxiety.

"Come!" he said, imperiously.

She did not move. He took her by the hand roughly. She felt that she was in the grip of an irresistible force, like a goat-kid seized by a lynx; the flow of her tears increased.

"Why weep?" he cried, harshly. "Is Tholrog not strong enough for the slave of the cowardly men of the lake?"

She had no reply ready—and, in truth, Tholrog's argument seemed irresistible; he was brave, strong and victorious. In a bitter abandon, she felt unable to refuse, and followed her imperious master—but her tears redoubled again, and Tholrog stopped.

He was overtaken by a strange sentiment. The struggle was not against Eyrimah. Tholrog did not feel the victory attached to his possession of the young woman so much as his defeat by a rival. The son of a proud race, he would rather that the image of the other be replaced in Eyrimah by his own image, or that he had actually killed his rival. At the same time, he felt disgust, weariness and hatred well up in him. He grasped Eyrimah's arm more roughly—and his savage eyes dominated her.

"You do not love your master, slave of the men of the water! Go—their race has corrupted your heart...the race of those that I crushed in the dry stream-bed!"

Eyrimah was overtaken by a confused regret, a near-desire to love the man of her own race—but the more precise that desire became, the more she saw the dusks of Re-Alg, the strolls over the pilings, the curly-haired head waiting for her by the water.

Tholrog looked into the young woman's eyes, and knew that their gaze was elsewhere, and his proud disdain was mingled with the regret of having been vanquished in that white bosom and the brightness of those eyes.

"Get away!" he cried. "You are merely a slave who must serve her master without looking at him!"

After Eyrimah had gone, he remained sullen. He wanted battles, dangers. Irritatedly, he contemplated the tall centenarian chestnut-trees, the fresh grass and the forests of oaks battling against the beeches. The emptiness of the day of rest weighed upon his barbaric imagination. A cloud of insects accompanied him into the shade, a buzzing cloud, a thousand minuscule lives determined to follow him. He swept them away with a slow gesture; he breathed in the terrible odor of vegetation, which was not the odor of their love. The florets of thorn-bushes and pools, the white unconsciousness of wild fruit-trees, the aroma of wild thyme, and the vapor of the mountain torrents troubled Tholrog. Instinctively, he had returned to the women's camp. He stood at the edge of the wood, behind a clump of raspberry bushes. A large white cloud cast a cool shadow there.

Suddenly, he was aroused, as he had been by the arrival of Eyrimah. A languorous and supple form had appeared on the tender grass. It was Rob-Sen's daughter, in her fiber tunic ornamented by freshly-picked flowers. She incarnated the beauty of foreigners, the profound charm of enemy women. Everything about her spoke of hostile blood: the blood of men who had chased the blond race into the mountains; the grim flesh that had wanted to kill Tholrog's people, and whom Tholrog's people had dreamed of annihilating for centuries. Before the prisoner, however, all hatred blossomed into charm. Virginal, she represented the joy of mingling with our own race those whom we find redoubtable, for the sake of the mystery of beauty.

With slow steps, Tholrog came around the bush to meet the young woman. She was alarmed by his appearance, but not like Eyrimah. There was certainly a little dread mixed in with her anxiety, but there was also manifest curiosity, astonishment and the admiration of his strength. Her gaze was so mysterious to the man of the mountains, so soft and so redoubtable, and some unaccountable artistry of attitude caused the anger that was tormenting Tholrog to vanish.

In the language of the lake-dwellers he said: "Do you miss the great lakes, daughter of Rob-Sen?"

"Yes, I miss the great lakes."

"Before nightfall we shall find new lakes. Would you like that?"

"I would like to see the lakes of my own tribe again...not those of my enemies."

"You will never see those of your own land again. You are Tholrog's slave."

She opened her eyes wider. Sadness struggled there with something vague, confused and infinite. Tholrog took pleasure in looking into them, as into the water of a precipice, and also with a tenderness as profound as that one feels before little children.

His bellicose spirit reacted against the soft languor, and, almost roughly, he said: "Tholrog will never give up the daughter of Rob-Sen!"

Her dark eyes beneath their networks of lashes and her red lips expressed a regret full of reproach. Then a tender malice appeared around her eyelids, almost a challenge.

"Tholrog would give up the daughter of Rob-Sen to save the prisoners of his own tribe."

"There will be no prisoners of my tribe. We and our friends, the Ariès, will take the lakes."

She bowed her head, as if beneath a yoke, remembering the massacre of the stream-bed. She was overcome by a frightful melancholy at the idea that Tholrog might do battle with Rob-Sen or In-Kelg—and yet, in her indecisive heart, she could not hate her master.

"You are strong," she said. "Rob-Sen is also strong—and our warriors cover ten lakes!"

"We shall take the ten lakes!"

This time she looked at him with a faint anger; rebellion appeared in her dark eyes.

"No one knows the will of the gods!"

Tholrog was intoxicated by the beauty of those wrathful eyes. He desired them even more ardently. "Your people's hour has come," he said.

"The gods have not spoken," she replied. Her somber gaze contained the plaint of the weak confronted by the abuse of the strong.

Tholrog, with the divinatory insight of savage natures, perceived that impression. His generosity stirred, but haughtily. "Your people are cowards. They massacred their guests!"

210

"Rob-Sen did not want that. Rob-Sen tried to save your people."

"Why not surrender the murderers to us?"

"He could not!" she replied, energetically but without bravado. "Ver-Skag aroused the men, and the priest approved. Rob-Sen spoke at length on behalf of your people."

Through her words, as through a vapor, Tholrog saw Rob-Sen speaking for the mountain men, and he saw Rob-Sen's son, who had caused Eyrimah to run away, his young curly head, his bold stance. He had wanted to kill him; he had challenged him mentally. Then again, he thought that his was the same blood as that of his captive. That calmed him; he placed his hand on Rob-Sen's daughter. "If Rob-Sen becomes our prisoner, I will speak for him."

She shook her head. Her face expressed filial pride. "Rob-Sen will not be captured."

"Have the gods spoken, then?" he said, ironically.

"The gods have not spoken, but Rob-Sen cannot be captured. He knows how to commit suicide."

At that thought, she softened. A feeble sob elevated her bosom. Her head fell back, like that of a warbler preparing to sing. Tholrog was considerably affected by that. Love took tender and protective forms within him. He felt the gentleness of certain powerful animals for a small creature taking refuge among them. He glimpsed the melancholy of the lost nest, the distant warm clutch.

"Are you afraid of Tholrog?" he asked.

Her master's gentleness made her shiver. A world of emotion rose up before her. "No," she replied. "Tholrog pulled me out of the abyss."

A delightful joy overwhelmed the young man, and then a savage timidity like the perfume of may-blossom. He drew his hand away from the young woman's shoulder. "You shall see your lakes again," he said, "if the route is free for the two of us—but Tholrog does not want you to see them again alone."

She knew perfectly well that he desired her. The malice of a little while before was sketched in her smile and the

211

blackness of her pupils. Then the pride of a chief's daughter made her dread impure slavery, in which she would merely be an inferior wife, submissive to another spouse. At the same time, the spirit of rebellion rose up more ardently, fear of the stranger mingling with the attraction of the stranger. Arming herself with coldness and incomprehension, she said: "The gods will decide the future!"

Her hands rose up in a mysterious gesture, toward the Sun. She remained collected and distant. Her attitude influencing Tholrog's mind, they drew apart from one another, all their words retreating like a landscape in the dusk.

Even that distancing was not without charm for the young man. It was like a necessary obstacle, a pause, a repose before a desirable object with which one is instinctively afraid to compromise. Timid, he no longer knew what to say.

Then the arrival of Dithèv extracted him from his embarrassment. He went back to the stream and, as on the night when he had crossed the threshold of the cave of Môh, Tholrog saw the silhouettes of Eyrimah and Rob-Sen's daughter fighting within him. They were the cloud passing overhead, the running water, the petal rolling in the wind, the bending grass, the peak eroded by inexhaustible forces. But Eyrimah vanished before the young lake-dweller. The diaphanous charm of her hair and her smooth skin and the finesse of her gaze haunted the young man less than the beauty of black eyelashes, strange pupils, dark hair and red lips—and he sighed like the poplars and the wind. His breast seemed full of a warmer blood and a more anxious respiration.

He lay down in the grass, and remained there in his confused intoxication.

Time passed. Tholrog went to hurry the preparations for departure. They were only waiting for the hunters.

Suddenly, in the distance, they saw them appear, moving rapidly in a disorderly fashion. Tahmen was in the lead, running at top speed, equal to that of a hind.

"The men of the lakes are less than 5000 meters away—numerous and well-armed!"

"That's all right!" Tholrog replied. Fretfully, he gave the order to leave. Anger born of great efforts made in vain rumbled in his breast.

After an hour's march, he climbed up on an eminence, and saw the advancing lake-dwellers for himself, on the horizon. There were 100 of them. In spite of the distance, he thought he recognized Rob-In-Kelg, the brother of Eï-Mor among them, by his gait and the details of his costume.

And the mountain men fled at speed, following awkward and rocky paths that their enemies, less practiced, would travel with difficulty.

Part Three

I. The Great Lake of the Ariès

It is morning: a young and mild morning such as there has been for thousands of centuries, and will be for thousands of centuries more. The great lake of the Ariès is waking up. The world is fresh and new for man and beast alike. Sleep has recreated the gentle illusion that everything is beginning again: foliage, moist corollas, stems and great tree-trunks are deceptive in the immense hatchery of light, in the embrace of that paternity which returns every morning and disappears at dusk.

Wings beat, the tails of fishes trace spirals, larvae crawl along with snakes and worms, paws march, draw back and pounce. There is joy, terror, love and wrath. Some are tenderly sheltered in their lairs or their nests; others are hiding beneath leaves or pebbles; others still are lying in wait for the enemy.

And humans too have woken up on the great lake of the Ariès. They are going to work, to fight, to love and to hunt. The will to live is active in their hearts. The race is proud and young; the water, the earth and the firmament are infinite treasures for them. The future opens full of force and bliss.

How beautiful a fatherland the great lake is! How vast are the plains and mysterious the forests! How confused and full of promise is the universe, how mighty the sky on winter nights, how voluptuous on the nights of summer!

The human dream is already elevated for the Ariès; from the lands of Asia and the plateau of the Himalayas, the emigrants have brought complex notions. Their brains hold an imminent civilization; they have learned to count animals, select plants, love flowers and trace the outlines of a few hieroglyphs.

Although the sky is still close, they have already grown tall; they have classified the stars. Gods roam in the winds; immense waters surround the Earth. They have industry and art, ingenious and naïve speculations regarding the nature of things, a marvelous sense of the ideal, a confused respect for everything that breathes, from which will emerge the gentlest religion that humans will know. The Earth, the Winds, the Dusk, the Waters, the Plants and their metamorphoses, the Beasts large and small, the Soil that bears everything that grows, the Star that always steers toward the Occident, Light and Darkness, Death and Life, Tools, Weapons, the domestication of certain animals, the Egg, key to Mysteries—on all of that, their elite minds have already reflected and divagated. The experience of their Sages, minutely transmitted, has taught them things that their more civilized ancestors have sometimes forgotten. They know secrets about life that are unmethodical, but fine and delicate, which will be lost in part when wisdom migrates to Cities, and when Wisdom forgets immediate nature.

It is morning. The night watchmen, standing on the shores and at the corners of aquatic villages have gone away to sleep. Other watchers are replacing them. On the distant hills a few warrior encampments can be seen; the Ariès are expecting enemies from the high lakes—the dark lacustrians they call the Ou-Loâ. Combatants are ready throughout their territory. The horizon is monitored; emissaries have gone down the river to warn the other tribes of the race. Already, 3000 men can be brought together at the first alert. It is war; the Ariès have accepted it, for themselves and their blond friends from the mountains.

In spite of anxieties regarding the numerous army of Ou-Loâ denounced by Kiwasar's envoys, the Ariès have not interrupted their customary way of life—and in the morning, the priests have sung to the Dawn-Gods, then to the Great God of light sprung forth from the mountains, the immense Egg of the World.

215

Tjandrinahr, the most subtle of the Ariès of the great lakes, thinks during the prayers. He knows that men are not alone in praying to the Sun. He knows that the birds have a religion, that the aurochs venerate the light, and that a beast exists—a beast that the ancestors have seen—which taught humans adoration.

The Sun has risen. An egg of red flame at first, the furnace of the firmament has become brighter. Tjandrinahr, knowing that the Sun sees every blade of grass and visits every seed, opens his own eyes wide in order to let in its divine caresses.

The Ariès have taken the first meal, of wheat cakes, fish and cream from goats or cows. It is a dulcet moment. In huts that are already intimate, families have the joy of shelter, the stimulation of caresses, the strength of paternity. Tjandrinahr has eaten with his own family. His sons and daughters are happy; he has the gravity of his great race. Happiness is within him. His strength protects and does not oppress. He accomplishes things more astonishing than other men with less effort. His one fault is an excessive love of watching plants, animals, the Earth and the waters. As subtle in war as in peace, he would have been the supreme chief if he had not wasted his time penetrating mysteries; he is only a tribal chief.

In the sacred morning, he contemplates the lake. The water is vaporous. The mists are rising slowly. Everywhere, one sees islets on pilings, human dwellings, groves covered with rushes and grass, straw and reeds. And Tjandrinahr's sensations have the vigor and imprecision of a child's; they are naïve and complex, mingled with delicate visions and erratic conclusions. His thoughts sometimes see logically, and then drift into chimeras or gross hypotheses. Life, which seems natural to others, astonishes him. Everything astonishes him.

Work was beginning, however. Women were weaving pale linen, the marvel of solid fabric made from the skillful alternation of threads. Men were carving bows and clubs, and sharpening bronze axes. Others were making fishing-nets or lance-heads, or milling wheat or barley between polished stones. Meanwhile, young girls were extracting milk before the departure of the herds. Soon, cows, urus, goats, black pigs and sheep were spreading out into the vast pasturelands, guided by skilled dogs. As it was not yet laboring season, the carts made of tree-trunks and sharpened branches remained idle on the shores of the lake.

Leaving the island, Tjandrinahr went into the fecund plain, thinking about the work of humankind. One group, which was driving pilings into the lake, caused him to marvel at the power of his brethren. He stopped to watch them dive and return, going down to the bed to dig with their tools. *Humans are strong*, he said to himself.

He sent emissaries to the hills, and gave orders to the herdsmen. The Sun rose higher. In the warm morning, hundreds of adults and children were swimming, chasing one another with the ease of semi-aquatic creatures. In the distance, some 50 young people were engaged in a swimming race. Like a living flotilla or a school of cetaceans they were cleaving through the blue water, diving and reappearing. Around them, pikes fled and vipers dived rapidly. The mass of swimmers thinned out, the quickest drawing ahead individually.

Elsewhere, fishermen were casting their nets; mothers were carrying new-borns; a party of hunters went in search of the flesh of deer, aurochs and wild boar. Some, armed with harpoons, were taking aim at pike in the clear water.

Walking on, Tjandrinahr arrived in the vicinity of a singular encampment. Slim people with copper-colored faces were standing around fire-pits. They were Immohys. With blue hair in ringlets, in the fashion of wild nomads, their expressions sharp and vague at the same time, their entire being expressed mysterious workings, and a formidable antiquity. Their hands were small, their gestures agile, their mouths cunning and obstinate. Their legends were full of caverns, expeditions deep within the Earth and unknown life-forms: animals,

217

gods and humans living in a universe with neither Sun nor stars.[13]

Tjandrinahr and the bronze-forgers greeted one another with friendly words. As was customary, the Ariès chief contemplated the work of the fire and the metal with admiration. That work was no longer a secret for the intelligent race of the Ariès. They had known about it for a long time, but they had not attempted to encroach on the work of their allies, more by virtue of tacit and loyal convention than necessity.

The Immohys extracted the copper and tin from remote regions, transporting it over immense distances in regular caravans of people of their species. Anyone who stole their materials would have been deprived of them forever. The anathema of the entire Immohys people, marvelously united in that epoch in spite of its dispersal—in bold and ingenious communication from the Ural mountains to the Alps, from the Ocean around the shores of the Mediterranean—would have enveloped the aggressor. Not warlike themselves, the Immohys charged other men with their vengeance, by arming them and telling them ancient secrets, illusory, but calculated to terrify enemies.

The swarms of the Occidental Ariès, still small in number, had the friendship of the Immohys. That amity was maintained by virtue of the profound respect of the race of agriculturalist warriors for the industrial race. The latter, a race with little future, almost uncivilizable, clung to its monopoly, seeing it as a superiority that was both effective and sacred, and the acceptance of their industrial superiority by the Ariès flattered the Immohys profoundly.

---

[13] Although Morel and Massé identify the Immohys with Frédéric de Rougemont's Semites, the resemblance stops with the mere notion of a particular tribe discovering the secrets of metallurgy and keeping them secret; Rosny's version is more reminiscent of Teutonic legends of metal-working dwarfs, fused with Greek legends regarding the forges of Hephaestus.

Tjandrinahr remained there for some time, then went on into the countryside, into the woods and pasturelands. He was thinking deeply about Work, Love and War. Gradually, he made his way into bleaker territory, of woodlands interspersed with grasslands, where a river ran. He was going to visit one of his tribe's observation posts, half-a-day's march away.

II. Tjandrinahr in the Wilderness

When Tjandrinahr found himself in the wilderness he walked as silently as a crawling worm. His marvelous eyes and his miraculous ears were examining the environment carefully. What he had learned for himself, and what he had learned from his father and grandfather, were recalled by his tenacious memory and mingled with recent things.

He found among the animals all the essential characteristics of humans, and others too, which he judged divine.

The plains and woodlands concealed innumerable living organisms. There were Herculean trees and graceful calices everywhere, an abundance of grass and roots, and animals unsubmissive to humans. Enormous aurochs passed through clearings and over grasslands. Still full of strength, their herds encountered no rivals, and all creation fled before them in the months when herbivores are bad-tempered. Tjandrinahr admired them, dreaming of animals more enormous still; glimpsed by his forefathers.

Horses were galloping, watched by large wolves or alarmed by the arrival of a bear descended from the mountains. The profound and quavering voices of old deer were audible, the grunts of wild pigs and the bleating of sheep with goats' horns. Hinds were leaping with their fawns, herons were abundant on the edges of fresh pools, water-fowl splashed around in the reeds near their delightful nests, rails fled through the grass and kingfishers were resplendent. Pigeons flew in infinite flocks, and geese grazed, while ducks, swans and storks dispersed; bands of crows were on the move beneath soaring vultures; magpies hunted; turkeys disputed territory with cocks and hens that had escaped from human care and reverted to the wild; magnificent pheasants screeched in the thickets.

An equally-fecund population swarmed in the streams: minnows, barbels, trout, bullheads, monstrous pikes and sticklebacks. More than one of the last-named was still guarding its young family—admirable fathers exhausting themselves for their offspring, having been brilliant in the days when they constructed their nests, waiting for females and persuading them to lay eggs in their ingenious nests, then watching over their brood for a month, defending it against large predators, wearing themselves out feeding the young family, multiplying their ingenious cares: a piscine paternity equal to that of birds…

The joys of hatching and the immense poetry of birth still extended through the whole landscape: shells scarcely broken, or in which frail beaks were still tapping at the door, preparing a way out; mothers listening for the tapping of young captives, delicately assisting them to open the door of the egg. Everywhere, males were bringing food back to the household or, perched on overhanging branches, cheering up the sitting by swaying in the wind. It was a sacred anguish, a vibrant delight: the moist hatchlings drying out in the shade; taut beaks raised agape for feeding; slender feet and bright eyes agitating; and, in the ocean of the air, a hundred thousand living skiffs ferrying seeds, larvae, worms, insects and fruits to the little quivering refuges. Almost all the artists had finished their work: the warblers had long since finished feathering their nests, the turkey-hens digging their holes, the republican sparrows establishing their rotundas, the goldfinches rounding their exquisite bowls, the orioles suspending their cradles, the herons building their heronries.

Meanwhile, in a more minuscule world, female tarantulas were dragging the sacks in which they have placed their offspring; wolf-spiders teaching their progeny to hunt; ant-nurses bringing pale foodstuffs to the edge of the nest; savage wasps setting forth to seize and paralyze living prey, equipping the nest with a provision of fresh numbed flesh on which the offspring will feed later—when larvae awake in their cells to discover spiders, caterpillars, bees or beetles—while parasites dispose their larvae in other nests, which live on the supplies of others or even devour those which hatch out with them.

War goes on alongside this poem of love. All these marvels, so slow to increase in force and finesse, at the price of so much hardship, experimentation, exploration and accumulated heredity, all these treasures of life—birds and chicks, larvae and spectacular beetles, mammals large and small—all that divine economy of forms and organs, all that inestimable labor, will be annihilated in an instant by bites, claws or stings, and cadavers will garnish maws, suckers, muzzles and mouths, to be obscurely interred in stomachs. War is so narrowly linked to love in nature that they shade into one another; against the prodigious fecundity that kills in itself, there is the prodigious voracity that regulates its thrust; against the delicate work, there is the eternity of hammer-blows, of brutal assassinations. Every terrain, immense or minuscule, hides ambushes, weapons, the fury and terror of life. Everything is slain, choked, poisoned, chewed up and devoured.

Two moles encountering one another at the intersection of their tunnels deliver themselves to a hideous battle, in which the victor devours the vanquished. The marten massacres pitilessly, and defends itself with a bloody heroism against an enemy ten times stronger than itself; the ferret sucks the brain out of a rabbit and devours its prey alive. The swallow only interrupts its carnage at nightfall. The pike and its rival, the perch, devour everything along the river; as soon as one hen is bloodied by a wound the others strike it down and eat it while it is still quivering. The falcon arrives over her heronry; cocks raise their hackles and precipitate themselves on one another in ardent skirmishes; the larva of the ichneumon fly awakes in its living nest, a caterpillar that it consumes at its leisure; the scarab beetle ravages its herbivorous kin; the wasp carries its conquests everywhere, laying low spiders, bees and caterpillars; and the little stickleback falls impetuously on fish 20 times larger than itself. Everywhere, the wolf makes war on the horse, the stag and the hind, and drinks the noble blood of handsome herbivores.

As he walked, Tjandrinahr witnessed various scenes of this vast love and this vast war. About the 11th hour, as he rested in the heat of the day, nature provided him with a spectacle. It was on the edge of a wood. The stream advanced in front of him through a grassland punctuated by trees and marshes.

Tjandrinahr was enjoying the shade of an ash-tree. A magpie was watching him from a high branch. An immense spider, having finished remaking its yellow-tinted web, was watching the movements of a buzzing swarm of flies. Larvae of every sort were flourishing in an old fallen tree, and minuscule masterpieces were blossoming there.

Beavers were gathered on the bank of the stream, constructing a dam. Already, one old tree was fixed across the watercourse. The artisans had divided up the work; some were cutting slender trees or thick branches, transforming them into similar pieces and sharpening them; others, working in groups, were fixing piles under water, holding the pieces against the old tree, preparing the ground with their feet and tail-trowels or plastering the interstices of the pilings. The little colony was working away in this fashion in the wilderness—and Tjandrinahr recognized the distant precursors of lacustrian humankind, the educators of those who constructed villages on the waters.

A small cry of distress distracted him; a few feet away he saw a viper appear, holding a little bird—a wren. The tiny creature was struggling in mortal terror. At a movement from the man, the viper turned back, intending to disappear into a bush, and a little spiny quadruped with a gentle physiognomy—a hedgehog—suddenly appeared. At the sight of it, the snake released its prey, hissed, picked up its prey again and fled—but the hedgehog caught up with it at a rapid run, and struck it with its paw.

The reptile accepted the battle, raised its slender head with bleak eyes, and displayed its fangs. The other, unintimidated, sniffed the venomous maw. Furiously, the snake struck and bit the quadruped's muzzle three times. Paying no heed, the latter made several efforts to seize its enemy, and received further bites. Then, suddenly, the viper was seized, its head crushed between the hedgehog's teeth; within an instant, the latter had devoured almost half the vanquished individual— after which, licking its lips, invulnerable to venom, it calmly carried away the rest: the stump of the reptile, quivering, twisting and coiling with a horrible vitality.

Tjandrinahr was thinking of getting under way again when he heard a whinny of distress, and a large wild horse ran over the crest of a hill. Its mane flew up with the speed of its progress, in ten-meter bounds, and its eyes were shining in anguish. Behind it was a chasing pack of large wolves, methodical and indefatigable. The horse had a start, however, and was able to hold and increase it, less weary than afraid.

The pack and its prey, running parallel to the stream, passed 100 paces from the man, with lightning speed. To continue the course it was necessary to skirt a little ash-wood, and as they got closer to it, the wolves scattered and spread out. There was a change of fortune; newcomers surged forth—a dozen wolves cleverly posted in advance in the wood.

Bewildered, the fugitive retraced its steps in part, and in a paroxysm of terror, and lust for life, the whole of its beautiful athletic body accelerated further, its legs launching the great body as rapidly as wings propel a falcon or a swallow— but the wolf pack surrounded it from all directions. It knocked some down, but others took their place; its course veered and turned back; it found itself within a great circle of howling beasts. Desperate, it tried to fight, charging frenetically. An old wolf leapt on its back, another bit its throat cruelly. It shook itself, and momentarily got free, neighing lugubriously. Then, all together, the carnivores covered it, tearing large wounds in its belly, its flanks and its breast—and the noble beast paid its tribute to the ineluctable law.

Tjandrinahr saw the victim get up gain two or three times, as the wolves drew out its entrails, its throat gaping, its hide and flesh ripped away, its bones laid bare; then it moaned painfully and gradually disappeared, shred by shred, into the wolves' bloody mouths, and into their sepulchral stomachs.

That battle, its whinnies of agony and howls of triumph, had attracted the attention of the whole world. Animals fled in panic everywhere. An astonished aurochs, roused from a drowsy torpor, raced away at hazard, heedless of its direction. The monstrous beast cut through the troop of carnivores. One wolf was unfortunate enough to be in its path; the aurochs took it by surprise. The wolf was powerful, expert and agile, but the powerful horns lifted it up without effort, hurling it through the air, helplessly—and all the predators were glad to flee, to get away from the implacable horns of the king of the forest and the savannah.

Then Tjandrinahr resumed his course. He left the woods and went over hills. Finally, he reached the Ariès outpost, not far from a large marsh. Twenty men were waiting for him there, the oldest of which said to him: "Father, men from the mountains have taken refuge in the marsh, pursued by the Ou-Loâ. Our allies are few in number, the Ou-Loâ more than 100…"

"We must gather the men from the nearest posts together," Tjandrinahr replied, "and attempt to rescue the men of the mountains."

III. The Marsh

The mountain-dwellers were in full flight. Initially, they had had an advantage of 5000 meters, but that advantage had diminished because of the women, although all of them marched with celerity. Eï-Mor, in spite of the approach of her own people, and Eyrimah, in spite of her fears, were faithful in their flight; Rob-Sen's daughter felt a sentiment of pride and admiration for Tholrog; Eyrimah's gratitude and love of her race, and also the uncertainty of her fate, combated her affection for In-Kelg.

The lake-dwellers gained ground continually. At first, they had only been glimpsed at intervals, at the hazard of climbs or descents. Now, in the plain sparsely strewn with hillocks, some of them were always perceptible. They often shouted threats, brandishing their spears or their large bows. The mountain-dwellers ran in a taciturn fashion, keeping as straight a course as possible, always guided by Tahmen, who had learned the rare and difficult art of not describing a curve when marching over a plateau or a plain.

The terrain was damp, strewn with small pools, which slowed the flight down. They were sometimes marching through actual mud, over rotten vegetation. Unfortunately, there seemed to be no end to it; the pools were accumulating.

Tholrog searched for some lateral exit; to the right and the left the country was similar in nature, or even more extensively submerged. It was necessary to continue whatever the risk, although progress was becoming almost impracticable. A veritable marsh extended before them, interrupted by islands where herons were perched on their long legs, some lost in the immobile dream of their race, others hunting. Frogs were croaking; slender reptiles could be seen fleeing amid the bulrushes, and water-fowl becoming agitated.

While the mountain-dwellers were hesitating, howls went up. On turning round, Tholrog saw the lacustrians 2000 meters away. He replied to their threats with a long trumpet-blast, searching with his eyes for some way forward or some combat position. Spurred on by the proximity of the adversary, the mountain-dwellers increased their efforts. The perfidious stagnant waters impeded them, full of tangled algae, filamentous plants and reeds.

One of the men marching at the head was nearly swallowed up; they were forced to deviate, following the edge of the marsh. The lake-dwellers were no more than 1000 meters away. Eyrimah and Eï-Mor had recognized In-Kelg among them. The lacustrians were also advancing less rapidly, however, and because of their greater number were not obtaining as much advantage from favorable places; often forced to divide up, they were losing time in waiting, ensuring the parallelism of their progress. Even so, the outcome of the pursuit was not in doubt; Tholrog's men could only move sideways along the marsh or turn back; both alternatives would lead to contact with the enemy. Their only hope was to find a passage across the marsh itself; they all searched for one anxiously, scrutinizing the sinister landscape.

"There!" a warrior suddenly cried. He pointed to a sort of narrow path that extended a long way over the waters. Tholrog, Irkwar and Tahmen tested it and found it soft on the surface but hard underneath. There was no time to hesitate; the lake-dwellers were almost within bowshot. Tholrog moved on to the little causeway. At its broadest, it permitted two or three men to walk abreast; often, it was necessary to go in single file.

In spite of these difficulties, the relative firmness of the ground allowed the fugitives to increase their lead slightly. On seeing that, the lake-dwellers fired arrows, but they did not reach the causeway, sinking into the algae. The mountain-dwellers only increased their pace, albeit apprehensively, for they did not know where they would end up. Masses of vegetation obscured the view.

A gap appeared in the bulrushes and tall reeds. Tahmen made an anxious gesture; the path was coming to an end. A kind of triangular near-island appeared, almost rocky, with sheer sides, covered by a few decrepit willows. Tholrog examined the terrain bleakly. It was the end; the flight having been interrupted, combat would become inevitable.

The near-island was, however, defensible. With its slightly-raised borders and its tangle of vegetation, they could take cover there. The narrow approach would only permit men to come through two abreast at first; the enemy would inevitably lose a great part of its numerical advantage. If the moun-tain men had had enough bows, arrows and javelins, it would have been almost impossible to force their retreat. Unfortu-nately, they only had a dozen bows, 30 arrows and a few jave-lins. Assuming that a third of the shots struck home, that was enough to kill a dozen enemies. They would still have stones, and branches convertible into arrows, but arrows with poor points picked up at hazard from the pebbles of the refuge and chiseled in haste. The lacustrians, by contrast, were abundant-ly provided with weapons of jet and ammunition.

In spite of the conditions of inferiority, Tholrog did not believe the peril to be insurmountable. While the defense was organized, a few warriors sent forth the mountain-dweller's challenge; trumpets roared over the bleak landscape, over the dull and funereal waters. Flocks of ducks took off and the he-rons on the promontories became uneasy.

A large black cloud, with a quivering phosphorescent nimbus at its pale borders, advanced across the face of the Sun, beginning to cast the marsh into the shade. The lake-dwellers took time to confer before starting out along the nar-row pathway.

The mountain-dwellers' best marksmen took possession of the available bows; Irkwar's and Tholrog's had a huge span and a vast range. Some of the others started shaping rare flakes of stone; the rest fashioned branches into crude arrows.

Eï-Mor and Eyrimah waited in anguish, afraid of the somber alternatives. As the prospect of combat came closer, Eï-Mor felt a considerable solicitude for Tholrog mounting within her, but she was also moved by the idea of seeing her brother again and finding herself back among her own people. She was only half-aware of her sympathy for the foreigner, sensing the intoxication she would have experienced in living with Tholrog, if he had been born of the people of the lakes.

As for Eyrimah, her love went invincibly toward In-Kelg, but her abomination of the lake-dwellers had increased considerably. She loathed and hated them; she was proud of belonging to the mountain-folk. Torn between these senti-

227

ments, her desire was unable to take precise form—or, rather, she wished vaguely that the lacustrian might be defeated, but that In-Kelg alone might survive the battle, and that the young man might be permitted to live among the mountain people.

The son of Talaun was also agitated as he thought about the outcome of the battle; the idea of losing the young women was particularly poignant among the miseries of defeat. In that lugubrious moment, they were still battling within him—but how dominant Rob-Sen's daughter was!

"They're coming!" a warrior shouted.

Bows in hand, Tholrog and Irkwar followed their adversaries' progress. Their approach was prudent. The vegetation fringing the refuge prevented them from seeing the mountain men, while the latter could see them quite well on the pathway. Eventually, one of the lacustrians extended a long-range bow and fired an arrow. The dart fell into the water a few meters from the shelter.

In his turn, Tholrog flexed his bow. The arrow whistled away, and flew straight to its target, the lake-dweller's throat. He fell. His companions retreated out of range. The throbbing voice of trumpets sang over the water.

"They don't have bows as powerful as Tholrog's!" cried the mountain men.

Another lacustrian warrior was seen to advance then, though not as far as the first. Tremulously, Eï-Mor and Eyrimah recognized In-Kelg. In a resounding voice, he shouted: "If you surrender Eyrimah and Rob-Sen's daughter we will let you go."

Meanwhile, Irkwar took aim at the young man. "He's not close enough," he said, irritatedly.

Tholrog, fearing that his companions might yield to In-Kelg's conditions, remained silent. With a shiver of gratitude he heard Tahmen say: "Do we believe the word of the lake-dwellers?"

The mountain men, excited by their leader's first success, replied with scornful shouts, and Tholrog, taking a step forward outside the refuge, answered: "Eï-Mor's fate will be decided after the war! And we shall never give up the daughter of the mountains!"

"Very well!" cried Rob-Sen's son—and he drew his bow, which was smaller than Tholrog's.

The mountain men jeered. In-Kelg fired, and his arrow, to everyone's profound astonishment, reached the refuge, brushing Irkwar's head. Instantly, the young lake-dweller fired another arrow, and Tholrog, pricked in the throat, uttered a cry of anger. Beside himself, he bounded forward, flexing his bow; his arrow buried itself in In-Kelg's shoulder. A few arrows fell harmlessly close to the mountain man; then there was a hectic clamor, as savage souls thrilled with battle-rage and tumultuous race-hatred.

Fearful of poison, Hogioé sucked her brother's wound forcefully; it was not deep. Eï-Mor and Eyrimah were frightened, their hands and breasts trembled; the abomination had arrived! Life seemed to them more sinister than the livid marsh, where the feverish shadow of huge clouds quivered.

An odor of storm and death was released by the putrescence of the water and plants; a wind of lamentation gusted at intervals, turning about with a splashing sound.

Then, a giant lacustrian came forward, as tall as Irkwar and even broader; his abrupt face painted with red dye, and his taut, profound and swollen torso, was suggestive of some kind of indolent monster, like a tiger, built for speed and for the employment of a rapid and ferocious strength. He raised his voice, full of insults. He spoke of the eternal victory of the men of the waters, the centuries-long defeat of the mountain folk.

"Who among you dares look me in the face?"

Tholrog, Irkwar and Wamb challenged him: "Do your men dare to go back to the edge of the marsh!"

The colossus instructed his companions to do so. At first, they refused, for the lake-dwellers did not like single combats, being an ant-like race, not an individualistic one. Before the insistence of their champion, however, and taking pride in seeing him so large and terrible, they gave in.

Tholrog wanted to meet the challenge, but his companions, especially Irkwar, prevented him from doing so. "You're wounded," Irkwar said. "Let me go."

Irkwar prevailed; armed with an oak-wood club and a stone axe, he went to face the lacustrian, who awaited him with an axe in each hand

They both exemplified rare types, superb humans created for battling against nature and their fellows. Infinite experiments were summarized in their dense and rapid musculature, their harmonious bone structure and their strong, light well-balanced heads. But the lacustrian was the squarer of the two in every respect, Irkwar more oblong. Their heads summarized that difference; the mountain man's was long, the forehead neatly-cut without lateral projections, the back of the head streamlined; the other's was round and compact, the forehead broad and the temples swollen.

Irkwar's face, his clear complexion reddened by fine pure blood, brightened by frank eyes that anger rendered resplendent, although somewhat confused, was abundantly covered with fair and silky hair. The lake-dweller's face, very short, with contracted and pre-eminent jaws, grim yellow eyes shielded by thick eyelids, a thick but sloping chin and dark hair, displayed stubbornness and the harsh courage of large carnivorous hunters.

With his eyes half-closed, crouching slightly, the lake-dweller watched his adversary approach.

As he did so, Irkwar became animated, bellicose wrath misting his blue gaze, his sanguinary arteries dilating, throbbing impetuously. He arrived thus within five meters of the lake-dweller. "I am here, man of the lakes."

The other did not understand him, but brandished his axes. Irkwar raised his club—and they looked at one another attentively, seeking to surprise one another.

Irkwar became impatient first. The great club whirled and lashed out. It fell back without striking home; the lacustrian had changed position. His entire being expressed strength, its musculature promising a lightning release. With a

230

natural instinct for combat, Irkwar saw that redoubtable pose and braced himself to receive the impact.

It was the pounce of a lion. Everything—the leap, the extension of the arms, the two axes—concurred in the same objective. Irkwar's gaze perceived each of the phases of the movement; his club was placed across the axes' trajectory, and his own axe was raised for a riposte—and everything happened like a collision of avalanches. The club was torn loose and rolled into the marsh, along with one of the lacustrian's axes. Irkwar's riposte was a trifle belated, for the mountain man had tottered; the dark-haired colossus was able to avoid the blow.

They recovered defensive postures, each intact but having measured one another's strength, full of respectful hatred for one another. Then their axes whirled, feinting and threatening, searching for an opening. As Irkwar took a step forward, the lacustrian uttered a howl to disconcert his adversary, parried a back-handed thrust, and precipitated himself forward. The blond giant retreated, struck. His thrust carried away part of the lacustrian's left ear and grazed the sloping shoulder, but in return, he had received a blow under the hip that, although deadened by a parry, had cut into the flesh.

Maddened then, they redoubled their attacks. Their crashing axes met one another several times, chipping one another—and again the lake-dweller howled and launched his terrible assault. Irkwar stopped him with a counter-move, and the axes, colliding frantically, shattered into smithereens.

Neither of them held anything now but a wooden stump. In tacit accord, looking one another in the eyes, they threw the debris away; they were unarmed, avidly ardent to match their naked strength—and each of them saw his antagonist's muscular splendor more clearly, and the uncertainty of victory. Force was inscribed in the arms hanging loosely from their vast shoulders: youthful, living, palpitating force. Their unblemished torsos swelled proudly, with fine hard pectoral muscles, square in the lacustrian, rounded in Irkwar. Their

231

whole flesh expressed a poem of superb humanity, worthy of vanquishing immense predators and colossal herbivores.

Irkwar resumed the combat. His fist lashed out at the enemy, making him reel—but he immediately received a redoubtable blow himself, and, renouncing all indirect action, they fell upon one another, gripped by the fury of hand-to-hand combat. Then there was the heavy vacillation of breasts, the dull impact of limbs, the cracking of joints, and the raucous challenges of renewed holds. On the narrow causeway, the conflict was complicated by the proximity of the marsh, into which each man tried to push his adversary.

The lacustrian, struck by a head-butt, staggered, and his knee bent. Irkwar grabbed him at an angle, weighed upon him heavily, and tried to force him down, but the other, keeping one knee on the ground, rapidly changed his grip and lifted the mountain man off the ground. Irkwar then took his adversary's head in both hands, twisted it, and braced himself for the fall. Thrown down with terrible force, he reacted by turning away; they both rolled on the ground, side by side, but Irkwar was slightly underneath.

Lying across the pathway, deploying their strength to the full, they remained motionless, mutually neutralizing their efforts. Suddenly, Irkwar gave in to the disadvantage of his position, and provided the impulse to roll over himself; in his turn, the lacustrian found himself half-vanquished. Breathlessly, he let go and struck Irkwar in the face violently. Irkwar returned the blow. They each came upright with a bound, and looked at one another as before, with as much hatred as admiration, fully conscious of the equality of their strength.

Their souls drifted in the gross warrior sensuality that balances lust. They were aware of a mysterious grandeur, a sentiment of funereal beauty, some strange reflection of infinitely remote times in which their ancestors had battled the power of forests and vast creatures. In the lacustrian giant, however, that stirred up nothing but an avid desire to defeat his enemy, to rip him apart and trample his cadaver, while in

Irkwar, an indefinable regret awoke, a dawn of fraternity for the splendid adversary.

Their fists extended, as at the beginning of the fight, the man of the lakes gathered himself, condensing himself for his predatory pounce, and Irkwar's rapid instinct reacted in a supreme defensiveness.

The dark body launched itself forward, both fists flying. Irkwar slipped sideways, struck near the temple—but while momentum carried the aggressor forward, the mountain man launched a flank attack with his knees and fists. He made a triple contact with the other, and precipitated him into the marsh.

The furious cries of the lacustrians and the roaring trumpets of the mountain men greeted this turn of events. Astonished, Irkwar's gaze searched for his antagonist; he had dived. Invisible for several seconds, he reappeared 20 meters away and leapt back up on to the causeway, dripping wet and soiled with blackish mud. Immediately, growling his challenge, he came back to resume the fight. Breaking the agreement, however, his companions invaded the causeway, several of them flexing bows. Irkwar only just had time to bear a precipitate retreat.

"Cowardly water-vipers!" he howled at the lacustrians. "Filthy worms!"

The mountain men joined their insults to his. They brandished their weapons at the entrance to the refuge, welcoming their champion triumphantly.

"Irkwar has vanquished the great auorchs of the waters!"

Meanwhile, the lacustrians had not advanced to within bowshot. To the insults of the mountain men they opposed other insults. Their colossus, still black with mud, launched a new challenge, and In-Kelg, in spite of his wound, added his own threats to those of his men.

"The men of the lakes are too cowardly!" cried Tholrog. "Their word is merely a magpie's cry!"

"We shall destroy your villages!" In-Kelg shouted, proudly. "We shall take your warriors into slavery. Nothing can withstand Rob-Sen!"

"Kiwasar will take the lakes!" Tholrog yelled. "Our allies in the west will destroy Rob-Sen's army!"

The trumpets sobbed again, and the marsh became darker. The great cloud was like the wing of an immense rook. The reeds and bulrushes sighed over the sinister water. The wind dropped, and then picked up again, swirling. The daylight was sullen and melancholy, the elements solemn.

In-Kelg, the giant of the lakes and all the enemies withdrew to the damp shore of the marsh, behind a curtain of willows. Only their sentinels remained, on watch like wading birds over the lagoons. And the mountain-dwellers were troubled by that silence full of ambushes...

IV. Tjandrinahr

Time went by. Heavy drops of rain began falling several times, then stopped. The huge cloud rotated, attacked by antagonistic winds. Broad and soft lightning-flashes cut through the background of the landscape. Very distant thunder released grave and long-drawn-out rumbles. A phosphorescent tint slid mysteriously over the viscous water.

The mountain men kept watch, anxiously. In-Kelg appeared at the entrance to the willow-grove, and then a company of lake-dwellers. At the first glimpse, the mountain-dwellers realized that the round-heads had united their little shields, fabricated from slender branches, into a sort of broad shelter, under the cover of which they would set themselves. They were protected against arrows fired vertically, either by the shields or leather-covered branches.

Tholrog and his companions were overtaken, not by dread but by a great bitterness, a confused hatred directed against excessively harsh destiny.

As they were meditating, In-Kelg advanced on to the pathway across the water. "Men of the mountain, do you not want to save your lives by surrendering Eï-Mor and Eyrimah?"

Tholrog darted a despairing glace at the women, Eï-Mor, meeting his gaze, returned it boldly, with a gentle expression on her face. Once again, he sensed that Rob-Sen's daughter had vanquished Eyrimah. "What answer should we give?" he asked.

The man-of-hidden-things got up prophetically. "Their words are lies. Even if we surrender the women, our lives will not be spared. I will reply!" In an arrogant voice, in a vague idiom mixing the language of the lakes with that of the mountains, he bellowed: "The men of the high country do not surrender captives, and Rob-Sen's daughter will die with us. She will die before your eyes, if you attack our refuge!"

Tholrog looked at the captive then. There was nothing in her black eyes or dull face—no protest against the declaration of the man-of-hidden-things. By contrast, he, the young chief, made a gesture of terror and anxiety, which she perceived, and which brought a faint girlish smile, tender and malicious, to her lips.

"Are the men of the mountains refusing to surrender Eï-Mor?" In-Kelg demanded.

"They are refusing to trust the words of lying beasts!"

There was a pregnant silence. Night seemed to be descending upon the marsh, so thick had the vast cloud become. The lake-dwellers moved their shelter of shields and branches forward.

Suddenly, the man-of-hidden-things began to vociferate terribly, proffering howling incantations and hurling stones into the sky. The lightning-flashes multiplied, and the thunder rumbled more closely. "I was holding back the storm!" cried the man-of-hidden-things. "Now, let it come!" With a wild gesture he seemed to be gripping the great cloud and drawing it down. Then he lifted his hand, holding a toad that he must have found in some cavity; he threw it into the water.

They all looked at him in admiration, partly believing in his power. "I launch the storm!" he roared at the lacustrians. "The men of the lakes will be sorry!"

The rain started falling. The mountain men howled enthusiastically.

The lake-dwellers continued their advance nevertheless, to within bowshot, to a place where the rocky path broadened out. There they fixed their shelter with the aid of stakes cut from the willows; it was about five meters high. At the base, they had furnished it with animal skins and fabrics, in such a way that it was perfectly secured against their adversaries' arrows. When that was done they brought forth a kind of crude platform made of ash-branches, and their most skilful archers hoisted themselves on to it, overlooking the mountain-dwellers' refuge. They could peer through the interstices of their shelter, select a victim, and fire rapidly, hardly exposing themselves at all, and for a very short period. Other warriors, inferior marksmen, protected their heads.

In these conditions, the mountain men's retreat became inadequate to protect them all. A dozen of them, crouching or lying down, would risk their lives by the slightest movement. Two warriors made the experiment. One stuck his head out from behind a jutting rock, the other thought he might be able to change his position for a better one. They were immediately seen by piercing eyes and three arrows were fired. One of the mountain men rolled on the ground, hit in the temple; the other drew an arrow from his arm.

A ferocious rumor from the lacustrians followed this success. The mountain-dwellers were prey to a shameful distress. "We're going to die like wolves in a trap!" Irkwar complained.

Soaked by the heavy rain, having eaten little since the morning, under the threat of death to which it was necessary to crouch down, without budging, the situation was intolerable. The bravest were more enraged than the others—and the cadaver of their companion, struck in the head, added to the desolation.

The storm increased its violence. The rain fell in resounding cascades; the view was obscured by a veil, a cataclysmic penumbra. The marsh splashed beneath an avalanche of stones—and immense lightning flashes lit up close at hand, like vast pale and fugitive suns.

The man-of-hidden-things cried into the tempest: "The men of the lakes will be sorry!"

An arrow replied to his bravado. Another warrior sprawled in death. Then, seized by frenzy, the man-of-hidden-things seized Eï-Mor, lifted her up and carried her to the front of the refuge, sheltering himself behind her. "The daughter of Rob-Sen will die!"

Tholrog, going pale, rushed forward. "Shut up!"

"The daughter of Rob-Sen will die," the other repeated, "if the men of the lakes do not withdraw out of bowshot!"

"If you touch the daughter of Rob-Sen, every one of you will perish!" cried a deep voice. "If you surrender the daughter of Rob-Sen, you will be freed. May Yar-Am strike us all, and our families, if we are lying!"

The mountain men looked at one another. Bitterly, Tholrog saw the indecision in their faces. The man-of-hidden-things murmured: "What do you want to do, son of Talaun?"

Tholrog's heart weakened. He could not sacrifice the lives of his companions to his desire to keep Eï-Mor. Taking a sudden decision, he said: "The word of the mountain-people is surer than that of the men of the lakes...what proof will the chief of the lake-dwellers give us?"

"If the men of the mountain promise to surrender Eï-Mor, we will withdraw 1000 meters from the shore. We will abandon our shelter of shields, behind which you will be safe from attack, and we will leave you provisions for two days. When Eï-Mor is with us, we will leave this land!"

The mountain men uttered exclamations, favorably surprised.

"Will the men of the lakes give us time to confer?"

"Very well."

Tholrog said to his companions: "Let those who wish to speak, speak!"

"We have to surrender Rob-Sen's daughter!"

"And if the men of the lakes don't leave?"

"We'll have their shelter, and provisions—the time to find a way out."

"What if they attack us by night, on rafts?"

"Can we too not construct a raft before nightfall," cried the man-of-hidden-things, "and pass by that means over these seemingly-deep waters?"

"Very well," said Tholrog, "let us reflect in silence—and if, thereafter, you want to surrender Rob-Sen's daughter, I will reply to the men of the lakes." His soul was as sad as the great lake; he never ceased contemplating Eï-Mor. The young woman was almost as somber as he was, caught between the instinct that pushed her toward the blond chief and the memories that called her toward the lake-dwellers.

The time approached. Tholrog's heart was beating tumultuously; confusedly, he interrogated the horizon; the rain that limited the view was no longer transpierced by lightning flashes. His entire being, taken by surprise, felt the force of the delicate, savage and unbreakable bonds of love.

"She must go!"

Suddenly, in the depths, in the squalls and the drifting mists, he seemed to hear shouting. It was coming from behind the refuge, where the waters were more clearly displayed. "Can you hear that?"

"Yes, we hear it." Tahmen replied.

The clamor was renewed: the clamor of numerous voices in the wind. Their eyes on the marsh, they shivered. Tahmen and Tholrog, renowned for the penetration of their sight, thought they could see something like an islet moving in the distance.

"Are they not enemies?" said Irkwar.

"We're in the Ariès' lands."

Extending his hand, Tahmen murmured: "Men!"

238

In the vague mist, Tholrog, and then Irkwar and other companions, also perceived them. The emotion of the besieged, equally prey to hope and anguish, was exacerbated.

The voice of the lacustrian chief interrupted them. "Are the men of the heights ready to reply?"

What should they do? What should they say? Uncertainty stifled them.

"The time has come to reply!"

The rain was easing slightly now; the view was clearer. Tahmen could see the outline of a huge raft, men clad in pale fabric, with elongated shields. "The Ariès!"

And Tholrog shouted, in an authoritative voice: "We will not surrender the daughter of Rob-Sen!"

The clamor on the waters was like an endorsement of their refusal: the mountain men, huddled in their refuge, replied to it forcefully.

Now, through the rain, beneath the pallor of the firmament, they could see the raft bearing 60 men. It was advancing slowly. At the tip of the prow stood a silhouette, with a pike in hand. Gradually, they recognized the bronze axes, doubly-pointed shields and the long lances of the Ariès.

The lake-dwellers watched that approach furiously, deliberating. Luck had turned against them. With the advent of the raft, they felt the absence of their fatherland more keenly, and all the ambushes of unknown territory. Already the newcomers could get behind them, while the mountain men charged from the front. Save for In-Kelg, grimly exasperated by the misfortune, they all became afraid of being so far advanced in unknown territory.

"Let's launch a surprise attack!" said In-Kelg.

"It would be slow!" the chief replied. "No more than three of us can go forward together. During that time, the men from the west will arrive—the men of the heights will probably kill Eï-Mor rather than surrender her now. Do you desire her death, Rob-In-Kelg?"

In-Kelg bowed his head before the force of these arguments.

The raft continued its approach. The Ariès were almost all standing upright, ready for combat, protected by their long shields. In the purified atmosphere, where nothing was any longer falling but a dwindling rain, and in which a divine light was filtering through a pale and fine cloud, as if through the vast petal of a water-lily, the silhouette of the man standing in the bow was clearly discernible; Tahmen and Tholrog could distinguish the gravity of his expression.

Irkwar's voice greeted him, shouting a welcome, and the Ariè extended his arms in a sign of alliance.

At that moment, the lake-dwellers decided to retreat. They were seen running away from their shelter in a precipitate withdrawal. Irkwar was able to shoot one of them down with an arrow; they did not even respond, accelerating their progress and putting all their energy into a safe retreat.

The raft arrived close by, amid the ardent enthusiasm of the mountain-dwellers. Their naïve, young and strong minds, admiring the allies, found them singularly handsome and heroically powerful.

The man standing to the fore came ashore. Tholrog and Irkwar advanced to meet him, stammering a few Ariè words with difficulty. Tjandrinahr put his hands on the shoulders of the two mountain men and replied in their own language. "The Ariès are glad to see you in their lands!"

"Father," Tholrog replied, "your son of the mountains offers you the life you have saved."

The Ariès looked at the tall mountain men sympathetically, recognizing that they were strong and redoubtable—and between the descendants of those who had come from the Land of the Seven Rivers,[14] the sons of the splendid and complex human race of the Ariès, and the vanquished sons of ancient Quaternary Europe there was a tender amity, like the prescience of superb destinies that would bring their united races to nothing thousands of years hence.

---

[14] i.e., the Indian subcontinent.

V. The Fusion of Races

A third of the night had elapsed. Tholrog was asleep in a cabin on the Ariès' great lake. He and his companions occupied the extremity of an island-village close to the shore. In a delightful post-pluvial sky, moonlight was shining on the lake.

A furtive noise woke Tholrog up. He sat up, and saw a black form in front of the hut, limned by moonlight. He was about to get up and grab a spear, but he suddenly recognized the silhouette of Eï-Mor. Then he lay down and shut his eyes again, cunningly feigning sleep. An extraordinary force dilated his heart.

The young woman drew nearer, leaned over silently. No longer blocking the moonlight, she examined Tholrog's face. She seemed anxious; then a half-smile creased her lips. She stayed there, looking and listening. Tholrog saw her neck lit by a bright moonbeam, her eyes softly attentive. She straightened up again, and left.

He listened to her light footsteps draw away, in a dream. Then he got up. He could see her, already some distance away on the islet. He called: "Eï-Mor."

She stopped. She did not turn round immediately. He caught up with her.

"Why have you come?"

"You're wounded. I wanted to see…"

"Why did you want to see?"

She did not reply. A pure breeze blew over the islet, lifting up the tresses of the young woman's hair; it was as if they had touched Tholrog.

"Why did you want to see?"

"I wanted to see if it was dangerous."

"It's not dangerous. Would you like it to be dangerous?" As he pronounced these words, he felt his contentment vanish. The suspicion they expressed seemed plausible. Knowing that

241

her own people were nearby, why should Rob-Sen's daughter not desire the death of an enemy chief who had declared his intention to keep her forever? That idea was emphasized by the slight fever of his wound.

Eï-Mor replied: "No, I wouldn't like it to be dangerous."

Standing up straighter, he said, sharply: "If it were dangerous—if I died—you would be exchanged. You would be free. Had you thought of that, daughter of Rob-Sen?"

"I hadn't thought of that!"

"Then why are you trembling?"

She fell silent. Tholrog's suspicions increased. The jealous vision of Eï-Mor returning to Rob-Sen's camp, glad to be given back to her own people, tortured him. He fastened his aurochs-skin cloak over his shoulders and growled: "How did you escape from Dithèv's custody?"

She recoiled, fearfully. "Why are you angry? I know remedies for wounds. Didn't you save me on the mountain?"

Her pure voice, the darkness, and the mysterious immobility of the Moon's rays on the ground began to mollify the young chief. "You wanted to heal me?"

"Yes, if your wound had been dangerous."

"Is that true, daughter of Rob-Sen?"

She nodded her head affirmatively.

They were outside the huts. An extraordinary splendor decorated the waters, the dormant water-lilies and their large floating leaves. The croaking of distant frogs was as charming as the bleating of ewes. Tholrog felt his suspicions vanish, as they had come, with the rapidity of ripples on the water. The foreign woman seemed to promise profound and inexhaustible joys. "Eï-Mor!" he cried. "Would Tholrog's death not be agreeable to you?"

"I do not desire Tholrog's death."

"Even if it set you free?"

"It would not set me free."

"You would be exchanged for prisoners. Tholrog will not exchange you!"

She turned away, troubled. She gazed at the lake. Marvelous nuances shimmered on the waters. The sky and the shores, vaster and more solemn, trembled in the light breeze as if they had been attached to supple and unbreakable cords.

At intervals, a slight gust of wind was seen to advance very slowly. Waves rose in the distance, the ripples growing, enlarging and expiring with a slight murmur against the shore. In the direction of the Moon there was a pathway of silver and sapphire. The odor of the water was fresh, and sometimes a trifle feverish. It awoke a delightful disturbance.

Insensibly, Tholrog and the young woman had drawn closer to one another on the edge of the platform. By leaning forward, they could see other villages, as if floating on the water. The roofs of huts were reminiscent of singular plants, and also of heaps of logs—large tree-trunks stripped of branches. Canoes were moored to the pilings of the islets; on the shore, patrolling watchmen passed one another by—for the entire lake was preparing for the war.

Meanwhile, the nervous noises of the night were audible: a frog leaping into the water; a startled fish taking flight; a mysterious rat passing over a promontory; an anxious, agitated water-hen. A bat, fleeing some peril, passed overhead with a shrill cry, carrying its offspring clinging to its breast. A village of beavers—animals sacred to the Ariès—was perceptible in a bright moonbeam: a village built on pilings like those of men. In the distance, an urus bellowed, followed by a wolf's howl. The splash of the waves still spoke its charming language.

Tholrog felt slightly feverish, and that fever refined his impressions. While Eï-Mor was silent, he saw Eyrimah's image take shape within him, but that image had scant power. In the contest of the two loves, Rob-Sen's daughter loomed large, dominant. The man would rather not have had his captive by right of force.

"Tholrog will not exchange you. Do you detest Tholrog?"

She gathered all of her boldness, with the sentiment of her youthful power. "If Tholrog does not exchange me, what does he want to do with me?"

"What one does with young and beautiful captives!" He adopted the tone of a conqueror, cold and rough. She shivered with pride and dolor. Her education as a chief's daughter, destined for the sort of union in which a woman retains privilege and pride, was reanimated within her.

"You are able to want that...and the daughter of Rob-Sen would no longer need to be exchanged."

Tholrog trembled. As a spark may set a forest ablaze, that reply convinced him to press on to the end. "You hate Tholrog, then?"

"Eï-Mor might not be a chief's first wife...others might be raised over her."

"What if no other were raised over you?"

Eï-Mor became paler than the night. Tenderness transformed her face.

Tholrog, captive of her imploring eyes, her young arms half-extended, said: "Among us, there is only one wife. Would you like to be Tholrog's wife?"

Eï-Mor's gaze expressed joy, love and frankness. "I would like to be Tholrog's wife!"

"Even if you were free?"

"Yes."

"Even if you were at home, on your lakes, with Rob-Sen?"

"Even if I were with my father!"

A youthful and powerful sense of good fortune overwhelmed Tholrog. He took hold of Eï-Mor. "You shall be Tholrog's wife!" He held her velvet body against him, those tresses whose caress had so often reappeared in his memory. He sensed a certain vertigo, and a weakness—but an even greater joy.

They stayed as they were. The immense charm of the lake mingled with their savage souls. The Moon and the pale stars were there for them alone: the entirety of the duplicated sky, above and below, and the poplars, the willows and the intermittent plaint of the waters.

He shivered.

"Go back inside!" she told him.

"Eï-Mor, are you happy with Tholrog?"

"Very happy—but you must let your wound rest. Tomorrow, I shall gather some herbs for you."

He went back inside. He watched Eï-Mor leave—and, shivering all the while, he had a confused sentiment of the splendor of life and the vastness of the future.

VI. The Great Battle

Rob-Sen, the conqueror of the Ariès advance guards, was camped within sight of the Great Lake. All night long, his army's fires had been reflected in the waters upstream, and all night long the lake remained illuminated by the Ariès' fires and the furnaces of the Immohys, who were forging desperately.

The Sun rose painfully; it was to illuminate one of humankind's decisive battles. Depending on the victory or defeat of Rob-Sen, the orientation of its races might swing toward the Ou-Loâ or the Ariès. The trail of the Ariès, from Asia to the western seas, was composed of populations of low density; the Ou-Loâ were still much more numerous; their tribes were in communication throughout the greater part of Europe. The news of a great victory over an important Ariè settlement could determine a general uprising to impede the previously-unvanquished invasion. Prolific and energetic, the Ou-Loâ would then be capable, within a century or two, of populating Europe strongly enough to resist the superior element, if not by force of arms, at least by force of numbers.

If, by contrast, Rob-Sen were defeated, it would add further momentum to the dispersal of the Ariès—and it would relieve the pressure on the ancient race of the tall fair-haired people of the Quaternary epoch, driven back into the North and a few mountain regions.

Rob-Sen's position was the better one; he was camped upstream. Hills protected his flank. His front was bristling with scattered rocks. He also had the moral force of his victories over the advance guards and superiority of numbers: 12,000 men against 7000 Ariès. His army was divided into two parts: 8000 men that he commanded himself, and 4000 whose command two powerful tribes had deferred—in spite of Rob-Sen's protests—to an old chief named An-Kar.

The Ariès had taken cover in a beech-wood that formed a sort of quasi-island between streams and minuscule lakes. Both sides observed one another curiously. The Ou-Loâ were seen circulating between the poplars, elms and beeches on the edges of pools. Most often clad in woven fabrics, they were armed with arrows with triangular points, harpoons, stones, axes, clubs and lances. Their shields were small and round. Their faces were painted with blood-red emblems in order to hide wounds.

The Ariès were armed with bronze weapons, catapults, bows and lances tipped with bronze or exceedingly hard stone. Their clothes were made of linen and leather. Their shields were long, with pointed ends. They were commanded by Visarmi, and, under him on either wing, Kouramas and Rova.

An-Kar commenced that attack against Kouramas; it was driven back. The Ariès advanced as far as the enemy's position.

Rova then attacked Rob-Sen and took a hill. Rob-Sen sent reinforcements and took the hill back. Visarmi ordered Rova to reoccupy it, and the great battle began. It was terrible. Three times the hill was retaken. It remained Rob-Sen's.

During this time, Kouramas took the offensive against An-Kar. At the head of 2000 men he drove the Ou-Loâ back, and subjected them to heavy losses. The battle intensified, a similar ardor animating the two races. Kouramas, however, succeeded in crossing a stream. His archers contrived profound ravages, while he attacked impetuously elsewhere. An-

Kar's hordes were cut in two; half found themselves pressed back against a marsh, while the other half were in a depression, in which Kouramas dominated them. Enraged, An-Kar was forced to ask Rob-Sen for help.

Now, at that moment, Rob-Sen, having retaken the hill for the third time, was mounting a forceful attack against Rova. He sent forth four successive columns of 1000 men, without being able to dislodge the Ariès—but the fifth time, they retreated.

The Ariès' supreme leader never ceased studying the battle. The silent grandeur and marvelous profundity of his race were alive in him. He had Tjandrinahr by his side, whose advice he held in high esteem. He sent 1000 men to help Rova.

Rob-Sen received An-Kar's messengers angrily; nevertheless, he gave him 1200 men. The day became solemn and grandiose. The whole of that corner of the Earth was filled with the anger of men. The races were measuring their past and future there, in death, courage and cunning. The ferocious will of nature was being accomplished there.

The conflict between Rob-Sen and Rova remained indecisive for a long time; by virtue of the superiority of arms and the influence of character, 3000 Ariès held firm against 5000 Ou-Loâ. Kouramas, however, lost part of his advantage over An-Kar with the arrival of reinforcements; he made this known to the supreme chief. Visarmi, holding no more than 2000 men in reserve, and fearful of some surprise from Rob-Sen, hesitated.

"What should we do, Tjandrinahr?"

"I think we should send 300 men—and if that isn't enough, 200 more in a little while, with Tholrog's mountain men."

"Are the mountain men braver than the Ariès, then?"

"No, Father, but I asked them this morning not to sound their trumpets. Hearing them unexpectedly, the Ou-Loâ might believe that we've received support from the mountains."

"Tjandrinahr is always the great sage of councils!" And Visarmi sent the reinforcements.

Meanwhile, Rob-Sen grew impatient with the enemy's resistance. He still had 2000 men in reserve. He launched half of them. After mounting marvelous resistance, Rova began to retreat—and in the meantime, Kouramas could make no progress against An-Kar, in spite of the reinforcements.

The battle continued in this fashion for a long time, slow and indecisive. The Ariè chief followed the course of destiny coolly, but the depths of his inner being were somber. Finally, he gave further reinforcements to both Rova and Kouramas; he only had 1000 men still in hand. These reinforcements fell on to the battlefield like wood into a stove. It heated up, howling at the sky. Rova held Rob-Sen; Kouramas began to grind An-Kar down again.

All of a sudden, amid the rumor of death, the mountain-dwellers' trumpets roared. Tholrog appeared on a ridge with his own men, including the giant Irkwar, and Ariès clad in animal-skins. Other trumpets roared in the valley. Then, An-Kar's warriors were troubled. They held firm, however, their anguish not manifesting itself as terror—but in response to an imperious charge by the Ariès, it revealed itself to be profound and irresistible. The men accumulated on the edge of the marsh—numbering 2000—collapsed and surrendered. Six hundred more were massacred in a ravine. The Ariès were, therefore, victorious on the right flank.

Visarmi's inner being was brightened. There was hope for the future of his race! He gave Rova all his reserves. Rob-Sen was similarly forced to exhaust his own. For an hour, destiny balanced 4000 Ariès against more than 6000 Ou-Loâ; the outcome remained doubtful, each side conserving its positions—but Kouramas, having completed his victory, came to Rova's aid.

Slowly, Rob-Sen was obliged to retreat into an encampment, a quarter of which he had lost. Thanks to men fleeing from An-Kar's rout, who had taken refuge with him and returned to the battle, he prevented the Ariès from advancing further, repelling their attacks.

At dusk, the battle was suspended.

The Ariès were victorious, having killed 2000 enemies, taken as many prisoners, and put one of the Ou-Loâ's wings to flight—but Rob-Sen was not yet defeated. He still had an army of 8000 men, strongly entrenched, against 6000 Ariès. He was thinking about resuming the battle the following day.

Fate did not want that. Messengers came to Rob-Sen during the night to tell him that the mountain men had retaken the plateau of Dap-Iwr—the mountain-dwellers' Iordjolk—and were threatening Lake Re-Alg.

Then, assembling the Council, Rob-Sen cursed the stupidity of An-Kar, the cowardice of the defenders of Dap-Iwr, and proposed to sue for peace while the strength of his position permitted him to do so on advantageous terms.

No one dared to raise a voice against him, and Rob-Sen acted in the capacity of supreme chief.

VII. Peace

Peace was made. It took nothing away from the Ou-Loâ's territory, but it was advantageous to the liberty of the mountain folk and increased the power of the Ariès. Rob-Sen ruled over his people and commenced a dynasty, to which In-Kelg and Eyrimah belonged, the young lacustrian gloriously bearing off the young woman.

The Moon had just risen. The great lake of the Ariès extended in infinite magnificence. A charm was in the air: the softness of things, the transparent quietness, the horizons that spoke the great language of mystery, and the beauty of the clear waters that always captivates the human heart.

Eï-Mor and Tholrog were contemplating their last night on the lake. They were sitting in silence. They had spoken, and were thrilling in a marvelous concordance, in the union of their gentle barbaric souls. The lake was within them—those silvery trails, its errant tiny creatures, its fugitive sounds—and so was the road through the mountains: the storm, the avalanche, the terrible marsh; all that was, for them, Love.

Their silence lasted a long time—a very long time—and their affection grew continually softer. In the end, however, Tholrog hugged the young lake-dweller more tightly, and drew her slowly into the shadows, toward the great eternal mystery that vanquishes Destruction.

NOMAÏ

To Paul Gallimard [15]

It was the time when men lived on lakes, in caves and in subterranean dwellings. Young Egypt had not yet stuttered her first hieroglyphs. Beasts were terrible, the elements obscure, formidable and fatal, and all atmospheric phenomena seemed to be the wrath, the vengeance or the ferocity of impenetrable beings.

In those days the tribe of the Sons of the Wolf lived on the Lake of Blood, and that tribe was powerful by virtue of the strength of its males and their cruelty. They had no gentle morality. Their virtue was finer the more murderous it was. To forgive an insult was a crime, sympathy for a stranger a sin; pity for the defeated was not even included among evil things, for no instance of it had ever been observed.

The family existed. Only the father was reckoned a human individual, and the sons, in order to liberate themselves, had to leave home or resort to bloody force. The daughters were sold, then becoming slaves without appeal, whose destruction would not invite any vengeance, or even any annoyance—but the sales could give rise to murder, by virtue of the conflict of lust and cupidity.

---

[15] Paul Gallimard (1850-1929) is nowadays best known as an art collector who helped secure the reputation of the Impressionists, but he was also a prominent member of the Societé des Amis du Livre, along with Gustave Geffroy, and Rosny probably met him at the Grenier. Although Rosny could not have known it when he penned this dedication, Paul's son Gaston was to go on to become a prominent publisher, founding Editions Gallimard.

Humans had not yet learned how to kiss from the example of the birds; there was only the savage and rapid love that had sufficed to perpetuate the generations of men for millennia.

Now, one morning in summer, when the leaves were still young, the daughters of the Bloody Lake were bathing in the lukewarm waters, and the warriors were watching them from the shore—for that was the way in which they were put up for auction.

The race was handsome. Among the adolescents, the ancestral form of the divine Hellenes and long-haired Iranians was perceptible. Then men armed with oaken clubs or lances tipped with flint chose their wives according to strength, plumpness and price. From time to time, a bather was summoned, and her purchaser, feeling her shoulders, rump and the firmness of her hips, would lead her away like an ox from the peat-bogs or a mountain goat.

Among them all, Nomaï, the daughter of the great lacustrian chief, stood out. The warriors admired her strong and flexible figure, the rounded cups of her breasts, and the agile vigor of her movements—but the magnificent softness of her gaze, the delicate curve of her jaw and the magical grace of her smile were made for the admiration of men who would only be born in future centuries.

She crossed the distance from the village to the shore twice, then appeared standing upright, her loins covered by a fibrous cloth, on a black islet in the shadow of an ash-tree. The chief looked at her proudly, like a warrior who had contrived a redoubtable axe or a long-range bow.

Next to the supreme chief stood Rochs, the chief of the young-men-who-preceded-the-war, who kept 30 enemy skulls in his house. Clad in a red hide, he was a giant in stature, his hand prompt in homicide and as heavy as a hammer. Suddenly, on seeing Nomaï standing on the black islet, he ceased bargaining with the chief of chiefs and shouted loudly: "Let it be as you desire, Zamm, son of Wor; you shall have amber, lances and the carved stones that quell the invisible powers..."

At these words, a warrior who was standing among the reeds let his arms fall and went pale. His eyes had not left Nomaï. Alone among those savage men, he had a notion of the beauty of a face and harmonious contours; he was the only one who liked the variable light of the virgin's beautiful eyes, her smile in which fugitive impressions were blended, and the charming gesture that renewed the harmony of her figure.

He had no reputation as a warrior. He had no taste for murder and was not manifestly avid for vengeance. And he devoted himself to meditation, which the Sons of the Wolf considered cowardly, shameful and sly. Only the priests had the right to indulge in it, because they mingled it with threats, blood, brutal celebrations and terrible chants—but they only admitted cunning men to their ranks, capable of maintaining the power of intelligence by malice, for they knew that gentleness was impossible and pity dangerous; martial might had no room for them.

Amreh was aware of his weakness. He regarded it with anxiety, sadness and even shame. He had struggled against himself, had joined in, as a matter of duty, with bloody celebrations and had taken vengeance against savage enemies, but he only took pleasure in wandering, ingenious contrivance and naïve reflections on the astonishing things that surrounded human life. Secretly, he denied many of the things that the chiefs affirmed. Thus, he did not believe that thunderbolts were the voice of the god of the air, but rather a fire that the clouds had taken from the volcanic mountains.

It also seemed to him that the gods ought to prefer the flesh of animals to that of men, and amber stone to warm blood. He thought, too, that water had been made by light, since it reproduced the images of things. Finally, he was convinced that the lacustrian tribes were not descended from wolves, but rather from a cross between bears and horses. He did not admit to any of these singular opinions; he knew that he would be immediately put to death if he made them known. Nevertheless, he took pride in having conceived them.

He loved Nomaï, and did not know the power of that love. He was unaware that the desire to be loved in return had been planted in his soul. Such a thing would have seemed more extraordinary to him than all his other sensations, as if he wanted to be loved by his weapons, the fruit he gathered on the lake-shore, or the fire that he lit in his stone hearth. He only dreamed of buying the chief's daughter, or carrying her off by force or trickery to the nearby mountains.

When he heard Rochs conclude the bargain with Zamm, Amreh was filled with fear and rage. He cursed the chief of the young men, and that was his only genuine hatred. Not as strong or as skillful in handling a lance, he flexed his bow, convinced that he could not avoid a conflict with the pitiless tribesman. And he removed himself from Rochs' presence in order to avoid too cruel an insult.

Meanwhile, Zamm had replied: "I also want two horns of war-paint and your large ash-wood bow."

Rochs hesitated, for he already thought the girl very expensive. Having looked at her again, however, standing on the black islet, he replied: "I'll take her!"

The lacustrian chief put his staff of authority on the other's shoulder as a sign that the deal was irrevocable—but Nomaï, having perceived the gesture, exercised her right as the chief's daughter and shouted: "I don't want to belong to Rochs!"

Such refusals were rare, occasioned by the fear of too brutal a master and not by reason of preference, which was inadmissible in a woman. Zamm and Rochs looked at her with surprise, anger and a savage disdain. The old chief, obliged to remain calm, asked his companion: "Will you consent to the swimming test?"

In that trial, the young woman received ten cubits start. She could refuse the man if he had not caught up that margin over the distance that extended from the point of a little promontory to the eastern extremity of the lacustrian village.

"I consent!" said Rochs, disdainfully—and his face showed that he would not forget the insult.

Meanwhile, Amreh had advanced toward the promontory. Nomaï's action astonished him as much as everyone else, but it filled him with delight. The obscure feeling that the woman had a "preference" for him became almost intelligible to him. With a fiery gaze he watched the beautiful young woman swim slowly back to the shore.

She was sporting in the waves like some goddess of the depths; her white shoulder threw a ray of moonlight into the blue water, while her long hair floated behind her like some marvelous water-weed.

She came ashore.

With a light bound, Amreh emerged from the reeds to stand before her.

Having stooped, in the attitude of a young hind ready to take flight, she offered the youth of her eyes and face to the warrior. He understood, confusedly, that she was imploring his help, and that she would not have claimed the swimming test against him. More inexpressible still, but with an invincible ardor, he had the impression that he would obey Nomaï like a slave, that he would betray the gods and humans alike, that he would exile himself from his native waters, if she would voluntarily rest her head upon his breast. And over that ancient savage drama of the Caves, over the lustful but solitary covetousness of the Sons of the Wolf, there rose up in that soul one of the first psychic desires of humankind, in which the desire to possess a woman was supplemented by a desire to be possessed by her—and that was also the dawn of the era when crimes committed *to obtain* women were supplemented by crimes committed *on behalf* of women.

Nomaï slowly detached her gaze from Amreh's. She ran to the point of the promontory, then lowered her arms toward the lake. "O Queen of the Gulfs, who brings forth the women of the land soaked in water, I will weave you ten tunics if you give me strength and speed!"

Her voice astonished Amreh, by its somber ardor and its melodious quality, while the anxious Rochs intoned the prayer: "Father, who brings forth men from the rock, I will kill two captives and offer their hearts to you if you refuse strength and speed to this woman!"

Then Nomaï leapt into the waves, and drew away to an extent of ten cubits. In response to the chief's signal, Rochs followed her.

She could swim better than any other daughter of the waters, as supple as a trout or a grayling. He cleaved the water with mighty sweeps of his arms. Their speed seemed equal. Rochs did not gain ground on the energetic maiden—and Amreh, breathless with hope, along with the bathers and the warriors, impassioned by the contest, and the old lacustrian chief, fearful of losing the splendid bride-price, watched the antagonists draw away.

Nomaï was no more than 100 cubits from the goal when a beam detached from the piling of a hut struck her on the shoulder. Surprised, she stopped—but she resumed the contest in spite of the pain. Rochs exerted himself to the full, however; with a wild movement and a savage cry of triumph, he caught hold of the charming maiden.

The warriors, always on the victor's side, howled Rochs' praises and the lacustrian chief rejoiced in the thought of the amber, weapons and amulets, while the somber Amreh, his heart full of murderous thoughts, lowered his head and leaned against a tree.

Meanwhile, Nomaï had escaped from the grip. She reached the village and stood up, resplendent, on the breakwater. Turning to Rochs, braving Destiny and Victory, she shouted: "I shall not bow my head to you!"

The young chief's laughter rippled over the water. "Whether you have the wings of an eagle or the feet of an ibex, I shall take you to my hut at sunrise."

She did not reply. She seemed crushed. Her face turned toward the tree where Amreh was standing—and the warrior felt hope bubbling up through his sadness, like the water of a spring through the hard rock.

It was dark. Amreh was awake in his hut. Several times, he had circled Zamm's large dwelling, but the dogs with wolves' heads all howled when he attempted to climb over the palisade—for Zamm lived in the village as if he were camped among man-eating beasts.

Amreh was listening to the cool voice of the lake, the intermittently-rising plaint of the breeze and the flutter of wings and the hum of insects. A slight scraping sound made him shiver; he saw a shadow appear in the door-frame. A low voice murmured: "Are you awake, Amreh?"

He recognized the movement and the voice. His heart beat tempestuously, and he replied: "I'm awake, daughter of Zamm."

He stood up. He was trembling in every limb. Taking a step forward into the hut, she said, in a low voice: "Close the door."

He drew a screen across and covered it with a fur. Then, Nomaï took from her tunic one of the phosphorescent stones that the Sons of the Wolf extracted from the mountain, with which they illuminated the dark nights. This one was large; it projected a blue light over the chief's daughter. Amreh could see her sparkling eyes and the sweetness of her face.

"I've come," she said, "because I do not want to belong to Rochs!" She fixed her gaze upon the young lacustrian.

He realized something that he alone of all his race was capable of realizing, and realized it quite clearly: the power of womanhood. Burning with the magical ardor of giving oneself instead of taking, servitude passed from his soul to his face. "You don't want to belong to Rochs?" he said, in a faint voice.

"No, I want to belong to you!"

He uttered a profound sigh; his joy made him unsteady on his feet—and he searched for a word that men had not yet created for women, but could not find it. Finally, he replied: "And I also want to belong to you." He drew nearer, and took her gently in his arms. They remained there, in a palpitation of tenderness. It was a prodigy for both of them, a legendary event—a legend that the tribe's storytellers had not yet sung.

She was the first to pull away. "Tomorrow, at sunrise, Rochs will claim me. How will you get me back?"

"I have no wealth," he said. "Wouldn't you like to flee far from the lake?"

He did not think of combat, not out of fear, but because of the certainty of being defeated—in which case Nomaï would be more surely enslaved. She understood that as well as if he had said it aloud.

"No," she said, "I don't want to flee far from the lake. We'd be recaptured by the Sons of the Wolf, captured by the Cave People, or hunted by the people who live in the trees in the Eastern forests."

The voluptuous energy of her speech left Amreh devoid of resistance. "What do you want to do, daughter of Zamm? Whatever you want, I want."

Savage and soft at the same time, she said: "We must kill Rochs. His life stands in the way of our lives; it will crush us as a millstone crushes grain. We cannot breathe easy while his heart beats."

"I'm not afraid of dying. I'd fight Rochs—but his weapons are better than mine, and he's more skillful in making use of them. I'd perish, and you'd be his prisoner."

Putting her hand on Amreh's breast, she said: "It isn't necessary to fight him, but to kill him by stealth. He has no male relatives apart from his grandfather, who is more like an ash-tree than a man. His brothers perished in the war against the mountain people. His father drowned. No one will claim the price of his blood. We'll take possession of his wealth and share it with Zamm."

Amreh could raise no objection against the act itself. "Red dogs guard him. If we touch his palisade, they'll bark— and their aid will render Rochs invincible."

She replied, in somber voice: "They won't bark again. The meat I threw them before coming to meet you has killed them. This is what we'll do: I'll knock at Rochs' house and call to him. He'll recognize my voice and come out, for he's possessed by my image. He'll want to hold me against him, and I'll extend my arms to him. You'll come up behind him in order to split his skull!"

The vision of this murder, shared with her, filled Amreh with a delightful and tender delirium. He looked at her, by the light of the blue stone, as he might have looked at a goddess, and he hugged her to his breast again with a sigh of ecstasy. "Go, daughter of Zamm...I shall do as you say, and I shall save you."

"Fetch your weapons," she said.

He chose his best axe and a sharp lance.

Nomaï silently removed the screen and fur sealing the hut. The black flesh of the night, and the stars, little sparkling stones, were tremulously reflected in the lake. It was the hour when human sleep is heaviest. Even the dogs were enjoying a more tranquil slumber. Besides, they only gave voice if someone touched the palisades, or if some stranger or carnivorous beast appeared on the lake.

Amreh and Nomaï marched silently over the pathways of planks and stones. Their souls were resolute. They followed their plan as a stone rolls down a slope, and they only paused to listen to vague noises that might have been the movements of a man—but they immediately recognized the passing of an owl, the footfalls of a marten or the flight of a water-rat.

They arrived in the vicinity of Rochs' house. It was massive, as large as Zamm's; the starlight drew a grayish gleam from it. It was surrounded by a high palisade of wooden stakes and bushes; no one could touch it without awakening the fury of the red dogs—but when Nomaï put her hand on it, silence persisted in the village.

"You see," she said, in a low voice, "the poisoned meat is reliable; they're dead. That's how we can cross the palisade."

They were both sufficiently agile and athletic not to reveal their presence. They found themselves close to the door. Amreh hid himself among the branches. Then Nomaï knocked on the door with her fist.

Rochs' terrible voice was raised in the silence: "Woe betide anyone who disturbs my sleep—death is already in their breast!"

Nomaï replied, softly: "I have come!"

Astonished, Rochs asked: "Why have you come?"

"I have realized your authority. In order that you will not beat me at sunrise, here is your slave."

He uttered a laugh of triumph, which was interrupted by suspicion and anxiety. "My dogs haven't barked…"

The young lacustrian woman had her answer ready, however. "They would have devoured me if I had not said the magic word of the wolf-god…they won't wake up before daybreak."

Rochs raised the fur covering his doorway. His piercing eyes peered into the darkness, but he only saw the recumbent bodies of dogs and the figure of Nomaï.

His flesh swollen with desire, drunk with audacity, and ever victorious, he could not imagine that any warrior in the tribe would stand up against him, even less that a woman might guide the will of a man. Only the silence of the dogs had troubled him—but he believed in magic words. He only picked up a lance, suddenly removed the screen, and appeared before the young woman—and he said, almost softly: "You have come."

Already, desire had advanced his mighty arms. Throwing her own arms around his neck, and clinging to him desperately, she cried: "Strike!"

Amreh emerged from the darkness. His axe glinted faintly as it was raised. It came down like a hammer.

Rochs uttered a cry like the howl of an aurochs in winter. He fell on to one knee, and then got up again, brandishing his lance—and he seemed still to be strong. A second blow from the axe cut into his shoulder, though; a third slashed his face. Then he collapsed to the ground with a dull groan.

"Strike his heart!" said Nomaï. "His life is our death."

With the tip of his lance, Amreh fumbled in the darkness, and when it reached the heart, the death-cry reverberated through the lacustrian village, amid the frenzied howling of dogs.

Men and women got up and ran toward Rochs' house— and Nomaï hid in the crowd while Amreh cried: "A duel to the death was declared between Rochs and me; one of us had to perish. The gods have given me the strength. Woe betide him who stands up against me!"

No one thought of standing up against him, but rather of admiring and fearing him—and the warrior continued: "I shall take his house, his weapons and his treasures, as is decreed by our ancestors—and I shall buy Nomaï, daughter of Zamm, paying double the agreed price.

And Zamm raised his voice in his turn, saying: "That is good. Let he who has vanquished his enemy take his place! You shall take the girl at sunrise."

Everyone cried: "That is good!"

The head priest, who had not wanted to initiate Amreh for fear of his gentleness, came forward. "The gods have spoken! Take possession, Amreh, of Rochs' house. Even so, you shall pay a tribute to the god of the clouds…"

"I consent to that," said Amreh, and, at a signal from the priest, he was left alone. His joy was as vast as the lake and the mountains. He was possessed by a confused and marvelous adoration. He yearned for Nomaï like dry ground for rain.

He was as glad to have obeyed the woman as to have won the victory. He sensed confusedly that his murder was a nobler deed than the murders of the men of his time, and less cruel. An instinct of justice, of defense of the weak and

261

thoughtful, was palpitating in his breast—and his love deepened by virtue of these obscure things.

He could not sleep, though—and he saw many stars glittering in the depths of the lake, and many others rising over the mountains. He thought about Nomaï's blue stone and wondered whether the stars might not be comparable to it—for they plunged into the lake and did not lose their brightness there.

Dawn silvered the horizon. The constellations became dull in the red twilight; they fled the copper Sun. He heard birdsong, and the breeze changed direction over the waves.

Then Amreh cried to the Sun: "Eye of Fire, joy of the world, gaze of the god who dried the Earth and gave it the trees, leave me the heritage of Rochs and the possession of Nomaï—I will offer you amber, aurochs, horses and long-horned rams!"

Zamm, meanwhile, brought his daughter to Amreh's house.

Around her neck and shoulders she wore a leather thong, the sign of servitude. In her right hand, she held a millstone. Arrowhead, iris and meadowsweet flowers sparkled in her hair. And Zamm led her through the midst of the Sons and Daughters of the Wolf, until he saw Amreh, when he cried: "Zamm, son of Wor, does not have two faces. He brings you, as he promised, the one who will bear your children. Remember your own promise."

In his turn, Amreh said: "He who breaks his promise is, among men, like a poplar without roots. Here is the amber, the lances, the engraved stones that quell the invisible powers, and the horns of paint." Then, indicating the crowd, he added: "May you all be witnesses!"

Zamm, full of joy, replied: "That is just."

And the witnesses shouted: "We have seen!"

Taking a piece of jade from his breast, the father made Nomaï open her mouth. Then, with an accurate blow, he broke one of her canine teeth, as was the rule. Blood sprang forth;

the young lacustrian woman offered her shining tooth to her master with her own hands.

"Thus have done the Sons of the Wolf for ten times ten generations," said Zamm. Handing over Nomaï, he said: "I no longer have a daughter!"

Then, according to the custom, everyone went away.

Amreh stood before the young woman, full of anxiety. Into his amorous soul, pity slipped like a subtle flower from the moist ground. It had been hard for him when the blood flowed from Nomaï's charming mouth—and he said something so sweet that no man, since the beginning of time, had ever said its like to a woman: "I would rather, Nomaï, that my blood were flowing instead of yours!"

She threw himself toward him, ardent with gratitude—and, leaning over, he steeped his mouth in the blood that was running over her red lips. It was a strange sensation, dissolving and delicious.

Their veins and their flesh seemed confused, and there came to them, obscure but profound, an intuition of the future caress of Love: a presentiment of the Kiss.

Afterword

Although *Vamireh* was not the first prehistoric romance produced in France, it had far more narrative energy than its lackluster documentary predecessors. Berthoud and Berthet had done little more than add a light fictional gloss to a description of life as they imagined it to have been lived in prehistoric times. Rosny did far more than that; he animated his picture, not merely with a lavish ration of violent conflict, but with a great deal of strangely-mixed emotion.

In their survey of Rosny's prehistoric romances, Morel and Massé likened *Vamireh* to the images of primitive existence featured in two of the classics of French Romanticism: Jacques Bernardin de Saint-Pierre's *Paul et Virginie* (1788), and René de Chateaubriand's *Atala* (1801). Although the comparison is not entirely apt, it is a great deal more perceptive than René Doumic's attempt to co-opt *Vamireh* into the Naturalistic straitjacket in which several contemporary critics attempted to confine Rosny (for their own convenience rather than his). *Vamireh* is, indeed, an unrepentantly Romantic work, and its Romanticism is quintessentially French, owing a great deal of its inspiration to Bernardin de Saint-Pierre's friend and inspirer, Jean-Jacques Rousseau. Although Rousseau never used or approved of the term "noble savage," it nevertheless described a significant archetype in his work, and that was the archetype that Rosny set out to embody in the character of Vamireh, which owes far more to Rousseau's speculations about the freedom and nobility of men untainted by civilization than it does to anything he can have found in the works of John Lubbock, Nicolas Joly or Gabriel de Mortillet.

Bernardin de Saint-Pierre's own study of savage innocence, *Paul et Virginie*, was initially published in the third edition of the fourth volume of *Etudes de Nature*, as an illustr-

265

ative dramatization of its principles. It is worth noting that Bernardin de Saint-Pierre went on from that work to produce the far more lyrical *Harmonies de la Nature* (1815), a partly-speculative essay that is one of the most significant precursors of Rosny's "La Légende sceptique." *Paul et Virginie* is an elegy for the lost paradise of innocence—here symbolized by a tropical childhood that is bound to be spoiled by adulthood—and an indictment of the corruption of civilization. *Atala*, similarly formulated as a tale of doomed love, is more specifically concerned with the morality of Christianity—the story was integrated into the author's *Le Génie du Christianisme* as an illustrative text, presumably in imitation of Bernardin de Saint-Pierre's use of *Paul and Virginie*—but displays a similar powerful nostalgia for the primeval in its celebration of the lush North American forest. *Vamireh*, written in a different era by a casual atheist, embraces a much less rose-tinted image of Nature than its predecessors, because Rosny's view of Nature invariably protests stridently and poignantly against its intrinsic violence—as in the entirely superfluous passage in *Eyrimah* describing Tjandrinahr's walk in the wilderness—and pays no heed to Christianity, at least overtly.

In *Vamireh*, the first and worst corruption of civilization is the development of religion, which Rosny sees as the parent of genocidal persecution and sadistic human sacrifice. Vamireh's own nobility of sentiment is entirely spontaneous. In this sense, Rosny's Romanticism is closer to Rousseau's than Bernardin de Saint-Pierre's or Chateaubriand's, and even more combative. The text of *Vamireh* is also more combative than its predecessors in tackling the question of propriety involved in its matching of lovers. Bernardin de Saint-Pierre and Chateaubriand are both sympathetic to the bonds of affection their characters form, but feel obliged in the end to break them by means of authorial murder. Not only does Rosny refuse that breakage, but he extends his sympathy to the union of Vamireh and Elem to the point of hypothesizing an "instinct of miscegenation" that brings them together. This invention is all the more remarkable given its origin in 19th century race theory, which often embraced a quasi-phobic horror of miscegenation. Rosny occasionally seems to subscribe to that horror in the identification of some of his minor characters as "half-breeds," but such thoughtlessness is far outweighed by the assumption of the innate attraction of different races in *Vamireh*—echoed, albeit less assertively, in the two central relationships featured in *Eyrimah*. Xenophobia is reckoned as another of the corruptions of civilization and religion.

From the viewpoint of modern paleoanthropological chronology, the most glaring "fault" in *Vamireh* is its juxtaposition of its two contending fully human races with two other semi-human species: the "men of the trees" and the "worm-eaters." It is, however, Vamireh's instinctive fellow-feeling for these distant kin, in contrast with the Orientals' murderous disgust, that marks him out as morally superior. His defense of the mammoth calf also displays his generosity, but that altruistic act is repaid in full, with abundant interest; his defense of the worm-eaters brings no reward, and holds out no possibility of any. His abrupt abduction of Elem might be held to count against him in that regard—and cannot be entirely excused on the grounds of her eventual consent—but Rosny clearly has an idea of innocence rather different from his predecessors, and it is worth noting that both Bernardin de Saint-Pierre and Chateaubriand eventually felt it necessary to kill their heroines in order to protect them from the implications of passion. Rosny evidently developed doubts about his assumption that the nobler sentiments of primitive humans might include a version of romantic love similar in all essential respects to the modern mythology of romantic love, and took care to provide a counterweight in his parable of the bloody origins of the first kiss—and he eventually carried those doubts to their logical conclusion in *Les Compagnons de l'univers* (tr., in vol. 6 as "Companions of the Universe")—but in respect of such sentiments, *Vamireh* is noticeably less compromising than *Eyrimah*, and makes fewer concessions to conventional literary expectation.

The presence of the men of the trees and the worm-eaters contributes greatly to making *Vamireh* a more interesting work than *Eyrimah* and "Nomaï"—both of which are exclusively concerned with human affairs—not only because they provide the hero with opportunities to demonstrate the particular pattern of his virtue, but also because they provide a fascinating illustration of Rosny's evolutionist ideas. Similar alternative species were to crop up in many of his later works, not only in such prehistoric romances as *La Guerre du feu* but also in many of his lost land stories, most notably "Nymphaeum" (in vol. 2), "Hareton Ironcastle's Amazing Adventure" (in vol. 3) and "Adventure in the Wild" (in vol. 5), but none of those later manifestations matched the peculiar nostalgic affection with which the two relevant species are viewed in *Vamireh*.

As I pointed out in one of the footnotes, Rosny evokes a concept that I translated as "organic potential" as a means of explaining the evolutionary predicament of the men of the trees and the worm-eaters, both of which species are scheduled for extinction (and are dimly aware of the fact, though quite reconciled to it). In essence, Rosny is suggesting that the two species in question have suffered a crucial loss of evolutionary impetus, which has condemned them to a slow but terminal degeneracy. He sees this as part of a curious process of "selection," in which the impetus preserved by the fully human species destined for dominance and glory is, in some mysterious sense, counterbalanced by a loss of impetus in its cousins—almost as if there were some kind of "law of conservation of evolutionary energy" at work, in which one species' gain is compensated by another's loss.

This kind of notion is a straightforward, if slightly peculiar, extrapolation of Lamarckian evolutionary philosophy, which imputed an innate progressive impetus to all living organisms, at both the individual and specific level. In Lamarck's view, all organisms and species were perpetually in a state of gradual and progressive evolution toward "higher" states of being—a thesis whose most glaring flaw, in the early 19th century, was not so much the assumption of the inheritance of acquired characteristics but its failure to account for the decline and extinction of so many past species. Not only did Rosny have far more fossil evidence to contemplate than Lamarck, but he lived in an era when ideas of decadence and degeneration were exceedingly fashionable, and much discussed, especially in their infection of literary philosophy. It is not surprising that Rosny should have thought that there was now abundant evidence in the data of biology and anthropology to support the notion that evolution was not always progressive, or that he should have imagined the phenomenon of evolutionary decline and eventual extinction in terms of the imagined loss or surrender of evolutionary impetus, whether conceived as "organic potential" or "vital spirit."

Although the phrase itself does not often crop up, the notion of "organic potential" tacitly or explicitly underlies not only the bulk of Rosny's prehistoric fiction, but also his various representations of relationships between humans and alien beings. In "The Death of the Earth" (in vol. 1), for example, the Last Men have lost all their organic potential along with the water that sustains Earthly life as we know it, and have become as resigned to their fate as the worm-eaters of *Vamireh*, while the inorganic "life-forms" fated to replace them, the ferromagnetals, still have a progressive impetus, whose ultimate effects are not yet calculable. The Martian Tripeds of "The Navigators of Space" (in vol. 1) are in a similar situation relative to the Zoomorphs and Ethereals, whose future is similarly uncertain in scope but nevertheless assured. Indeed, one could probably make a case for the covert presence of a notion of organic potential in his naturalistic accounts of contemporary human manners and mores, even if it is only manifest there by virtue of his incessant use of animal analogies rather than by virtue of any explicit philosophical commitment.

A further example of this way of thinking is provided in *Vamireh* in its peculiar depiction of dogs, which are seen as social creatures living in "villages" with a capacity for hierarchical organization; although it is not explicitly stated, the implication is that they might have gone on to develop intelli-

269

gence had they not surrendered their organic potential by permitting their domestication by humans. Rosny may not have meant this entirely seriously; although he usually maintained a tone of deadly earnest in his writings they are not without wit and a certain sly humor—as "Nomaï" clearly illustrates. Although there is far less trace of satire in Rosny's prehistoric fantasies than many other examples of the subgenre, there is a certain malice in his unemphasized revelation that the "worms" the "worm-eaters" eat are, in fact, mollusks, and that *escargots* [snails] are specifically mentioned at one point as an element of the diet that has awakened such contempt in their persecutors.

The fact that Rosny followed *Vamireh* so rapidly with *Eyrimah* probably resulted from his enthusiasm to take advantage of the publicity generated by Dubois' discovery of "Java Man," and it is not surprising that it seems to have been composed in a hurry; it provides one of the most glaring examples of the author's tendency to wander from his initial prospectus, eventually shoving the love story of Eyrimah and Rob-In-Kelg to the sidelines in favor of the rather different love story of Tholrog and Eï-Mor. In the process, the villain Ver-Skag is entirely forgotten—a fate shared by numerous characters in Rosny's work, who are introduced as if they will have an interesting role to play but vanish into the wings, never to return to the stage. This gradual but excessive drift in the narrative does no favors to the novel's plot, but does serve to illustrate the strength of an undertow continually effective in Rosny's creative flow, which drew him inexorably away from the partly-civilized lake-dwellers toward the nobly barbaric mountain men, so that the celebration of their innocent world-view eventually displaced the initial concern with lacustrian politics.

In spite of the fact that his early reputation was partly founded on a study of nihilists, anarchists and revolutionary socialists, Rosny was never much interested in politics, and whenever he embarked upon a story in which imagination was to guide him he was magnetically drawn, whether he initially intended it or not, to hypothetical lands in which politics were drastically simplified. The fact that the elementary battle between Nature and Culture was fated to be settled in favor of the latter was, to him, bittersweet knowledge, because it seemed obvious to Rosny that if only Nature had done a better job of organizing herself, then Culture would never have been forced to develop the excessive complications of advanced civilization, and most or all of its horrid corruptions might have been avoided.

Given its actual context, Rosny was well aware of the fact that organic potential had to imply strength and violence—that the noble savage's savagery was as essential as his nobility—and he could not entirely regret that fact, because he was well aware of his own authorial delight in detailing battles of every sort. He knew that the intimate association between sex and cruel violence that he found everywhere in Nature—and never tired of pointing out in his fiction—provided a context for human life, as for any other, no matter how our myths might strive to obscure the configuration of the linkage, and the fact that the current of his imaginative works drew him repeatedly and incessantly to the theme of abduction is surely evidence of the extent to which he found that linkage deeply problematic.

SF & FANTASY

Guy d'Armen. *Doc Ardan: The City of Gold and Lepers*
G.-J. Arnaud. *The Ice Company*
Aloysius Bertrand. *Gaspard de la Nuit*
Félix Bodin. *The Novel of the Future*
André Caroff. *The Terror of Madame Atomos*
Didier de Chousy. *Ignis*
C. I. Defontenay. *Star (Psi Cassiopeia)*
Charles Derennes. *The People of the Pole*
Harry Dickson. *The Heir of Dracula*
 Sâr Dubnotal *vs. Jack the Ripper*
Alexandre Dumas. *The Return of Lord Ruthven*
J.-C. Dunyach. *The Night Orchid. The Thieves of Silence*
Win Scott Eckert. *Crossovers* (non-fiction)
Paul Féval. *Anne of the Isles. Knightshade. Revenants. Vampire City. The Vampire Countess. The Wandering Jew's Daughter*
Paul Féval, *fils. Felifax, the Tiger-Man*
Arnould Galopin. *Doctor Omega*
V. Hugo, Foucher & Meurice. *The Hunchback of Notre-Dame*
O. Joncquel & Theo Varlet. *The Martian Epic*
Jean de La Hire. *Enter the Nyctalope. The Nyctalope on Mars. The Nyctalope vs. Lucifer*
G. Le Faure & H. de Graffigny. *The Extraordinary Adventures of a Russian Scientist Across the Solar System* (2 vols.)
Gustave Le Rouge. *The Vampires of Mars*
Jules Lermina. *Mysteryville. Panic in Paris. To-Ho and the Gold Destroyers*
Jean-Marc & Randy Lofficier. *Edgar Allan Poe on Mars. The Katrina Protocol. Pacifica. Robonocchio. Tales of the Shadowmen* (anthos.; 6 vols.) *Shadowmen* (non-fiction; 2 vols.)
Xavier Mauméjean. *The League of Heroes*
Marie Nizet. *Captain Vampire*
C. Nodier, Beraud & Toussaint-Merle. *Frankenstein*
Henri de Parville. *An Inhabitant of the Planet Mars*
Polidori, C. Nodier, E. Scribe. *Lord Ruthven the Vampire*

P.-A. Ponson du Terrail. *The Vampire and the Devil's Son*
Maurice Renard. *Doctor Lerne. A Man Among the Microbes.*
The Blue Peril. The Doctored Man. The Master of Light
Albert Robida. *The Clock of the Centuries. The Adventures of*
Saturnin Farandoul
J.-H. Rosny Aîné. *The Navigators of Space. The World of the*
Variants. The Mysterious Force. Vamireh
Brian Stableford. *The Shadow of Frankenstein. Frankenstein*
and the Vampire Countess. The New Faust at the Tragicomi-
que. Sherlock Holmes & The Vampires of Eternity. The Stones
of Camelot. The Wayward Muse. (anthologist) *The Germans*
on Venus. News from the Moon
Kurt Steiner. *Ortog*
Villiers de l'Isle-Adam. *The Scaffold. The Vampire Soul*
Philippe Ward. *Artahe*

MYSTERIES & THRILLERS

M. Allain & P. Souvestre. *The Daughter of Fantômas*
Anicet-Bourgeois, Lucien Dabril. *Rocambole*
A. Bisson & G. Livet. *Nick Carter vs. Fantômas*
V. Darlay & H. de Gorsse. *Lupin vs. Holmes: The Stage Play*
Paul Féval. *Gentlemen of the Night. John Devil. The Black*
Coats: The Companions of the Treasure. Heart of Steel. The
Invisible Weapon. The Parisian Jungle. 'Salem Street
Emile Gaboriau. *Monsieur Lecoq*
Steve Leadley. *Sherlock Holmes: The Circle of Blood*
Maurice Leblanc. *Arsène Lupin: The Blonde Phantom. The*
Hollow Needle. Countess Cagliostro
Gaston Leroux. *Chéri-Bibi. The Phantom of the Opera. Roule-*
tabille & the Mystery of the Yellow Room
William Patrick Maynard. *The Terror of Fu Manchu*
Frank J. Morlock. *Sherlock Holmes: The Grand Horizontals*
P. de Wattyne & Y. Walter. *Sherlock Holmes vs. Fantômas*
David White. *Fantômas in America*

www.ingramcontent.com/pod-product-compliance
Lightning Source LLC
Chambersburg PA
CBHW030358020726
47493CB00003B/862